The Territory of Lies

CIANA STONE

DEDICATION

As always, for my partner in life, my true love.
Thank you for supporting and believing in me.

Chapter One
Wednesday, April 20

It was a beautiful spring day in Akron. Halfway through the work-week people were already beginning to make plans for the upcoming weekend, looking forward to spending time with their families, playing golf, taking a bike ride or just doing yard work. For the most part, it was an average day, with people going about their normal routines. Until four minutes after nine, Central Daylight Time, that is. Then the beautiful spring day became a hellish nightmare.

The sounds of traffic on the street and conversation of people on the sidewalks were drowned out by a deafening explosion. The blast was immediately followed the sound of rushing air and the splintering of thousands of panes of glass. Moments later, black billowing clouds of smoke and debris darkened the sky. The once stately John F, Seiberling Federal Building and U.S. Courthouse was now a burning mass of destruction. The five-story structure was in flames, ceilings and floors collapsing in on one another; walls falling and furniture flying.

For one split second there was total silence, as if the entire city had come to a sudden halt. Then the sounds of screams filled the air. The fear was once more reality. But how? And more importantly, why?

Fifteen Days Earlier
Wednesday, April 6
Washington, D.C.

The man with thinning gray-streaked hair sighed and leaned back to stare at the ceiling. "Dr. Forrest, I'm trying to explain it as best I can. It's just that ..." His voice trailed off and his eyes closed.

"It's all right, Senator Tyler." Dr. Forrest spoke in a soothing tone. "Just relax and breathe. Take a few long slow breaths. We have plenty of time. You're under no pressure here."

As the Senator followed the suggestion, Dr. Forrest studied him. He had aged considerably since the first time he had walked into the office. At that time he'd appeared a robust fifty-eight year old man with slightly thinning hair, graying at the temples. Now he looked ten years older. Dark circles marred the skin beneath his eyes and the wrinkles that creased his cheeks resembled crevices on a crumbling stone wall.

Senator Ned Tyler opened his eyes and focused on the doctor once more. "I don't know how to say this any other way. The truth is, my problem runs much deeper than marital problems or work related stress. I find myself in the tenuous position of having to make a formidable decision, one that — well, to be blunt, one that the balance of many lives depend upon."

Dr. Forrest sat quietly watching the Senator, until a full minute had passed. "Is this not part and parcel that goes along with your position, Senator? Forgive me if I seem to put this in a light vein, but since I know little of the decision to which you refer, I must assume you're speaking of some proposed legislation. Considering that, I feel it necessary to point out that all decisions made by the Senate affect the lives of many. So, is this decision is any different from many of the others you've made in the past?"

Senator Tyler looked up with a haunted expression in his eyes. "You don't understand, Doctor. This isn't just something that just affects lives. It's something that destroys them. I'm talking about something that is going to kill, hundreds, maybe thousands of people."

Dr. Forrest blinked in surprise at his words and forced aside alarm. Chances were he was dramatizing the impact. There was, however, genuine anguish in his voice and that could be addressed.

"Senator, it doesn't take a medical degree to see that you're distraught and I'd like to help you through this, but there is very little I can do if you aren't open with me. I understand how difficult it is to establish a rapport with a stranger, but unless you can be open and candid with me — help me to understand what's distressing you - then I have to say, in all fairness that therapy will prove to be of little help. I do want to help you, but I don't want to waste your time or money."

Senator Tyler lowered his head into his hands. A shuddering sigh passed through him then the sounds of soft weeping filled the room. Doctor Forrest reached over to lay one hand on the Senator's shoulder. It was going to take some time for him to be trusting enough to open up. Hopefully, he would not suffer a breakdown before he did.

∞

On the other side of the city a man waited anxiously in the penthouse suite of the Watergate Hotel. He had no idea why he had been invited and the unknown made him nervous.

The door leading from the study opened and a man with regal bearing entered, dressed as if he had just stepped off the cover of a men's fashion magazine. Tall and lean, his hair was dark and straight, worn in a style favored more by the young than a man in his fourties. His complexion was a strange mixture of olive and bronze as if his ancestry was mixed. The vivid green of his eyes was incongruous with the dark skin and black hair.

He smiled as he crossed the room. "Congressman Blackman— Sloan, my friend. Good of you to come at such short notice. How is your lovely wife, Mary?"

"Fine, but let us come to the point. Why did you wish to see me, Adrian?"

Adrian Zayne ignored the question. "I trust my request for a meeting did not inconvenience you?"

"No. It was something of a surprise, however."

"Yes, I imagine it was," Adrian replied with a chuckle. "Please, do have a seat."

As soon as Sloan sat, Adrian took a seat himself. "Really, Sloan, there is no need for you to be so anxious. There is absolutely nothing wrong with you being seen here. After all, am I not one of the largest supporters of the United States Congress?"

"Yes, I suppose you are."

"Let me come to the point of this meeting. I understand that one of your old acquaintances has an upcoming birthday this weekend."

Sloan's eyebrows drew together in a puzzled frown.

"Larry Anderson." Adrian provided the name. "You know, he has become quite the social butterfly since he left the Senate, what was it, five years ago. I hear he took a position as a lobbyist for the dairy industry."

"Oh, yes. I haven't seen Larry in… why it must be close to two months. So, he's having a birthday?"

"Yes, and I thought it might be nice to arrange a little party for him," Adrian said as he stood. He crossed the room and picked up an embossed leather folder from the antique desk. "As a matter of fact, I've made all the arrangements. What I want, Sloan, is for you to act as host for the party. I've taken the liberty of having the invitations delivered and I've taken care of the financial matters, of course. All the information is in here."

Sloan took the folder and looked up at Adrian. "Why?"

"Why what?

"Why have a party for Larry? I didn't even know you were acquainted."

Adrian laughed and sat down again. "No, as a matter of fact we're not. But that is not important since I'm not hosting the party. As you well know, Congressman, parties are most excellent means of meeting and making new friends."

"I take it there's someone on the guest list that you are interested in."

A sly smile took hold of Adrian's handsome face. "Let's just say that I'm looking forward to the party, Congressman."

Saturday, April 9

Sydney was just walking out the door of her apartment when the phone rang. She started to ignore it and let the voice mail answer but decided at the last second against it. Not many people called her home phone. She ran back inside and picked up the extension in the living area, hoping nothing was wrong.

"Hello?"

A man's voice came over the line. "Syd? Hey, I can't believe I caught you at home."

"Blake!" Worry turned to delight. She took a seat on the arm of the couch. "Where are you?"

"Right now, in an airport in Charlotte, North Carolina. How are you?"

"Fine. Busy. How about you?"

"Tired. And looking forward to getting home."

"When do you think that'll be?"

"Sometime next week, hopefully. Listen, I only had a second. I just wanted to say hi and that I miss you."

"That's sweet." she said softly. "I miss you, too. You take care."

"You, too. I'll give you a call when I get home."

"Okay, talk to you soon."

Sydney hung up the phone and stared at it for a moment. She was starting to think that he was becoming more serious than she was comfortable with. She'd been divorced for less than a year and was in no hurry to get into a serious relationship; and definitely not a relationship in which the other party was looking for marriage. Her first attempt had been such a disaster that she wasn't sure she would ever want to get married again.

That was something she'd made clear to Blake when they first met. At the time he said he understood. He was divorced after having been married for sixteen years. He told her that his marriage reached a point where there was no use in continuing with it. Neither he nor his wife was happy and so they'd decided to call it quits and part as friends.

He had been divorced for a little over four years. Sydney thought perhaps he'd reached a point where he missed being married and having a wife to come home to when he did get a chance to be home.

Oddly, while she had no desire to get married again, she had found herself thinking about having children. She'd always wanted to have a family and still did but the time had never been right. Her energy had been focused on school and then on establishing herself in her practice and there was little time for anything else.

That hadn't been a problem in her marriage. Her husband, Evan Mallory, was consumed with his career and had paid little attention to anything else, including her. She'd not really noticed his lack of attention until they had been married over a year. By then her practice was established and while she was still primarily centered on work she had a little more time to pay attention to what was happening in her personal life.

It was at that point she realized that Evan wasn't interested in her for anything more than an attractive decoration when he attended social events. Not only that, she'd discovered that he was involved with another woman, and had been the entire time they were married. It seemed that Evan had married her not only because she was attractive and 'socially acceptable' but also because she was the daughter of Republican Senator Jack Forrest. The day she found out she packed her things and moved out. She had not spoken with Evan except through their attorneys since that day.

After the separation, she put all her energy into her work. She wouldn't even consider dating until she had her divorce papers in hand and even then she dated infrequently. Eight months ago she went with a friend to a party and there she met Blake.

She thought about their meeting as she left the apartment and got in her car. Once in route, she allowed her mind to travel back to that night.

She stood on the balcony, looking out over the lights of the capital. The din of the crowd mixed with the blare of music from within the apartment was beginning to give her a headache. She wished she hadn't agreed to come to the party with her friend, Celeste. This was a party for people who were hunting — for lovers, husbands, wives or mistresses. She had no desire to be counted among the participants.

Celeste was having a ball, but Celeste always did. She skipped from one man to the next as quickly as using the Uber app on her phone. Sydney wasn't into that sort of thing. Not only was she acutely conscious of the risk of sexually transmitted diseases but she simply wasn't the kind of woman who indulged in casual sex.

As she continued to look out over the city someone stepped out onto the balcony behind her. She turned to look. The handsome man smiled and inclined his head toward the interior of the apartment. "It's kind of loud in there. Do you mind sharing your balcony?"

"It's not mine," she said with a smile, admiring his rugged good looks.

Standing at least two inches over six feet he was a big man. Not heavy or stocky, just big, like someone who had worked out most of his life. His hair was medium brown, straight and thick, worn short around the sides and back, and longer on top. He had the kind of face that was attractive but not classically beautiful. It was a rugged face with slightly chiseled features, housing beautiful hazel eyes. He had the kind of looks that made cause a woman to fantasize about bedding him and man feel envious of his looks and stature. She estimated him to be around forty.

"Well," he replied in response to her comment. "Do you mind sharing whoever's balcony it is? My name's Blake Edwards."

"I don't mind at all and it's nice to meet you, Blake Edwards. I'm Sydney Forrest."

"Any relation to Senator Forrest?"

"His daughter."

"Well," he said with raised eyebrows. "I'll admit to being a fan of your dad's. He's what politicians should aspire to be — honest and straight forward. I like that in a person."

"I'm sure he'd be flattered to hear that." She liked the sound of his voice. It was deep yet soft, like someone who didn't feel the need to be loud to make a point. "And, what do you do, Blake? Are you of the next generation of politicians to the capital or perhaps one of the new breed of lobbyists out to change votes?"

"Neither," he said with laugh that started as a deep sound in his chest that rose to emerge as an amused chuckle. "I'm just your average government worker."

She raised her eyebrows at him. "Somehow I don't think so."

"Oh? Why not?"

"Well," she said as she considered him. "To begin with, you speak well, in the manner of someone accustomed to presenting ideas in some type

7

of public forum. Your body language says that you're self-assured yet not arrogant, confident yet not brash, and your eyes tell me that you have a sense of humor. That's not exactly how I'd describe an average government worker."

"So, if I'm not a government worker then what would you guess me to be?"

She thought about it for a second. "Ummmm…An attorney, perhaps, or… well, I'm not sure. Why don't you tell me?"

"You're pretty good." He smiled and leaned his forearms on the balcony rail. "I'm with the FBI."

"With the FBI as in administration or agent?" she asked then held up her hand. "No, wait, don't tell me. You're an agent."

"Special agent Edwards, at your service. So, now we know who I am, who are you Sydney Forrest? And is that Miss, Ms., or Mrs.?"

"It's Ms."

"Okay, let me think." He turned toward her. "Ms. Sydney Forrest. Daughter of a senator, astute in reading people, not into the meat market scene, obviously intelligent, a classy dresser and one of the most beautiful women I've ever seen, if you don't mind me saying. You must be… I have no idea."

Sydney smiled at his compliments. "I'm a psychiatrist."

Blake's eyes widened then he surprised her by laughing. "Well, I'd never have guessed that."

"I take it you don't have a very high opinion of psychiatrists."

"No, quite the contrary. I think very highly of your profession, but like a lot of people I'm a bit uneasy about someone accessing my psyche. I suppose it makes me feel a little vulnerable and that's something I'm not at all comfortable with."

Sydney admired his honesty and her attraction to him rose. "I see, and I understand. At least you're honest about how you feel. That's a rare quality."

"It should be a common one, don't you think?"

"Yes. Unfortunately should and is are rarely the same. It's difficult for people to be honest. We're all so busy trying to protect ourselves and hide behind our facades that honesty becomes something that threatens our security. It would be nice if we didn't feel compelled to hide but could simply be honest and open."

His voice lowered slightly as his eyes met hers. "I think we can. At least I can. And the truth is, Dr. Forrest that I find you one of the most interesting women I've met in a long time. Do you think there's a chance that you would have dinner with me?"

"Now?"

"Unless you'd rather go back in and join the circus." He nodded his head toward the apartment.

"No, I don't think I want to do that." She realized she'd like to spend more time with him and get to know more about him. She hadn't been intrigued with a man for a long time but Blake Edwards intrigued her. "And I think dinner would be lovely."

Blake offered her his arm. "Shall we?"

She smiled and took it. "By all means."

A smile took shape on her face as she thought about that night. Blake had been a gentleman in the true sense of the word. They had a lovely dinner at a small, quiet restaurant and talked for hours. He was interesting and witty and easy to talk to. When he took her home he didn't even suggest that the night continue. Instead he kissed her at the door and left with a promise to call her soon.

Sydney still remembered that kiss. It had been a very long time since she had been excited by a kiss the way she was by his.

Blake hadn't pushed her to get into a physical relationship but had understood her wanting to wait until they knew one another better. She'd appreciated his willingness to take things slow. Sometimes she wished she hadn't been so cautious. There were times when he kissed her, she wanted to throw caution to the wind, rip off his clothes and make passionate love to him. So far she hadn't found the courage to be so bold.

There were so many things about Blake that she liked, but she was still afraid of making another mistake. She pushed aside thoughts of herself and Blake. Trying to analyze her own life was not her favorite pass-time. Especially considering all the other people she had to think about.

Being a psychiatrist had its advantages. It kept you from dwelling on yourself too much. And it made you realize that no matter how bad you think your own problems are, there is always someone else whose problems make yours look like a day in the park.

When she pulled up in front of Loews L'Enfant Plaza Hotel she got out of the car and handed her keys to the valet. She accepted a claim ticket, put it in her purse and walked into the hotel. A sign on a large easel in the lobby told her where she wanted to go.

Sydney still wasn't sure if it had been a wise decision to accept the invitation to Larry Anderson's party. She was acquainted with the host, Congressman Blackman. He and her father had been friends for many years, but she knew Larry only in passing. She'd almost declined the invitation, but her mother had convinced her otherwise with the reasoning it was important to her father that the whole family be present.

She wondered if her brother would have shown up if he was in town. Sylvester, or Sly as everyone called him, wasn't much for Washington society gatherings. In fact, he detested them. Sly was the family radical. Instead of going into the family firm when he graduated from law school, he'd joined the Peace Corps.

Sydney walked into the ballroom that had been reserved for the party, gave her wrap to the woman at the cloak room, and then greeted the host, Congressman Blackman and his wife, Mary. After a moment of idle conversation she excused herself and wandered over to the bar.

"A glass of wine, please." She gave a smile to the bartender. "Preferably white."

He returned the smile and poured her wine. After sampling it, she turned and looked out at the crowd. There were numerous well known Washington personalities present, ranging from Capitol Hill notables to members of the new administration, along with members of the press and local television celebrities. She saw many people she was acquainted with but made no move to speak with any of them. She was content to stay on the sidelines and watch.

As she looked toward the entrance her eyes widened slightly. A tall, raven-haired man dressed in a well-cut evening jacket and white shirt entered the ballroom. He appeared to be alone. She smiled. He was striking. Not handsome, but unique, almost patrician. No that wasn't right.

Sydney shifted position once more and moved to an empty table, still watching. She sat down and after a few minutes realized that she was still holding the glass of wine. He was different. Just as she started to try and pinpoint what the difference was a voice called from behind her. "Sydney! Darling, whatever are you doing over here in a corner all alone?"

Sydney turned to her mother. "Hi, mom. You look beautiful."

Mrs. Forrest kissed her daughter and smiled. "Likewise, darling. Now, tell me. Who are you with?"

"I came alone. Blake's still on assignment somewhere."

"That FBI fellow? Honestly, Sydney! When are you going to find yourself a nice man with a promising future? Why, I was just telling your father this very morning that—"

"Telling me what?" Jack Forrest interrupted as he came up behind them.

"Hi, Dad," Sydney said with a grateful smile and hugged him. "Thanks," she whispered. "You're just in the nick of time."

Jack Forrest pulled back and looked at his wife with an expression that Sydney knew was mock sternness. "Ah, the old 'get a good man' speech again, hmm, Shirley?"

Shirley smiled and patted his cheek. "Now, darling. Don't get all fierce on me. You know I'm only trying to look out for our daughter's future."

Jack smiled and took his wife's hand to kiss it. "Yes, of course. But right now I need you by my side, dearest. We must express our best wishes to the man of the hour and you know how difficult I find it to be ingratiating to that little worm."

"Of course, darling," Shirley replied and looked at Sydney. "Excuse us, dear, the Senator needs a watchdog to wish Larry happy birthday."

Sydney smiled and watched her parents move away. Her father was one of the best actors she had ever seen. He might personally detest someone but if that person could help him get what he wanted, then sugar would not melt in Jack Forrest's mouth. She had always supposed that was what made him such a successful politician.

She started to take her seat then decided against it. She was there so she might as well make the best of it and mingle.

Across the room, Adrian Zayne stood talking to a short man with a swarthy complexion. "And can you point this doctor out to me, Rico?"

Rico Cordelli smiled and looked around. "Right over there, with Senator East and his wife."

Adrian smiled and patted Rico on the shoulder. "Excellent. Thank you so much, my friend. We will speak soon. Do enjoy the evening."

Adrian walked over to the bar and got a drink, watching Senator East and the young woman with him. He watched her as she talked, noting the way light danced off her strawberry blond hair and the graceful arch of her neck as she tilted her head back and laughed lightly. She was not a tall woman, perhaps around five-five. Her figure was not the thin frame of a model, but reminiscent of pin up girls of the past. The curves were very evident in the elegant creme colored dress. He admired her shapely legs and full breasts and wondered what delights were hidden beneath the material.

She was, by all standards, beautiful. With creamy skin and dark lashed blue eyes she drew many admiring glances from the men around her.

Adrian smiled to himself and moved from his place at the bar as the music started. As he made his way through the people he watched Senator Forrest approach the woman and ask her to dance.

Sydney smiled up at her father as he led her into the swirl of dancers. "You seem to be my knight in shining armor tonight."

Jack raised his eyebrows. "Old Ralph boring you into a coma with one of his stories?"

"No, his wife was driving me to suicide with one of her attempts at matchmaking."

Jack laughed and twirled her around. "Your mother tells me you're still dating the FBI fellow. Are things getting serious between you two?"

Sydney's smile faded. "I'm not ready for anything serious. After what I went thought with Evan I don't think I'll ever be ready, to tell you the truth."

"Well, you know what they say about saying never," Jack said with a chuckle. "As soon as you do, you'll find yourself hip deep in the very thing you swore you'd never do. Besides, not every man's like Evan Mallory, honey. Some of us are even human."

Sydney laughed. "As opposed to what?"

"Sub-human?" he asked and raised his thick eyebrows comically.

Jack stopped moving and Sydney looked up in surprise as the tall man she had been watching earlier tapped Jack on the shoulder. "Senator, do you mind if I cut in?"

Jack stepped aside. "I suppose I can allow it. But keep in mind - this is my daughter."

"Then I shall be on my best behavior," Adrian replied and took Sydney's hand.

"So, you're Senator Forrest's daughter," Adrian said as he took her in his arms and moved her around the dance floor.

"Yes."

"And do you have a name, beautiful lady?"

"Yes, but my father always taught me not to give my name out to strangers, sir."

"Then let us rectify that. My name is Adrian Zayne and you are the most beautiful woman I have ever seen."

Sydney smiled and looked up at him. "I'm Sydney Forrest and I don't think I've ever heard that line spoken quite so convincingly. Tell me, Mr. Zayne, are you an actor?"

Adrian smiled down at her and pulled her a little closer. "No, actually, I'm just your ordinary, run of the mill businessman, trying to make a dollar where he can."

Arching one eyebrow in disbelief she pulled back and looked at the cut of his expensive suit. "You'll have to do better than that, Mr. Zayne. Run of the mill businessmen trying to make a dollar where they can, can't afford suits like this. Why your shoes alone would set most people back a month's pay."

Adrian laughed and swung her around. "I can see that you are not easily fooled, Sydney Forrest. I like that. I think you and I are going to get along extremely well."

"Is that so?" she bantered.

Adrian leaned down close to her, so that his breath brushed her face when he answered. "Yes, most definitely. I guarantee it."

Wednesday, April 13

Senator Tyler arrived fifteen minutes late for his appointment. He looked as if he had not slept in a week and he was extremely agitated.

"Why don't you have a seat and try to relax," Sydney suggested as she closed the blinds in the room and turned on a soft reading lamp between the two chairs. "Would you care for something to drink? Tea, water?"

"No, nothing." Tyler sat down and wrung his hands in his lap. "Doctor, I don't know how much longer I can take this. I can't sleep, I can't eat, I can't concentrate . I think I'm losing my mind. I just don't know how much more I can take"

"Senator, I want to help, but I can't do that unless you let me."

"I just don't know–I don't know who I can trust. If anyone finds out–I don't know–if anyone knew what I've done . . ."

"Senator," she said softly and leaned forward toward him. "To begin with, in this room it doesn't matter what anyone thinks. Here there is no blame. I represent neither moral nor judicial authority. I don't sit in judgment on you. My only concern is for your mental well being. Also, I must stress to you once again that nothing said here will leave this room. Our conversations are protected by the doctor patient confidentiality and I assure you that I take that very seriously."

Tyler nodded, but for a few moments his eyes darted around the room. "Okay," he said at last. "Okay."

Sydney settled back and waited for him to begin. "Well," he said and heaved a sigh. "It all started a couple of years back. I was running for re-election and you know how expensive that can be."

Tyler paused and stood. After a moment he started to pace. His words, which had started haltingly, poured in a torrent. "I was approached by a man. His name is unimportant. He offered to contribute quite heavily to my campaign. All he wanted in return was a little assistance.

"I don't know if you're aware of what happened in the mid 2000's with the housing market boom, but this man and an associate of his had become involved in lending and wanted a bit of help with securitization."

"I'm sorry, I don't know that term." Her words had his steps halting, but only for a moment.

"Oh of course. Securitization is a process where we take an illiquid asset or group of assets and through financial engineering, transform them into a security. Do you understand?"

"No, not at all."

"Let me give you an example. A typical example of securitization is a mortgage-backed security or MBS, which is a type of asset-backed security that's secured by a collection of mortgages. Get it?"

"In a general sense, yes."

"Okay, so this man, he just wanted a bit of assistance, you know?" He halted and looked at Sydney. "It didn't seem like such a big thing at the time. We all do it, you know. So, I agreed. Only I didn't know what I was getting into at the time."

He sat down and mopped his face with a handkerchief. Sydney considered what he had said for a moment. "Then what you are afraid of is that someone will tie you and this help you gave the man together and that your career will suffer?"

Tyler looked at her and she could see the fear in his eyes. "If only it were that simple, doctor. But I'm afraid that's only the tip of the iceberg."

She did not comment but waited for him to say more. When he did not speak she prompted him gently. "Would you care to continue, Senator?"

"I can't," he said with a shake of his head. "Not now. I have a meeting that's very important."

"Very well, but I'd like to up our sessions to two a week."

"I'll have my secretary check my schedule and call you."

"Senator, I think you should try to get some rest. Maybe take a few days off and get away, relax. Sometimes distancing ourselves from the situation so that we can look at it more objectively can be very beneficial."

He nodded and walked to the door. "I'll think about it. In the meantime, do you think you could prescribe something to help me sleep?"

Sydney hesitated. She did not like to prescribe drugs, but the Senator looked as if he was about to come apart at the seams. She picked up a pad from her desk and wrote on it. "Take this to any health food store and they can find this for you. It's a tea that will help you relax. There's no side effects and it's very pleasant tasting. If this doesn't help then I'll consider something stronger."

Tyler took the paper from her. "Thanks, Doctor Forrest. It helps being able to talk to someone."

She smiled and took his hand. "There's always a way out of any situation, Senator. A way that's best for everyone. Together, we'll work on finding that way for you."

He forced a smile and left. Sydney went to her desk and started to key in notes on her laptop from their session. She paused to think. She was not sure there was a good way out for the Senator. If what she suspected was true, then he had been taking payoffs, and that was enough to get him booted off the hill at the very least; if not booted into a river.

◌

Adrian looked at the man seated to his right. "You are quite sure this information is correct?"

"Without a doubt."

"Then make contact and set it in motion."

The man nodded and stood. When he left the room Adrian looked at the other men seated around the polished marble table. "Well, gentlemen, it appears as if phase one is about to be set into motion. If there is no other business, I suggest we adjourn."

A man spoke up from the other end of the table. "There is one other thing."

Adrian turned his attention to the tall, stocky man. "Yes, Senator?"

"Tyler," the man said. "Do we know if he's talked?"

"I have decided to handle that matter personally."

"But what if he has? Everyone here knows that we can't afford a leak. If anyone finds out what Tyler knows then the results could be disastrous for us all. I don't even want to think the hell the Oval would rain down on us. No, I don't think we can afford to take that risk. I think we should deal with Tyler and the –"

"I said I will deal with it." Adrian interrupted in a soft but firm tone. "There will be no more discussion on that aspect."

The Senator did not comment and after a moment Adrian looked around at the others. "Gentlemen, this meeting is adjourned. Have a pleasant day." He got up and walked out of the room.

The Senator who had opposed him looked around at the others. "I still say we need to do something about Tyler."

"And I say we do like Adrian says," Richardo Cordelli spoke. "If he says he'll handle it, then consider it handled."

"Easy for you to say! You have far less to lose if this thing blows up in our face."

Richardo smiled and stood. "And you have far more to lose if you cross Adrian, Senator. Think about that."

◌

Sydney punched the intercom button on her phone. "Yes?"

"A Mr. Zayne for you on line three."

"Thank you, Julie," Sydney replied, picked up the phone and punched line three. "Hello, Mr. Zayne."

"Mr. Zayne? I thought we had agreed to drop the Mr. and Ms.?"

"Adrian, I'm surprised to hear from you."

"I said you would. Did you think I would lie?"

"I don't know what to expect from you. I don't know you."

"Exactly the reason I called. Are you free for dinner?"

"Tonight?"

"Yes. Around seven?"

Her first instinct was to say no because she was involved with Blake. But then she had dinner with associates and friends who were men often and never gave it a second thought. Since she wasn't interested in a relationship with Adrian and Blake was out of town, there was no reason to say no. "All right. Where shall I meet you?"

"I'll pick you up. See you at seven"

"But you don't even know where I live."

Adrian laughed softly. "Sydney Forrest, you'd be surprised at the things I know about you."

Surprised at his remark and a little disconcerted she hesitated a moment. "See you at seven."

"I am in anticipation," he replied and hung up.

She replaced the receiver and stared at it thoughtfully. Adrian Zayne was an enigma. Nothing about him fit into any mold or standard. She didn't know what to make of him.

The night of Larry Anderson's birthday party he had stayed with her the entire evening. They had danced and talked and the hours had flown by. He was extremely interesting, well-read and even more well-traveled. He could talk about almost any topic intelligently and knowledgeably and that impressed her.

Moreover, he listened to her when she talked and treated her as if she was more than merely an attractive woman. She felt he was interested in the whole person which was, in her experience, a rare quality in a man.

Adrian was different. While he looked at her with apparent interest in her appearance, he also listened with apparent interest to her thoughts and opinions.

"Almost too good to be true," she murmured. A little voice inside her head spoke up. *And you know what they say about that, Syd. If it looks too good to be true, then it probably is.*

Sydney pushed the thought aside. It wasn't like this was a date.

And what about Blake? The little voice in her mind asked.

She told herself that she wasn't hurting anyone by having dinner with Adrian and while that didn't appease her conscious, it did at least divert it. She turned her attention to her work and finished the rest of her notes on the session with Senator Tyler. Her secretary buzzed her to let her know that her next appointment was there. Wrestling with her conscience could wait, she had patients to attend to.

Later That Evening

Blake dropped his bag beside the door as he pushed it closed with his foot. It felt both good and strange to be home. He had spent the last four months on a case in cooperation with the DEA and for the past month he had been in Jacksonville, North Carolina, working undercover.

He raked his hand through his hair as he walked across the room. It was definitely time for a hair cut. While he'd been working undercover, he'd let it grow out longer than regulation and he felt uncomfortable about showing up at headquarters with long hair and a full growth of beard.

He was still a little surprised that he had been asked to go to North Carolina to work on the case. There were plenty of qualified agents in the area who could have taken the job. But he had not questioned the opportunity. He went where he was sent and did the job he was sent to do. He never had been one to question orders.

After turning on the lamp beside the couch he sat down, loosened his tie, kicked off his shoes and propped his feet up on the coffee table.

He checked his personal voicemail. There were three messages. The first was from his former wife, reminding him that his son Michael wanted to fly up and spend part of his spring break with him. A return call was expected.

The next message was from one of the guys at the bureau, one of his closest and definitely oddest friends; George We'zel. George was without a doubt the smartest man Blake had ever met, especially when it came to computer systems. There was not a system in the world that he could not hack his way into. And if there was anything going on it was a sure bet that George knew about it.

George was one of those guys who probably wore white button-down shirts with pocket-protectors every day to school. He was short, only five- seven, thin to the point of being skinny, and glasses so thick his eyes looked magnified out of all proportion.

He was also very quick, physically as well as mentally. His movements always seemed to be rapid darts here and there, like a small animal that is accustomed to being seen as prey and so moves in rapid nervous bursts. Mentally, he was faster than greased lightning. He could weasel his way into anything.

That trait, coupled with his odd name, We'zel, had earned him the nickname, Weasel. He did not seem to mind. In fact, he seemed to like the name.

Blake was one of the few people in the bureau who genuinely liked Weasel. Almost everyone else merely tolerated him for his brilliance and skills.

As he listened to the cryptic message Blake smiled. Weasel had called to remind him that technology became obsolete very fast. In the world of technology you either were literate or dead. There was no in-between. He suggested Blake join the living.

Blake had no clue what the message meant so he erased it and listened to the last one. It was from a woman named Dyan Milton, someone he had dated for a short while. He had't seen her in several months. They had gone out a few times after he had started seeing Sydney but as his interest in Syd grew stronger he stopped calling Dyan. She had called to remind him that she had not heard from him and suggested that they get together.

Blake erased the message, called his ex-wife to confirm Michael's visit, then tried to call Sydney. There was no answer. He hung up before her voice mail picked up. He would try her later.

It did not take long to unpack his suitcase and shower. When he made it to the kitchen he found the only thing he had in the refrigerator was a wilted head of lettuce, a molded container of fruit, spoiled milk and a couple of beers. He called out for a pizza then went back into the den and flopped down on the couch.

For a while he channel surfed, but could not find anything he wanted to watch. Bored, but having no desire to go out he wandered around the apartment.

As he walked by the spare bedroom his eyes fell on the desk. On it was the new tablet. It was a gift from Sydney. She was one of those people who was online a lot, too much in his way of thinking. But he had to admit he was constantly amazed at the things she discovered online and by communicating electronically with the other net-bugs, as she called them.

Blake wasn't a novice to technology and the internet, but also wasn't interested in using either as anything other than what, in his opinion, they were designed for. Tools. But he had expressed a mild interest in finding out what the appeal was about all the new "Pro" tablet one evening while at dinner with Sydney and the next day she had presented him with one along with a printer.

Since that day he had not touched the tablet. Now, having nothing else to do he picked it up and carried it back to the couch, sat down and turned it on.

"Okay, let's see," he looked at the screen. "I want . . . what do I want? Check email? Yeah, why not."

He was just clicking on the mailbox icon when the doorbell rang. He went to the door, accepted delivery, paid the pizza boy then returned to the couch with his pizza.

His mail consisted mainly of what he could only describe as the same kind of junk that littered his physical mailbox. There was only one message he did not delete. It was from We'zel and read simply: Dude do you ever check your email? Weasel.

Blake smiled, deleted the message and leaned back, chewing and staring at the screen. He finished one slice of pizza, still staring at the screen then rose. Sydney might think playing around online was fun, but he didn't know anything he was interested in seeing, reading or watching.

He put the tablet aside and picked up his phone. Sydney's number was answered by voice mail. "Hi, this is Sydney. I can't come to the phone right now. Please leave a message and I'll get back to you as soon as I can."

"Hey," he said as he heard the beep. "It's Blake. I just got in and wanted to say hi, but since you're obviously not there I guess I'll talk to your voice mail instead. Give me a call when you get a chance. I missed you, Syd and I'm looking forward to seeing you."

Blake lay back on the couch and turned on the television. Coming home to an empty apartment was starting to wear thin. He found himself thinking how it would be if he and Sydney were together. Maybe not married. She was adamantly against that. Maybe just living together. It would be nice to have her curled up beside him to watch television, and even nicer to feel her next to him when he woke up in the mornings. He wondered what that would feel like to wake up beside her. Since they had never spent a night together he could only imagine. Fortunately, there was nothing wrong with his imagination. With his own imagined scenario floating through his mind he drifted to sleep.

CR

While Blake was spending a lonely evening at home, Sydney was having one of the most unusual evenings of her life.

At exactly seven her doorbell rang. She opened it to find Adrian standing , dressed to the nines and holding an enormous bouquet of long stemmed roses.

He bowed his head slightly as he presented her with the roses. "For you."

"Thank you," she said as she accepted them. "They're beautiful."

"They pale in comparison to your beauty," he replied as she stepped aside for him to enter.

"My, you are very good at that." She turned to take the flowers to the kitchen.

"At what?"

"Flattery," she said as she put the flowers on the counter and got a vase from the cabinet.

"I am completely sincere." He walked up behind her as she ran water into the vase. "You are even more beautiful than the memory I have been carrying in my mind."

Sydney turned around to look at him. He did not move so she was forced to tilt her head back to look up at him. He traced his fingers down the side of her face to her throat and she felt an uncomfortable chill skitter down her spine.

Adrian smiled and moved aside as she put the flowers into the vase. "Would you care for a drink?"

"I have a bottle of champagne on ice, waiting for us," he replied. "Are you ready?"

"I suppose I am." She walked into the living area to pick up her wrap from the back of the couch. Adrian took it from her and draped it around her bare shoulders.

"Then let us be off, my lady."

They left the apartment and took the elevator downstairs to find a long white limousine waiting. The driver was standing by the door. Sydney and Adrian got in and he picked up an iced bottle of champagne and poured two glasses.

She accepted a glass and took a small sip. She was surprised to find herself feeling nervous. Normally she had no trouble meeting or being around men, but Adrian had an unusual effect on her. Something about him seemed to hint at a sense of controlled power lying just beneath the surface - something that suggested deep and fierce passions. That not only intrigued , it frightened her a bit.

He smiled and draped one arm along the seat, letting his fingers play idly along one shoulder where the wrap had slid to expose the skin. Sydney tried to suppress the unease that his touch inspired and took another sip from her glass. She knew from the label on the bottle, the champagne was expensive, but there seemed to be a bitter bite to it.

"Where are we going?"

"To a very nice restaurant. After that - well, I suppose we will just have to see what develops, won't we?"

She smiled and raised her glass but did not drink. "I suppose we will, Mr. Zayne."

She turned the conversation to him, asking about his business. He answered very forthrightly, telling her about his various enterprises.

"My goodness, I had no idea. It sounds as if you own half the country."

Adrian laughed and moved his hand from her shoulder to the back of her neck. "Not quite, but I am working on it. Ah," he said with a smile as the car slowed. "Here we are."

Sydney looked out the window at the row of planes and helicopters parked on the tarmac. "The airport?"

"Come." Adrian took her hand as the driver stopped the car and got out to open the door. He led her to a sleek helicopter where a pilot was waiting. They got in and after a few moments the craft rose into the air.

Sydney looked around, wondering why Adrian had gone to such trouble and where they were headed. It was not long before she found out. They landed a short distance from the town of Blue Ridge in Virginia where another Limousine was waiting. Within minutes they were pulling up in front of The Inn at Little Washington. Sydney had been there only once, with her father, many years ago. The restaurant at the inn was booked months in advance. Getting a reservation on short notice was next to impossible.

How Adrian had managed to accomplish that task in such a short amount of time piqued her curiosity. *Just who is he?* She wondered as he escorted her inside.

They were greeted by the owner and shown to a table by the window in the lovely wood-paneled dining room. Dinner was wonderful and Adrian was both attentive and entertaining.

He suggested they have coffee and brandy in the courtyard. The owner once more showed them to a table then left them alone. Sydney took a seat and looked around at the lovely surroundings. "This has been wonderful," she said as she looked at Adrian. "Thank you. I've really enjoyed it."

"You sound as if the evening is over," he commented then turned to give the waiter their drink order. "And it has only just begun."

"Just begun? What do you have planned next?"

"That is a surprise."

"Really? What makes you think I like surprises? You don't even know me."

Adrian laughed. "Sydney Forrest, I know you better than you know yourself. I have from the first moment our eyes met. You, beautiful mistress of my fantasy, are an adventure waiting to happen. Beneath that cool demeanor and detached clinical professionalism beats the heart of a rogue, a woman who would dare to defy the elements, the fates themselves. In that savage heart you psychiatrists try to obliterate is the potential for the most intense emotions, the deepest passions. You not only like surprises, you adore them. And I am going to fill your days and nights with new and unexpected delights and adventures."

23

For a moment she was speechless. The words he had spoken would have sounded false, arrogant, and presumptuous in the extreme from anyone else. From Adrian they sounded both sincere and a bit menacing.

"I hardly know what to say in response. I must admit that I've never been told anything quite like that and while I cannot say I agree with your diagnosis of my psyche, it certainly was interesting."

Adrian's smile faded and his hand moved to her face. He took her chin in his fingers and lifted her face slightly to look into her eyes. "Don't play games with me, Sydney. I'm quite serious and in your heart you know that I'm right. Haven't you grown tired of commonplace men - men incapable of matching your intellect, your passion? I think you have, just as I think you've been waiting for me for a very long time."

"That's very presumptuous, don't you think?"

"Not at all, it's simply the truth. You don't have to admit it to me, but you should at least admit it to yourself."

What he said was not true. She had not been waiting for someone like him to come along. But perhaps he was playing her. The question was, why? "So, you're the answer to my dreams? Very well, I'll play along. If that is so, then what am I to you, Mr. Zayne? Your latest diversion?"

"My only diversion," he said and moved closer to her. "Believe me, Sydney, I'm as surprised and overwhelmed as you. I never expected this to happen - but it has. You see, I've been waiting for you as well and I don't intend to let you get away."

Even if Adrian had given her a change she would not have had a reply. His lips met hers. She turned her head to one side and he drew back, lifting her hand to his lips. "Am I moving too fast for you?"

"Yes."

"Then you would prefer me to back off - take things slower?"

She thought about it for a moment. "Adrian, all I agreed to was dinner. With a friend. I'm involved with someone. And you-"

"Yes?" his asked, his eyes sparkling as he raised his eyebrows in question. "What about me?"

She hesitated a moment, choosing her words with care. " You're intelligent and worldly, fascinating and mysterious. You're what women dream of finding in a man - attentive, passionate, with intrigue and a hint of hidden danger beneath the surface. You're a puzzle that hasn't been solved and I'm not sure ever will. But the temptation to try is compelling. I do enjoy your company, but you need to know that friendship is as far as it will ever go."

Adrian smiled and kissed her hand again. "Are you quite sure about that?"

"Yes."

"I appreciate your honesty. And I believe in the old adage, that you can never have too many friends, so a toast. To friendship."

With a smile, she raised her glass.

Chapter Two
Thursday, April 14

At five minutes after nine in the morning George We'zel sat at his normal place in front of his console in his cubicle at FBI headquarters in Washington, D.C. A middle-aged woman with salt-and-pepper gray hair, wearing a severely cut dark blue suit entered the room.

"Hey there, Weasel, anything new happening?"

"Hey, Stella," Weasel responded with a smile. "Nothing major – except..." he swiveled his chair around to face her. "You won't believe this. Guess who went online last night?"

"Who?"

"Blake Edwards."

"No way!" she exclaimed. "Blake?"

"Did I hear you say Blake went online?" Ken, a man at a console nearby joined the conversation. "As in Blake 'the Rake' Edwards?"

"One and the same," Weasel said with a smile.

"No, couldn't happen!" Ken exclaimed. "He's too busy with all those good looking babes he always has hanging all over him to have time to putz around online."

"Not only that," Stella added. "He can find his way around the NCIC and he's a smart guy but I have to say that being adept online would be analogous to a monkey performing brain surgery."

"Scoff if you like," Weasel laughed. "But it's a fact."

"I'll believe it when I see it," Stella commented then walked over to Ken. "I need to get a copy of that info that was downloaded from the DOD last night."

Ken nodded and turned to his keyboard. "I'm on it."

Just then Blake walked in. "Hey, Weasel."

Stella and Ken turned at the same time Weasel looked around at Blake. "Well, well," Ken quipped. "Rough night, Blake? Or are red eyes and dark bags genetic in your family?"

"Late night," he replied without elaboration.

"Yeah, I'll bet," Stella laughed and winked at Ken.

Blake gave her a scowl and everyone laughed. "Late night?" Ken quipped and hooted a laugh. "You mean a late night online?"

Blake snorted and looked away. He had no idea how they could know he was online, but he was sure not going to let them know about his social life, or in the case of last night, the lack there of.

"I've got better things to do with my time."

To cover his discomfort he pulled a pack of cigarettes from his pocket and took one out. He'd just recently started smoking again and wasn't exactly pleased with himself for it, but it had fit his last undercover role. Now he needed to put them down again. "I do have a life, you know."

"Blake you know you can't smoke in here!" Stella exclaimed.

Blake ignored her and flicked his lighter several times. Nothing happened. But he didn't expect it to. He hadn't deactivated the safety feature.

"Have you lost it man?" Weasel asked and pointed to the sign on the wall. "No smoking!"

Blake did not acknowledge him, but continued flicking the lighter. Now no one was giving a thought to what he was or was not doing last night.

"Blake, what do you think you're doing?" Another man asked as he walked into the room.

"Trying to get this damn lighter to work!" he exclaimed and threw the lighter down on the floor.

Everyone watched as he snorted and stomped out of the room, passing the Assistant Director who was walking in. "Blake."

"Morning," Blake said in passing and continued to his office across the hall.

"What's going on in here?" The Assistant Director asked as he looked around. "What was all that shouting about?"

By the time the words were out of his mouth everyone had already hurriedly returned their attention to their work. Weasel turned around in his chair. "Shouting, sir? Was there shouting? I must have been too involved in what I was doing to notice. Would you like me to ask around and see if I can find out?"

The Assistant Director frowned. "No, thank you. Now, Stella, did you get me a printout of that info from the DOD?"

"We're working on that now, sir," she replied and gave Ken a nudge. "I'll have it in your office in five minutes."

"Very well, " he said then turned and left the room.

"Whew!" Ken blew out his breath. "That was close. Man did you see Blake with that lighter? Flick, flick, flick - didn't anyone ever tell him what child-safe means? If you ask me . . . "

"Weasel!" Blake stuck his head in the door and Ken fell silent. "I want to see you in my office. Now!"

Weasel smiled as Blake stomped off.

"What's that all about?" Stella asked as Weasel stood and started for the door.

"Curiosity, my friend," he replied. "Overwhelming curiosity."

He walked across the hall to Blake's office. As soon as he opened the door Blake looked up from where he sat at his desk. "Weasel! How long did you have that email in there?"

Weasel smiled and took a seat in the chair placed in front of the desk. "God, I don't know. Months - years maybe."

Blake frowned and leaned back in his chair. "Man, I have no idea why you people get so into the whole online thing. I don't even know where to start. It's like a maze. And those so-called social sites definitely aren't for me. Not to mention some of those private chat things. Have you read some of that garbage?   If that's all there is to it, you guys are definitely wasting your time."

"Unless…" he pinned Weasel with a hard stare. "There's something meaty you want to share."

"What?" Weasel took off his glasses and cleaned them with a handkerchief he pulled from his pocket. "Man, where have you been? Ain't nothing like that on the Web."

"Come on," Blake scoffed. "I know you, and you wouldn't still be ragging me about this if there wasn't something you wanted me to find."

Weasel put on his glasses and returned the handkerchief to his pocket. For a few seconds he was perfectly still and quiet then he sighed and nodded. "Okay, this is probably a big mistake, but I'll give you an address."

He picked up a pen from Blake's desk and jotted something down on a memo that was lying nearby. "But remember, you didn't get this from me. It's kind of Top Secret, so keep your mouth shut about it."

"Sure." Blake agreed and looked at what was written on top of the interoffice memorandum. "This is it?"

"Indeed," Weasel smiled. "Gotta get back. Catch you later."

"Yeah, later," Blake murmured and looked again at what Weasel had written. It did not make any sense. He tore off the top of the page with the writing on it, stuck the paper in his pocket then put himself to the task at hand. Endless reports and paperwork.

⊂⊃

Sydney frowned as she looked at the computer screen. She did not remember ever seeing anything quite like this.

Since she had a little extra time before her first appointment she decided to check on the files she had secreted online. The files were still encrypted and she did not detect any tampering attempts.

She's set up various locations a couple of years ago for certain files she considered particularly valuable. All entries made were encoded so that anyone stumbling accidentally on them would think they were nothing more than gibberish. There was only one person besides herself that knew the locations and how to decipher the information. And that person was someone she'd trusted for many years.

Most people would have been surprised to discover the person's identity as well as their friendship. Even Sydney would admit that they made an unlikely pair. Their interests aside from hacking were very different. But their love of hacking had brought them together during their freshman year of undergraduate school and that friendship had withstood the years.

She wondered if GW had seen at what she was looking at. During the last couple of weeks there had been some odd chatter online. Several times she had seen cryptic messages, alluding to 'something big' that was going to happen and then there were disquieting messages from several groups; information about terrorism and how to make bombs and the like. She didn't know what to make of it but kept an eye on it. She figured the chances were good that it was nothing more than malcontent voices using the deep web as a forum for proselytizing.

As she looked at the screen she wondered if she should flag GW to take a look at the message that talked about harboring fugitives from the law if the need arose.

Sydney looked up as her secretary entered the room. "There's a man here to see you, Doctor. He says he's from the FBI and that it's important."

Sydney quickly logged off her computer. "The FBI?" It must be Blake. "Very well, show him in."

The moment the dark-haired man in the navy suit appeared, she reached for the button to do a hard shut-down of her computer and then pressed a button under the lip of her desk to activate the room recorder.

"Dr. Forrest? I'm Special Agent Robert Wells, FBI." He pulled his identification from his inner coat pocket as he spoke and handed it to her. "I'd like to speak with you about one of your patients."

"Oh?"

"Senator Ned Tyler."

"What makes you think I'm treating Senator Tyler?"

Wells frowned then gestured toward the two chairs set on the other side of the room. "May I sit?"

"Of course." She rose and crossed the room to take a seat facing him.

"Senator Tyler has been observed coming to your office on five separate occasions, Wednesday afternoons at two o'clock on March fifteenth, twenty-second, twenty-ninth, April fifth and yesterday, the twelfth."

"Is the FBI in the habit of following all of the senators around, Mr. Wells?"

"I'm not at liberty to discuss such things with you doctor."

"I'm sorry, Mr. Wells, but I'm afraid you're wasting your time. I don't discuss my patients - with anyone."

"Dr. Forrest, I am afraid you misunderstand. You are not being given a choice in this. You will turn over all transcripts, tapes and other records to me now concerning your sessions with Senator Tyler."

"I most certainly will not." She stood. "Please excuse me, Mr. Wells, but I have patients to see. I'm sure you can find your way out."

"Dr. Forrest, you're making this more difficult than it has to be. I can have federal agents come into this office and confiscate all your files, but I don't want to have to resort to that. If you cooperate we can avoid such unpleasantness."

"What is said in this office is a matter of the strictest confidentiality. Perhaps you've heard of it, Mr. Wells. If not, I suggest you do a little research. You can't order me to turn over anything to you or divulge any information about my patients any more than you can order a priest to testify to something said in a confessional. So, in that light, I'll have to ask you to leave."

"Dr. Forrest, are you concerned with the welfare of this nation?"

"What kind of question is that?"

"A very simple one. Are you concerned with the safety and welfare of this nation?"

"Of course."

"Then I ask you again, turn over all relevant information on Senator Ned Tyler to me."

Sydney sat down and stared at him. "Just what do you hope to find, Mr. Wells? What do you suspect the Senator of?"

"Like many members of the Senate, Senator Wells is privy to highly classified information," he answered. "Consider for a moment, Dr. Forrest. Hypothetically, what could happen if a person in such a position were to become mentally unbalanced. Wouldn't you think that would be cause for alarm? What if this mental aberration or condition led him to do something with certain information that threatened the security of this country?"

"I can assure you that nothing of that nature has ever been discussed here," she replied. "Senator Tyler is suffering from - personal problems. Nothing more."

"I'd like to take your word on that, Doctor. Unfortunately, I do have my orders."

"Then I'm afraid you're not going to be able to carry those orders out, Mr. Wells. Tell your superiors that I will not now, or ever, turn over any privileged information to anyone - not you, the Secret Service, the NSA, DIA, CIA or even the President himself. Now, I must ask you to leave. I have a patient to see."

Agent Wells opened his mouth then closed it. He walked to the door, stopped and turned back to her. "You leave me no choice, Doctor. I'll see you tomorrow morning with a court order. Have a nice day."

Sydney watched him leave then waited a few moments and buzzed her secretary. "Julie, call the rest of my appointments for today and say something has come up. Apologize for me and reschedule then you can take the rest of the day off. Please lock the reception area when you leave."

She ended the conversation before Julie had a chance to question her on what was going on. Sydney then stopped the recording, turned on the computer to download the audio and copied it to a flash-drive. She added all of her notes on the Senator to the drive and deleted them from her computer. After that she keyed in a security program to protect the files on the hard drive, preventing them from being accessed.

She had no idea what was going on, but it obviously involved more than just some payoffs from unethical businessmen to the Senator. She removed his printed patient file from the file cabinet and put it in her briefcase.

The last task was to alter her appointment schedule, change the Senator's name on all of his appointments as well as his name on the billing information. Should anyone search for his name they could come up empty-handed.

Satisfied she'd done enough to throw agent off if he did, in fact, return, she grabbed her purse, let herself out through the private entrance in her office and went down to the parking deck. She got in the car and drove straight home. Once there she went directly to the computer in her study. She had to hide the information in a place no one would think to look and the best way she knew to do that was in the last place someone would think to look; right in plain sight – on the Internet

CR

By the time Blake finished his reports it was almost noon. Since he had nothing else pressing, he decided to take the afternoon off. By the time he got home he had forgotten all about the slip of paper in his pocket with the Internet address Weasel had given him.

The moment he entered his apartment he tossed his jacket on the couch, pulled his phone from his pocket and dialed Sydney's cell phone. When he got no answer he called her private line at her office. After a dozen or more rings he hung up and called the main office number. The answering service picked up. He told the operator he had no message to leave, hung up and dialed her home phone.

It was odd for Sydney to be away from her office. *Unless she's sick or something. Maybe that's why she hasn't returned my call.*

The phone rang four times before she answered. "Yes?"

"Syd? You okay?"

"Blake, hi." Her voice sounded like she was either distracted or upset. "Yes, I'm fine. I just—I just decided to take a few hours off and catch up on some work at home. How are you?"

"Okay. Did you get my message?"

"Oh! Yes, I did but it was late when I got in and I didn't want to wake you and then things were crazy at the office this morning so—"

"It's okay," he interrupted. "You don't have to explain. So, where were you last night?"

"Having dinner."

"With who?"

"A friend."

"Anyone I know?"

"No, I don't think so."

"New friend or old?"

"Yes."

Blake frowned. It was unlike Sydney to be so evasive. In all the time he had known her she had been very up-front and straightforward. He got the feeling that she was trying to keep something from him.

"Is everything okay, Syd?"

"Just fine, why?"

"I don't know, you just sound a little funny."

"It's nothing. Just work."

"So, why don't you forget about work for a while and let's go do something?"

"Umm, well - I don't know. I have something I have to do this evening and it's almost one now."

"So, we'll have lunch and maybe take in a matinee or go to the park," he suggested.

"Okay," she said after a moment's hesitation. "Give me twenty minutes to change and I'll meet you at that deli near the mall - you know the one I mean."

"Sure, see you in a little while."

Blake hung up the phone with a smile. He was really looking forward to seeing Sydney. Last night he had made up his mind about asking her to move in with him. With the decision made, he was eager to get her answer.

♋

Adrian's butler opened the door to admit two men. He showed them to the library where Adrian stood as the men entered, and gestured toward the couch. "Gentlemen, good afternoon. Can I have Alran prepare you a drink?"

"No, thank you," Congressman Blackman declined. "Thank you for seeing us on such short notice, Mr. Zayne."

"You indicated it was a matter of some importance," Adrian said as he took a seat.

"Yes," Greenland, spoke up. "It came to my attention that the FBI is having Senator Tyler followed. Not only that, an agent was sent to see Doctor Forrest today, demanding that she turn over all tapes and transcripts of her sessions with Tyler."

"Really?" Adrian commented with raised eyebrows. "And what was the good doctor's response?"

"She refused," Blackman answered. "But you can bet they'll be back - with a court order."

"And what is it that you want from me?" Adrian asked.

Greenland and Blackman looked at one another then back at Adrian. "We can't afford anything falling into the wrong hands, Mr. Zayne. And we can't be sure that Tyler hasn't told the doctor what he knows."

"Yes, that is true."

"So," Greenland said then hesitated. "We obviously have to take action to keep things from getting out of hand. The Oval has specifically instructed that we get this matter buttoned up."

Adrian smiled in apparent unconcern. "No cause for alarm, gentlemen. As I have previously stated, I will handle Senator Tyler and the doctor. All you have to worry about is fulfilling your parts of the arrangement. I'll deal with the Oval. Now, is there anything else?"

"But how can you insure that he or his doctor won't talk?" Greenland blurted.

"I have my ways," Adrian said in a voice as soft as the whisper of a viper. "Do you question that, sir?"

"No, not at all. But - well, you can understand how this development would cause a certain amount of consternation," Blackman replied hastily.

Adrian's smile returned. "Yes, of course. But there is no need for concern. Now, if you will excuse me, there are matters that require my attention. Alran will show you out. Have a pleasant day."

The men stood at the dismissal and left the room. As soon as they were outside they looked at one another. "So, you think we should do like he says and forget about it?" Greenland asked.

Blackman shook his head as they walked to his car. "I think it'd be wise to have someone put on Tyler. Let's keep him under close eye. If it looks like he's going to be a problem we'll take care of it ourselves."

Greenland nodded. "Good idea. And I have just the man for the job." He started to turn away but Blackman stopped him.

"You have to be careful about how you work this. We can't let anyone know."

"I know," Greenland replied. "Don't worry. I'll take care of it. I'll talk to you later."

The two men got into their cars and pulled away from the house. Inside Adrian stood at an upstairs window, watching them. He turned away from the window with a smile. Keeping Tyler under control was no problem. He was so scared that he would not dare divulge anything to the authorities.

As far as Sydney Forrest was concerned, he had every intention of making sure that she had no desire whatsoever to divulge anything the

Senator might tell her. Before long she'd be of the opinion that anything that spilled from Tyler's lips fell squarely into the territory of lies

He smiled as he contemplated the task before him. He had never had any trouble at all controlling women and getting them to do exactly what he wanted them to. But he had to admit that Sydney was different from most women. Putting aside her compelling beauty, her mind was sharp and quick and she was very firm in her convictions. It would be a challenge to conquer and control her.

It had taken him less than five minutes to realize that he wanted her. From the first moment he had sensed there was something special about her. Now he knew that he would make her his and when he was done she would do anything he asked of her. As would her father, and that was the real prize in this game. Jack Forrest would insure that the country moved forward in the correct direction.

Thoughts of Sydney and the evening he had planned made him smile in anticipation. He picked up the phone and asked his assistant to join him in the study. He wanted to make sure the plans for the evening were perfect.

ख़

Sydney saw Blake as he got out of his car. He was dressed in a faded pair of jeans, worn sneakers, and an old Harvard T-shirt. His hair was longer than he normally wore it but she liked it the way it brushed his collar and thought it made him look younger. She watched him, as if for the first time noticing the strong lines of his face and the muscular physique beneath the clothes. The way he moved was powerful and sexy. She found herself becoming aroused.

He looked around and smiled as he saw her sitting at the sidewalk cafe. She waved and returned the smile. "Hi," he said as he walked up to the table. He leaned down and kissed her lightly. "Been here long?"

"Just long enough to get a table. I ordered iced tea. I hope that's okay?"

"Sure, fine," he said as he sat down. He took her hand. "So what've you been up to while I was away?"

"The usual," she replied then paused as the waiter returned with their drinks. They placed their order and the waiter left.

"So, you were saying," he said and took a drink of tea.

"Oh, yes. Well, let's see. Aside from work I went to the Kennedy center one night with Celeste, you know, my old college friend? And I had dinner with Sly while he was in town. Oh, and I went to a party for one of the lobbyists."

"Sounds like fun," he said and made a face.

"Actually it was," she replied. "But enough about me. What about you? Have you talked to Michael lately?"

"No, I spoke with Jessica though. Michael's coming up this weekend to spend a couple of days of his spring break with me."

"Blake, that's wonderful!" She gave his hand a squeeze. "I know how much you miss him. Hey, Sly got a couple extra tickets to a concert for this weekend and gave them to me. I'm not particularly into the group. They're really for the younger generation so Michael might like it. You can have the tickets if you want."

"I'll ask him."

"You've let your hair grow." She reached over to to run her fingers through his hair at the temples, combing it back.

"I was going to get it cut, but I forgot to call and get an appointment."

"I like it," she said with a smile, letting her hand move briefly to his face.

He smiled and took her hand in his to give her knuckles a kiss. The waiter brought their lunch and they chatted about inconsequential things as they ate. After they finished Blake suggested they take a walk. They wandered over to the mall enjoying the fresh spring air.

"Syd," Blake said and grasped her hand. "I've been doing a lot of thinking lately."

She turned and looked at him but did not speak. "About us, I mean," he said. "And I wanted to run something by you—see what you thought about it."

"What?"

For a moment he was silent. "I was thinking it'd be nice if maybe we—well, if we started thinking about getting a little more serious—maybe even move in together."

She stopped walking and took both his hands in hers. "That's a lovely offer but I can't. Now, before you say anything, let me explain. I'm just not ready for anything like that."

"I'm not talking about getting married, Syd. There'd be no commitment or obligations."

"But there would," she argued quietly in a calm tone. "Don't you see? If we lived together we'd feel obligated to report to one another everything we do. Our lives would no longer be our own. We'd have to check with one another before we made decisions about what we wanted to do. Like, for instance—what if one of your friends called and asked you to go out for a few beers. You'd feel like you had to clear it with me first. You see what I'm getting at?"

"Yeah, I see," he answered in a gruff tone. "You're saying that you see it as having to give up your freedom and that I'd be in your way."

"That's not what I said, but essentially you're right."

He looked at her in surprise and she smiled gently. "Blake, I care about you and I enjoy being with you very much, but I made it clear in the very beginning that I'm in no hurry to get into a that type of commitment. I haven't changed my mind about that."

He shrugged and looked away. "No big deal, it was just a thought. Anyway, like you say, it works pretty good the way it is. Long as you're not putting me off for some other guy."

He laughed but she didn't. His laugh faded and he looked at her with a frown creasing his brow. "That's not it, is it, Syd?"

"No, that's not it, Blake."

"So, you're not seeing someone else?"

"No. Like I said, I had dinner with a friend but it certainly wasn't a date."

"You sure? "

"Yes, positive. But I didn't think we had to answer to one another about who we see or where we go. And I'm sure you've been out with other women since we've been dating."

"Maybe in the beginning," he admitted. "But not now."

"Well, I certainly don't have the right to tell you who you can and can't see and I wouldn't presume to expect you to center your entire existence around my wants. I care about you a lot and I'd like to find out if we are going anywhere from here but I'm not going to try and box you up by our relationship. But if on the off chance this is a fishing expedition because you're interested in someone else..."

"I'm not interested in anyone else!" he insisted then narrowed his eyes. "That's what this is all about, isn't it? You've met someone and you've got the hots for him."

"That's crude and completely out of line."

"But it's true, isn't it? There is someone else."

"I told you I had dinner with a friend. That's it. I'm not interested in any more than that."

Blake dropped her hands and jammed his into his pockets. "I don't do competition too well, Syd, and to tell you the truth I'm just too old to start trying. I don't think I want to be played against this guy so I won't stand in your way."

"Blake!" She grabbed his arm as he started to turn away. "Wait!"

He stopped and she looked up at him, suddenly afraid that he would just walk out of her life completely. "Please, don't do this. This isn't you. You're a bigger person than this. Don't make this a 'it's my way or the highway' choice. Don't just throw our relationship out with the trash because I've shared a meal with someone along the way."

Blake shook his head. "It's not that, Syd. It's just that I thought what we had was more than just being friends. I guess I wasn't seeing things too clearly. Listen, I've gotta go. I have things to do. Catch you later."

She hung onto his arm as he tried to turn. "Blake." She put her arms around him and hugged him. "We are more than friends, much more. You know that. And I do care. But you have to try and understand. It's hard to build a relationship even if you are around the person all the time. We're lucky to see each other a few times a month with the way your job is. That doesn't mean that I want to give up on us. I don't. I want to find out where we go from here. I just don't want to rush into something before it's time. But I do care - more than you know. Please believe me."

He wrapped his arms around her and held her close for a moment then released her. "Yeah, me, too. Now, I have to go. I'll talk to you later."

Sydney watched him walk away. Why couldn't she be honest with him? And with herself. Blake had taken much more of her emotions hostage that she was comfortable with. And she wanted him in a physical way more than she had ever wanted a man. Which was one of the reasons she was hesitant to initiate things in that department. She feared it would make her too attached to him. And with emotional attachment came the potential for pain. Pain she wasn't prepared to deal with.

She was a coward. Plain and simple. She knew that. What she didn't know was how to change it. She sighed and started back in the direction she had come. Suddenly the spring day was not quite so lovely.

Later That Evening

Sydney got out of the limousine in front of the mansion in the suburbs of Maryland and stared at the enormous house and landscaped lawns. She'd been surprised when Adrian's driver arrived to pick her up, expecting Adrian himself. For a moment she just looked around, wondering once more just who Adrian Zayne really was, then she walked up the steps to the massive double doors.

They swung open before she had a chance to knock. Adrian stood framed in the opening. "Welcome to my home," he said as he extended his hand to her.

She smiled but didn't take his hand. "It's - magnificent."

"As are you," he said with a smile and grasped her wrist to pull her to him. "I've missed you, Sydney."

She tensed and gently extracted herself from his embrace. "Are you teasing me, Mr. Zayne?"

"Never," he replied solemnly. "Have you been thinking about me?"

"Yes, I have." It wasn't a lie. Ever since her lunch with Blake she'd thought about what to say to Adrian. She found him interesting and it was possible they could be friends, but it wasn't worth losing Blake. She'd made up her mind to tell him that she wouldn't be seeing him anymore.

His face brightened in a smile. "Come, let me show you my home."

Sydney was impressed with the house. It was decorated very tastefully and she could tell that no expense had been spared. Of the thirty rooms she saw not one could be described as anything less than perfect.

When the tour was completed Adrian took her outside onto the terrace where a table had been set. A bottle of champagne waited with two glasses between the candles that fluttered in the breeze. All around the terrace tremendous bouquets of spring flowers had been placed along with candles set in small glass globes to prevent the breeze from extinguishing them. It was a thoroughly romantic setting.

She smiled up at him. "Why Mr. Zayne, if I didn't know better, I'd think you were trying to seduce me."

"And supposing, hypothetically, of course, I was?" he asked, taking her hand to lead her to the table. "Would I succeed?"

"Honestly? No. Nothing has changed, Adrian. I'm still involved."

Adrian laughed and sat down close to her. "But not married. Champagne?"

"Yes, thank you."

They sipped champagne and watched the last of the day's light fade from the sky. The scent of flowers filled the air and from inside the sounds of soft music filtered through the opened doors.

"Would you care to dance?" Adrian stood and offered his hand.

"No."

"It's just a dance, Sydney."

"No, it's not."

"Fine." He appeared annoyed and she watched with interest to see what he would do next. Abruptly he smiled. "I have a surprise for you."

She raised her eyebrows. "A surprise?"

"Come with me."

She rose and followed him out into the garden beyond the terrace. In the middle of the garden was a lovely Victorian gazebo surrounded by graceful willows and delicate flowers. A shimmering pond dotted with lily pads lay between them and the gazebo; a graceful wooden bridge spanning the water, sheltered with wisteria covered arches.

"Adrian, it's beautiful!" she exclaimed. "It's like something from a fairy tale!"

He smiled and led her across the bridge. Once on the other side she could see that the gazebo was screened to keep out insects. Inside the flames of candles swayed gently on stands surrounding an enormous canopy bed covered in white silk and draped in filmy white lace. On the bed lay the dress of a princess from old romantic legends.

"What's this?" she asked as she walked to the bed and touched the dress.

"Your outfit for the evening."

She looked at him in confusion. "My outfit?"

"Yes," he said with a smile. "I will leave you to change in privacy. An attendant will come to assist you. I will rejoin you shortly."

"Adrian! Wait! What is all this?"

"A surprise," he said over his shoulder. "I will return."

Sydney watched in perplexity as he disappeared through the garden. A few seconds later a slender elderly woman came down the path.

"Good evening, my name is Elsa. I will assist you."

Sydney was not so sure about the whole scenario. But the dress was absolutely divine and she had to admit that she was dying to try it on. "Hi, Elsa, I'm Sydney."

"A pleasure, Miss," Elsa said and nodded respectfully. "Now, let's get you into that dress."

A few minutes later, Elsa directed Sydney's attention to a large dressing mirror behind the bed. Sydney walked over to look at herself and gasped. She looked like she had just stepped out of a storybook. The tight bodice of the dress pushed her breasts up high and cinched her waist tightly, flaring out into a multi-layered shirt of sparking beadwork and scattered sequins over a surface of thin white satin. The dropped sleeves hung low on her upper arms, leaving her shoulders bare.

Elsa walked up behind her and put a sparking diamond necklace around her neck then took the pins out of her hair, letting it fall loose and free down her back. "You look just beautiful," she complimented. "Please make yourself comfortable. Mr. Zayne will be with you shortly."

Sydney watched the woman leave then looked once more at her reflection. What would Blake think if he saw her in this outfit? A noise from outside drew her attention and she walked around to the side of the bed.

Adrian stood at the door. Dressed in a white shirt with billowing sleeves that laced down the center and black pants he looked like a pirate, ready to whisk her away to his ship and sail away.

"So, the princess Sydney. At last we meet face to face."

Sydney hesitated momentarily, unsure what to say. But the sparkle in Adrian's eyes and sly smile made her overcome her uncertainty. There seemed little harm in going along with the game.

"Pirate," she said contemptuously. "How bold you are, but how foolish. My father will see you drawn and quartered for having the audacity to intrude upon me in my private chambers."

He walked to her, lifting her long hair in one hand to move it behind her right shoulder. "Ah, but worth every measure of pain, my lady."

Sydney was shocked at the way her skin crawled at his touch, but also comforted. Blake had nothing to fear when it came to Adrian. She was not in the least attracted to him physically. In fact, his touch verged on repulsiveness.

She could end the game now, but didn't want to make a scene. Perhaps the kindest way to end the beginning of their friendship was to play along but make it clear that she wasn't interested in anything else. "Think carefully, sir. The king does not take lightly his daughter's virtue being stolen."

"But it is not your virtue I desire to steal, my princess," he whispered as his fingers moved lightly over the swell of her breasts. "It is your heart."

"Then you shall fail, Pirate, for the heart of the princess belongs to another."

"Or so she thinks," he countered. "Princess, it seems that you will be my prisoner tonight." In a move so quick Sydney was caught off guard, Adrian lifted her up and slung her over his shoulder like a rag doll.

"What are you doing?"

"As I said, you are the prisoner of Captain Zayne, the most feared of all pirates. And as my prisoner, dear princess, you shall be submitted to multiple and diverse forms of delicious torture."

The word torture grabbed Sydney's attention. The playfulness of being thrown over a man's shoulder as if weightless was quickly replaced with apprehension. Refusing to give into her fear, she chose to play along.

"Well, Sir, though I may be your prisoner I still have two very fine feet and can walk to whatever destination you choose. I will not be carried like a common rug going out for wash."

Adrian continued to carry her out of the gazebo. After only a few steps he deposited her into a chair. Once upright Sydney could see that a lovely table had been set with candles and champagne. There were various platters of appetizers, all her favorites.

"Now my princess. Your torture will begin." He filled a flute with the chilled champagne, "You must be parched," he said as he put the glass to her lips. She took the glass, sipped and suppressed a grimace. His taste was apparently very different from hers when it came to selecting champagne because just like the flute they'd shared in his car on the previous evening, this left a bitter taste in her mouth.

She took the glass from him when he pressed it to her lips again and set it aside to select a canapé. "These look wonderful."

But tasted odd. She set the canapé aside after one bite. She washed the bite down with champagne, suppressing a shudder at the bitter bite of the drink."Not to your liking?" Adrian asked.

Sydney shrugged. "You know how it is, sometimes you're in the mood for something and sometimes you're not."

"I hope that does not extend beyond food."

The look on his face told her that it was a mistake to be there. She might not be interested in a relationship that extended beyond friendship, but clearly he was.

"I think I should go."

"Forgive me. I was pushing again. Please, stay."

"No, I really need to go. If you'll excuse me, I'll go change."

Before he could argue, she left the table. Her clothes were folded neatly on a chair, waiting for her. She changed quickly. Just as she was sliding on her shoes, she heard his voice behind her. "I would like for you to stay."

Sydney turned to face him. "Adrian, this isn't going to work."

"Why?"

She considered giving him a nice lie, coming up with an excuse. But that wasn't fair to either of them. "Because I'm involved. Emotionally involved with someone."

"And is this someone as emotionally invested in you?"

"Yes, he is."

"I see."

"I'm sorry, Adrian. I have to go."

He reached for her as she started by him and but she evaded his grasp and hurried through the house and out to her car. As soon as she started the engine she turned the AC on. It wasn't that warm but she could feel the perspiration on her skin, and a slight nausea bubbling in her stomach.

She had not consumed that much of the champagne. Maybe it was just a case of anxiety. She'd feel better once she got home. The evening had been a mistake but it had also been a wake-up call. As wealthy, charming and interesting as Adrian might be, he was not the man for her. Blake was.

Now, if she could just find the courage to let their relationship move forward, to let go of the past and look to the future.

Friday, April 16

It was almost noon by the time Sydney arrived at her office. As she got off the elevator her thoughts were on Adrian and their evening together. A shocked gasp tore from her throat as she turned the corner and saw the door to her office standing open and two men walking out, laden with boxes.

"What is the meaning of this?" she demanded, barring their way.

One man brushed by her, bumping into her shoulder and pushing her out of his way but the other stopped and turned around and walked back to the office door. "Sir?"

Special Agent Wells stepped out into the hallway and Sydney glared at him. "Would you care to explain what is going on? What are these men doing in my office and what are they taking out?"

He reached in his pocket and handed her a folded sheet of paper. She unfolded it and quickly scanned it. "This is incredible!" she fumed and marched passed him, shouting to the others in the office. "Everyone hold it right where you are!"

Obviously surprised by her appearance, the people in the room did just that. They all stopped and looked at her. She snatched up the phone on the secretary's desk and viciously dialed a number. "Hello, this is Sydney Forrest. Put me through to my father immediately."

"Don't you move!" she snapped at a man who bent over to pick up a box of files from the floor. "Dad! There's a bunch of FBI men in my office ransacking it. This agent Wells handed me some bogus court order giving them authority to take everything. You have to do something! This is illegal —okay, hold on."

She turned to agent Wells. "Senator Jack Forrest would like to speak with you."

"I have nothing to say to the Senator," Wells replied then looked at his men. "Okay, let's get finished up here. Jamison, you and Hardwick clear out the rest of these cabinets. I'm going to check on Williams and Talbot."

He ignored Sydney and walked into her private office. After a moment of stunned silence she put the phone back up to her ear. "He won't even come to the phone, Dad. What am I going to do? The judge? Yes, hold on."

She unfolded the paper Wells had given her. "It's Judge Walton Frieze—okay, thanks. Yes, I will. Bye."

She hung up the phone and walked into her office to find Wells leaning over another man's shoulder as the man typed away on the keyboard of her computer.

"Where are the files?" Wells looked at her.

"I don't know what you're talking about," she replied.

"The computer files. We can't get into them."

"How terrible for you."

Wells gave her a hateful look then turned his attention back to the man at the keyboard. "Try going directly from the system prompt and do a directory."

"I've already tried that," Talbot said. "Every time I do it locks the system up and I have to reboot."

He looked up at Sydney. "What have you done to this system?"

"Why nothing," she said sweetly. "Now, if it's not too much of a bother, could you give me some idea how long it's going to take you people to finish tearing up my office? I do have work to do."

Wells cursed. "Just turn off the damn thing. We'll take it with us."

"Just let me try one more thing," Talbot said.

Sydney walked over and watched him. As he typed she smiled to herself but yelped out loud. "No! Don't do that!"

Both men looked at her in surprise then Wells tapped Talbot on the shoulder. "Do it."

Talbot smiled and hit the enter key. The screen blinked several times then the disk made a soft whirring noise. Talbot started keying in one command after another but to no avail. The whirring sound of the disk drive went on for a few seconds then stopped and the screen went blank.

He looked up at Sydney. "What was that?"

"Beats me. I'm a psychiatrist, not a computer specialist."

Talbot cursed and stood. "I think she built some sort of self-destruct into the operating system. The entire system's dead."

Wells snorted and yelled at the man who was working on the wall safe. "Williams, you get that safe open yet?"

Williams pulled the door to the safe open with a smile. "Yes sir!"

Wells walked over and looked in the safe. It was empty. "Where are the tapes?" he turned to Sydney.

"What tapes?"

"Dr. Forrest, I warn you, you are in direct violation of a court order. I suggest that unless you want to be arrested for obstruction of justice you turn over those tapes to me."

"I can't turn over what I don't have, Agent Wells."

Wells turned to Talbot. "Take her in. Maybe she'll feel a little more cooperative after she's had a chance to think about it."

Sydney jerked away as Talbot tried to take her arm. "I'm not going anywhere with you people!"

"I'm afraid you are, Doctor," Wells disagreed as Talbot grabbed her arms to pull them behind her back.

Sydney scowled as he fastened restains on her wrists. "I believe I'm entitled to a phone call," she said as Talbot nudged her towards the door.

"You'll get your call, doctor." Wells took her arm and walked her out of the office. "Just as soon as we get those tapes."

Sydney gave him a hateful look but said nothing. Now she had to figure out how she was going to get herself out of this mess.

CR

Blake picked up the phone in his office. "Edwards."

"Blake? It's Sydney. I'm in trouble and I need your help."

"What's wrong?"

"I've been arrested. Can you do something to get me out?"

"Where are you? Why were you arrested?" Blake felt his heart thud rapidly.

"It's a little hard to explain. The FBI seems to think they have the right to come in and take my patient files without my permission. They wanted the tapes of my sessions and I refused so they arrested me."

"The FBI?" If she had been taken in by the bureau it was not going to be so easy for him to just walk in and bail her out.

"Blake, please get me out of here!"

"Okay, Syd, hold on. I'll be there as soon as I can."

He jumped up, grabbed his jacket and was headed out of his office when the phone rang again. Thinking that it might be Sydney he ran back and jerked it up. "Edwards–Sir?--Yes sir, right away."

"Damn!" He slammed his hand down on his desk. His supervisor wanted to see him and there was no way to refuse.

He walked down the hall and knocked on the supervisor's door. Once he heard the voice directing him to enter he opened the door. "You wanted to see me, sir?"

"Come in, Agent Edwards." His Supervisor, Paige replied. "Have a seat."

Blake sat down as ordered. "Agent Edwards, I understand you have become involved in a matter out of your area."

Blake's eyes flew open wide. He had only just spoken with Sydney. Her call must have been traced and someone had notified his supervisor. *Holy shit. Whatever she's mixed up in must be big.*

"Uh, yes sir. In a round about way. A friend - a woman I know - a doctor - has been taken in for refusing to turn over her patient files. She called and asked me to come down and–"

"I don't think that would be wise, Agent Edwards. This isn't your case and you'd be well served to leave it in the purview of those in charge. That is all."

"But sir!" Blake blurted. "I can't just let her sit there and . . ."

"That's exactly what you are going to do Agent Edwards." Paige stood. "Do I make myself clear?"

"Yes, sir," Blake said tightly.

"Then you may go."

Blake left the office and stood in the hall for a moment, wondering what was going on and how he could find out. An idea occurred to him and he ran back down the hall and into Weasel's office.

"I need your help," he whispered as he leaned over beside George We'zel.

Weasel turned with a frown. "What kind of help?"

"Something that only someone with a brain as big as yours can do. I need you to break into a computer system for me."

Weasel's eyes brightened behind the thick glasses. "Sounds interesting. Why don't you tell me more."

જ

Sydney sat alone in a room inside the FBI headquarters of the J. Edgar Hoover building. She had no idea even what part of the building she was in. She had gotten lost after only a few minutes. Aside from two chairs and a small table the room she was in was empty. Outside the door two agents stood on either side.

It had been hours since she had called Blake and there had been no word from him. She had refused to talk to anyone and for the last half hour she had been left alone.

At first she had been filled with righteous indignation. Now that was beginning to fade and fear was starting to rear its head. She didn't know what to do. She couldn't turn over the information they wanted. Not because she had anything of such importance. So far all she knew was that Senator Tyler had been taking payoffs from someone apparently involved in the big mortgage scandal around 2008. It was not that she thought the information was so damaging. It was more than that. She took the doctor patient privilege very seriously and to turn over the information was against everything she had sworn to hold true to.

The door opened and Agent Wells walked in. "Do you feel like talking now, Doctor Forrest?"

"No, actually I feel like going to the bathroom and making a phone call."

He stared at her for a moment then nodded. "Very well, Agent Sellers will escort you to the ladies room then to a phone. I will be back shortly."

He left the room and one of the men posted outside the door looked in. "Doctor Forrest? If you will come with me."

He walked with her to the ladies room and positioned himself just inside the door. She gave him an irritated look but he ignored it. Slamming the door of the stall she relieved herself then washed her hands and ran her fingers through her hair. "Can I make that call now?"

"If you'll please come with me," he gestured ahead of himself.

Sydney walked out of the restroom and went with the agent to another office. He motioned to the phone then took his position outside the room. For a moment she hesitated. She had no idea who to call. She considered her father, but dismissed the idea. She could not get him involved in this any deeper than she already had by calling him earlier.

Another possibility came to her and she picked up the phone and dialed, hoping she remembered the number correctly. After two rings a deep voice came on the line.

"Yes?"

"Adrian? Thank god. It's Sydney. I'm in big trouble and I didn't know who else to turn to."

"Tell me what's happened," his voice was calm and low.

She quickly explained the situation. "Just remain calm and do not answer any questions," he instructed. "I promise I will have you out of there within the hour."

"I hope so," she whispered. "Thanks,"

She hung up the phone and the agent took her back to the room where Agent Wells waited. "Are you ready to tell me where those tapes are Doctor?"

She shook her head and sat down, hoping that she had not made a mistake in calling Adrian. He might be wealthy and know a lot of important people but she had no idea if he had the kind of contacts it was going to take to get her out of this.

Chapter Three
Friday, April 14

Blake looked over Weasel's shoulder as he worked. The display flashed so quickly from one screen to another that Blake could not begin to read what was on it. After ten minutes Weasel looked up at him with a smile. "Here we are, dude."

Blake looked at the information on the screen. "Senator Ned Tyler? She was arrested for his patient files? That doesn't make sense. I haven't heard any dirt on Tyler, have you?"

Weasel shrugged and cut a look around. "You get a chance to check out that address I gave you?"

"No, not yet. Weasel, we need to find out what Tyler's up to. You have any ideas on how to do that?"

"I just might," Weasel's fingers danced on the keyboard. A few seconds later the screen filled with information. It was an article from the Associated Press about the Subprime Mortgage Crisis and hedge funds who manipulated politicians with illegal campaign contributions. Blake read through it then looked at Weasel. "I don't see what you're getting at. His name isn't even mentioned."

"That's right," Weasel exited the screen and keyed in a new address and search command. "But look right here."

Blake's eyes widened as he read the small article telling of a social event held at the home of banker who played a key role. There were quite a few notable figures attending. "So he is connected!"

"Could be," Weasel exited the screen.

"But it still doesn't make sense. If he was taking payoffs then he should have been named in the first article, so obviously his alleged involvement hasn't been made public. And anyway, if he were being investigated for something like that wouldn't it be by a Senate Investigative Committee? Why the FBI?"

Weasel shrugged and looked at Blake expectantly. Blake scratched the back of his neck and blew out his breath. "So what now?"

"Now I get back to what I'm being paid for," Weasel answered as he turned his attention to the computer. "And you do what you're trained to do."

"Which is?"

"Investigate."

Blake snorted but patted Weasel on the shoulder. "Thanks for your help pal."

"Anytime," Weasel did not look up but continued to click away on the keyboard. "You know what I always say – the deep web is where it all comes together. You just have to know where to look."

Blake thought about the comment as he returned to his office. He searched his pockets and finally located the piece of paper with the address Weasel had given him in the inner breast pocket of his suit jacket. After logging onto his computer, he opened a browser window and typed in the address into the search bar.

The screen went blank for a moment then a message printed at the top, letting him know that he was connected. He had no idea what he was suppose to do next.

Just as he was ready to forget all about it the screen changed and content displayed . It was a list of articles written about things like derivatives, securitization, collateralized debt obligations and criticisms for US trade policies and the country's involvement in NAFTA and the UN.

"What the hell?" he murmured as he leaned back and stared at the screen. "Why did Weasel give me this?"

ରଙ

Sydney looked up as Agent Wells and another older man walked into the room. "Dr. Forrest, my name is Raymond Sanders. I am the Assistant Director of the Criminal Investigative Division of the Federal Bureau of Investigation. I wanted to apologize to you personally for this unfortunate misunderstanding and tell you that you are free to go."

She stood and looked from Mr. Sanders to Agent Wells. "And my supposed tapes? Am I going to be harassed about that again?"

"No." He shook his head and cut a look at Wells. "And again I do apologize. It seems that our agents were a little overzealous in the performance of their duties. As we speak your files and records are being returned to your office."

"Well, thank you so much," she said sarcastically and started for the door.

Mr. Sanders stepped in her path. "There is one thing I would like to ask you, Doctor. If at some future time you suspect that any of your patients are indeed a threat to national security will you please contact me directly? I realize this is an unorthodox and possibly even unethical request but you must understand that we take our jobs very seriously and rely on many resources in order to do the job of insuring the security of this country. As a citizen and a patriot I am asking you to consider my request."

Sydney studied him for a moment then nodded. "I will consider it, sir. Now, could you possibly call me a cab? I find myself without transportation thanks to your subordinates."

"That will not be necessary. I have been informed that a car is waiting to take you home. Agent Wells will escort you outside."

"Thank you," she replied and walked to the door, followed by a very taciturn, hard-faced Wells. Neither of them spoke until they walked outside. He pointed to a long white Limousine then looked at her.

"I think it only fair to tell you that this isn't over, Doctor. We will find out what we need to know."

"I'm sure you will," she replied frostily. "Now, if you will excuse me, I've had enough of your delightful company for one day."

The limousine driver opened the rear door for her and she got in the car. As soon as he was behind the wheel he looked around at her. "Where to, Doctor Forrest?"

"Wherever I can find Adrian," she replied. She wanted to find out what he had done or what strings he had pulled to get her released from custody before she did anything else.

☙

After half an hour Blake leaned back in his chair and stared fixedly at the computer screen. He had been going through the information and there seemed to be no end to it.

A knock at his door made him look around. "Hey, Blake! What's shakin'?"

"Not much Steve, how 'bout you?"

"You know, the usual," Steve replied as he closed the door and took a seat in front of Blake's desk. "What're you working on?"

Blake made an expression of disgust, "Paperwork." He was not about to tell anyone he was conducting his own investigation on bureau time. Especially not Steve. He was a true-blue, to the core company man. At one time, Steve and Blake had been partners. Back when both of them were working for the Special Operations Group in New York. When Blake transferred to Washington, he had requested reassignment and had been working drugs ever since. Steve was still a SOG man, but now that he was in Washington, he was part of the TTS, or Technical Support Squad.

Like the Special Operations Groups elsewhere in the bureau, the TTS was a surveillance group. These agents did nothing but surveillance; break into homes or offices and install bugs, bypass alarm systems, break into computers, put tracking devices and bugs on vehicles, install wiretapping devices, program suspects answering machines to play back messages for them and pilot surveillance planes. In Washington, the TTS was in big demand; so much so that they had to turn down a great many requests for help. They were the best of the best.

"So what can I do for you?" Blake asked after a moment's reflection on the old days working SOG with Steve.

"I have an assignment for you if you want it."

Blake raised his eyebrows. "Really? Where?"

"Right here, old buddy. A nice cushy surveillance job."

"Surveillance?" Blake grimaced. "Doesn't sound too appetizing."

"You don't know who it is yet."

"So tell me."

"Senator Ned Tyler."

Blake's heart jumped in his chest. That made twice in one day Ned Tyler's name had come up. "Tyler? Why? You think he's into drugs?"

Steve shrugged. "Not exactly. At this point we don't know what he's into but there are rumors he's associated with some pretty unsavory types - certain shady businessmen. We just want to see what we can turn up. You interested?"

Blake pretended to consider it then nodded. "Maybe, but I'm not part of your squad. You get it cleared for me to switch over for this gig?"

"It's all taken care of, old buddy. It'll be just like the old days. So, you in or not?"

"Sure," Blake agreed. "Why not. When do I start?"

"Right now."

"Who's working with me besides you?"

"Like I said, it's just like the old days - just me and you." Steve put a folder on Blake's desk. "Paper work is all here. You finish up here and meet in front of Tyler's place at six. You got the six to one shift. He gets home by half past five."

"I'll be there," Blake agreed.

Steve left and Blake stared at the closed door for a long time. *This is too much to be coincidence. First Sydney gets hauled in by the bureau for refusing the turn over Tyler's records, then Weasel shows me the information on Tyler and some guy that was part of one of the hedge funds involved in the mortgage scam, and now he bureau is having Tyler watched. Something is definitely up.*

"So how do all these things tie together?" he mumbled as he looked back at the computer screen.

No answer came to him and he had no real desire to spend the rest of the afternoon reading through the files. He found a thumb-drive in his desk, plugged it into a USB slot and burned the information to it.

After checking through the paperwork Stever had left and finding it in order, he slid the folder into the top drawer of his desk. He rose, put on his jacket and stuck the drive in the inner breast pocket and turned off his computer. Might as well go home and change and grab something to eat before he met Steve at Senator Tyler's.

ℭℛ

Adrian was on the phone when Sydney was shown into the study. "We will have to continue this conversation at a later time. I have something that requires my immediate attention."

He hung up the phone, stood and walked to her, enveloping her in his arms. "My poor princess," he murmured and kissed the top of her head. "Are you all right?"

"I'm fine," she replied as he released her. "Just angry and confused. How did you get me out?"

"Actually I did very little."

"Well, you must have powerful influence."

"Nominal," he said and took her hand to lead her over to the leather couch. "I have thought of little else but you since you left last evening."

She sat down next to him. ""Adrian, I . . . " She shook her head and stood to walk to the window. After a moment of gazing out over the immaculate grounds she turned to find him watching her. "Adrian, I'm on unfamiliar and uncertain ground here. You're . . . well, to be honest, you're a little overwhelming and as I said, I'm involved with someone."

"Sydney, please, come here," he held out his hand to her.

She returned to the couch, ignoring his outstretched hand as she sat down beside him. "You have nothing to fear from me." He said in an earnest tone. " I will never betray you, I will never do anything but give you pleasure and happiness. I will give you what you want - what you really want in your secret heart."

"Adrian, that's very . . . well, it's quite a declaration," she said hesitantly. "But there's the matter of the man I'm seeing. Not to mention the fact that we barely know one another."

"Then we must rectify that," he pulled her close to him and moved his hand to her leg.

Sydney stopped his hand as it started up her leg. "I don't think this is the time or place, do you?"

He looked around as if surprised by her question then looked back at her. "Actually I think it's the perfect time and place."

His hand moved higher and she stopped it. "Adrian, no."

"No?" His eyes widened slightly in surprise then narrowed. "I do not like that word."

His hand started up her leg again and once more she stopped it. This time he grabbed her hand in his and bent her arm behind her back so that she arched forward against him. "You want me," he breathed into her face as his free hand moved to her breast.

Sydney felt fear race through her. She tried to jerk free just as the butler walked into the room. "Forgive me, Mr. Zayne. There is a call for you."

"Say that I will return the call later," Adrian answered without bothering to release Sydney or remove his hand from her breast.

Her embarrassment at being fondled in from of the butler made her fear diminish and she pushed at him in anger. "Stop!"

After a moment he released her and she straightened her skirt and stood. "I really have to go. My office is in a shambles and I have to call my patients and–"

"I understand," he interrupted. "But I must ask. Why were you arrested to begin with? Are you involved in something that I should know about?"

"No. I haven't done anything. They wanted me to turn over records from one of my patients and I refused."

"Has this patient done something that threatens the national security?"

She hesitated for a moment. "Adrian, I'd love nothing better than to tell you everything I know, but the truth is I don't know anything - and even if I did, I couldn't talk about it. What my patients tell me in therapy is private and confidential. I won't divulge anything like that to anyone. Not even you. I hope you understand."

"Not only do I understand, but I commend you," he said with a smile. "I would not have you betray that confidence, Sydney. You do not have to explain. I was merely concerned for your welfare."

"Thank you for helping me. "I have to go. Will you have your driver take me to my office?"

"Certainly." He stood and picked up the phone to inform the driver she was ready to leave.

"Will you come back when you finish?" he asked as they reached the front door. "I will have dinner prepared."

"I don't think that's a good idea."

"As a friend," he said then added. "Certainly I've earned that."

All right," she agreed after a moment's hesitation. "But I want to go home and change first."

"All right. And while you're there why don't you pack some things to bring with you?"

Her eyebrows drew together in a puzzled frown and he chuckled. "I would prefer that you not leave until morning."

"No. I'm not going to spend the night with you."

"But what pleasure might you miss if you decline?" Hhe ran his hands down her sides as he spoke.

"Looks, I thought I was clear on all this. Friendship is all I have to offer."

After a moment he agreed. "Fine."

"You're sure?"

"Absolutely."

"Okay, then I'll see you later."

As she got in the car she settled back and looked out of the window thinking about things. She didn't really believe he would be satisfied with being friends and the smart move would be to call him later and cancel dinner. But she did owe him. He'd come through for her when she needed it. Maybe she was reading more into it than she should. It was just dinner with a friend. Nothing else.

Monday, April 17

Sydney yawned as she unlocked the door of her apartment. It had been a very long day and she was looking forward to taking a long hot shower before she went over to Adrian's for dinner. She had not really wanted to but when she tried to refuse he said he would come to her apartment. That changed her mind. By going to his house at least she could leave when she was ready.

She did not know what it was about Adrian that concerned her. He seemed to have accepted that their relationship would never move beyond friendship and had not pressured her at all for more.

Maybe I'm just tired, she thought to herself. The weekend had been trying. After she left Adrian's on Friday she went to her office. Just as Mr. Sander's had promised, all of her files and records had been returned. Dumped in the middle of the reception room floor, to be exact. She had worked on putting everything back in place until after nine and had just started out the door to go to Adrian's when her father called.

He was understandably upset and wanted to see her. The meeting with her parents had been tense. There was nothing she could tell them that they did not know, except of course that she had called Adrian to get her out. That had opened a whole new can of worms. And her mother, had, of course wanted to know everything about the new man in her life. By the time the visit ended, Shirley had talked her into calling Adrian and planning a family dinner for the following evening. When she got home she found Adrian's limousine parked in front of her apartment building.

He had tried to talk her into inviting him to her apartment but she got out of it by telling him about the dinner at her parents' the next evening and promising to go over to his house after the dinner.

Saturday she had spent the entire day finishing up at the office and rescheduling all the appointments she had canceled. Blake had called and left a message that he would get in touch with her another time but said nothing about the incident with the FBI. Sydney thought it just as well that she had not spoken with him. Not only did she not want to say anything about going out with Adrian but she was a little put out with the way he had left her stranded when the FBI had taken her in.

The evening with her parents went as well as she expected but had a few surprises. Her mother was extremely impressed with Adrian and made a point of saying so. That was no surprise, especially after Sydney listened to her mother and Adrian talk about all the important people the two of them knew. The surprise was her father. Jack was uncommonly quiet and reserved the entire evening and she got the feeling that he did not share Shirley's enthusiasm for Adrian.

They had just left her parents' house when Adrian got a call and had to leave town on business. She had not seen him on Sunday, but he had called several times during the day and left messages that he wanted to see her as soon as he returned. Late that night she was wakened by him calling to say he was back and ask her to come over. She refused and told him she would see him the next afternoon.

As she let herself into her apartment she thought about how persistent he was. She didn't understand why he was pursuing her so ardently. It was flattering but puzzling. She checked her messages then started for the bathroom. She had just taken off her shoes when the doorbell rang. She opened the front door to find Blake standing there. She was startled to see him and also a little aggravated that he had left her stranded the way he had.

"Blake! I didn't expect you."

"Can I come in?"

"Oh, yes."

He walked in and turned to her as she closed the door. "Syd, what's going on? Why is the bureau interested in Ned Tyler and why were you taken in?"

"A better question is what happened to you?" she asked as she walked by him to the living room.

Blake followed her and sat down on the couch beside her. "I was on my way out the door. God as my witness. The phone rang and I thought it might be you so I picked it up and it was my supervisor. He ordered me to stay away."

"He ordered you?" She raised her eyebrows. "But how did he even know about it?"

"I asked myself that same question. Syd, is the Senator into something heavy? Are you in danger?"

"In answer to your first question, you know I can't say anything in regards to a patient. As to the second question, no, I'm not in any danger, as you can see."

"I didn't just abandon you," he said earnestly.

"I understand." She felt the knot of irritation dissolve. She could understand his position. Sometimes one's job placed obligations that could not be ignored and his obligations were to the bureau. "It's okay, it all worked out."

"How?"

"It just did," she evaded answering. "So how was your visit with Michael?"

"Good. He left this morning. But back to you - exactly how DID you talk them into letting you go?"

"Well, I'm glad you got to spend some time with Michael." She ignored his question and stood. "Want something to drink?"

"No, I don't want anything." He grabbed her hand as she started by him. "Syd, what's up?"

"Nothing," she said and left the room to go into the kitchen.

Sydney took a glass from the cabinet and turned toward the ice maker but Blake stepped in front of her and took hold of her arms. "You want to tell me what's going on or do you want me to guess?"

"I said it was nothing," she said, refusing to meet his eyes.

"Syd, look at me."

After a moment she looked up. "Blake, I-" she hesitated for a moment. "I-I'm sorry, it's nothing earth shattering. I had to call a friend to help me out. I didn't want to talk about it because I didn't want it to come between you and me and–"

He let go of her and stepped back. "Well, it must be pretty intense if you're so shaken up about it. Who is this friend?"

"That's not really important." She did not answer his question directly. "What matters to me is that you understand that this has no bearing on our relationship. I still–"

"Syd, let's cut the crap, okay? Obviously, you're pretty important to this guy for him to pull the kind of strings he did to intervene with the bureau. And you wouldn't have called him unless he was pretty important to you."

"In case you've forgotten, I called you first," she reminded him. His tone of voice was making her own anger rise.

"And I told you what happened."

Sydney bit back a sharp retort and took his hand. "Blake, I don't want to fight with you."

"What do you want?"

"I want –" she hesitated. "I want you to try and understand that just because I get together with a friend occasionally doesn't mean that I don't care about you. A lot of people have friends of the opposite sex and–"

"Just stop right there!" he interrupted her as he pulled his hand away from hers. "Syd, I'm not stupid and to be frank, you're too smart to try such a lame ploy. Whoever this guy is, he's not just some platonic friend. I personally don't think those kind of relationships are possible. Sex always comes into play somewhere along the way."

"I disagree." She jumped on the opportunity to change the subject. "There are many people of the opposite sex who are very close friends and sex is never an issue."

"Right. Name me one."

"My friend GW," she said with authority. "We've been friends since our freshman year in college and there's never been one thing about sex mentioned. We just happen to like one another and share a –"

"Common interest," he finished her sentence. "Yes, I know but I don't think that's what's happening with you and your mystery man and right now I don't want to talk about it anymore."

"Blake!" She ran after him as he turned and walked out of the room. "Wait!" She grabbed his arm as he headed for the door. "Please."

He stopped and turned to her. "I do care about you," she said softly. "Can't you please believe me?"

He put his hand on the side of her face and looked at her for a moment then nodded. "Sure, Syd. Listen, I've got to go. I'll see you around."

Sydney knew from the tone of his voice that he was telling her good-bye. She felt tears building up in her eyes and quickly looked away. She didn't want him to see her cry. His thumb stroked once over her skin then his hand fell away from her face. She didn't look up as he walked out of the door but as soon as the door closed she raised her head and stared at it.

She wanted to run after him but she knew it wouldn't change anything. Blake was a stubborn man and in his current mood would not listen to anything she had to say. She had to give him space and hope he'd realize that he was wrong.

One thing was for sure. Being friends, however uneasy, with Adrian had far too high a price. It was time to close that door.

ʘ

Blake got in his car and sat without moving, staring vacantly out the window. Part of him felt like smashing his fist through a wall. Another part wanted to crawl up in a dark corner somewhere and hide from the hurt in his heart. But he did neither because the most dominate part of him, the part that was always reasonable, would not allow him to move.

After a few minutes he sighed and lit a cigarette. This was not the first time a relationship had ended for him. The demands of his job put a strain on relationships. He was gone a lot and when he was home there was always the chance that his plans would be interrupted if something came up. That came with the territory.

During the years since his divorce he'd been involved with a number of women and all of those relationships had ended. But it was the first time the end made him feel so miserable. He knew that it would take him a long time to get over Sydney.

The beep of his watch reminded him that he didn'tt have time to sit around feeling sorry for himself. He was already late to relieve Steve at the Senator's.

When he reached the Senator's street in Georgetown he pulled up in front of the house across the street from Senator Tyler's. Steve's car was parked in the driveway.

Blake made his way to the side door and let himself in with the key Steve had provided. Steve was in the front room, staring out of the window, smoking and thumping his ashes in an ashtray that overflowed onto the floor.

"Anything happening?"

Steve turned and shook his head. "He got home about half an hour ago. So far there's nothing on the audio except him and his old lady arguing about him eating too much red meat and drinking too much scotch. I'll relieve you in the morning."

Blake nodded and took a seat in the chair by the window. It was going to be a long night. Not only was surveillance a lonely and boring job, but now he had his own personal problems to torment himself with. Or so he assumed. Ten minutes later he changed his mind. The Senator's car was backing down the drive.

He left the house, went quickly to his car and pulled out onto the street, following the Senator at a discrete distance. The Senator drove to the Watergate Hotel. He left his car with the valet and went inside. Blake parked his car in front of the hotel and showed his identification to the valet, telling him not to bother the car. He followed the Senator to the elevator and got in with him.

"What floor?" he asked over his shoulder.

"Penthouse," Tyler replied shortly.

Blake pressed the button for the fifth floor and got off when the doors opened. He took the next available car down to the lobby and went directly to the desk. "Excuse me." He showed his identification to the desk clerk. "Could you tell me who is registered in the penthouse suite?"

"No one is there at present," the clerk replied. "That suite is reserved exclusively but is not being used right now."

Blake frowned. "Reserved by who?"

"Mr. Zayne."

"Thank you," Blake made a mental note of the odd name and walked back outside to his car. A few minutes later Senator Tyler emerged from the hotel. The valet brought his car around and he got in.

Blake followed him from Washington, across the river and into the suburbs of Maryland. The Senator stopped in front of the entrance to an enormous estate and Blake drove slowly past him, seeing him talking on his cell phone.

He made a left turn at the next corner, stopped and looked back. The Senator was pulling away from the house, headed back the direction he had come. Blake turned around and drove back by the estate, making note of the address. He had gone less that a block when his attention was taken by a car coming toward him.

His eyes widened as they passed. It was Sydney. He looked into the rear-view mirror ande saw her pull up to the gates of the estate where the Senator had stopped. A moment later her car disappeared through the tall iron gates.

Blake frowned tightly and pulled out his cell phone to call the Bureau. "Put me through to George We'zel," he said as soon as the call was answered. "It's Blake Edwards. . . . Weasel, hey. Listen I want you to run down a name and also an address for me. The name's Zane . . . No, I don't know how it's spelled. . . As soon as he had relayed the address he added, "and I want that as soon as possible, okay? . . . yeah, call me on my cell. Thanks."

He ended the call, lit another cigarette and inhaled slowly. Maybe this assignment would not be so dull after all.

◌

Adrian was waiting at the door when Sydney pulled up in front of his house. She got out of the car and walked up the steps to him.

"I'm not going to like what you have to say, am I?" he asked.

"Probably not."

He sighed and stepped aside, gesturing for her to precede him inside. "Then let's get it over with, shall we?"

She nodded and entered the house. She wasn't going to enjoy it either, but it was necessary. Once she ended the friendship, she might be able to convince Blake to give their relationship a chance. At least that was her hope.

Wednesday, April 19

John F, Seiberling Federal Building Akron, Ohio

As the city filled with cars; people hurrying to their jobs and to drop their children off at day care, a yellow Ryder truck pulled up in front of the north side of the John F, Seiberling Federal Building. No one paid much attention to the man who got out of the truck and walked away.

Minutes later an explosion rocked the city. Intense light flashed as the force of the explosion ripped up through the federal building. The first massive boom was followed almost instantaneously by the deafening roar caused by the collapse of the building. One after another, the floors collapsed onto the next below in a domino effect. With the flying glass from the windows rained down a barrage of office furniture, chunks of concrete, tangled wires and human bodies.

On the second floor of the building, just moments before the bomb exploded, people sat at a conference table, laughing and talking as they waited for a meeting to begin. When the explosion occurred, the windows imploded. Many of the people in the conference were tossed, still in their chairs, across the room, others burned by the heat.

On the fourth floor of the building a sixty-two-year old secretary for the Department of Housing and Urban development crawled dazed and bloody toward the stairs. Two floors below a man crawled free from where he was trapped beneath a table to see daylight instead of walls surrounding him.

The normal sounds of traffic were not to be heard. Instead there was the sound of groaning metal, shifting concrete, falling glass, wood, and plaster and worst of all, screams of pain and fear.

The destruction did not stop at the federal building. On the opposite corner of the street in a day care center, children sat at rows of tables in front of the windows, eating breakfast, filled with the enthusiastic joy that only children seem to possess. Workers raced to get the children outside to safety, heedless of their own safety or injuries. In wide-eyed terror the children huddled around their day-care teachers, desperate for some measure of assurance that the world had not suddenly turned into a place they could not understand. But that was exactly what had happened.

Around the point of the explosion there was other damage. Cars that had been overturned were on fire in the streets. Windows that were blown out of buildings added glass to the debris. The center of the city had abruptly changed from a normal spring morning to a terror stricken scene from a nightmare.

Almost immediately a call was placed to the police. Seconds later a message was entered into the NCIC, the FBI's massive computer system. Before the first emergency vehicle could arrive on the scene, bureau offices all over the country were receiving the news, as was the White House and other government offices. The unthinkable had happened again.

ଓ

At five minutes after nine in the morning, Blake was sitting at the kitchen table with the laptop in front of him. He'd been there for hours, going over everything time after time. He lifted his cup to his mouth, grimaced at the taste of cold coffee and set it back down. As he scrolled down the list he'd composed he frowned.

After he saw Sydney turn into the same estate he had followed Senator Tyler his curiosity had run wild. What was she doing there? Was it coincidence that she had shown up right after the Senator or had they planned to both be there? Who owned the estate? And why had the Senator not been allowed in? Who had he called on his cell phone?

The questions had kept him busy half the night until Steve showed up for the next shift. Blake picked up his cold cup of coffee and went into the kitchen to get a fresh cup. As he did he continued to think about the events of the previous night.

Weasel had finally gotten back to him with the information he'd requested, but it led only to more questions. He wasn't sure how any of it fit together but he was sure that he was going to do whatever it took to find out.

Blake retuned to the computer and sat down to read over what he had entered:

1. Senator Ned Tyler: possible illegal campaign contributions from someone involved in the big mortgage sandal of mid 2000s. No evidence to back up allegations, but proven acquaintance between Tyler and several big hedge fund owners who were involved.

2. Sydney Forrest: Tyler's psychiatrist. Taken into custody by FBI for refusing to turn over Tyler's patient files and tapes of sessions. Suddenly released. Someone with clout pulling strings - but who and why?

3.   Senator Tyler put under surveillance by FBI – no firm reason behind surveillance other than allegations of possible bribes being accepted from hedge fund owners.

4.   Tyler goes to Watergate Hotel to see Adrian Zayne. Zayne not there. Tyler then goes to an estate in Maryland owned by Zayne and is refused entrance. While in front of gate he makes a call from his cell to Maryland number of Zayne.

5.   Tyler leaves at almost the same time Sydney shows up. Why was she there? Is this her mystery man?

6.   Adrian Zayne: Age 42, never married, no children. Billionaire, no arrests, no traffic violations. Record squeaky clean. Graduated Harvard Law with honors – took over family empire. Parents both deceased - killing in IRA terrorist car bombing in London when Zayne was 18. Zayne has connections with numerous politicians as well as connections to the White House specifically through the president. They were both at the openings of two golf courses in Russia and Zayne contributed heavily to the President's election campaign. He has been referred to as an advisor on more than one occasion. No political aspirations of his own and registered as a Republican.

Blake finished reading and leaned back in his chair to frown at the screen. After reading what he had entered he was struck with the thought that maybe it was all just some strange coincidence. It was not beyond the realm of possibility that Tyler and Zayne were simply friends. Or Zayne could be one of Tyler's campaign contributors. Tyler was Republican.

But how does Sydney figure in? Did Tyler introduce her to Zayne or did Zayne recommend her to Tyler? Why would the FBI be interested in Tyler for no more than illegal campaign contributions - or is there more to it than that? If so, then where does Zayne play into things?

"Same questions - over and over," he mumbled and reached for the keyboard to clear the screen. "This is getting nowhere fast."

The phone rang and he reached for it instead of the keyboard. "Yeah?"

"Report in immediately. We have a situation."

Blake did not bother to ask why or what. He hung up the phone and went into the bedroom to change from his jeans into a suit and tie. Five minutes later he was on his way out the door.

He had not made it to his office before he met Steve in the hall. "What's up?"

"That's what we're about to find out."

They made their way to the meeting room where a number of people were already gathered. For the next ten minutes as the room filled to overflowing there was much speculation as to the reason they had all been called in. Blake saw Weasel come in the door and motioned him over.

"You know what's going on?" he asked as Weasel took a seat beside him.

Weasel cut a look at Steve who leaned forward to look at him then shook his head and faced forward in his seat. Blake got the distinct feeling that Weasel did know something and opened his mouth to question him further. At that moment a hush fell over the room and he turned his eyes forward.

The Director of the Federal Bureau of Investigations, Robert Mueller took a position at the front of the room. He took one look around then began to speak. "At approximately nine o'clock this morning, Central Daylight Time John F, Seiberling Federal Building Akron, Ohio was bombed. At present we do not know the number of fatalities or the extent of the damage. The ATF and this bureau has people on the scene and will forward updates as soon as more is known. At present, we believe the device used to be a car bomb but no confirmation has been made."

Blake could feel the sense of shock and consternation from the people around him as Director Mueller looked out over the assembly. "I do not need to stress the seriousness of this matter nor the importance of locating the responsible party or parties as quickly as possible. Attorney

General Gonzales assures me that we will be given every assistance we need from the U.S. Attorney's Office. We will be working in cooperation with the ATF and local and state authorities. Your individual assignments will be posted at the end of this meeting.

"Ladies and gentlemen, I have given the President my personal guarantee that we *will* get whoever is responsible for this heinous crime. I have every intention of keeping my word. Thank you."

Mueller walked out of the room and for a moment there was complete silence. Blake thought about what the Director had said. He did not doubt his declaration of intent for one moment and he suspected no one else in the room did either. If Meuller gave his word you could take it to the bank that he would do as he promised. That was the kind of man he was.

The Deputy Director stepped forward. He called several agents' names, directing them to meet him in his office after the meeting to go over their assignments in Akron, Ohio. Blake hoped to hear his name but was disappointed. When the meeting was concluded, he made his way to the front of the room where the Assistant Director of the Criminal Division was speaking with several of the agents whose names had been called.

"Excuse me, sir. Could I speak with you?"

"What can I do for you, Edwards?"

"Sir, I'd like to request that I be assigned to the scene."

"The assignments have been posted, Agent Edwards. You will proceed with yours as directed by your department supervisor."

Blake started to protest but the assistant director turned away. Disappointed, Blake headed for the exit. He found Weasel waiting for him.

"Bummer, huh?" Weasel asked. "You wanted to go."

"Yeah," Blake grumbled.

"Well, cheer up. Just because you're not there doesn't mean you can't work on the case."

Blake looked at him with a puzzled frown. "You trying to make a point, Weasel?"

Weasel smiled and shrugged as he started towards the door. "Seems to me you're already one step ahead of everyone else, Blake. You already know where to start looking."

Blake stopped and looked at him in complete confusion. "I do?"

Weasel did not stop or even turn around. "Surf's up, dude. Ride the wave."

Blake watched him leave the room, wondering what in the world he was talking about. Then it dawned on him. Weasel was right. He was already one step ahead of the game. If it was a car bomb then it had to be terrorism and he had the file on all the groups in the U.S.. That was one of the things the address Weasel had given him had provided. Blake had downloaded it to his computer.

If he just had it with him. The beginnings of a scowl changed to a smile. He did not need the drive. He had a computer in his office. All he had to do was like Weasel said. Get back online and find the site again. Feeling once more like a man with a mission he headed for his office.

Once there, he turned on the computer in his office and logged onto the Internet. He keyed in the address Weasel had given him and tapped his fingers impatiently on the desk top. "What the hell?" he mumbled. The address was no longer active. There was nothing.

He picked up the phone and dialed Weasel's extension.

"Speak." Weasel's voice came on the line.

"Weasel - Blake. Listen I was trying to get to something online and I can't find it. It's like it's not there anymore. An address can't just disappear, can it?"

"People pull the plug all the time," Weasel replied. "Think of it like the ocean, man. Today you might surf a couple of regular waves and catch one killer ride. Tomorrow you go back and there's no guarantee the same killer wave will return. The tsunami comes and goes, dude. You ride it as long as you can then move on to the next one. Just look for the next wave and be ready to copy and save. "

Blake frowned at the analogy. "Thanks."

He hung up the phone, sat back and stared thoughtfully at the screen. The only thing he could do was to go home and get on his own machine. He needed to look at that file more closely.

☙

The phone buzzed and Sydney punched the intercom button. "Yes?"

"Doctor, Senator Tyler is here. I think you should see him."

Sydney sat up straight in her chair. "Yes, of course, send him in."

She stood up and started for the door. It opened before she reached it and Ned Tyler stumbled into the room. She caught him and helped him to a chair. He was trembling and crying and mumbling incoherently. At first she thought he was drunk.

" Senator." She knelt down in front of him. "Try to listen to me. You have to calm down. Do you hear me?"

"It's my fault!" he suddenly shouted. "I should have done something. Oh, God! My fault, all my fault."

His words dissolved into another fit of crying. Julie returned with a glass of water and gave it to Sydney. "Hold all my calls," Sydney directed. "And reschedule my last two appointments."

As soon as Julie left, Sydney sat down across from the Senator. "Here, have some of this, sir."

Tyler lashed out verbally. "You think that's going to help? How stupid can you be? Don't you get it? It's my fault. All those people are dead and it's my fault."

Sydney realized that he was not drunk, as she had initially assumed. "I have no idea what you're talking about," she said as she set the glass on the table between the two chairs. "Senator, look at me. I can't help you unless you can talk to me calmly and rationally."

He turned his red eyes to her and she leaned forward closer to him. "Listen to me carefully. I want to put you under hypnosis. It will help to calm you so that we can talk. Will you agree to that?"

After only a moment's hesitation he nodded. She smiled gently and spoke in a slow even tone. "Good. Now I want you to concentrate on the sound of my voice. Only that."

He blinked a couple of times and swayed slightly but kept his eyes on hers. "Good, now on my command you will take long slow deep breaths. Inhale. That's good. Now exhale, slowly, slowly. Inhale. Good, exhale.

"Now as you continue to breath slowly, taking long deep breaths you will concentrate on the sound of my voice. I'm going to help you feel calm so that we can speak about what is bothering you. You're going to feel very calm and relaxed. In fact, you're beginning to relax now. Very good. Just let yourself relax.

"Lean back comfortably and feel the tension ease from your muscles . A feeling of relaxation is stealing over you. I want you to close your eyes. I'm going to count to ten. With each number your relaxation will deepen. You will feel calm and relaxed but your mind will be alert and focused.

"One, you are very relaxed, your muscles are beginning to lose some of their tension. Two, the feeling of relaxation is increasing. Three, the tension in your body is dissipating like a light fog in the morning sun. Four, your mental tension is dissolving. Five, you are going deeper into relaxation. Six, you are reaching a place where tension does not exist. Seven, you are safe and protected. Eight, calm and protected and relaxed. Nine, you are sinking into this protected state of relaxation. Ten, you are there."

She fell silent and regarded him for a moment then got up and turned on the recorder. "Senator?" she sat down again. "Do you hear me?"

"Yes."

"Very good. I want you to tell me what was troubling you when you first arrived."

"All those people dying."

"You feel responsible for deaths?"

"Yes."

Sydney frowned. "Senator, I want you to think back to our last session. During that session you told me that taking money from some unethical businessman was the least of your problems. Do you remember that?"

"Yes."

"Can you tell me now what those problems you referred to are?"

"Yes."

"Then tell me."

The senator licked his dry lips and cleared his throat. "I started back in '2004 . . . the first week of July . . .

Senator Tyler walked into the private conference room at the Watergate Hotel to find four other men waiting. An expensively dressed man with unusual green eyes at the head of the table stood and smiled.

"Senator Tyler, thank you for agreeing to meet with us. Please, have a seat. I believe you know these gentlemen?"

Tyler nodded at the rest of the men, all of whom he was acquainted with, and took a seat. The man reclaimed his seat and turned his attention to the man to his right. "General?"

The heavy set man with short iron gray hair nodded and looked around at everyone. "As you all know this country is at present under the threat of another eminent terrorist attack. 9/11 was a merely a warning of−"

"Excuse me," Tyler interrupted. "Under threat of eminent attack? Forgive me, General, but I have heard nothing of any threats."

"Then you are very ill informed," a fellow by the name of Greenland spoke up. "General, if you would allow me to preempt you for a moment."

The General nodded and Greenland turned to Tyler. "Senator, let me give you a little reality check. 9/11 is hardly an isolated act of terrorism in this country. The Federal Bureau of Investigation thwarted a terrorist plan to detonate bombs in the Lincoln and the Holland tunnel under the Hudson river, in the United Nations headquarters and the Manhattan building where the New York office of the Federal Bureau of Investigation is located."

Tyler blanched at the news and swallowed nervously. "But I never heard anything about that!"

"Nor would you ever," Greenland said. "My point is, Senator, that terrorism is not a remote possibility, something that *could* come into our lives. It is here. Luckily, the FBI had an informer on the inside and was able to prevent the scenario I just described to you. But next time we may not be so lucky. And let me assure you, sir, there *will* be a next time.

Tyler looked around at the men. "I don't understand. Why exactly are you telling me this?"

The General took the floor. "Ned, we're old friends and you know that I don't scare easy. But this time, I'm starting to sweat. You have to understand. Terrorism is on the rise on a global scale. And as the superpower on the globe we are in eminent danger. We are the focal point of tremendous hope as well as deep resentments. Not only do we have to worry about the Islamic fundamentalists who see us as Satan, the evil protector of Israel, but we have just as many threats from within our own borders. Subversive and anti-government, anti-military groups are gaining in strength daily. In short, we are sitting ducks."

"Hardly!" Tyler scoffed. "Why we're the strongest nation on—"

"Are we?" The General interrupted. "I don't think so. Terrorists can come and go in and out of this country with no trouble at all. We have tens of thousands of people going in and out of this country from all over the globe. Who's going to spot a terrorist among all these numbers? And explosives can be purchased by almost anyone without ever raising suspicion. Just consider the kind of bomb that can be built with no more than diesel fuel and certain fertilizers that can be purchased at any corner hardware store. And what about the enemy from within? Like the serial bomber? The man who is responsible for sending mail bombs to the University of California professor and the Yale University associate professor? The same man who is suspected of being responsible for twelve other bombings? Are we safe from him?"

Tyler shook his head. "No—I mean, I don't know. I'm not—just what is your point?"

"My point is that this country is vulnerable and unless the government takes swift and drastic action our people are in eminent danger."

"What kind of action are you referring to?"

"Wide ranging. First we need to elect a leader who will help us to rebuild the might of our military," the general replied and gave a nod to the fourth man of their group. Tyler wasn't friends with the man, but had met him and knew he moved in powerful circles and not just in this country.

The General continued. "And Ned, you and I and everyone else in this room knows that the military's budget has being slashed dangerously low. Along with that, we're being placed in the role of international policemen - expected to go on foreign soil and police a foreign population. I'll be straight with you. Our troops are not prepared or trained for that type of role. Look at our success rate thus far. The media is full of stories. We cannot be expected to perform at optimal levels without optimum training and equipment and that - as we all know - is not possible without funding."

"So that's what this is all about? Funding?" Tyler looked around.

"Essentially, yes," the General replied. "What we - and many others within our respective groups want is to see – among other things – the military budget increased."

"I don't think that's going to happen," Tyler responded. "Wes, let's be reasonable. I - we people of the Senate and Congress - we can't go to our constituents and say "hey, I've decided to cut education and clean air and welfare and give that money to the military. The public simply won't go for it. The Cold War is over and Americans just don't see the need to spend billions of dollars of their tax money on a fat military."

"Exactly," the man who had first greeted him spoke up. "You've cut right to the heart of the matter, Senator."

"I have?" Tyler was confused.

"Yes," the man smiled. "What is required is a change in public opinion. And a change in leadership."

"A change?" Tyler looked around. "Well, I know a lot of people want to get the Democrats out of office and perhaps if we had a strong enough candidate we could do that. But something that will make the people want to increase the military budget? Well, color me stupid but I can't think of anything short of world war three that would do that."

The man laughed quietly. "Perhaps not, Senator. But I can."

"I can still remember the smile on his face when he said that," Tyler said. "I looked into those damn jungle cat green eyes of his and part of me wanted to run out of that room. But I didn't. I should have. I should have run as fast and far as I could."

Sydney listened with a sense of growing horror. When Senator Tyler fell silent she was so stunned by what he'd said that for a moment she couldn't speak. Finally, she cleared her throat. "And so after this meeting - were you ever contacted by these people again?"

"Many times. He's a demon from hell, Doctor - the devil himself. He said he would change the mind of the people. That there would come a day when I would see the tide turn. And I did. We all did.

"Just look at who's sitting in the White House. Did anyone ever dream that was a real possibility? But it happened. So the devil came through on that and now on this. I just never dreamed that he would do something like this. My god, how can I live with all those deaths on my head. If only I had had the courage to go public - expose them - all of them. I could have brought down the entire house of cards."

He paused and she waited in expectant silence, anticipating that he had more to say. "But it would have brought everything down with them," he said softly. "How could I do that? The country would be in chaos, there would be no government - no one to head the military. Anarchy would reign and we would truly have been vulnerable - completely without protection. What could I have done but a prisoner in this territory of lies I find myself inhabiting..

"But the children, Doctor, the children. How can I ever look at my grandchildren without seeing the faces of those who died today? How can I live knowing that I didn't have the courage to try and stop it? How —"

Tyler started to gasp and his face paled. Sydney jumped up and grabbed his shoulders. "Listen to me," she tried to be very calm. "The anxiety you feel is going to subside. Breathe slow and evenly and feel the anxiety diminish. You must concentrate only on my voice. I'm going to count backwards from ten to bring you out. When I finish counting you will be calm and completely coherent."

Tyler was still breathing heavily but not in heaving pants and gasps like before. She counted evenly but quickly. After she reached the number one she sat back in her chair. "Senator?"

Tyler blinked and looked at her with the eyes of the condemned. "Doctor Forrest, what am I going to do? How can I live with myself?"

She leaned forward slightly. "Senator, we all make decisions we later regret and the only way to resolve the regret is to take steps to right whatever wrongs we might have done. I'm not convinced you are responsible for the things you claim, and I think you should take some time to think about that. I'd like for you to come back tomorrow, if possible. I think that with more frequent sessions I may be able to help you."

He barked a harsh laugh. "Therapy? You think therapy's going to change anything?"

"No, I don't. But I think it can help you see things objectively and clearly. That's what you came to me for, isn't it?"

He nodded and stood up. "Yes. I'll be here, but it will have to be later in the afternoon around five."

"That's fine, I'll see you then."

He started to go to the door but stopped and looked at her. "Doctor, do you think I'm a monster?"

"No, Senator, I don't. I think you're a person with a problem and my only concern is helping you see a way out of that problem."

"Thank you," he nodded. "I'll see you tomorrow."

Sydney watched him leave then ran to her desk to stop the recording. She quickly copied the audio file to a flash drive and then deleted it from her computer. "Deaths?" she whispered. "What is he talking about?"

She put the flash drive into her purse and left the office to go home where it was private. She didn't know where all this was leading, but she felt it was important to record what Senator Tyler had told her and put the information where it would not be found.

The moment she arrived at her apartment she went straight to the computer. It took her almost half an hour to transfer and review the data and then hide the file along with the others. After leaving a message for GW to retrieve the file and store it with the others but not to decode it, she went into the bedroom to change clothes. She turned on the television set as she took off her jacket and unzipped her skirt. When she heard the word "bomb" she turned to the set.

Her hand flew to her mouth as her legs turned to rubber. Sydney sank down on the end of the bed and stared in horror at the screen, hearing for the first time the news about the bombing in Akron.

A lump formed in her throat as the camera switched to show a still shot of a fireman carrying the body of a small child from the destruction. The child's hair was matted with blood and its body was covered with stains. The child's small body hung limply in the strong arms of the fireman. His face wore an expression of grief, compassion and deep sadness as he looked down at the tiny child.

The scene switched to show video footage of people running out of the building after the explosion; people bloodied and terrified. But the most heartbreaking scenes were that of the children; innocence that could not understand but could only experience the horror and pain, huddled together with those who had brought them to safety, looking like victims of a war no one knew had started.

The newscast was interrupted by a briefing from the White House. The President had just signed an Executive Order, shutting down all entry into the United States by anyone other than a US citizen with a permanent residence. He was quoted as saying that it was time to close the borders, suspend immigration and put the safety of the nation first.

If need be, he would declare a state of martial law, issue a national curfew and suspend all travel with the States.

Sydney felt a sickness take hold in her stomach as she watched. She didn't know whether to support the travel ban or not. All she could think about were Tyler's words. *The children. What about all the children, he said. My god, he knew!*

Chapter Four
Wednesday, April 19th
Akron, Ohio

While rescue teams worked frantically to get to the people trapped inside the federal building other specialists were hard at work to discover clues that would lead them to the person or persons responsible. Four FBI "fly-away teams", their computers and forensic equipment had been dispatched to the scene. At the Strategic Information Operations Center in FBI headquarters in Washington, D.C., the mood was one of confident optimism. Those who were experienced in such investigations understood one very fundamental truth about people who commit such terrible crimes. Regardless of who they are or how careful they might be, they always leave clues.

Two blocks from ground zero in Akron, the first clue came in the form of a piece of hard evidence. An FBI agent finds a twisted piece of charred metal; a piece of a truck axle with a vehicle identification number on it. He immediately took the fragment back to the command center and gave it to his superior who fed the VIN into the computer.

Within moments the FBI had its first lead. The truck was a Ryder vehicle, manufactured in Detroit by Ford, and assigned to a rental company in nearly three hundred miles from Akron.

Meanwhile the news media was jumping. A Palestinian-American man was reported to be traveling from Akron to the Middle East. He was spotted in Atlanta at the airport and detained. The news media reported that he was an interpreter who had been in the employ of the government for over a decade, but the NSA scooped him up and secreted him away for what the White House Press Secretary was calling "high level interrogation."

There were groups outraged by the man's arrest and protests already springing up over it, claiming it to be just another example of racial prejudice.

Immediately around the country, supporters of the administration were beginning to point accusatory fingers. Every middle-eastern group in America was being looked at suspiciously. Many were quick to point out that it had been middle-easterners who were responsible for the World Trade Center bombing and 9/11.

Like a tidal wave, mistrust and suspicion washed over the country, fueled by news reports and speculation. Neighbors began looking at each other through the eyes of prejudice and bigotry. The explosion had destroyed much more than was originally thought. Now it threatened to sweep the country into the kind of fear and racism that precipitates violence.

Washington, D.C.

Sydney had no idea how long she had been sitting on the bed, watching in horror as the reports continued from. When at last, the network returned to the regularly scheduled program that was in progress she remained fixed in place; her eyes staring vacantly at the television screen while her mind was filled with Senator Tyler's words.

But the children, Doctor, the children. How can I ever look at my grandchildren without seeing the faces of those who have died this day? How can I live knowing that I did not have the courage to try and stop it?

Sydney's mind was in a whirl. Without realizing it she jumped up and began to pace the floor in rapid, nervous steps. If Tyler really did have foreknowledge of this unspeakable act of savagery–if his story was true–then it was clear this was not, as the media hinted, the work of some fundamentalist middle-eastern group. The plot had not originated somewhere thousands of miles across the world. It had been hatched right here in this country. And aside from the others involved with Senator Tyler she was the only one who knew the truth.

"Oh, my god!" Her legs suddenly felt as if they would collapse beneath her. "I'm the only one who knows!"

Fear and uncertainty rose like a wave of nausea, threatening to overwhelm her. She didn't know what to do. She couldn't break the doctor patient privilege and reveal what she knew. But how could she remain silent?

"God, help me," she whispered. "Somebody tell me what to do." *First you need proof,* a small voice inside her head spoke up. *Right now all you have are the ramblings of a mentally disturbed man. You need more.*

Yes! She grabbed onto the thought with desperation. *That's it. I need proof. Names and dates—something I can verify. I can start at his session tomorrow. But I have to be careful how I handle this. What I'll have to do is—"*

The ring of the doorbell interrupted her thoughts. She quickly pulled on on a robe over her blouse and pantyhose and went to the door. Senator Tyler stood outside. She could smell the alcohol on him.

"Senator! What are you doing here?"

"I—I didn't know where else to go," he stammered. "Doctor, I can't take it anymore. I have to talk to someone!"

"Come in." She stepped aside. "Please, have a seat. Let me change and I'll be right back."

Sydney ran back to the bedroom, threw on a pair of jeans and took off her blouse, replacing it with an old tee-shirt that Blake had given her. The words, "shrinks do it in therapy" wrinkled across the front. She grabbed her phone and returned to the living room to find Senator Tyler sitting on the couch with his head in his hands.

He looked up momentarily as she entered the room. She took a seat in the chair that was adjacent to the couch.

"Doctor, what am I going to do?" Tyler sighed despondently, dropping his head back down.

"I can't tell you that," she replied softly as she access the record function on her phone and slid it behind a picture on the end table. "That's something you must decide for yourself. I can only listen and hopefully help you to be able to reach that decision."

He looked up at her with red, tear-filled eyes. "I once used to wonder about men such as Hitler, Mussolini—how they could close their eyes and go to sleep at night knowing the atrocities they had allowed to happen, the lives they had let be destroyed. Now, here I am, in that same position and I find myself asking, how can I ever expect to sleep again. How can I ever live with this?"

Sydney consider it for a moment and then leaned forward. "Senator, I'd like to put you under hypnosis, like we did this afternoon. If you can go back to when this started, remember it clearly; perhaps you can find some clue as to how you became enmeshed, whether it was truly your choice. Perhaps we can find a way for you to extricate yourself from the problem."

He did not speak for a long time then finally he nodded. It did not take long for her to guide him into a hypnotic state. When he was relaxed and ready she began. "You previously told me that someone at the first meeting told you that there was a way to change the opinion of the people concerning increasing the budget of the military."

"Yes,"

"Was the subject of subsequent meetings the same—the military budget?"

"Essentially, yes," he replied. "Normally the subject of the budget would be mentioned. Especially in the beginning. But then it started to change."

"In what way?"

"He would start talking about terrible things—saying things like "suppose, hypothetically a bomb were to go off in, for example, a skyscraper in the middle of New York, or Los Angeles?" He would use different examples each time and after each example he would ask me what I thought the American people would think. If their lives were in danger, if there was no place that was safe, would they welcome the presence of the military on every street corner, in front of every building and in every shopping mall? Would they welcome a leader who wanted to close our borders, cut off trade with other countries? Would they then be so against increasing the budget if the President had the military standing guard over them to insure their safety?"

Sydney thought about it for a moment then directed another question to him. "And these men—I believe you named a General and a man by the name of Greenland? Was there ever anyone else at these meetings?"

"At the meetings?" he shook his head. "Wes and Greenland were only at the first meeting. I'd see them around, with the others. The General was always there along with - well, never mind. There are a lot of people in this, you see, a great many. If the American public knew . . . they wouldn't trust any of us from the city mayors to the President. We'd all be hanged at dawn. But the entire contingent never met formally. I knew who they were because I saw them with him from time to time. I didn't have to ask what it was about. I knew. It was just like the times I was with him. He would tell me what was going to happen—without actually coming out and saying it. It was always posed as a hypothetical situation, a 'what if.' But I knew what he meant. I just didn't want to believe that he'd go through with it."

"You keep saying he," she responded quietly. "Who is this person?"

"The devil!" his voice rose in volume and filled with emotion. "A demon from the blackest hell, a creature with no conscience, no compassion, no feelings. He– "

Sydney moved beside the Senator as his breath became labored and strained. He pushed her away as she sat down. "He found out about the money I took from that – that damn hedge fund and used it against me."

"He threatened you?"

Tyler laughed harshly. "Oh, he's too smooth for that. He never comes right out and says anything straight. He implies and insinuates. But he made himself clear. He reminded me how my career would suffer, maybe even be over if anyone ever found out. How my wife and family would be cast out. How they'd lose their friends and social standing. How we'd be exiles in our own neighborhood. How our lives would be over."

"He, you keep saying he. Who is this man?"

Tyler fell back against the couch and breathed rapidly. Just as he opened his mouth the doorbell rang. Sydney whirled around to look in the direction of the door then turned back to Tyler, quickly bringing him out of hypnosis. "Senator, there's someone at my door. Either you can wait in my study or you can remain here. The choice is yours."

He looked from her to the door then over at the bar. "Can I have a drink?"

She was not sure he needed more alcohol but at the moment she didn't know what else to do. "Sure, help yourself." She jumped up and walked to the door. "Blake!"

"You busy?"

"Actually, I do have a guest. Bbut you're welcome to join us."

"Your boyfriend? His tone was sarcastic.

"Hardly, young man." Senator Tyler turned from the bar with a glass of Scotch in his hand and looked in Blake's direction. "Although that is a lovely dream for an old man. Please, join us. I was just entertaining–or should I say boring my lovely hostess with tales of her father and I in the old days."

Blake walked in and extended his hand. "Blake Edwards, sir."

"Good to meet you, Blake," Senator Tyler shook his hand. "Ned Tyler."

Blake was experienced enough to hide his surprise at finding Tyler here. "A pleasure sir." He inclined his head then looked at Sydney. "I hate to intrude but I needed to talk to you about something. Do you think I could speak to you in private for a moment?"

She looked from him to the Senator then nodded. "Why don't we go into the kitchen. Senator, if you'll please excuse us?"

Tyler nodded and Sydney walked into the kitchen. "I didn't know you were so chummy with your patients," Blake said as soon as they were alone. "Isn't this a little unorthodox?"

"According to who?" she asked, wishing that he had not shown up while Tyler was there.

He looked away for a split second then back at her. "I don't know. But the point is—"

"The point is," she interrupted. "Why are you here, Blake?"

"Syd, I just—look, regardless of how things stand between us I just don't want to see you get mixed up in something that'll land you in trouble. I know the bureau wanted Tyler's files and there has to be a reason. Have you stopped to consider that he's probably being followed?"

She inhaled sharply. "The FBI is having him watched?"

"It's possible."

"Then they know he's here!"

Before he had a chance to speak she left the room and walked into the living room. She picked up her phone from behind the picture on the end table. "Excuse me," she said to the Senator as she dashed down the hall.

Blake followed her as she went into her study. "What's that?"

She whirled around, putting the phone behind her back. "What?"

"That." He grabbed her arm and pulled it from behind her back. "What's going on, Syd?"

"It's none of your concern," she said defensively. "This is a professional matter and I'm not disposed to discuss it with you. Also, I don't believe you have any right to ask. This is my home and what I do here is my business."

"Then why are you acting so paranoid?"

"I'm not!"

"Oh, no?"

"No!"

"You know something, don't you?"

"Know something?" she repeated and backed up. "About what in particular, or just about things in general?"

"Cut the crap! Come on, Syd. Tyler's into something and you know what it is."

"That's absurd!" she protested, turning her back on him.

He stepped behind her and whispered in her ear. "Is it?"

She looked up over her shoulder at him. "Blake, he's just a patient with a problem. That's all. And you know I can't talk to you about it."

"I don't think that's all it is." He took her by the shoulder and turned her around. "And your eyes tell me I'm right. Something has you rattled."

Sydney dropped her gaze. She wished she could tell him what she knew but she couldn't tell anyone. *And besides, you don't have any proof,* she reminded herself. *And without proof it's still just a story from a troubled man.*

"I'm just tired," she said at last. "That's all."

After a long silence she looked up at him. His hazel eyes were filled with worry and caring and her heart swelled with feeling. At that moment, she wished he would put his arms around her and hold her. She wished she could put her arms around him. The feelings that had been building up for him over time came to the surface and she was shaken by it.

He stared down at her in silence then nodded. "Okay, Syd, whatever you say. But when you get in over your head, you know where I'll be."

"Yes," she whispered, "I know."

"So." He gave her a strained smile. "I guess you better get back to your company."

"Want to stay and have a drink?" she asked as she put the phone on the desk.

"Okay, sure," he agreed after a moment. "But I need to make a pit stop. I'll be there in a sec."

She smiled and left the room to return to the Senator. He was sitting on the couch, morosely nursing his drink. Blake walked into the room just as she was pouring a glass of wine. "Wine?" she asked, holding up the bottle.

"Got any beer?"

"In the frig."

"I think I can find it." He started for the kitchen. The doorbell rang and he called over his shoulder. "I'll get it." He opened the door and looked at the tall dark-haired man. "Yes?"

"This is Sydney Forrest's apartment, is it not?"

"Yeah. I'm a friend of Syd's, Blake Edwards. Come on in."

"A pleasure to meet you, Mr. Edwards." The man smiled and walked inside. "My name is Adrian Zayne."

Blake covered his surprise. Suddenly all three of the players in his little mystery were together in the same room. He closed the door as Adrian walked in and saw Senator Tyler suddenly turn white as a ghost. His drink sloshed out over the rim of his glass as his hand started to shake uncontrollably.

Sydney noticed his reaction and ran over to him. "Are you all right?" she asked as she took the glass from his hand and put it down on the coffee table.

Tyler didn't seem to hear her. He just stared at Adrian like he was scared to death. Sydney looked from Tyler to Adrian to Blake then back to Adrian.

"Adrian, what are you doing here?"

"We were supposed to have dinner, were we not?" he asked as if everything were perfectly normal.

She frowned for a moment. She hadn't agreed to have dinner with him. "No. I don't think so." But as you can see, I have people here and—"

"I can see it slipped your mind, darling," he said with a smile and looked at Senator Tyler. "Ned, I must say that you do not appear to be at your best this evening. In fact, " he paused and looked at Blake and

Sydney. "All of you seem a little—let me think, how can I describe it . . . uncomfortable."

"Didn't you hear about the bomb in Akron?" Blake asked when no one else seemed willing to speak.

"Yes, dreadful, isn't it?" Adrian replied and walked over to Sydney. "Darling, I can't tell you how much I've missed you."

She drew back from him as he tried to kiss her and he chuckled. "Forgive me, I forget how shy you are—in public that is."

Her jaw clenched at the remark. Blake wondered if Adrian Zayne knew that he had just struck a nerve. He looked at the man to see him smiling with apparent unconcern, cool as a cucumber.

Sydney moved away from him toward the bar. "Blake, would you mind getting me a beer when you get yours?"

Blake cut his eyes around at the people in the room then nodded. "Sure, I'll be right back." As he turned to leave the room he saw Sydney look at the Senator with a concerned expression on her face.

More curious by the moment, he thought as he walked into the kitchen. If he was lucky, he just might find out what was going on between those three.

Sydney sat down beside Senator Tyler as soon as Blake left. "Senator, why don't you let me take you to the guest room. I think you need to get some rest."

Tyler looked from her to Adrian and blanched again. "No," he shook his head. "I think I should go."

Sydney took his arm as he tried to stand and his legs gave out. "I don't think you're in any shape to go anywhere just now. Come, let me help you."

Once she had him on his feet she steered him in the direction of the hall. "I'll be right back," she said with a look over her shoulder at Adrian.

She took Senator Tyler to the guest room and helped him sit on the edge of the bed. "Can I get you something? A glass of water—anything?"

He shook his head and refused to look at her. Sydney knelt in front of him and looked up into his lined face and frightened eyes as she took his hand. She knew there was something very wrong. He had taken one look at Adrian and looked as if he were going to have a cardiac arrest.

"Senator, I really do want to help you. Isn't there anything I can do?"

He was quiet for a long time and just as she started to stand, thinking that he was not going to answer, he squeezed her hand. "Are you involved with Adrian Zayne?"

She immediately opened her mouth to tell him that her personal life was not open for discussion but something in his eyes made her change her mind. "He's a casual acquaintance. Why?"

"Then God help you," he whispered and released her hand to lie back on the bed. "God help us all."

Sydney stood and looked down on him, confused and somehow frightened by his remark. For a moment, she debated whether to press him on what he meant then something he had said earlier came to mind.

...those damn jungle cat green eyes of his...

Her own eyes widened and she felt a cold sweat break out over her body. She hurried to the door, closed and locked it then returned to the bed. She sat down beside the Senator and leaned over to look at his face.

"Senator, I have to ask you something and I need yu to be honest with me. Is Adrian Zayne the man you were talking about earlier?"

Tyler actually jerked at the question and his eyes grew round and scared. Sydney held her breath as she waited for a reply. For several very long seconds he didn't speak. Then he pushed himself up into a sitting position. "Dr. Forrest, I'm going to do you a big favor - give you the most important piece of advice you've ever been given in your life. If you're half as smart as I think you are, you'll take it."

He paused long enough to take her hand. "Get as far away from Adrian Zayne as you can and don't ever let him near you again."

"Why?"

"Just take the advice." He released her hand and lay back down.

"But why?" she persisted. "*Is* he the man?"

Tyler closed his eyes and breathed heavily. "I think I need to get a little rest if you don't mind. I don't feel very well."

Sydney considered pushing him for an answer, but inside she knew she didn't have to. Adrian was the man he had been talking about; he was involved in what had happened in Ohio. She felt like she was going to be physically ill.

God, what am I going to do? She didn't have time to ponder the question. Blake called out to her from down the hall. She jumped up and unlocked the door. His voice triggered something inside her, something she had been running from for a long time.

"Sorry," she said as she walked out into the hall and saw him at the other end. "I was just showing the Senator where he could lie down."

"You're out of beer," he said as she walked up to him.

"That's okay, I didn't want one anyway" she replied, wishing there was some way she could tell him what she knew. But there wasn't. And besides she had no proof. All she had was the Senator's story and her own suspicions. That was hardly proof.

Blake looked down at her with a puzzled expression. So that he would not see the confusion and fear in her face she dropped her eyes as she gave his hand a squeeze in passing and returned to the living room.

Adrian turned toward her from his seat as she entered. "Darling, I called and made reservations for−."

"Adrian, I'm not leaving the Senator alone," she interrupted him, trying to keep her distaste for him out of her voice. "It'd be best if you leave."

"Why don't I have my driver take him home?" Adrian stood to face her. "We can have dinner brought in and spend the night here."

Sydney felt like she would scream if he touched her but she did not want him to know that she suspected him so she did not react as he took her hand in his and lifted it to his lips.

"No." She finally responded when she felt she could speak without sounding nervous. "He needs me right now and I can't turn my back on him. I'm his doctor."

Adrian's eyes narrowed fractionally for one split second then he smiled. "Yes, of course, I understand completely. We will reschedule."

She nodded." Let me see you out." She walked outside with him and he took her in his arms.

She stiffened and he released her. "Are you quite sure you are all right? And shouldn't your friend be leaving as well?"

"I'm just worried about Senator Tyler." She steered the subject away from Blake. "I'll be fine."

"Try to rest. I would not want you to overtax yourself, even if it is for such a noble cause."

"I'll be okay. But thank you for being so concerned."

He smiled and cupped the side of her face in his hand. "I will call you in the morning. Do be sure not to let your friend stay too long. By the way, what is he doing here?"

She said the first thing that popped into her mind. "He came by to take a look at my computer. Blake's just—well, you just wouldn't believe his knack for computers and I've been having a little problem so I thought I'd get him to look at it."

Adrian looked at her for a moment with a hard expression in his eyes then smiled. "Of course. Well, good night."

"Good night."

She waited until he got in the elevator, then ran back inside. Blake was sitting on the couch but stood and turned to her as she came into the room. Sydney stopped abruptly and looked at him for a moment then her legs took control and propelled her across the room to him.

Blake did not expect what happened next. She flung her arms around his neck and clung to him tightly, trembling fiercely. For one moment he did not move then he wrapped his arms around her and held her. "Syd, what's wrong?" he whispered softly.

"Just hold me," she whispered against the crook of his neck. "Please, just hold me."

"Okay." He pulled her down on his lap as he sat on the couch. "It'll be okay - everything's going to be fine."

"You promise?" she whispered shakily.

"Absolutely," he replied, wondering what had her so frightened. He had never seen her that way before. She was normally so in control and seemed so strong and confident. But now she was shaking like she was scared out of her mind.

He held her until the trembling ceased. Just as he loosened his hold on her to ask her what was wrong, the Senator walked into the room.

"Oh, excuse me," he apologized.

"It's okay." Sydney stood. "What can I do for you?"

"I called my aide and he should be here in a few minutes. I think I should go home. There are some things I need to think about. Mr. Edwards, it was a pleasure to meet you. Please forgive my behavior this evening. I assure you it is not typical."

"The pleasure is mine, sir," Blake replied.

Sydney walked the Senator to the door and spoke softly to him. "Senator, I'd like to see you in my office in the morning."

"Doctor, I really don't think therapy is going to do any good at this point," he said dejectedly.

"Perhaps not," she agreed.

He looked at her in surprise and she continued. "But you and I both know that we're in an unusual position here, Senator. We both have information that could be potentially dangerous and we have to decide what to do with it."

"You mean we have to decide how to save our own hides," he said despondently with a good measure of fear in evidence.

Sydney didn't know how to answer. Her concern was not so much for herself but for the innocent people whose lives had been destroyed by what had happened. If there really was some secret group within the government that had planned the bombing incident then they had to be exposed.

"I think we both need to consider this very carefully," she responded with a noncommittal answer. Before she had finished her sentence one of the elevator doors opened and the Senator's aide stepped out.

Sydney nodded to the man then gave the senator what she hoped was a comforting smile. "I'll see you in the morning."

He nodded and walked away. Sydney went back inside the apartment and closed the door, leaning back against it and closing her eyes. *God, what am I going to do? And more importantly, who can I trust?*

As if in answer to the question she heard Blake's voice. "Syd?"

She opened her eyes as he walked over to her. "Is there anything I can do?" he asked softly, reaching for her hand. "If you're in some kind of trouble I'll help you anyway I can - you know that, don't you?"

Sydney nodded and went into his arms. "Yes, I do know that, and it means more to me than you realize. But this is something I have to work out on my own."

For a few moments they simply stood holding one another. With no small measure of surprise, Sydney realized that the change she sensed in herself was dramatic, and she suspected, permanent. She thought it ironic that she should spend her days trying to help other people get in touch with themselves while she had been so busy running from herself. Ever since she found out that her ex-husband, Evan was having an affair she had tried to build a wall around her emotions so that there would be no chance of her getting hurt again. She'd hidden behind that wall, hiding from life and from herself.

But somehow Blake had eroded those walls without her even being aware of it. Now she saw that the walls had crumbled and that she couldn't continue to hide from her feelings. And for the first time in a very long time she didn't want to.

As she was thinking about her personal revelations Blake stepped back from her. "I guess I better get going."

"No." She held onto his arms. "Don't go. Please."

"Okay." He looked at her in surprise. "You want to go grab some dinner or something?"

"I'll call out for something if you're hungry. Or I'll cook if you like."

"I'm not really hungry."

"Then why don't we just sit and talk or something?"

They went into the living room and Blake sat down on the couch. Sydney turned on music then sat down beside him.

"So, what do you want to talk about?" he asked as she looked up at him.

Sydney looked at him for a few moments, trying to summon the courage to be honest. He smiled gently and took her hand, raising his eyebrows in question and she knew that if she chickened out she might never have the nerve again.

"Blake, will you stay here tonight?"

"Spend the night?" he asked with confusion clear in his voice. "You're afraid to be alone?"

"No, I'm not afraid." She placed her hand on the side of his neck. "I just want to be with you."

He opened his mouth then closed it, looking at her with a perplexed expression on his face. "Let me get this straight. You want me to stay here–with you–tonight?"

"Yes." She ran her fingers up his neck to caress the side of his face. "Very much."

"Why? I mean, just a few days ago you said–"

"Just a few days ago I was still running," she said softly and moved closer. "But now I'm not. I'm through running, Blake and I want more than anything for you to stay here with me tonight. If you want to, that is."

He looked at her for a long time before answering, as if searching for some answer in her eyes. Finally, he nodded. "Yes, I want to. If you're sure."

"Very sure," she breathed as she moved to loop her arms around his neck and straddle his lap.

Their lips met and she felt her breath catch at desire that rose inside her. Blake's hands moved to her shirt to pull it up. Their lips parted only long enough to pull the T-shirt over her head and toss it aside. Then he claimed her with another kiss.

Sydney pushed aside everything else but the feel of his hands on her. There was plenty of time for other things later. Right now all that mattered was that they were together.

The kiss soon became frenzied. Clothes were quickly removed and tossed aside. They explored each other's body with hands and mouths, tasting, touching and experimenting with one another.

When finally they were spent, bodies slick with sweat, Blake and Sydney curled into each other, unwilling to break the contact. Sleep claimed them, still wrapped in one another's arms.

Thursday, April 20

Washington D.C.

It was several hours before the first rays of light would streak the morning sky. Adrian Zayne stood in front of the window in the dark room of the penthouse suite of the Watergate Hotel, looking out at the lights of the Capital.

A knock at the door had him speaking without turning away from the sight. "Enter."

Two men walked into the room. "I think we may have a problem," he said without bothering to look at them.

"Tyler talked," one of the man stated, rather than asking.

"Possibly. However, considering that he talked to his psychiatrist, I do not think we have cause for alarm in that quarter at present."

"Then why did you summon us?" the second man asked.

"We have a new player in the game . One that may prove to be very troublesome."

He turned and pinned the second man with a hard stare. "I expect you to handle this problem personally."

The man swallowed and cleared his throat. "So, do I get a name or do I have to guess?"

Adrian's eyes glittered dangerously in the dim light. "Blake Edwards."

"What do you want done with him?"

"Use your imagination. Just neutralize him before he becomes a problem."

He turned to the first man. "And I think it's time you made an appointment with the doctor, considering the stress you've been under lately."

"You want me to talk to the doctor?" the man asked with surprise in his voice. "About what?"

"About the dangers of spreading unfounded rumors. And do make sure she is properly intimidated."

"What if she runs to the police?"

Adrian chuckled. He had no doubt that she would run to someone. But he fully intended that someone to be him. By the time he got through, Sydney Forrest would not trust anyone but him. "Just do as I tell you."

The man inclined his head and Adrian turned away. "That will be all."

Without another word the men left the room. Adrian looked out over the city with a smile.

CR

Sydney untangled herself from Blake's arms and sat. He rolled over but did not wake. After a moment she got out of the bed, put on his discarded shirt and went into her study. She she turned on the computer and took a seat in the desk chair.

Only the light of the computer screen lit the room, bathing her face in blue light and turning her strawberry blond hair into a cascade of silver-blue.

She accessed the deep web and keyed in an address. It was a chat room she had opened some time ago. In all the times she had checked it, no one aside from herself and GW had been in it. She typed quickly, hoping that she was not making a big mistake in what she was doing.

After she and Blake made love she fell asleep and dreamed that Adrian was chasing her through a park. The dream woke her and she started to think. In a way, he was chasing her. He was very persistent about wanting to be with her and she didn't understand it. She didn't believe that he was in love with her and it didn't make sense that he would pursue her the way he did.

Then it came to her. It made perfect sense. If Adrian was involved in this secret group the Senator spoke of and if he knew the Senator was having second thoughts then it followed he would want to find out if the Senator had talked. And how better to do that than to seduce the one person the Senator talked to, his psychiatrist.

I've got to do something! Her mind raced *Somehow I've got to find a way to make the authorities take notice of Adrian without breaking the doctor patient confidence. But how?*

The answer to that question came to her in a flash and she knew what she was going to do. It was risky and there was a chance that she would get not only herself in trouble but others as well. But at this point it was the only thing she could think to do.

As soon as the message was complete she exited, then keyed in another address. She emailed herself the recording she made of her conversation with Tyler earlier in the evening and uploaded it to the new site.

As soon as she finished she erased the recording on her phone. She shut down the computer and started to put the phone on the charger when a thought occurred to her.

The phone wasn't scheduled to back up until four am, so the recording had not yet made it to the cloud. If she reset the phone back to factory defaults it should erase all trace of the recording.

But that didn't satisfy her. There were ways of retrieving deleted data. She looked around and her eyes fell on a small metal statue her mother had given her.

Perfect. She hurried across the room for the statue

Blake woke and found himself alone in bed. He got up and walked out into the hall. There was light coming from the study. He padded down the hall to see Sydney sitting on the floor in front of her computer desk, pounding something with a statue.

For a moment he did not speak, but merely stood and watched her. She looked like a beautiful apparition in the eerie blue light of the monitor, her skin seemed to glow and her hair looked like molten strands of polished silver.

She'd surprised him. He thought things were over between them, that she was becoming seriously involved with Zayne. When she had asked him to stay he was shocked.

He was glad she had asked, more than he cared to admit. He'd not told her, but he knew he loved her. After making love to her he was convinced beyond all doubt. She was so beautiful and uninhibited in the act of love, responding to his touch as if her body were made especially for him.

A sense of curiosity broke through his thoughts of love. "What are you doing?"

She jumped and looked at him. Her expression of surprise changed as she took in his appearance making him realize that he had not bothered to put on any clothes.

"Just keying in some notes on a patient," she said as she turned off the computer.

"With a little metal statute. In the middle of the night."

"Sometimes I don't sleep." She left the statue and what looked like the remains of a cell phone on the floor and walked over to him. "And I didn't want to wake you."

"Are you sure there isn't something bothering you, Syd?"

She looked down. "No—yes, I mean I don't know how—I want to tell you but I don't know how."

"We don't have to talk if you don't want to," he said when she remained silent. "We can just listen to music or —"

"No, I want to talk," she interrupted.

He fell silent and once more she hesitated. "So?" he asked, feeling confused and a little anxious as well. A thought that maybe she was going to tell him that she'd changed her mind and didn't want to see him anymore made his hands sweat. "What is it you want to talk about?"

"About—" she paused and looked down at her hands clenched in front of her. "About us."

"What about us?" His voice sounded harsh, even though he did not mean to sound that way.

He could see the anxiety on her face. "I wanted to tell you that — Blake, I don't care about Adrian Zayne and I don't want to have anything to do with him and…"

"And what?" Blake asked when she fell silent.

"And nothing. He's not important. But you are, Blake. I know that I've been the one who's been putting on the brakes in our relationship and I can only say that I felt like I had to. I've been through one rotten relationship that made me feel betrayed and used and I was afraid of letting myself care about someone again because that would set me up to get hurt again."

"I'm not like Evan Mallory," he said softly but firmly.

"No, you're not," she agreed. "You're the most caring, compassionate, giving person I've ever known. You're strong but gentle, smart and funny and—"

"This is starting to sound a little like a 'dear John' send off. Look, Syd, if you want to get rid of me you don't have to build me up to let me down. Just say it straight out."

"Straight out?"

"Yeah." He looked into her eyes. "Just say it."

"Okay." She took a deep breath then looked into his eyes again. "I love you."

"You—wait a minute, you love me?"

97

"Yes. I love you."

He looked at her for a moment then took her hands in his. "I never thought I'd hear those words coming from you."

"I never imagined I'd ever say that to anyone. And I wouldn't say it now if I didn't mean it. But I'll be honest with you. It scares me to death and right now I feel like I'm standing in front of a firing squad waiting for the hammer to fall—not knowing how you feel."

"I feel like −" He released her hands and pulled her close so that their gazes were locked. "I love you too, Syd. More than you can imagine."

"Then will you please love me now?"

"Most definitely."

She accepted his kiss eagerly and he scooped her up in his arms and took her back to bed. He gave no thought to Adrian Zayne or Senator Tyler. The only thing on his mind was Sydney and how grateful he was that she loved him.

Chapter Five
Thursday, April 20
Washington, D.C.

Blake picked up the dirty clothes from the floor and tossed them into the hamper. He looped a tie around his neck, and knotted it, making a mental note to take his shirts to the cleaners.

He put on his jacket and started out into the hall. As he started by the guest room he stopped and looked in at the computer. He only considered it a moment before he walked into the room. He turned on the computer and accessed his mailbox. There were two messages in it. One was from Weasel.

Time to cruise. Click on this. A URL followed.

Blake scribbled down the address and read the next message. "What the hell?" His eyes flew open wide as he read what was on the screen.

What does a billionaire, mortgages, campaigns, ammonia nitrate and diesel fuel have in common with the military?

He leaned his chair back on two legs and crossed his arms over his chest, thinking. For several minutes he tried to come up with something, but he drew a blank. Finally he gave up and wrote down the message on a pad by the computer. Then he went back to Weasel's email and clicked on the link. A popup window opened, asking for a password."Great!" he complained and reached for the phone. He dialed and waited. A few moments later Weasel picked up.

"What's up?"

"You didn't leave me the password."

"What password?"

"Come on, Weasel! The message you left with the address. You didn't leave a password."

"I didn't leave you an address."

Blake's eyes flew open wide. "You're jerking me around, right?"

"No way, my man."

Blake looked at the address on the screen above the password block and frowned. "Weasel, listen, I need a favor. Could you swing by my apartment after work? I want you to help me out with something. I'll spring for damn!"

"What?"

"I'm suppose to have dinner with my girlfriend at her place."

"Well I wouldn't want to mess with your love life."

"No." Blake considered it for a moment. "Listen, stop by and after we finish we'll go over to her place. I'll call and clear it with her. Besides, I'd like you to meet the lady I'm going to be living with."

"Whoa! This sounds serious, dude. I'll be there. Any lady who can tie you to one corral I definitely have to meet. See you around five."

"Thanks," Blake replied and hung up. Now all he had to do was convince Steve that he needed to take the day shift permanently. He wanted to have more free time in the evenings to be with Sydney.

He'd called Steve on his cell last night after the Senator left and gotten him to pick up the tail on Tyler from Sydney's apartment. He didn't mention that he was at her apartment, himself. He just said that something had come up and he needed Steve to fill in for him.

Blake checked his watch. It was almost nine. He had to get moving. He turned off the computer, tore off the top piece of paper from the pad and put it in his pocket then grabbed his suitcase and left.

He hadn't been able to tell Sydney the Senator was being watched and he was one of the watchers. Blake felt bad about keeping it from her. In a way he felt like he was using her. Because of her he knew where the Senator was going to be this morning at nine o'clock and if Steve had done his job Blake would be able to hear everything that was being said from his car.

CR

Blake sat in his car watching the building where Sydney's office was located. As he watched the building a car pulled up behind him, halfway down the block. Inside were two men wearing dark glasses.

As a car parked behind him and the driver got out to open the door for Senator Tyler, Blake turned on the portable recording unit on the front seat of his car and put the earphones in his ears to check the sound. Senator Tyler got out of the back seat of the car and entered the lobby of the building.

Blake picked up a magazine from the car seat and opened it, flipping through it to an article about how quick the public and the media were to jump to the conclusion that the bombing in Akron had Mid-East origins. He got involved in the article as he listened to the chatter of Sydney's secretary greeting the Senator and telling him that Doctor Forrest would be with him shortly. Because of that, he paid little attention to the traffic on the street.

ʖ

Sydney stood as the receptionist showed the Senator in. "Good morning, Senator, I'm glad you could make it this morning."

Senator Tyler took a seat, flopping down in the chair as if the muscles in his body were turning to jelly. Sydney could tell by his face that he hadn't slept. Large dark blotches stained the sagging skin beneath his bloodshot eyes.

"I still don't see what good this will do," he replied as she took the seat across from him.

"I agree," she said quietly. "Therapy won't change what happened. Nothing will. That isn't the reason I wanted to see you. This isn't a session, sir. I think we need to speak frankly, person to person, not doctor to patient."

"And that will do about as much good as therapy," he mumbled.

"Senator, Tyler, I'm in a precarious position. I'm walking a tenuous line right now and to be honest I don't know what to do. If what you've told me is true then it's very possible that you and I may have knowledge of something that should be reported to the authorities. Now, I know you haven't come right out and said this in so many words, but I'm under the distinct impression that the people you mentioned are responsible for what happened. Am I correct?"

"You know you are." His voice sounded old and fragile.

"Then I need to ask you a few questions. Will you answer those questions for me?"

"To what end? Even if I tell you everything I know, there's nothing you can do. Who will you go to with the information? Doctor Forrest I don't think you understand the full implications of my position, or yours either for that matter. Right now my life is worth about two red hot cents if those people think I've talked. And considering that I've been coming to see you, it's a very distinct possibility that your life is in danger as well."

Sydney hadn't considered that she might be in danger until that moment. The realization swept over her in a wave of almost paralyzing fear. For a moment she couldn't speak or move. But she forced herself to push the fear into the background. She might not be trained to handle such a situation but she was smart enough to know that if she was in danger then her best bet of surviving was to get as much information as she could and get that information into the right hands.

"All the more reason for you to be candid with me, wouldn't you say?" she asked as soon as she found her voice.

Senator Tyler looked up at her for a long moment then nodded. "Yes. I've got enough deaths on my conscience. I don't need any more. I'll answer your questions."

"May I record it?"

"If you wish."

Sydney fetched her new phone from her purse then took her seat again. "Okay, let's get started."

¦

Blake heard the Senator's voice through the earphones and put down the magazine. As he looked up he saw a shapely blond walking down the sidewalk in front of him. As she started by a dark Nissan a couple of cars ahead, two men got out of the car. One man got in front of the woman, blocking her path while the other closed in behind her.

Blake was out of the car with his gun in his hand and reaching for his credentials by the time the first man grabbed the woman's arm.

"FBI" he barked as he ran up behind the man with his back turned.

The man whirled around faster than Blake anticipated. His foot shot up and out, knocking the gun from Blake's hand. Pain shot up Blake's arm but he recovered fast enough to block a punch the man threw at him and counter with a solid right to the man's stomach.

By this time, the woman was screaming as her assailant tried to pull her towards his parked car. Blake could not take time to pay attention to the woman, however. His punch had doubled the man over, but the man came at him again, wrapping his arms around Blake's midriff to lift him up and slam him against the parked car.

Blake grunted and balled up his fist to pound down hard on the back of the man's neck. He was released as the man backed away. He lashed out with a sidekick. His foot caught the man in the center of the body and sent him reeling backwards into a newspaper vending machine.

Blake started to turn towards the screaming woman but before he could the woman broke free from the second man and threw herself on Blake, wrapping her arms around his neck as she screamed and cried for him to help her.

He couldn't see. It was like the woman was trying to climb up on his shoulders. "Lady, calm down!"

He grabbed her arms and tried to pry her off him. Just then a second man attacked from behind. Blake felt his breath catch as the man's arm tightened around his neck and he reacted quickly, elbowing the man in the ribs with all his strength. The man fell back and Blake whirled toward him but before he could make another move he felt something hard jab into his back. "Don't do anything stupid," the woman ordered.

A split second later another car skidded to a stop in the street. "Let's go." The woman prodded him with the gun.

Knowing better to argue with a loaded weapon, Blake got into the back seat of the car. The passenger in the front seat, a man about thirty-five with dark hair, wearing dark glasses, turned and leveled a gun at him as the woman climbed in beside him. As soon as she was in the driver swerved out into the traffic.

"What's this all about?" Blake asked.

"No questions," the man with the gun snapped.

"I do hope you know what you're doing," Blake quipped. "Kidnapping a federal officer, assault with a deadly weapon--"

"Shut up!" the man barked.

Blake fell silent and watched as they drove to the Potomac Boat Club on the river. He put up no resistance as he was ordered out of the car and escorted to a large pleasure boat that was moored nearby.

The two men and the woman escorting him did not board the boat. Blake faced the three men on board. "So, anyone want to explain what's going on?"

"Agent Edwards." An older, portly man with a regal bearing stepped forward. "Please have a seat."

Blake sat down as the boat pulled away from the dock. The older man did not sit, but swayed with the motion of the boat as if he had spent many years on the water.

"Agent Edwards, you are interfering with a highly classified operation and I must insist that you terminate your surveillance on Senator Ned Tyler."

"Why?" Blake looked from the speaker to the other two men. "Who are you?"

The older man took a seat beside him. "I'm afraid I don't have many answers for you, Agent Edwards. All I can tell you is that your interference could be very detrimental to our investigation and your surveillance must cease."

"Again, I ask why," Blake said firmly. "What authority do you have to not only kidnap a federal agent and demand that he cease an investigation? Moreover, how do you know that I am running surveillance on this Senator you speak of?"

"We know a great deal," the man replied then looked at the other two men. "Why don't you have a drink and let Agent Edwards and I speak in private."

As soon as the two men moved below deck, the man turned his attention again to Blake. "We are with the DIA, Mr. Edwards. That's about all I can tell you except that our investigation is of the highest priority and our authority comes straight from the top."

"Then why not go through normal channels and have the order for the termination of surveillance come from bureau officials?"

The man chuckled. "You FBI chaps are so naive at times, Mr. Edwards. There *are* matters that you're not privy to, areas in which your jurisdiction does not extend. That is the situation right now. The DIA has complete autonomy in this matter and is neither required nor inclined to discuss it with the FBI."

"Then why come to me?"

"Because you're a man who can understand duty and loyalty and the good of the many."

"I don't follow."

"I think you do. "You see, Agent Edwards, our country is moving towards what many years back President Bush called "a new world order." The cold war is no more. The two Germanys have become one, the USSR is fragmented, the arms race was cut back and communism has been discredited. We are taking steps to replace the superpower rivalry that has long divided the globe, the rivalry that fueled the cold war. Our military's role has been subjugated to that of international policemen operating under the jurisdiction of the UN."

"I am aware of the current world situation, sir."

"Perhaps. But let's examine for a moment that "new world order" and the way it is viewed by a great many people."

"To begin with let's look at the UN peacekeeping missions. Consider, if you will these past events. One: the operation in Somalia. This country was in anarchy. International famine-relief agencies found it almost impossible to operate there and people were starving by the hundreds, the thousands. So, the Security Council voted to establish an operation in Somalia. What happened when in the first 500 troops arrived? I'll tell you - they were unable to operate. So, the Council votes to send in more troops. Within one month over 15,000 US troops were in Somalia. We did what we were sent to do. Soon food supplies were reaching most of the people. But then the UN steps in and takes command of the operation from the US From that point on it was one mess after another. Somali rebels killed 23 Pakistani soldiers - reinforcements were sent in to capture the rebel leader and what happened? They failed and once more the UN steps in to reemphasize the needs to reach a political solution."

"I do hope there is a point to this lesson in history," Blake commented.

"Yes, there is - if you will allow me to continue. Let's consider another scenario. Bosnia. Need I say more? That situation was out of control."

"Which brings us to?" Blake was trying to figure out where this was all leading.

"To United States citizens who are vehemently opposed to a world united under the auspices of the United Nations. There are citizens in this country who see the government as *The Beast*, Agent Edwards. They view any cooperation with the UN as anathema. They look on Democratic politicians as being little more than liberal elitists and see them as daily betraying tradition American values. GATT, NAFTA, the General Agreement on Tariffs and Trade - these are not seen as positive measures. No, quite the opposite. These are viewed as more evidence that the United States of America is surrendering without a fight to "the new world order" and it scares the hell out of them."

Blake frowned slightly. "You're talking about extremist groups, sir and they do not constitute the majority of the American public. Besides, I hardly see how that has any bearing on why I have been brought here."

"Then perhaps you are not nearly as smart as I thought you were," the man said as he stood.

"Excuse me?"

"You heard me, Agent Edwards. And since you are obviously unable to grasp the importance of what I've been trying to tell you, I see no need to continue this conversation."

"Fine," Blake agreed. "If you'll just drop me at the dock, I'll be on my way."

The man turned and walked away to speak to the man piloting the boat. The boat turned in a wide arc and headed back in the direction it had come.

"I trust that I can depend on you to cease your investigation and surveillance on Senator Tyler?" Ihe older asked Blake.

Blake considered his words for a moment. "Let's say, hypothetically, of course, that I refused."

"That would be very unfortunate."

"Then I guess it's in my own best interests to agree." Blake decided his best course of action was to go along with the man and try and find out who he was and what he was up to.

"Yes, it would indeed, Agent Edwards. As well as rewarding."

"Rewarding?"

"All patriots find reward in serving their country," the man replied. "Don't you agree?"

"Yes, I do."

"Excellent Then there will be no further need for me to contact you, will there Agent Edwards?"

"Not that I see."

"Very good. Please, have a pleasant day." The man turned and walked below. Blake stared at him then looked around as the boat pulled up next to the dock. One of the men he had seen when he first boarded the boat came up from below deck to tie the boat to the dock.

Blake got off and walked down the dock, looking around for the car that had brought him there. It was nowhere to be seen. He pulled out his cell phone and called a cab. Now he had another mystery to solve.

☙

Sydney had just hung up the phone when her secretary buzzed her. "Doctor, there's someone here who says he was referred to you by Senator Tyler and insists that he must talk with you today."

"Could you come in here please," Sydney responded.

A moment later the door opened and her secretary walked in. "What's this man's name?" Sydney asked.

"Ralph Needham."

"Needham?" Sydney could not remember ever meeting anyone by that name, nor could she remember the Senator ever mentioning anyone named Needham. "Well, okay, I have a few minutes so send him in."

The secretary opened the door. "Mr. Needham? If you'll come in the doctor will see you now."

She left as the man entered the office. Sydney rose as she looked at him. He was of medium height and build, dressed in a dark blue suit. If it were not for his nose, which looked like it had been broken several times and eyes that seemed more animal than human he would have been completely nondescript.

"Mr. Needham." She walked around her desk and held out her hand. "How do you do? I'm Doctor Forrest. I understand Senator—."

A gasp cut her sentence in half as the man grabbed her hand and jerked her to him to wrap his free hand around the front of her throat.

"I understand you like to talk about your patients, doctor," he whispered menacingly.

Sydney clawed at the hand around her throat with her free hand, trying to draw air into her lungs. The man tightened his grip on both her throat and her hand and she felt like she was surely going to pass out; either from lack of oxygen or pain. She was afraid that he was going to kill her.

"It's not very smart to tell other people's secrets," he whispered in her face.

"I haven't," she wheezed, her voice sounding little more than a choked hiss of air.

"And you better not if you want to keep that pretty face of yours. You'd be surprised what a soldering iron can do to human skin."

"Please," she rasped.

He eased up on her throat and she gasped greedily, pulling air into her lung in huge gulps. "Don't make me have to come back," the man warned, shoving his face close to hers, making her recoil at the smell of garlic and onions on his breath now that she could breathe. "I'd enjoy teaching you all about pain but I don't think you'd like it very much."

"I haven't said anything to anyone about anything!" she insisted. "I don't know what you're even talking —"

His hand tightened again, cutting off her voice. "Don't play that game with me, doctor. I'm not nearly as stupid as I look. Just remember what I said. You talk and I come back. Got it?"

She nodded her head and he sneered at her then shoved her backwards. She fell back against her desk, throwing her arms out behind her to keep her balance and in the process sending things flying off the desk as she scrambled to stay upright.

The man laughed and straightened his jacket. "Thank you so much, doctor Forrest. You've been a big help."

She watched in frozen silence as he left the office. For a few moments she could not move. She was petrified with fear. When she did get control of her body she ran to the private bathroom adjoining her office and turned on the cold water, cupping her hands and splashing it on her face.

When she straightened and picked up a towel to dry her face her gaze moved to the mirror and fell on the red marks on her throat. She raised one hand to touch them as she stared at her reflection. *What have I gotten myself into?* She winced at the tenderness on her neck. She did not know how the man that called himself Needham knew that Senator Tyler had talked to her or what he had told her.

Her eyes widened and she whirled around. There was only one way someone could know. Her office had to be bugged!

◌

Blake found his car parked where he had left it with the keys still in the ignition. The equipment was still in the front seat but the tape was missing. His gun was lying in the floorboard.

He leaned over to pick it up, thinking to himself that it was beyond strange that whoever the people were he had tangled with would retrieve his gun for him.

Now what? he asked himself as he started the car. He could not decide if he should go to Steve and tell him what had happened or go to headquarters.

An uneasy feeling took hold of him and he turned the car off and got out. He wanted to make sure Sydney was okay before he did anything. .

The receptionist looked up as he walked in. "May I help you?"

"I'd like to speak with Doctor Forrest."

"I'm sorry, the doctor is not in," the woman said with a flirtatious smile. "Would you like to make an appointment?"

"No, thanks. This is personal."

She raised her eyebrows. "Oh! Well, in that case, would you like to leave a message. She should be back in an hour or so."

"No, thanks anyway," he said and turned to leave then stopped. "Did she say where she was going?"

"To lunch with an old friend, I think."

"Okay, thanks." Blake replied then left the office and returned to his car.

&

Sydney spotted GW as he started up the steps of the Lincoln Memorial where she sat waiting. He looked much the same he had the first day she had met him. The only difference was that his frame was now lean rather than scarecrow skinny.

She'd been surprised to reach him when she called. Getting in touch with GW was like trying to spot Elvis. She knew where he lived, but he was rarely there. And she had no idea where he worked. That was the one thing he wouldn't tell her. She didn't know why he wanted to keep it a secret but she respected his privacy and so didn't question him.

She stood up as he reached the step below her and leaned over to give him a hug. "It's good to see you. Where've you been hiding? I've tried to call you a couple of times but you're never in."

"Well, you know how it is. So, what's going on with all these encrypted files you've been uploading, Syd?"

She frowned and sat. He sat down beside her and she looked out at the reflecting pool at the reflection of the monument mirrored on its surface. She trusted GW more than anyone else in the world but she couldn't divulge what the Senator had said in her office even to him.

When she turned to him, she saw the curiosity in his dark face was tinted with concern. "I think I stumbled onto something that's—well, it has to do with someone or some group doing something unlawful."

"So why not go to the police?"

"I can't. And I can't tell you more than that, GW. I wish I could, but this information came from a patient's session and you know as well as I that I can't talk about it."

"Then why encrypt the files? Is this patient giving you trouble?"

"No, actually it's the government. An FBI agent - Wells, was his name, showed up at my office and took all my files."

"Then it would seem that the problem's already been taken out of your hands."

She bit her bottom lip for a second with a slight frown on her face. "Well, he didn't exactly get this particular patient's files. I erased all the information on the office computer and destroyed all printed records."

GW shook his head at her. "Syd, you aren't that stupid. You know that erasing the files doesn't mean diddly. The data can still be recovered."

"Not if I had the system set to do a low level format."

GW laughed, "Syd, my sly friend, I do love the way that mind of yours operates."

"I learned at the feet of the master," she said with a smile and a slight bow of her head.

GW's smile faded. "So what do you want from me?"

"I just wanted to make sure the data's safe and to remind you that it must stay encrypted."

"You cut me to the quick." GW put his hand over his heart and made a mock expression of pain. "Would I ever mess with your files?"

Sydney gave him a look tinged with skepticism, "I know your curiosity old friend and I know how much you love a challenge. But this time I really need you to contain your natural inquisitive nature."

"I'll leave them just the way they are right now. But let me ask you something. What exactly are you going to do with the information you have? If the FBI is on this patient's case then it's a sure bet they have some reason to be. Are you sure it wouldn't be better just to give them what they want?"

"No, I don't think so. And besides, at this point I don't have any proof that what I know is true. And that's what I have to find out."

"So now we get to the real reason you called. You want me to break into some computer somewhere, right?"

"Get that look of excitement out of your eyes. I don't want you to break into anything … yet. But I would appreciate a little tutorial in how to do a couple of things."

GW smiled. "Ah, grasshopper, what can an old monk teach?"

Sydney laughed at him. "GW, if I could drain your brain I could run the entire world from my iPad."

"True," he agreed with a chuckle. "So tell me what you need to know."

It took a few minutes for her to explain what she needed and even longer for him to explain how to do it but at last she had what she came for.

"I really appreciate this," she said as she took his hand. "I mean it, GW. You're the only —"

Both of them looked up as a portly woman in a floral print blouse and white polyester pants passed by them, speaking loud enough to be heard by everyone within earshot about how the country was going to the dogs and the younger generation had lost all it morals. Everywhere you looked you saw white people with black people and it just was not natural.

Sydney's eyes narrowed at the woman's words. She slid over close to GW and put her arms around him. "Oh, honey," she crooned loudly. "I can't wait to get you home."

The woman's eyes grew round as silver dollars and she gave Sydney and GW a look of utter contempt then stomped on up the stairs. Sydney laughed and released GW.

"Hey, does this mean you don't want to take me home?" he asked teasingly.

Sydney gave his shoulder a playful push. "I couldn't handle it. Besides," she added, her face lit in a happy smile. "I have a man in my life."

"So tell Uncle GW everything."

Her smile grew wider as she thought about Blake. Being with him last night had confirmed her feelings. She was in love with him and she felt like she wanted to shout it from the top of the world to let everyone know.

"He's wonderful, GW - smart, funny and gentle. He's everything I want and I can't believe I found him."

"So this is the one, huh, Syd?"

"Yes," she replied dreamily, looking back over the reflecting pool below them. For a moment she indulged herself in fantasy, thinking about her and Blake together. Then reality intruded and her expression changed to one of anxiety.

"GW, what if I'm protecting someone who's responsible for that bombing?"

He jerked his head around to look at her. "Is that what you think?"

"It's what I'm afraid of," she admitted. "And it's eating me up. All those innocent people . God, what if in a round about way I'm protecting one of the people responsible? Is my career worth more than all those people's lives who have been lost or destroyed?"

He took her hand in his. "I can't answer that. But I can tell you that if you want me to I'll help you get to the truth."

"How?"

GW raised his eyebrows and gave her a half-smile. "Well, to begin with, give me permission to decrypt the files and I'll see what I can come up with."

"I can't do that!" she insisted.

"Okay, whatever you say," he said as he stood. "Listen, I've gotta go. You know where I'll be if you need me."

She stood and hugged him. "I always seem to run to you with my problems. Maybe you should've been a therapist. You always seem to be counseling me and in case I haven't told you lately, I do appreciate it. You're my best friend, GW. I don't know what I'd do without you."

"Well, let's just hope you never have to find out," he said and gave her a hug then released her. "Now, get out of here and go find that honey man you're so worked up about. I'll talk to you soon."

She smiled and watched him walk away. She had no doubt that from the questions she had asked, GW knew exactly what she planned to do. What surprised her was that he had not voiced any objections to her plan. But then GW was always surprising her.

ભ

Blake let himself in his apartment and went straight to the bathroom. After showering and putting on clean clothes he went into the kitchen to get something to drink. Just as he was opening a soft drink the doorbell rang.

"So, what's the problem, dude?" Weasel asked as he walked in.

"Want something to drink?" Blake asked as he closed the door.

"No, thanks."

"Okay, come on." Blake said and led the way to the spare bedroom where the computer was. He had put the paper with the address and the message on the desk beside the computer.

Blake picked up the piece of paper and handed it to him. "Are you sure you didn't leave this message for me?"

"Time to cruise. Double click on this." Weasel read the first note. "Nope, not me, dude. You tried the address?"

"It was passworded and I couldn't get in."

"So, what's this next thing - a riddle?" Weasel read the note aloud. "What does a billionaire, mortgages, campaigns, ammonia nitrate and diesel fuel have in common with the military? Strange combo. What's the answer?"

"You tell me," Blake replied. "Have a seat," he gestured to the chair in front of the computer as he pulled another chair over.

Weasel shrugged and put the paper down on the desk as he took the seat Blake offered. "Well, where do you want to start—figuring out this riddle or finding out the password to that address?"

"The address."

Weasel nodded and went to work. He keyed in the address then leaned back and studied the screen for a moment as the password request was displayed.

"What?" Blake asked when Weasel did not move or speak for several seconds.

"Just thinking."

Blake looked from him to the screen then back at him. "About what?"

"The password."

"Can you figure it out?"

Weasel scratched his chin. "It'll take me a few minutes. Why don't we work on the puzzle while I do this."

"You can do both at the same time?"

"Just look at me like a multi-processing unit," Weasel said with a smile as his fingers started flying over the keyboard. "Now what was that first clue - a billionaire?"

"Yeah," Blake answered absently as he watched Weasel's fingers dance on the keys and the screen flash as it switched from one display to another. "So?"

"So, how many billionaires do you think there are in this country?"

"I don't know."

"Then maybe we should find out."

Blake picked up a note pad from the desk, and jotted down a note. "Okay, item number one. Number of billionaires."

"And now mortgages," Weasel said, never taking his eyes off the screen as he talked. "Have any ideas?"

"Well, uh." Blake asked, tapping his pen against the desk as he thought. "I guess there are different kinds right? "

"Yep. Got any caffeine, man? I need a jolt."

"Sure, I'll put a pot on."

Blake left the room to go to the kitchen. He started the coffee then looked around in the cabinet for some sugar. There was a bag of sugar in the back of the cabinet beside a box of artificial sweetened his ex-wife had brought with her when she came up last year to drop Michael off.

While he waited on the coffee to brew he returned to GW.

"Next we have campaigns." Making a notation beside the word he looked up at Weasel as he lay the pad on the desk.

Weasel looked down at the pad, seeing what Blake had written.

Billionaire	Adrian Zayne and how many more
Mortgages	
Campaigns	Senator Ned Tyler
Ammonia nitrate	
Diesel Fuel	
Military	DIA?

"You want to elaborate on that?" Weasel asked as he turned his attention back to the computer.

"Okay." Blake collected his thoughts. "First of all, I was just handed a new assignment - totally outside my area. Steve asked me to help him out on something he's working on. They're interested in Senator Ned Tyler. Seems like Tyler might have been taking illegal campaign contributions from some guys involved in hedge funds. And I followed Tyler to an estate in Maryland owned by Adrian Zayne."

"So?"

"So?" Blake gave him a surprised look. "There's bound to be a connection."

"But it means nothing," Weasel pointed out. "It's not new - you and I both known the bureau's already nailed the connection between Tyler and the hedge fund. And this Zayne guy if he has connections here, then he's one of many. Besides, how does that tie in with the rest of the clues?"

"Ammonia nitrate, diesel fuel and the military," Blake mumbled. "What do they have in common?"

"Well, ammonia nitrate and diesel fuel make bombs and the military uses bombs."

"Bombs!" Blake jumped up from his seat. "Christ all mighty, that's it! Ammonia nitrate and diesel fuel!"

Weasel turned from the computer to look at him. "Maybe you should have a look at this, dude."

Blake stepped over and leaned down to look at the screen. "What's all that?"

"Things that have come in the last few week," Weasel replied. "From various locations. Someone collected them and put them here."

Blake looked at the list of files displayed. The names did not make any sense to him. "Display one of the files."

Weasel highlighted one of the selections and double-clicked on it. Blake's mouth fell open. "The Terrorist's Handbook? People download stuff like this??"

"Looks like it. You got card or flash drive?"

Blake pointed to a desk drawer. Weasel rambled around and found a flash drive. He downloaded all of the files onto it as Blake stared thoughtfully at the screen.

"So," Weasel exited the screen and logged off.. "You have any ideas?"

"Afraid so." Blake took his seat. "Weasel, what if this riddle is from someone who knows something about the bombing in Ohio? Suppose these people - Zayne and Tyler - are somehow involved?"

"If you follow that line then you have to consider the last item," Weasel pointed out. "The military."

Blake started at the idea. "No way. There's no way the military's involved in this thing. Could they?"

Weasel shrugged and waved the flash-drive in his hand. "And how do extremist groups play into the equation?"

"I wish I knew." Blake rubbed his forehead then jerked his head up to look at Weasel again. "Who's leaving these clues? And why me? And–damn! That guy at the river this morning!

"What guy?"

Blake quickly filled Weasel in on what had happened while he was on stake-out and finished with, "so what if this is all connected? Where do we go from here?"

"You're the investigator." Weasel turned off the computer and stood. "And my brain can't operate without fuel. Didn't you say something about food earlier?"

"Damn!" Blake looked at his watch. "Yes, I did but I need to call Syd and—"

"Syd?" Weasel's eyebrows rose.

"Yeah, Syd," Blake gave him a funny look then smiled. "As in Sydney - the most beautiful woman you've ever seen."

"Hey, man, I think maybe three's a crowd. Why don't you go see your lady and I'll catch you later."

"No," Blake refused and picked up the phone to call Sydney.

"Hello?" She answered on the second ring.

"Hey, it's me. Listen, I'm sorry I'm late. I got kind of tied up at work and —"

"It's okay," she interrupted his explanation. "I understand. But you're still planning on coming aren't you?"

"Yes, but I have a friend from the bureau here and I wanted to check with you and see if it was okay if I invited him for dinner. I kind of promised to feed him."

"Sure, that's fine."

"Great, we'll see you in about half an hour."

"Okay, I'll be waiting."

Blake hung up the phone and turned to Weasel. "We're set. You ready?"

Weasel shrugged with a smile. "As I'll get."

ɒ

Sydney ran to the door and threw it open, thinking to herself that she needed to give Blake the extra key so that he could let himself in. She opened her mouth to greet him but stopped short as she looked up at Adrian.

"Adrian! What are you doing here?"

He leaned over and kissed her on the cheek then walked passed her to enter the apartment. "I tried to call you numerous times and your secretary simply refused to put my call through." He said and turned to her. "Why is that, my darling?"

Sydney closed the door and faced him. "I was extremely busy and I asked her to hold all calls."

"Even mine?" He tried to take her in his arms.

"Everyone." She evaded his grasp and backed up into the living room. "So, what did you want?"

"What an odd question." He advanced on her. "Surely you do not have to ask."

Sydney backed up into the sofa and he took hold of her arms, pulling her to him. "I have not been able to think of anything but you, my love," he whispered into her ear as his hands moved to caress her. "I longed to feel you pressed against me, hear you cry my name."

A feeling of contempt and loathing rose inside her, making her want to shove him away. But she could not afford to let him know that she was on to him. She tried to be gentle as she pushed back from him and smiled. "I've been thinking about you, too, and I'd love to show you how I feel but right now I'm expecting company and I really need to get ready."

"Company?"

"Yes, and they should be here any minute."

"Just who is this company?"

"A couple of friends." She tried not to sound stiff and nervous. "I wish I had known you would be free and- I wouldn't have made plans. Maybe we can get together another night soon."

Adrian looked at her for a few moments then jerked her up against him. "Are you trying to put me off, darling?"

"Put you off?" She looked up into his eyes and wondered how anyone so perfectly beautiful could be so perfectly rotten and evil inside. "No, of course not. You know better than that."

"Do I?"

"Yes." She lowered her eyes and put her hands against his broad chest, running them up to his shoulders as she pressed against him. "You know I've never met anyone like you."

He grabbed the back of her hair and pulled her head back then claimed her lips in a rough kiss. She did not welcome the kiss but she pretended that she did, wrapping her arms around his neck and holding him tightly.

At last he released her. "I will expect you very early tomorrow."

"How early?"

"No later than ten in the morning."

"Adrian! I have patients to see."

"Are you saying that your patients are more important to you than me?"

"No, not at all."

"Then cancel your appointments and be at my house by ten." He spoke as if commanding her.

She dropped her eyes and nodded, fully intending on making up some excuse tomorrow as to why she couldn't make their date. "Okay, if that's what you want. I'll be there."

"Now that's the way I like my princess to behave," he said smugly.

Sydney was sure that if she had not been looking at the floor at that moment he would have been able to see the anger and contempt in her eyes. She meekly followed him to the door and he gave her one last hard kiss then left.

She closed the door and ran to the bathroom. She squeezed enough toothpaste on her brush to clean an elephant's tusk, scrubbed her teeth then rinsed her mouth twice with mouthwash. As she was drying her face she looked at her reflection in the mirror.

You're not cut out for this. She didn'tt know if she could play the kind of game it would take to trick Adrian into telling her something she could use against him. Then she remembered the faces of the people she had seen after the bombing and she knew that she had to try.

The doorbell rang and she ran down the hall. When she opened the door she saw Blake standing outside with a suitcase in his hand. She threw her arms around his neck and he wrapped one arm around her, lifting her up and hugging her as he walked inside.

"I'm so glad you're here." She buried her face in the crook of his neck.

"Me too," he replied and set her down then dropped his suitcase. "I want you to meet a friend of mine."

Sydney looked around and her mouth dropped open. The man standing in the doorway had the same expression on his face. Blake looked at the two of them with a curious expression as he made the introductions. "Sydney Forrest, this is George We'zel - Weasel to some of us at the bureau. Weasel, this is Sydney."

Weasel extended his hand and Sydney stepped forward to take it. Weasel winked at her as their hands clasped. "Nice to meet you, Sydney."

"The pleasure is all mine, Mr. We'zel," she said with a twinkle in her eyes. "And why don't you just call me Syd."

"Sure, Syd, and you can call me . . . well you can call me just about anything, but don't call me George." Weasel nodded and let go of her hand then looked at Blake. "Well, dude, you weren't lying. This time you picked a winner."

Sydney turned to Blake with her eyebrows raised. "This time? You mean I'm part of some group?"

He smiled and put his arm around her. "Don't pay any attention to Weasel. He's just pulling your leg."

"Is that so?" Sydney cut a look at Weasel. "Well, I can see that I'm going to have to keep an eye on you ...Weasel."

Chapter Six

Thursday, April 20

Washington, D.C.

"Anyone want coffee?" Sydney asked as she stood to gather up the plates from the table.

"Sure," Blake answered and looked at Weasel. "What about you?"

"You know me," Weasel replied with a smile. "I'm always on for caffeine."

Sydney took the plates to the kitchen and started cleaning up. She still could not believe that GW worked for the FBI and was friends with Blake. And why GW had not told Blake he knew her was question she intended to be answered. The only problem was getting GW in private for a few minutes.

As she opened the trash compactor to toss something in an idea occurred to her. She closed the bag, lifted it from the compactor and walked to the kitchen door. "Blake? Would you do me a really big favor?"

"Sure, what?" He stood and started to her.

"Take this down to the trash?" she asked sweetly. "I can't stand for it to pile up."

He smiled and took the bag from her. As soon as she heard the door close she went into the living room. "You want to tell me what's going on?" she asked to GW's back.

He turned from his seat on the couch and looked at her. "What do you mean?"

"You know exactly what I mean *Weasel*."

He shrugged and followed her into the kitchen when she walked away. "I can't believe you didn't tell Blake that you knew me. And not only that, why didn't you tell me you worked for the FBI?" she scolded him.

"It never came up."

"Never came up?" She slammed a glass into the dishwasher and turned with her hands on her hips. "Nice try, but that evasive crap won't cut it. You're supposed to be my best friend and now I find out you've been playing me for a fool all along. I could strangle you. How could you let me keep downloading those files like that? God, I can't believe you did this to me. You used me, you—you—"

"Hey!" Blake's voice came from the doorway. "What's going on?"

Sydney ignored him completely. Now that she was started, her anger was in control. "You're a real piece of work, GW. All this time I thought you were helping me when—"

"GW?" Blake interrupted, looking from her to Weasel in confusion.

"Yes! And he's been lying to me. All these years - how long has it been, GW? You've been with the FBI for how long and not bothered to mention it?"

"Who's GW?" Blake asked again.

"Him!" Sydney pointed to Weasel.

Blake's facial expression changed from confusion to surprise and his mouth fell open. "GW?" he looked at Weasel then back at Sydney. "Why didn't you tell me you knew Weasel?"

"Because I didn't know anyone named *Weasel*," she replied caustically. "I know GW." She turned on Weasel again. "Just what kind of game *are* you playing, GW? And why weren't you honest with me when we were talking about—"

She stopped abruptly, realizing that she was just about to spill the beans. Blake looked from her to Weasel. "Someone want to tell me what's going on?"

Weasel's face split in a wide grin. "Sydney Forrest, I'd like you to meet my friend, Blake Edwards. Blake works with me at the FBI. Blake, this is my oldest friend, Sydney Forrest. Syd's a shrink. Now, is everyone happy?"

Sydney sputtered and rolled her eyes. "Cute, GW, very cute. But this time cute won't cut it. What are you up to?"

His smile did not fade but it did change into one of slyness. "I think a better question is what are *you* up to?"

Sydney's eyes widened. She did not know if he was going to tell Blake about her files. Blake frowned at the comment and turned to her. "Syd, *are* you up to something?"

She looked at him for a long moment. After what had happened with the man calling himself Needham this morning she was not sure about trying to find out more about Adrian on her own. Right now the idea of having Blake around to protect her sounded very appealing. And maybe it was better that Blake knew what she was up to.

"Well, maybe a little something," she finally answered. "And I guess it's time we were all honest. So, why don't we go in the living room and sit. This might take a while."

They all returned to the living room and sat down. Weasel took a seat in the recliner, throwing one leg over a padded arm while Blake sat down on the couch and pulled Sydney down beside him. For a few moments no one spoke.

"You were saying?" Blake verbally prodded her.

Sydney took a long slow breath then let it out. "It started when I began therapy with a new patient - Senator Tyler. At first I thought he was suffering from stress. But he kept hinting that he was party to something horrible - something he couldn't live with.

"I put him under hypnosis and he revealed something. Something unbelievable. According to what he said, he was approached by someone after he took illegal campaign contributions from someone involved in the mortgage scandal back in 2007 or so. This person used that o blackmail Tyler into attending a meeting. There were three people besides the Senator there; a General, and three men apparently connected with the government.

They told him that it was time for the military budget to be increased. He told them they were dreaming, that the people would never stand for it - that there wasn't a need. That's when the man who arranged the meeting told him that he had a way to change the attitude of the people."

She stopped and looked at Blake then at Weasel. "Tyler insinuated that this group is behind the bombing."

"What?" Blake barked.

Sydney nodded. "That's what he thinks and I'm starting to believe him, Blake. He's scared to death and ever since he told me what he thinks is going on strange things have been happening. First, I suddenly meet Adrian and he starts chasing me like I'm Cinderella to his Prince Charming; then the FBI want me to turn over my patient files and then . . . well, then this morning a man who said his name was Needham came to my office and threatened me."

She reached up and pulled down the mock turtle-neck collar of her sleeveless top to show him the bruises around her neck. "I thought he was going to kill me. He said if I talked that he'd come back and I'd find out what kind of damage a soldering iron can do to human flesh."

A shudder passed through her as she remembered the encounter. Blake put his arm around her. "Why didn't you call me?"

"I couldn't. At least I didn't think I could. Blake, I haven't talked to anyone about what I know until now. So, if someone knows what's been said in my office it's because the office is bugged."

Blake looked away from her and she wondered what was wrong. "I'm sorry," she apologized, thinking he was upset with her for not calling him. "I should have called you but I just didn't know what to do. I thought I could take care of this on my own - find out if what Tyler said was true. But now I know that I can't."

He looked at her again. "Do you have any idea who's behind this plot the Senator talked about?"

She nodded. "Adrian."

"Tyler told you that?"

"No, not exactly. But the night you were here and Adrian showed up while Tyler was here, he told me that I should get as far away from Adrian as I could and not let him anywhere near me."

Blake leaned back and stared across the room. Sydney looked from him to Weasel, wondering what he was thinking. Weasel snapped his fingers a couple of times. "Hey, dude! I see the wheels turning. You want to share?"

"Just thinking," Blake replied then looked at Sydney. "You were right about your office being bugged. It's part of the surveillance the bureau has on Tyler."

"How did you find out?"

"I'm part of the surveillance team."

"You? You mean you've been bugging my −is the apartment bugged? Are my phones tapped?"

"No. Not yet, anyway. But they may be before it's over. Syd, we have to take this to the bureau."

"No!" She grabbed his arm. "Blake, you can't. I can't turn over those files and without them you have nothing."

124

"You can't or you won't?"

"It's essentially the same thing. Look, you have your obligations and I have mine and I can't turn over those files. There has to be another way to stop Adrian."

Blake didn't say anything for a moment then he nodded. "I never thought I'd hear myself say this, but you might be right. This thing may be a lot bigger than any of us think."

"What makes you say that?"

"Maybe it has something to do with the DIA snatching him while he was on surveillance this morning in front of your office," Weasel spoke up quietly.

Sydney's eyes flew open wide as Blake turned to Weasel with an angry expression on his face. "Hey, don't get your knickers in a knot, my man." Weasel looked completely unperturbed by the anger on Blake's face. "If we're going to put a stop to whatever's going on we're all going to have to be honest with each other. So, why don't you fill Syd in on what happened?"

Blake blew out his breath. "Maybe you're right. But before I say anything more, I want you both to realize that if we go any further, we'll be operating without the support or authorization of the bureau. In other words, we'll be on our own."

No one commented and after a moment he started to relate what had happened that morning. When he finished, Sydney jumped up and started pacing back and forth. "This is all starting to fit together. Tyler said that a general was at the meeting and now suddenly when you're assigned to his surveillance someone saying they're with DIA suddenly grabs you and tries to talk you into scrubbing the surveillance."

She stopped and looked at the two men. "But what do we do now?"

"Protect the Senator." Weasel's voice was soft.

Blake and Sydney both looked at him and he shrugged. "He's at the center of this and it seems to me that if someone is worried about him talking then the best way to insure that doesn't happen is to take him out."

"You're right," Blake agreed. "But without going through the bureau how can we protect him?"

"I may have a way," Sydney offered. "What if I have him declared mentally unstable or say that he's had a breakdown and have him committed to some private institution somewhere. That way, not only will the FBI stop their surveillance, but whoever the Senator's afraid of won't have to worry about him. They'll figure that even if he does talk no one will believe him. He's crazy. Not even his own psychiatrist believed him."

"Good idea," Weasel said. "And that brings us to the next issue at hand."

"Which is?" she asked.

"Adrian Zayne. We have to throw him off our track."

"You have any ideas on that?" Blake asked as Sydney sat down again beside him.

"You know me." Weasel smiled. " I alway have ideas. And this one is perfect. The way to get to Zayne is to have someone on the inside - right?"

Blake nodded and Weasel's smile widened to a grin. "And fortunately for us, we already have that. He's already hot for Syd so we just let her play up to him and see what she can come up with."

"No!" Blake's voice was loud and harsh. "Absolutely not!"

"Why not?" Sydney questioned him. "GW's right. I can just pretend to stop running and let him think I've fallen victim to his charms."

"No," Blake argued. "Syd, this isn't a game and this guy could be dangerous. I can't let you go in. You're not trained for this."

"But who's better trained to play mind games than me? Think about it, Blake. He already knows me, and–" she smiled and she pointed out, "–I can let things slip about Tyler and manipulate Adrian so that the suggestion to commit Tyler comes from him. When I act on his suggestion, he'll think he has some kind of control over me and he won't be suspicious."

"And, as you pointed out," Weasel added. "Since we're operating unofficially, it's the best chance we've got."

"Okay, I'll agree," Blake said grudgingly. "Provisionally. But I think we need more than just Syd on the inside. We need something we can use as evidence to take to the bureau."

"Then why not give Zayne another fish?" Weasel asked.

"A fish?" Sydney asked, not understanding what he meant.

"Yeah," he looked at her. "See, Tyler's been his fish. Why? Let's think about it. Tyler has a lot of connections and a lot of clout as well. If this Zayne and his group wants something done on the hill they need someone like Tyler–someone who can influence votes. But now, Tyler's going to be out of the picture, which throws Zayne's plan out of sync. So, we offer him another fish. One we control."

Blake grumbled and leaned back to rake his hands through his hair. "Nice idea, but it's impossible. There's no way we're going to convince some Senator to go along with an operation that is not even sanctioned by the bureau."

"Don't be too sure," Sydney said excitedly.

Blake looked at her with a puzzled expression. "Are you forgetting who my father is?"

"Your father? You want to bring your father in on this? Syd, that's crazy! He'll never go for it."

"I think he will. He doesn't care much for Adrian and if we tell him what Adrian's up to he'll be furious. I think he'll be more than willing to go along with us. And besides, who better than Jack Forrest? No bragging intended, but he is one of the most powerful men in Washington. He's been around a long time, people trust him and he's head of a very powerful committee. Add all that up and what do you have? The ideal man to have on your side if you want something to get done."

Blake looked over at Weasel who smiled and nodded. "She's right. Jack's the man."

"There's one thing you seem to be forgetting about this little scenario," Blake said. "Just how are you going to get Zayne focused on Senator Forrest?"

Weasel's brow knotted together in a frown at the question but Sydney knew how they could do it. "How about though me?"

Both men turned their attention to her as she explained. "You know how political conversations go–this person says this and that person says that–everyone repeats what the people they support have to say. So, I fill Adrian full of stuff like "my father thinks this that or the other." Whatever we decide to feed him to get him interested on focusing on my father. Then if he does show an interest, maybe he'll want me to set something up."

"Yes." Weasel agreed. "Now, the next step requires some hardware. Can I use your computer?"

"Sure, you know where it is. Need any assistance?"

Weasel scoffed at the idea. "Get real, girl. You just sit there and make eyes with honey man and I'll take care of the next phase."

"Which is?" Blake turned to look at him as he started out of the room.

"Let's just call it a little creative programming," Weasel said with a laugh, then stopped at the puzzled expression on Blake's face. "Man, if we're gonna stop Zayne we need to get the scoop on him. And how better to do that than to talk with his little empire's computers?"

A smile formed on Blake's face. "You can do that?"

Weasel looked at Sydney. "Syd, explain it to the man. He still thinks I'm human."

Blake turned to Sydney as Weasel left the room. "What did he mean by that?"

"It's an old joke, sort of. When we were freshman in college, I stayed in an apartment close to the campus. My roommate dropped out after only a month or so and I put an ad on the bulletin board outside my computer class. GW was looking for a roommate and answered my ad.

"We hit it off like we'd known each other all our lives and so he moved in with me. When my parents found out I was rooming with a man they were very unhappy. When they found out I was rooming with a black man they almost went into shock so I explained by telling them that GW really wasn't human, that he'd been dropped here by an alien civilization to study humanity and also improve our computer technology."

"And they went for it?"

"Not until they met GW, then it didn't matter anymore. They came to look at him like a son. In fact, my dad helped him out his senior year when his father was killed and money was tight."

"What happened to his dad?"

"Mr. We'zel was a policeman in New York. He was killed during a robbery."

"I didn't know Weasel's father was a policeman."

"He doesn't talk about his dad very much. They were real close and George, his dad's name was George - anyway, he was like GW's hero. He was big and strong and smart and above all - honest. GW never felt like he measured up to his dad until the last time he saw him.

"His dad had been shot and the doctor's just couldn't pull him out. GW's mom called and GW was in a panic. He had no car and little money and he was afraid he wouldn't make it. I called my father and he had a helicopter take us to the hospital.

"GW's dad told him that he never felt he had measured up to GW, that he always wished he could have been as smart and he told him how proud he was. Then he died."

"That's a pretty sad story. You'd never guess by being around Weasel, either. He always seems so–"

"Nonchalant, unemotional and unaffected?" she finished his sentence. "That's just his way of protecting himself, Blake. GW's feelings are all hidden but they're there and they're very deep."

"So, I guess you and he must be pretty close."

"I thought so." She considered the words she spoke and shook her head. "No, I know so. He didn't mean anything by not mentioning to us that he knew the other. He was just having fun. He's a very special person, Blake. More than people realize. Most people see him as being some nerd brain trust and they make fun of him because–well, because he's different and smarter than them. But he's a lot more than that."

"I agree."

"I'm glad." She took his hand with a smile. "I shouldn't have blown up at him the way I did. I guess it was just all the stress of what's been going on. You and he being friends is really wonderful for me because next to you I guess I love him more than anyone else in my life aside from my family. We've had a lot of good and some kind of strange times together."

"Like?"

She laughed as she remembered. "Once, during our junior year, someone reported us to the apartment manager - something about us being different sexes, different races and living together. See, when GW first moved in with me we had a young woman as a manager and she never had a problem with us living together. But she got married and moved away and this older man took over and he was - well, he was very narrow-minded.

"Anyway, he called and chewed me out and threatened to evict us. Apartments were hard to come by that close to campus and I didn't want to lose mine so I kind of said that GW wasn't a guy but a girl. That his name was Georgina Winifred We'zel but she usually went by her initials, GW."

Blake smiled. "And the guy fell for it?"

"Not exactly. He'd seen GW but he'd never really paid any attention to him. So, he said he'd come over and see for himself. GW was crashed out from an all-nighter at the computer lab and I ran in his room and pulled him out of bed and made him let me put makeup on him. We were all ready for the manager and when the doorbell rang GW threw the door open and there stood this girl he had been trying to get a date with for weeks. She took one look at him all decked out with eyeshadow, eyeliner and lipstick and literally ran. Needless to say, it took a lot of explaining from both of us to convince her that he wasn't a cross-dresser or something."

"And what about the manager?"

"Oh, him." Sydney laughed. "He came over and talked to GW and later he told me that my room-mate, Georgina seemed very nice but she was the ugliest girl he had ever seen."

Blake laughed for a second then his laugh faded. "Uh, Syd—you and he haven't ever… you know."

"No," she replied with a soft laugh. "Things have never been that way between us. We're more like computer nerd friends, brother and sister - that sort of thing. Why? Would it bother you if we had?"

"I don't know, I guess not," he replied then winked at her. "I just like to know who my competition is."

"You don't have any competition."

"Not even from Adrian Zayne?"

"Especially not from him. I love you, Blake. Completely and permanently. Nothing will change that."

"I hope not. Syd, I really have misgivings about you being the inside man with Zayne. I've seen the way he looks at you. Do you really think you can handle it?"

"I think I have to try," she said then searched his eyes. "But that's not all, is it? You're really wondering if I'll sleep with him."

Blake looked down for a split second then met her eyes. "That thought did occur to me."

"Blake, I don't want Adrian," she whispered softly. "Once, I thought I did – for about five seconds. But then my vision cleared and I saw him clearly and I no longer did. I only want you."

"But what if he pushes it?"

Sydney didn't want to consider that so she pushed the thought from her mind and tried to reassure herself as she reassured Blake. "Then I guess I'll just have to have a permanent case of PMS."

Blake made a face of mock horror. "Oh, no, not that!"

She laughed and pulled his face to hers. "Just promise me that if I call for help you'll be the shining knight that comes to my rescue?"

"You got it," he promised just before he claimed her with a kiss.

"My hero." Sydney smiled at him as the kiss ended then stood. "Come on, let's go see what G . . . Weasel's up to."

◌

By two a.m. everyone was tired, almost to the point of being punchy. They'd gone over and every aspect of their plan, refining it and analyzing it in detail.

Sydney told Blake and Weasel about Adrian showing up before they arrived. Blake was a little upset she hadn't mentioned it earlier but tried not to make an issue out of it.

As Weasel finished going over with Sydney things she should bring up in conversation with Adrian when she saw him next, Blake leaned back in his chair and rubbed his eyes. He felt like he needed to take a break to clear his head and fill his stomach which was growling.

"Why don't we take a break and stretch our legs?"

Weasel looked up from the keyboard that seemed to be attached to his fingertips and nodded. Sydney walked over to Blake, running her hands down his chest as she leaned over and whispered in his ear. "What did you have in mind?"

131

Blake cleared his throat as Weasel's white teeth shown in the incandescence of the computer screen like a flash of ivory against the darkness of his skin.

"I was thinking about taking a walk down to the diner and getting a bite to eat."

Sydney straightened up with a mock pout on her face then winked at Weasel before she smiled at Blake. "Sounds like an excellent idea. Let me grab my purse."

Weasel chuckled to himself as he logged off the computer and leaned back to stretch. "You buyin', lover boy?"

Blake cut him a look and stood up. "I guess so, Georgina."

"Georgina?" Weasel bounded to his feet and took off out of the room. "Syd!"

Blake chuckled to himself as he started down the hall, listening to Weasel asking Sydney just what all she had told Blake and her insisting that she only told him that one thing, then Weasel threatening to tell some of her old secrets. Blake shook his head and herded them toward the door. Working with the two of them could prove to be very interesting.

They walked the four blocks to the diner with Weasel telling a story about Syd that she was not eager for him to tell.

"So, picture this." Weasel held his hands up like he was framing a shot for a video. "Here's Syd, all dolled up like something out of Sports Illustrated's Swimwear Issue, determined to impress this jock that she had talked into going with us."

"I was not all dolled up!" she argued.

Weasel rolled his eyes and gave Blake a look. "Man, she was looking fierce. Anyway, we get off the bus at the river and the guides tell us to divide up into eight per raft. Since there were twenty three of us, one raft was going to be shy. So, the jock jumps in the raft with his buddies and Syd shoves me over and we get in. We're paddling down—"

"Do you have to tell this story?" Sydney interrupted him again.

He ignored her and kept talking. "Like I said we were paddling along, having a good time. Syd was batting her eyes and flirting with the jock all morning. About an hour before lunch she suddenly gets this weird look on her face and scrambles to the back of the raft to whisper to the guide. He shakes his head and she looks like she's going to faint. I didn't know what was going on, but she was suddenly very quiet and subdued, sitting in the back and not saying a word. We went through one pretty decent rapid and the raft filled up with water. Only our water was red."

Blake's eyes went from Weasel to Sydney and she just shook her head as Weasel continued. "You should have seen those guys. The jock looked at Syd and saw her seat full of blood and the raft full of bloody water and he just dove over the side. It didn't take long for the others to follow him. Syd looked like she wanted to die and I just sat there thinking to myself whether I should bail with the rest of the men or hang with her."

"And what did you do?"

"He bailed," Sydney answered.

Blake put his arm around her shoulder. "Sounds pretty embarrassing."

"You can't begin to imagine," she muttered, and gave Weasel a scornful look. "And it looks like I'm going to be forced to remember it the rest of my life."

He shrugged as if unaffected by her look. "Well, what can I say? It's a true story."

"So what happened with the jock?" Blake asked.

Sydney and Weasel both burst out laughing and he looked at them curiously. "Believe it or not, today he's a gynecologist," she said between giggles.

Blake smiled and shook his head as he opened the door of the diner for her. They entered and as Sydney led the way to an empty booth Blake made a mental note of everyone in the place and were they were sitting.

An old man wearing a blue uniform shirt like that of a factory worker sat at the bar sipping a cup of coffee. The man's face seemed vaguely familiar, but Blake couldn't place him. It was the kind of face you see in passing but never bother to learn the name.

A young couple sat in one of the middle booths, looking through a stack of brochures. Tourists, no doubt, he thought as his eyes passed over them to a man in the back booth that piqued his interest. The man was like the loner most people have seen from time to time; dressed in dark clothing and wearing a face built of sharp angles that had been etched with deep lines by the dark forces of life.

"Blake!" A voice drew his attention away from his moment of suspicion.

He turned toward the slight blond woman with the bright smile and sparking eyes as she moved over to him. "It's about time you showed up. Where've you been hiding, stranger?"

The events of the past few days melted into the background as he smiled down at Bonnie, drawing in the good feelings that always emanated from her in strong waves.

"Been away on business. How's my girl?"

"Oh, you know." She waved her hand. "It's the same ol' story - one of my girls quit to move back home and now I'm shorthanded."

"You're always short-handed, Bonnie," he commented in a friendly tone as he slid into a booth beside Sydney. "And yet you always manage to fix the best breakfast in Washington - not to mention the best cup of coffee I've ever tasted."

"Still the same flirt," Bonnie laughed. "And it still won't work, handsome. You still pay full price. So, what'll you have?"

"My usual," he replied and looked at Sydney.

"Coffee, please," she said with a smile.

"Same here," Weasel added.

Bonnie moved away to get their drinks and Weasel took the opportunity to look at the menu. When she returned with their coffee, Bonnie was not hesitant to speak up about Blake's companions. "So, you going to introduce me to your friends, or do I have to do it myself?"

"Oh! I'm sorry!" he apologized immediately. "Bonnie, this is doctor Sydney Forrest and George Washington Weasel."

"Weasel!?!" Weasel squawked indignantly and turned to Bonnie with a regal nod. "It's We'zel, madam," he pronounced his name correctly so that it sounded like Weh-zell with the emphasis on the last syllable. "And it is my pleasure to make your acquaintance. And please, call me GW."

Bonnie smiled at him as his face lit up in a smile that stretched from ear to ear. "Nice to meet you, GW." She looked over at Sydney. "Doctor, eh?" Then she gave Blake that look that mothers often give their sons when they finally bring home a girl the mother likes. "So, what can I get you two?"

"I'll have scrambled eggs with cheese and an order of toast," Sydney replied. Weasel ordered one of almost everything and Bonnie left to fill their order.

As Weasel and Sydney got into a discussion about Weasel's meat intake Blake let his mind wander over all the things they'd discussed.

The man in the blue work shirt sitting at the bar threw down a dollar and got up to move to the register. Bonnie hurried down the counter to take his money and Blake dug his fingers into his eyes. They felt like they were full of sand.

In the recesses of his mind he heard the sound of the register drawer opening. Sudden tension gripped him as he opened his eyes and saw the expression on Weasel's face. From that point on, everything seemed to move in slow motion, even though in reality it took only a matter of seconds.

Sydney lifted her coffee cup to put a paper napkin under it, unaware of any danger. Blake looked up at the window behind Weasel's head and saw a reflected view of the man who had been sitting at the back of the diner now. He now held an assault rifle. How had he gotten that into the diner without notice? The long baggy coat?

On instinct, Blake reached for his weapon, only to come to the bleak realization that he didn'r have it with him. Weasel's facial expression changed from one of surprise to one of cold calculating composure.

"He's carrying an AK47, basic version with a fixed wooden stock. Gas operated, it'll fire at a rate of 600 rounds per minute and is equipped with a 30-round magazine. Normal male reaction time is a little over two seconds."

Blake heard Weasel's words as he gauged the distance between himself and the gunman. It was too far travel. He would never make it before the gunman reacted. Therefore, a straight-forward assault was out of the question.

He picked up his coffee cup and stood. "Bonnie, I'm going to get more coffee," he stated loudly.

"Hey man, sit your ass down!" The man wielding the gun shouted. "This is a hold-up!"

Blake pretended to be surprised; throwing his mouth open and widening his eyes as he let his coffee cup drop to the floor. The gunman's eyes flickered momentarily to the cup and Blake made his move. Unfortunately, he was a moment too slow.

Bonnie, however, was not. As the gunman caught Blake with the butt of his weapon, Bonnie whacked him a solid blow to the head with her big iron skillet.

The gunman hit the ground with a thump. The eggs that had been frying in the pan when the pan became a weapon sailed several feet into the air and plopped down right on top of Weasel's head. The uncooked yolks exploded, splattering Sydney and filling Weasel's dark curls.

Sydney jumped up and ran to Blake who was holding his ribs as he picked up the weapon from the floor. "Are you okay?" She pulled his hand away from his ribs and started feeling him for broken bones.

"I'll make it." His voice was less strong than he would have liked. He made himself straighten and look around at Bonnie who was still standing above the gunman with the frying pan in her hands. "Nice work. Ever considered a job in law enforcement?"

"Naw." She smiled and lowered the pan. "Too boring. Okay." She looked around at the waitress who was peeking over the counter with wide eyes. "Let's get moving. We have customer's to serve."

She gave Blake a wink and he smiled. "You have anything we can use to tie this guy up, just in case he comes around before the police get here?"

"Won't catch me wasting anything on scum like that," she commented then pointed to the man's dirty sneakers. "Use his shoe strings."

Blake knelt down and quickly unlaced the man's shoes. After he had fastened the man's hands behind his back securely and tied his ankles together he stood, trying to ignore the pain in his ribs.

Sydney knelt down beside the gunman as Blake placed a call to the city police. "Blake?" she looked up at him. "You better have them send an ambulance. He's bleeding pretty badly."

Blake relayed the request then escorted Sydney back to the booth where Weasel was mopping egg off his head. He had to laugh as he looked at Weasel and Weasel looked up at him with a scowl. "Does everyone who goes out with you have so much fun?"

"Nope, just my special friends," Blake replied with a laugh as he slid into the booth after Sydney. "I don't know about the rest of you, but I'm starving!"

Sydney and Weasel looked at one another then at Blake. For a moment neither one of them said a word then Sydney shook her head and spoke teasingly. "You know, Blake, maybe we should enlist Bonnie's help on this little project. She might come in handy if one of us needs protection."

Blake rolled his eyes as Weasel laughed.

Friday, April 21, 1995
Washington, D.C.

Sydney rolled over, fumbling for the clock as the shrill, persistent beep shattered the silence. "What time is it?" Blake asked as she rolled back over next to him.

"Five, thirty," she said with a yawn.

"Five thirty? God, who gets up that early?"

"Me." She snuggled over closer to him. "I normally run, but I think I'll skip it this morning. After an hour's sleep I don't think I have the energy."

Blake yawned and ran his arm beneath her. "I don't have the energy for anything."

"Nothing?" She raised her head and looked at him with a suggestive smile as she ran her hand down his body.

"Well, maybe that," he agreed and rolled over with her beneath him.

"Ummm," she purred as his hands moved over her body. "That feels delicious."

"You are delicious," he murmured as he moved his lips down her neck.

Sydney sighed in pleasure, forgetting about the lack of sleep and all the plans and plots and schemes.

The ring of the phone pulled Sydney from a sound sleep. She untangled herself from Blake's arms as reached for the phone. The lighted display of the clock on the nightstand announced that it was after ten.

"Hello? . . . Yes, I'll be in. No, I'm fine. I just overslept. Tell Mrs. Harding that she can either wait or reschedule her and apologize for me. . . . yes, in about an hour."

She hung up the phone and sat. "I've got to get to work."

Blake groaned and pushed himself into a sitting position. "What time is it?"

"After ten."

"God, I'm late," he grumbled. "Where's my phone?"

"Use the landland if you want," she replied as she stood and padded naked to the bathroom. "I've got to shower but there's plenty of room if you want to join me."

"As soon as I make a call."

"Okay."

Blake waited until she closed the bathroom door then picked up the phone and dialed. "Steve? Blake. Listen, man, I'm sorry about last night...no, I'm fine, but something came up yesterday and I think we should get together and talk about it...no, I'll be there...yeah, give me about an hour."

He hung up the phone and swung his legs over the edge of the bed. He hadn't discussed his decision to talk to Steve with Sydney or Weasel, but felt he had to. Steve was one person he knew he could trust and he needed to talk to someone who wasn't so close to the situation, to get an objection opinion.

Blake wasn't arrogant enough to think that his personal feelings didn't come into play in all this. He had an emotional investment in Sydney and he knew that colored his thinking. What was more, the plan he, Weasel and Sydney had come up with stood a good chance of falling apart around them if any part of it went sour and he was very hesitant to take chances with Sydney's life - or Weasel's either, for that matter.

He thought about how he was going to tell Steve what was going on as he got up and walked into the bathroom. Sydney was in the shower. He watched her for a moment through the glass doors, admiring her as she stood with her face turned up to the spray of water.

He thought how ironic it was that she should realized that she loved him in the midst of all that was going on. Would she would have ever come to that realization if things were different? He hoped so. He didn't want to think that her love for him was precipitated by fear and a need for security.

Pushing the doubts aside, he opened the shower door and stepped in behind her. She turned with a smile on her face and pulled him under the water with her. "Have I told you today how much I love you?" she asked as she pressed close to him.

"No, I don't think so."

"I love you, Blake." Her voice changed from a tone of teasing to one of total seriousness.

"I love you, too," he replied, wishing that he could find the words to express just how much he did care.

But she didn't seem to require elaboration. With a smile and a quick kiss she released him. Half an hour later they were parting at the front door, ready to set the first phase of their plan into action.

◌

Sydney returned to her desk after seeing her patient to the reception area. The intercom buzzer sounded and she reached for the phone when the door to her office opened.

NShe looked up in surprise. Two men entered the office. "Dr. Forrest, we're here to escort you to Mr. Zayne's estate," one of the men announced as the other walked over to her.

Sydney looked up at the man beside her as he pulled her chair back and reached to take her arm. "Just one minute!" She jerked her arm away. "You can't just come barging in here and expect me to drop everything to–"

The man beside her grabbed her arm and hauled her to her feet. "If you will please come with us, Doctor."

"No, I won't!" She tried to jerk her arm free again but this time the man didn't release her. "Let go of me! I don't know who you think you are but you can't walk in here and harass me this way. If your boss wants to see me then he can call and make arrangements, but there's no way I'm going anywhere with you!"

The man standing in front of the door stepped forward to take her other arm as she was pulled forward by the first man. "Mr. Zayne doesn't like to be kept waiting."

Sydney couldn't believe what was happening. People didn't send goons to grab someone from their work and drag them off. *At least not normal people,* she considered as the men escorted her from her office into the reception area.

"Doctor?" Her secretary looked up in surprise.

Sydney didn't want to cause any undue alarm. If her office was still bugged then Blake knew what was going on and he wouldn't let anything happen to her. Besides that, she was the one who had been so adamant about being able to handle her role in their little plan. She couldn't chicken out before they even got started.

She composed herself and spoke as calmly as possible. "I have to leave for a little while Julie. Please reschedule the rest of my afternoon appointments. Thank you."

She didn't have time to say anymore. The men escorted her outside to a limousine parked at the curb and helped her into the back seat.

Sydney didn't say a word during the ride. She was busy trying to figure out how she was going to deal with Adrian.

ᘓ

Blake walked into the front room of the house and waited until Steve took off the headset before speaking. "Steve, I'm going to cut straight to the chase. Exactly why is the bureau having Tyler watched? I get the feeling that this is more than just a case of a crooked politician taking illegal contributions."

Steve took a drink of coffee from a styrofoam cup then lit a cigarette. "What makes you think that?"

"Don't play that game. This is me you're talking to. We go back too far for that crap."

"Yeah, we do. And I'm not playing. I told you from the start it's a straight surveillance job. Tyler has proven connections to people we know are associated with organized crime and we want to know how deep that association is. There isn't any more I can tell you because there simply isn't any more to tell. So, back to my question. What makes you think there's more?"

"Let's just call it instinct." Blake wondered if talking to Steve might not be such a good idea after all. If he did confide what he knew then he ran the risk of Steve taking the information to the bureau. And if his suspicions were wrong he was sure he would be the one that wound up with egg on his face.

Creating an outlandish tale about some shadow group run by a billionaire who was out to chance public opinion about the military by blowing up federal buildings was not the sort of thing that was going to earn him a promotion. Add to that the fact that he had nothing to back up the allegations, and it might only serve to earn him a padded cell right beside Tyler. But then again, the bureau had launched investigations based on far less in the past.

But the real truth was that he just was not comfortable playing behind the bureau's back. He had given it a lot of thought and he knew that he was not going to function as well as he could unless he was honest and forthright about what his suspicions were and what he wanted to do. The problem was how to go about getting approval.

"Well, old buddy." Steve yawned then stubbed out his cigarette. "Maybe you're instinct's wrong this time."

"Maybe so." Blake fanned the smoke that drifted up from the smoldering cigarette. "But I don't think so. And I don't think you will either when you hear what I've got to tell you."

"So, let's hear it." Steve's face assumed a more serious look.

Blake started talking and didn't stop until he'd told Steve everything that had happened and his theory about it. Steve was completely silent until Blake finished, chain-smoking and watching him intently. When Blake finished, Steve tossed his last cigarette into the cup of cold coffee.

"And you have what kind of proof on this Zayne character?"

"Nothing – exactly. Except Doctor Forrest's notes and session tapes with Senator Tyler."

Steve stood and walked a few paces then stopped and spoke without looking at Blake. "Why didn't you tell me about your little run-in outside the doctor's office?"

"I should have." Blake walked over so that he stood in front of Steve. "And I really have no excuse except that–"

"You're more than friends with this Doctor Forrest, aren't you?"

"Yes, I am. And I was trying my best to keep her out of this. She's dead set against turning over those records, Steve - even to me. I just wanted to help her but I realize that the best way to do that is with the bureau's help and approval. So, will you go with me to the brass?"

"No." Steve reached in his pocket for a cigarette and came out empty-handed. "But I will set up a meeting for you. I'll call you later and let you know when and where."

"A meeting with who?"

"Do you really need to ask that question? Or have you been out of the loop so long that you've forgotten how things work?"

"Got it." Blake realized what Steve was trying to tell him. There were people in the bureau you went to if you wanted something done and you wanted it done fast. Like any other organization, there were always ways to by-pass middle management. "So, next item on the agenda. How about switching shifts with me?"

Steve raised his eyebrows. "You want to give me a reason I should?"

Blake smiled and took a seat in a folding chair beside the window. "It's personal."

"Personal? As in a woman, personal?"

"Something like that."

"Well, well." Steve grinned knowingly. "The little shrink's finally done what women have been trying to do for years. She's tamed Blake the Rake. Will wonders never cease? So, do I get to meet this babe or is she exclusive property?"

Blake didn't really like Steve's tone of voice. In the past he might have been guilty of having extremely casual relationships and he might even have been guilty of thinking about women as 'babes' now and then, but he could not ever think of Sydney in that way. "She's special Steve, and I don't want to blow it."

"Okay," Steve agreed after a moment. "I guess I owe you one. I'll take the six to one, but you better not let me down again, partner. I'll expect you at one o'clock sharp."

"I'll be there," Blake agreed, "and again, I'm sorry about today. It won't happen again."

Steve stood and picked up his jacket from the back of the chair. "I'm headed home to grab a couple hour's shut eye. I'll be in touch about the meeting. Let me know if anything turns up in the meantime."

"Will do." Blake settled into the chair Steve had vacated and checked the equipment. It was going to be a long shift.

Chapter Seven

Friday, April 20
Washington, D.C.

Sydney marched up the front steps ahead of her escort. The door of the mansion opened before she reached the top of the steps to reveal a man she'd never seen before.

"Doctor Forrest? If you will come with me. Mr. Zayne is waiting."

She did not reply but followed in silence, trying to decide how she should act. Even if she didn't have any suspicions about Adrian she would be angry at being taken from her office by force and brought to him. In order to be convincing in her role she had to follow that line.

The man led her through the house to a massive set of double wooden doors. He knocked on the door and waited for a reply from within before opening the door. "Sir, Doctor Forrest is here."

"Show her in." Adrian's voice came from inside the room.

The man stepped back and nodded to Sydney. She walked in the room but gave a glance back as the door closed behind her.

"Darling." Adrian started across the room to her.

"Don't you darling me!" She held up one hand, palm out. "How dare you send those– those men to my office like that? In case you're not aware of it, Adrian, kidnapping is a crime."

He smirked and continued toward her. "But no one has been kidnapped, my pet. I simply sent my men to fetch you for our date. In case you haven't noticed, you *are* late. I do recall telling you to be here no later than ten and it is now . . ." He turned to look at the massive Grandfather's clock on one wall. " . . . almost half passed three."

"I don't care if it's midnight! You have absolutely no right whatsoever to have me abducted and brought here like I'm some kind of servant. I won't tolerate this from you or anyone. Do you hear me?"

"And I do not tolerate being stood up." He closed in on her and took hold of her arms. "Do you understand?"

Sydney had to force herself not to retreat. Something about Adrian's tone of voice frightened her but she couldn't let him know.

"Then perhaps you should refrain from issuing orders and try asking for a change," she said stiffly.

"Why are you being so difficult, darling?" He pulled her with him to a leather sofa and pushed her down.

"I'm being difficult? I find it incredible that you could even utter those words. In case you're having some trouble with your short-term memory, you're the one who started all this by commanding me to be here in the middle of a work day just to suit you.

"You had no regard whatsoever for me - not to mention a complete lack of respect. I'm a physician and I have patients to see. My work may not be important to you, but it is to me and I will not have you disrupting it."

"I grow weary of this conversation." He stood and walked across the room to a wooden bar to fill two glasses with a deep red wine. When he returned to the couch he offered her a glass.

"I don't want any wine." She refused the glass. "And I don't want to be here, so please notify your driver that I'm ready to leave."

Adrian put both glasses of wine on the table in front of the couch then sat and tried to take her in his arms. She was stiff and unyielding. "Come now, my precious - surely you know that I did not mean to upset you. I only wanted to be with you. Lately I've begun to feel rather neglected. With your time being so taken up with patients and old friends there seems to be no time for us."

Sydney pushed at his chest to keep him from kissing her. "Adrian, I want to see you, but I do have other things that are important as well. I can't just drop my entire life and hide out here with you."

"Why not?"

"Come on. You're not stupid. I have a practice to run and I have family and friends."

"And those things are more important than me?"

She looked down as she spoke. "Adrian, I told you that I like you - maybe I feel more than that for you, I don't know. But I do know that this isn't the way to find out. I'm not the kind of woman who wants to be pampered and sheltered; who just does nothing. I'd go crazy in a day. I have to be who I am and if you can't deal with that then it's obvious that I'm just not right for you."

"But you are right for me." He argued and pulled her closer; his fingers digging into the flesh of her arms. "And I am the only man for you, Sydney. You know that."

"Maybe," she agreed with a grimace of pain. "Adrian, you're hurting me."

"As you are me." His grip tightened instead of loosening. "You know how I feel about you and you use it like a knife in my heart."

"That's not true," she said then gasped as his grip increased even more. "Please, stop!"

"And will you return the favor in kind? Or will you persist in hurting me?"

"I never meant to hurt you, Adrian, I just don't want to rush into something. Surely you can understand that. I havet one failed marriage behind me and I just don't want to rush into another relationship and it end up badly."

"I was not aware we were rushing." He leaned over to brush his lips against hers.

"I guess I just need a slower pace than you. Will you please try and understand?"

"If you take off your clothes," he said with a smile.

"What?"

"I want you." He reached for the top button of her blouse. "And you want me even if you don't want to admit it."

"This isn't the time." She grabbed his hand to stop him. "I really do have to get back to work, Adrian."

"Then go!" He pushed her and send her tumbling off the couch. "If your precious job is so important then go. Get out of my sight!"

Sydney felt a sinking feeling in her stomach that mixed with her fear. If she alienated him she would never be able to get any evidence on him that Blake and Weasel could take to the FBI.

She straightened her skirt as she knelt in front of him. "Adrian, I'm sorry." She looked down as she spoke, hoping she looked convincingly meek and apologetic. "I didn't mean to hurt your feelings. I do want to be with you. It's just that I have to see my patients."

"Your patients, your patients!" he barked irritably. "I am so tired of those words. Go to your damnable patients, Doctor Forrest. Go and listen to their woes and be sympathetic and solve all their petty little problems. And when you are lying alone in bed, then ask yourself why your bed is empty and perhaps you will discover that you already have given your life up to someone else - your patients."

"Adrian, please." She took his hand in both of hers. "Okay, look, I'll call my office and have my appointments rescheduled. Will that make you happy?"

"No." He pulled away and stood to look down at her. "Now, you will have to ask to stay."

"What?" She started to stand but he put his hands on her shoulders and forced her back down.

"Ask."

She looked up at him, feeling anger bubbling just below the surface. She was tempted to tell him to go to hell but she couldn't. That wouldn't further her purpose. "Okay, can I stay?"

He just looked at her with an arrogant expression on his face. "Please?" she asked as sweetly as she could manage.

"Very well," he said pretentiously and extended his hand to her. She put her hand in his and he pulled her to her feet. "Now, why don't we try to put this behind us and begin again?"

"I'd like that."

"Excellent." He reached for the wine glasses. "Then let us toast to a new beginning."

Sydney took the glass he offered and touched the rim to his. Adrian smiled as the glasses clinked. "Bottom's up, darling."

◌

Blake found Weasel waiting outside the door of his apartment when he arrived. "How'd you manage to get away from work? I thought you were filling in for Mac."

"Ulcers." Weasel put his hand to his stomach. "How 'bout you?"

"I'm off duty until noon," he said as he unlocked the door. "So, did you come up with anything?"

"Actually, yes." Weasel pulled a couple of memory cards from his pocket. "You want to see?"

146

Blake checked his watch. "I don't have that much time. I told Syd I'd pick up something for dinner. How about you just fill me in and we'll look at the data this evening?"

"Sure." Weasel returned the cards to his pocket. "To begin with, Zayne is a very big contributor - to a wide array of organizations. He gives big bucks to everything from MS to the Humane Society to the Presidential campaign."

"How noble," Blake groused as he opened the refrigerator and pulled out a couple of sodas.

"He's also a member of the NRA," Weasel said.

Blake turned around and looked at him sharply. "A lot of people are so that's not saying much."

"Unless you realize what faction he's backing in the organization."

"Oh?" Blake opened a kitchen drawer and got out a pack of cigarettes. "Well, now you're got my attention."

"There's some unrest in the NRA right now. And from what I found out Zayne was quite supportive of the, let's say, more extremist faction. But his support was very quiet, if you get my drift. Lots of money and behind the scenes string pulling but nothing public. Seems our boy wants to keep his name out of things."

"Then how did you find out?"

Weasel raised his hands in front of him and wiggled his fingers. "Just call me Mr. Magic."

Blake laughed. "Okay, Mr. Magic. Did you find anything else?"

Weasel's smile faded. "Yeah."

"So, share."

"I don't have anything concrete yet." Weasel turned away and took a seat at the kitchen table. "You remember the big poop about that big investment group who peddled some forty billion in securities backed by something like two hundred thousand risky home loans?"

"Yeah," Blake said. as he thumped his ashes in the sink. "Why?

"Well, it seems like our boy was involved."

Blake's eyes widened. "You sure about that?"

"You cut me to the quick," Weasel put his hand over his heart. "Zayne's had his fingers in pies ranging from that piece of nastiness to the election of several very high ranking politicians."

"And you have evidence of that?"

"Yes, Mr. By the Book." Weasel paused and took a sip of his drink. "Only you can't use it as evidence."

"Why not?"

"Because of the source." Weasel smiled sheepishly.

"And that is?"

"The horse's mouth." Weasel's smiled widened. "Or should I say horse's computer system."

"Then what good is it if we can't use it?"

"Did I say we couldn't use it? No, I said we couldn't use it as evidence. There's a difference."

"And that difference is, oh wise one?"

Weasel shook his head and rolled his eyes. "Okay, consider this. Suppose we need an ace in the whole, say a contact to get Zayne to take someone into his confidence. What would be better than a little doctored info to make it look like that someone was playing in the same ballpark all along?"

Blake polished off his soft drink and tossed the can in the trash. "What makes you think we'll need something like that?"

"Boy Scout motto. Always be prepared. Speaking of which, have you talked to Syd? I called her office on the way over and her secretary said she'd left with two men."

"Two men?" Blake frowned. "Did her secretary know who the men were?"

"Nope."

Blake picked up the phone and dialed Sydney's private office number. After a dozen rings he hung up and called the main office number.

"Doctor Forrest's office. May I help you?"

"Julie, hi, is she in? This is Blake Edwards."

"Mr. Edwards, hi. I haven't talked with you for a while. I'm sorry she's out right now. You want to leave a message?"

"Did she say when she'd be back?"

"No, actually she didn't. And to be honest, it was a little weird. She had a full schedule today and . . . well, to tell you the truth, those guys were kind of like thugs and she didn't look too happy when she left but she told to reschedule her afternoon appointments and . . . excuse me, but can you hold on a sec and let me catch the other line?"

Blake waited for a few seconds until the secretary came on the line. "Hi, sorry to make you wait but it's lucky I did. That was Doctor Forrest. She said to tell me that she wouldn't be back in today and for me to reschedule all her appointments."

"Didn't you say she told you that when she left?"

"Yeah, strange, huh?"

"Maybe she just forgot she had mentioned it. Did she say why she wanted you to reschedule?"

"No, just that she had a pressing personal matter."

"Oh, okay. Thanks."

Blake hung up the phone and looked at Weasel. "I've got a feeling that Zayne didn't take getting stood up this morning too well. According to her secretary two men came and 'escorted' her out of her office. Two guys that looked like thugs, she said. Syd told her to reschedule all her appointments then she just called again and told her the same thing."

A distant look took hold of Weasel's face that Blake recognized as the expression he wore when he was going over all the angles of a problem in his mind. After a few moments his eyes focused sharply on Blake. "Is her office still bugged?"

Blake's eyes widened momentarily. "Yes! Steve told me he'd taken an office on the same floor and set up the equipment."

"Then maybe we should get our butts over there and get the files," Weasel said. But Blake was already headed for the door.

Maryland

Sydney was sitting on the terrace, picking at a fruit salad when the first wave of nausea hit. The fork slipped from her fingers and clattered onto the plate. She ignored it and dabbed at the sudden burst of perspiration that broke out on her face.

"Is there something wrong with the salad?" Adrian asked from across the table.

"Would you excuse me for a moment?" She stood unsteadily feeling as if she was going to be sick. She didn't bother to wait on a response but went inside to the restroom.

She turned on the water in the sink and splashed cold water on her face. Her skin was flushed and hot like she had a fever and she felt slightly disoriented. Fortunately, the nausea was dissipating but leaving her with a vaguely unsettled feeling in her stomach.

Must be nerves, she thought as she dried her face and ran her fingers through her hair. *Maybe Blake was right. I'm just not cut out for this spy business.*

Sydney stared at her reflection for a moment as she pressed the cool towel to her skin. If what she felt now was an example of what some of her patients went through then she would be much more sympathetic in the future when they talked about their stress-induced symptoms.

Adrian was still sitting on the terrace when she returned. He stood as she walked out and held out his hand to her. "Darling, are you all right? You're positively flushed."

"I'm fine." She took his hand. "It was probably just the effects of the wine on an empty stomach."

Even as the words came out of her mouth a suspicion rose in her mind. She remembered feeling ill before when she was with Adrian and that time she had been drinking wine. She also remembered how sexually aroused she had become. Just as she started to wonder if he could possibly have drugged her, he pulled her to him and claimed her lips in a passionate kiss.

Her own response alarmed her more than his advance. She knew not only intellectually, but mentally and emotionally as well that she did not desire Adrian. The problem was that her body didn't seem to realize it. Shivers of desire ran over her as his hands moved down her body.

God, I've got to get out of her! She tried to suppress the lust that was asserting control over her. "Adrian, I really don't feel very well. Maybe I should go home. There's some kind of flu bug going around and I might be coming down with it."

"Why don't you let me take you upstairs?" He took her hand and raised it to kiss her palm.

Sydney felt herself weaken and it scared her. He had to have drugged her. There was no way she would be so turned on otherwise. She was one hundred percent sure of that.

She did not have to pretend to decline with regret. The whole time her mind was screaming for her to run, her body was screaming for her to accept his offer. "That sounds almost irresistible but, no, I can't. I really don't feel well. I really want to go home, please."

"Very well," he agreed after a momentary pause. "I will have the car brought around."

She walked into the house as he picked up the extension on the terrace and ordered the driver to bring the car to the front door. Her heart was beating entirely too fast and her skin felt like it was on fire.. Only a sex-starved nymphomaniac would understand how she felt and that frightened her. She'd read the literature on the so-called sexual arousal stimulants as well as the case studies of people who had undergone the experimental treatment. Many people experienced severe reactions, ranging from gastrointestinal distress to cardiac arrest and even one documented case of cerebral stroke.

Adrian walked in behind her and wrapped his arms around her, nuzzling her neck. "I'm going to miss you."

Sydney's breath quickened despite her intentions to not let herself be affected. "Same here." Her voice was husky when she spoke.

"Are you sure I can't talk you into staying?"

"You probably can," she said and turned to face him. "But please don't. Just let me get over whatever this is so I can enjoy myself without distractions."

He smiled and took her hand. "Very well, let me walk you out."

The car was waiting when they walked outside. Adrian kissed her passionately as the driver opened the car door for her. She found herself returning the kiss more enthusiastically than she wanted. "I'll see you soon."

"I will be waiting," he whispered and kissed her hand. "Hurry back to me."

"I will," she whispered then turned and got in the car.

The driver closed her door then got in behind the wheel. "Where to, Doctor Forrest?"

"My office." she leaned back and closed her eyes, wondering if it might not be a better idea to go to the nearest hospital. But how would she explain having a drug in her system if she really had been drugged? No. She'd have to come up with another way to find out if her suspicions were correct.

ભ

Adrian hung up the phone and rose to pour himself a drink. The butler knocked on the door. "Sir? There is someone at the gate."

"Thank you." Adrian walked over to the phone and pressed the extension to the gatehouse to inquire who was waiting admittance. When he received the information from the guard on duty he gave permission for the car to enter then took a seat and sipped at his drink.

A few minutes later the butler showed the two men into the study. Adrian did not bother to rise as they entered the room.

"I have the information you requested," the younger man said as he set down his briefcase and took a file folder from it.

Adrian accepted the folder and opened it to look at the stack of black and white surveillance photos inside. "Excellent."

"Do you want me to move on this?"

"Not just yet." Adrian closed the folder with a satisfied smile. "Let's give our little friend just a little more rope so that when the noose tightens he will have farther to fall."

The older man cleared his throat. "I must admit to some feelings of misgiving about this, Adrian. If this backfires it could draw unnecessary attention to us. Attention we can't afford."

"That is not your concern. Just do as you're told and there will be no problems."

"But –"

"But what?" Adrian stood.

"Nothing." The older man backed down. "Nothing at all."

"Good." Adrian smiled. "Now, I believe you gentlemen have things to attend to. I'll let you know when I need you."

With that, he strolled past them and out of the room, leaving them to see themselves out.

൙

Sydney arrived at her office to find it dark and empty. That wasn't a surprise. She normally closed at five and it was now after six. She didn't bother to turn on the lights in the reception area but continued through to her office.

She went directly to her reference books and gathered up an armload to take to her desk. After taking off her jacket and hanging it on a chair, she started going through the books. It was not long before she reached for the phone.

"Is Doctor Howard in?" she asked when the phone was answered. "This is Doctor Forrest."

She was put on hold for a few moments then a female voice came on the line. "Sydney? This is a surprise. How are you?"

"At the moment not too good. Jackie, I need to see you."

"Now?"

"Yes. I know it's late but it's important. I'm still in the office so I can be there in a second if you can wait."

"Okay, fine. I was planning on catching up on some paperwork anyway. Come on down."

Sydney hung up the phone and grabbed her keys. She locked the office door behind her and took the the stairs to the next floor above . Her destination was a door J.M. Howard. It was unlocked so she walked in. A middle-aged woman with slightly graying dark-brown hair and warm brown eyes was waiting.

"So, what's up?"

Sydney raked her hand across her face then wiped it on her blouse, leaving a dark spot. "I think I've been drugged and I need to know for sure. Can you do the blood work?"

"What kind of drug?" Jackie motioned for Sydney to follow her into the lab.

"I'm not sure. That's why I'm here."

"Okay, let's find out," Jackie motioned to a chair then turned away to get the necessary implements.

"You're burning up." She commented as she withdrew a small vial of blood from Sydney's arm. "What are your symptoms?"

"Aside from an elevated body temperature—accelerated pulse, nausea and . . . " Sydney paused as Jackie withdrew the needle from her arm. " . . . what you might call a case of the hots."

Jackie whirled around and gave her a curious look. "Are you telling me you're on one of those damned designer drugs? Sydney, you know they're illegal. No ethical physician would ever give—"

"I wasn't drugged by a physician."

With a nod Jackie set to work.

∞

In an office a couple of doors down from Sydney's, Blake and Weasel were fast forwarding through the audio. They reached the spot on the tape when the two men came Sydney's office and listened to what was said. Blake's expression grew angrier by the moment as he listened.

"Those sorry sons-of –" he started as he turned off the tape.

"Hey man, let's see what else is on it." Weasel interrupted and reached over to start the playback.

Blake stood and paced pacing back and forth but stopped abruptly as he heard Sydney's voice on the tape telling someone named Jackie she needed to see him.

Weasel looked up at him as he stopped the tape. "That was about twenty minutes before we got here. Want to check her office?"

Blake nodded silently and they left to walk down the hall to Sydney's office. The door was locked but Blake had no trouble getting in. His years with SOG had provided him with skills that came in very handy in such situations.

The lights were not on when they entered but Blake saw light underneath Sydney's office door. He crossed through the reception area and opened the inner door. There did not appear to be anyone inside but her computer was on and her desk was piled with books.

Just as he was walking over to the desk Sydney walked in. "Blake!"

He barely had time to turn around before she had run across the room and thrown herself into his arms. He could feel how hot she was. She felt like she was running a high fever and her skin was damp.

154

"Syd, are you okay?" He pushed her back to arm's length and looked down at her.

Her eyes were dilated as she looked up at him and the expression on her face transformed from one of fright to one of desire. He did not understand why she would be looking at him with lust filled, hungry eyes and she did not give him time to ask.

"Blake." His name came out of her mouth like a husky growl just before she pulled his face down to hers and kissed him hungrily.

"Syd!" He pushed her away gently. "What's wrong with you?"

"Blake, I –" She suddenly noticed Weasel sitting in the chair in front of her desk. "I'm sorry."

"Where were you?" he asked. "And who's this guy Jackie?"

"A doctor." She walked over to the small galley in the alcove in one corner to get a handful of ice cubes from the ice-maker. "And she's not a he."

"Not a–why did you need to see a doctor? And why are you smearing ice all over your face? Are you sick?"

"Drugged." She lifted her hair in the back to put the ice against her neck.

"Drugged?" He bounded over to her and pulled her to her desk to push her down in the chair. "With what, by who?"

"Adrian." She answered then pointed to a listing in one of the books on her desk. "With this."

Blake glanced up as Weasel stood and leaned over to pick up the book and start reading.

"Zayne drugged you?" Blake knelt down beside her. "Should you be in a hospital?"

"No." She shook her head and dropped the ice to reach out and grab his shirt and pull him closer.

"Syd!" he pried her hands off him as she started running them down his chest to his pants. "What's with you?"

"Horny drugs," Weasel spoke up.

Blake looked up at him, thinking that he had not heard him right. "You want to run that by me again?"

"Essentially, it's a horny drug according to this." Weasel tapped the book. "Illegal as hell but very effective if I read this right. Kind of turns you into a walking sex machine for about six hours."

Blake looked back at Sydney. "You let him give you that crap?"

"No, I think it was in the wine. I started feeling nauseous and–"

"And what?" Blake almost did not want to know. If she told him that she had gotten all worked up over Zayne he was not sure he could take it.

"And I told him I had to leave, so his driver brought me here and I called Jackie." She pushed herself up, pulled her blouse free from her shirt and started to unbutton it. "I'm going to spontaneously combust if I don't get cool."

Blake grabbed her hands to keep her from taking off her blouse and Weasel headed for the door. "Hey man, call when you get her detoxed."

Blake nodded and turned to Sydney as Weasel closed the door on his way out. "Let's get you home and you can take a nice cool shower, okay?"

"Let's forget the shower and play doctor," she said in a sexy tone, reaching this time for his shirt.

"Syd," he took her hands in his.

"Blake," she purred, moving sensuously against him. "I want you."

"No, you don't, it's the drug."

"I want you without the drug," she argued and pulled her hands from his to reach for the button on his slacks. "But we might as well take advantage of it."

"I can't do that." He captured her hands once more. "I love you, Syd but I can't do this."

For a moment she didn't say anything. He was afraid he had hurt her when he saw a tear slide down her face but she smiled and put her hand against his face. "What did I ever do to deserve you, Blake Edwards?"

He smiled and took her hand. "Just unlucky I guess. Now, come on, let's get you home."

Monday Morning, April 24

Washington, D.C.

Sydney came in from her run to find Blake sitting at the table in the dining room with papers scattered everywhere. He turned as she came in. "Good run?"

"Umm." She nodded and went into the kitchen to get a cold bottle of water from the refrigerator. She drank half of it as she walked into the dining room and looked down at the papers that littered the table. "When did you get in?"

"A few minutes ago." He put his arm around her waist and gave her a hug. "I found your note. Thanks. I would've been concerned if I'd come in and found the place empty."

She smiled and kissed his forehead. "I've got to get a move on. I'm running late. You want some breakfast?"

"I'll fix it," he said as he made a note then looked up. "You go shower and I'll have it ready when you get through."

She blew him a kiss and headed for the shower. The weekend had been both wonderful and miserable. It had taken her well into the evening hours for the drug to wear off and much to her embarrassment she had pestered Blake unmercifully. He'd been gentle but firm with her, refusing to make love to her or even kiss her while she was under the influence of the drug.

Sydney thought that was the kindest, most caring thing anyone had ever done for her and it made her realize that he really meant it when he said he loved her. Her love for him had grown even deeper because of it.

Saturday morning Blake announced he'd told Steve what they were planning. Sydney wasn't happy at the news and they spent a couple of hours arguing about it. In the end she understood that he was only doing what he thought was right and she stopped protesting. But she reaffirmed her convictions about her patient files and made up her mind she was going to take care of Senator Tyler before Blake got the entire bureau involved. If she could get Tyler committed and out of the way where he would be safe then he wouldn't have to face dealing with the FBI. She felt that she owned him that much.

The rest of the morning they had spent with Weasel, going over everything. Both he and Blake were skeptical about her continuing as the 'inside man' with Adrian after what he'd done but she had argued that now she would be on her guard and he wouldn't get a chance to drug her again.

Weasel accepted her word but Blake was harder to convince. She understood how he felt. If the situations were reversed she'd have problems with it as well. Being a fair man, Blake gave in and agreed to continue as planned if he got permission to continue with the investigation from the bureau.

Weasel asked him point blank what he was going to do if the bureau turned him down and Blake had no answer. Sydney suggested that Weasel go with Blake to the meeting. He hadn't seemed keen on the idea but Blake had. Weasel was highly respected in the bureau; everyone knew he was one of the true geniuses of the age and if he had an opinion it was normally listened to very carefully.

Sydney did not and could not admit to Blake that she was beginning to be very afraid. If Adrian would stoop to drugging her then she wasn't safe at all with him. She started to think that it might be a good idea for Blake to go to the bureau with their suspicions. Maybe then she could just go back to being a doctor and stop all this role playing. She wasn't a good actress and was afraid it wouldn't take long before Adrian saw through her act.

Later in the afternoon, Adrian showed up at her apartment. She made Blake and Weasel hide in the study while he was there. It took far longer to get rid of him than she anticipated; three hours longer. By the time he left, Blake was fit to be tied and even Weasel had a sour attitude. They both left to go out and have a couple of beers and she went to the gym for a while.

By Sunday, she and Blake had worked through things. He admitted that he had a problem with her being with Adrian. She was flattered that he was jealous and assured him that she was not attracted to Adrian. He seemed a little unconvinced at first but after spending the rest of the day in bed she thought he was beginning to lose his jealously.

As she turned off the water, she also turned off her thoughts of the weekend. She took care with her appearance and left her hair loose around her shoulders the way Blake liked it. Her outfit was one of her favorites, a sea blue silk tank-top and a white skirt with a matching jacket.

Blake was setting a plate of toast on the table when she walked into the dining room. "You look gorgeous." He smiled appreciatively as she lay her jacket across the back of a chair.

"Thank you." She walked over to the table to give him a kiss. "This looks wonderful."

She sat down and sampled the eggs. "Umm, it's good. So, what's on your agenda for today?"

Blake didn'tt answer for a moment and the way the smile disappeared from his face made her stomach knot up. She lowered the fork of eggs back to her plate and she reached for his hand. "Blake?"

"I'm okay." He gave her a smile that appeared forced. "Just wish I'd hear from Steve. I'll feel better when we have the bureau behind us on this."

Sydney almost reminded him there was a chance the bureau wouldn't stand behind him but she changed her mind. Last night she woke to find him staring at the ceiling and he admitted that if the bureau was against his proposal he might not continue with it. He just couldn't play the role of renegade very well and if the bureau didn't think their suspicions were grounded then maybe they weren't.

She could understand why he felt that way. Blake was a very honest, loyal man and the bureau had been part of his family for a long time. He couldn't betray his honor to them or to himself. But despite what happened with the bureau, she was going ahead with her plan to commit Senator Ned Tyler. On an instinctual level she was sure that his life was in danger and she wasn't going to stand by and do nothing when there was something she could do to protect him.

"Well, maybe he'll have some news for you today when you see him," she said after a moment, then changed the subject. "Say, would you like to meet me after work for some Chinese? We haven't done that in a while."

Blake smiled and gave her hand a squeeze. "At Fortune's in Virginia? Sure, how about six-thirty?"

"That sounds great!" she replied and picked up a slice of toast as she stood. "I've got to run. Just leave the dishes. I'll get them tonight. But thanks again for breakfast. It was wonderful."

"But you didn't finish—" His words were cut off as she leaned over and kissed him.

"See you later!" She didn't give him time to say anymore before she was out the door. Sydney hurried to her car and headed away from the city.

◌

Blake pulled into the driveway of the surveillance house across the street from Senator Tyler's. Steve was headed toward his own car as

159

Blake parked. "I've been trying to reach you," Steve said as he walked around the front of the car and got into the passenger seat of Blake's car. "Come on, we've got a meeting."

"Where're we going and who're we meeting with?" Blake looked over at him.

"We're going to breakfast," Steve replied as he lit a cigarette. "And we're meeting someone who's willing to listen to this theory of yours."

Blake knew from Steve's tone of voice that his best bet was just to close his mouth and not ask any more questions. Just the fact that Steve had arranged the meeting told Blake that he did believe the somewhat unbelievable story he had told. Not only that, it told him that Steve was behind him. Otherwise he would not have gone out on a limb to arrange this meeting.

"Let me bum a smoke."

Steve handed him the pack and Blake took one and lit it. "So, anything exciting happen after I left this morning?"

"You might say that." Steve gave him a sidewards glance. "Tyler left and met someone."

"Who?"

"You're lady friend, Doctor Forrest."

Blake jerked around in surprise to look at Steve. "Sydney? You sure it was my Sydney?"

"Unless there's two drop-dead beautiful shrinks in D.C. by the name of Sydney Forrest, yeah pal, it was your Sydney. And by the way–that possessive tone of voice is a dead give away. This woman's got you hooked."

"So, they met at her office, right?" Blake ignored the comment. "That's not so strange. She *is* his doctor."

"But they didn't meet at her office. Take the next right. They met in the parking lot of the Airport."

"And?"

"And nothing." Steve frowned. "If they talked in either car I'd know something, but one of them was savvy enough to avoid that. I tried the parabolic mike but there was too much interference. You have any idea what it was about?"

Blake put out his half-smoked cigarette. "None. She didn't mention Tyler to me." He looked at Steve. "But I intend on finding out."

"Good." Steve nodded approvingly. "Cause if we're going to have any chance of pushing this proposal through you're going to have to have all the players under control. We can't afford a wild card."

"Don't worry." Blake hoped he sounded more convincing than he felt. "I can take care of her."

Steve laughed and lit another smoke. "Yeah, how many men have gone to their graves with those words on their lips?"

ℂℜ

Sydney found Weasel waiting for her when she arrived at the deli. He didn't smile as she slid into the booth and looked across the table at him. "Sorry it took so long. I had to cut a session short. What's wrong?"

Weasel's expression was grim. "Blake got the go-ahead to proceed with the investigation."

"Well, that's good, isn't it?"

"That depends."

"GW, would you just tell me what's bothering you?"

"I found out something." He paused as the waitress walked over to their booth. "A club sandwich and fries. And iced tea."

"I'll have a salad with oil and vinegar and iced tea," Sydney placed her order then looked at Weasel as the waitress left. "What?"

Weasel leaned forward and lowered his voice. "Syd, you were followed this morning."

Sydney felt her eyes widen and fought to keep the surprise off her face. "Are you sure?"

"Absolutely. Your car's bugged."

She leaned back and studied his face. "Do you think Blake had anything to do with it?"

"You don't seem too surprised. Doesn't it bother you?"

"I'm not surprised. The bureau already knows I'm treating Tyler so why wouldn't they bug my car or house or office? But what's this about me being followed?"

"That's all I know. In fact, all anyone knows is that you met with Tyler this morning before eight, spoke for about half an hour then you went to your office building but didn't get to your office for another half hour and Tyler went straight home and didn't talk to anyone but left home right before lunch and was driven to the airport where he boarded a commuter flight for Charlotte, North Carolina."

Sydney didn't comment right away since the waitress returned with their drinks. If that was all the bureau knew then it would take them a while to figure out where Tyler had really gone. He'd disembarked from the commuter flight just before take-off and had been taken to Virginia by car. Aside from Sydney and Mrs. Tyler, no one knew where he was; not even his aide.

"Why are you telling me this?" she asked after a minute of silence.

"Because I know what you're up to," he said with a hint of a smile.

"Oh?"

"Don't play that game with me, Syd. I'm on your side."

"You're FBI," she pointed out. "And I've recently come to discover that the bureau instills great loyalty in its ranks."

"True," he agreed. "But one doesn't necessarily have to negate the other."

"Not necessarily. But I get the feeling that there's more to this than you're saying."

Weasel chuckled. "You know, sometimes I think we know each other too well. You're right. There is something else. I think Blake's been asked to more or less recruit you to act in the capacity we had already planned - as the inside man with Zayne. But don't let that fool you. They don't trust you as far as they could spit you. There's still the issue of the session notes with Tyler and your tapes and your little meeting this morning."

"So you're saying that I'm some sort of suspect?"

"Anyone associated with Tyler is suspect," he pointed out. "Don't forget there was an investigation on him before Blake went to the man with his proposal."

"What do you think I should do?"

"To begin with how about telling me what that meeting with Tyler this morning was about?"

Sydney considered it for a moment then nodded. "Okay, but I don't want you to mention this to Blake. I'll tell him myself."

"Mum's the word."

Sydney quickly filled him in. Just as she was finishing the waitress arrived with their order. Weasel dug into his sandwich but Sydney had lost her appetite. She pushed the salad aside and watched Weasel for a reaction. He chewed thoughtfully then dabbed at his mouth with a paper napkin and looked at her.

"I hope you know what you're doing, Syd."

"So do I," she agreed. "So do I."

☙

Adrian picked up the phone and lifted it to his ear. "Yes?"

"Edwards got the green light. He's got five men, four field agents and some computer genius. They gave him complete authority to run things and from what we've been able to determine, he just might start by looking in our direction."

"Then he will have to be dealt with, won't he?" Adrian asked acerbically. "Is there anything else?"

"No, sir. What do you want us to do?"

"What I always want. Take care of it."

"You can count on it."

"I'm sure I can." Adrian said with a smile. "Now, do you have any other news to report?"

"Just one thing. Six o'clock at the Fortune Chinese Seafood Restaurant on Leesburg Pike at Arlington Boulevard."

"Excellent." Adrian hung up the phone and smiled at his reflection in the gilt-edged mirror that hung on the opposite wall. Aside from a few minor irritations things were progressing very nicely and after tonight those little irritations would no longer exist. Then everything would be perfect - just like he had planned.

Chapter Eight

Monday, April 24
Washington, D.C.

Blake sipped his beer as he waited for Sydney at the restaurant. He felt like he had just run the gauntlet and lived to tell about it. The meeting Steve had set up had been tense. Blake had been as honest and straightforward as he could be, answering all questions put to him and outlining the plan he and Weasel had devised.

The breakfast had stretched into the lunch hour and beyond before the man they came to meet was satisfied he knew all that Blake knew. Then he had surprised both Blake and Steve by giving the go-ahead to proceed. What was more surprising was that Blake had been put in charge. Steve was going to proceed with his investigation of Tyler and act as backup for Blake.

But the biggest surprise was that Weasel had been assigned as part of the team, along with four other men Blake had worked with a couple of times in the past.

After the meeting concluded, Steve had Blake take him back to the surveillance house to get his car then Blake went to the bureau where the four agents he had been promised were waiting to meet with him, as was Weasel.

By six that afternoon everything was mapped out and everyone had their assignment. Blake was both keyed up and nervous. It was a big opportunity for him to head up an investigation of this nature and he didn't want to blow it. But he wasn't looking forward to questioning Sydney about why she had met with Tyler this morning.

He was just finishing his beer when he saw her being escorted to the table. He stood as she walked over to him. "Hi," she whispered as she stood up on her toes to give him a kiss.

He returned the kiss then held her chair for her as she sat down beside him. "How was your day?" she asked. "Did you hear from Steve?"

Blake started to answer but stopped long enough for her to place a drink order. "The investigation's official," he answered as the waiter left.

THE TERRITORY OF LIES

"You don't sound particularly pleased. I thought that's what you wanted."

"It is and I am. It's just—Syd, I have to know. Why did you meet with Tyler this morning and what happened to him? He's vanished."

Sydney looked at him for a long moment. "How did you know I met with him?"

"Tyler's under investigation. He's being followed."

"I see." She nodded. "So that's why my car and my office are bugged."

Blake looked down momentarily then met her eyes. "Yes. So, the meeting this morning?"

"I talked to him about going to the clinic and he agreed."

"And?"

"And I made the arrangements. He's safe and out of the picture - just like we planned."

"I wasn't aware that you planned on doing it quite so soon. Why didn't you tell me this morning?"

"Because I was afraid you'd tell me to wait until you had your meeting and I didn't want to wait for that to happen. No, that's not true. The truth is, I was afraid that once you went to the bureau either they'd turn you down and Tyler would be in the same predicament or they'd give you the green light but not want to go along with having Tyler committed and he would still be in danger. So, I decided to make sure that he was safe. He's not a bad man, Blake. He's just someone who was duped and used and he doesn't deserve to be tormented. Besides, he told me that he's already tendered his resignation. He won't be part of the Senate any longer."

Blake wasn't particularly thrilled that she had made a unilateral decision to take matters into her own hands. Especially now that the investigation was official and he'd been put in charge. He remembered his words to Steve that he could handle Sydney and wondered if he had spoken too soon.

"Syd, I understand your concern and I know we planned to do just what you did. But I've been put in charge of this investigation and I can't have you making that kind of move without getting clearance."

"You mean permission, don't you?"

Blake could tell from her tone and the stiffness that came into her posture that she didn't like the idea that she had to ask anyone for permission and he could understand her feelings. But he had to find a way to make her understand his position.

"Look, I don't think this is the time or place to–"

"Darling!" A deep male voice interrupted from behind him. Before Blake could turn Adrian Zayne walked around him and leaned over beside Sydney to take her hand and lift it to his lips. "What a remarkable coincidence. I've been trying to reach you all day."

"Adrian." She smiled somewhat stiffly then looked at Blake. "You remember Adrian, don't you, Blake?"

Blake nodded. "Mr. Zayne."

"Ah, yes." Adrian smiled but didn't release Sydney's hand. "Mr. Edwards, isn't it? The FBI chap. Delighted, I'm sure. Sydney, darling, I have a table waiting. Won't you join me? I'm sure your friend won't mind. After all, an FBI agent has so many important matters to concern himself with. Isn't that so, Mr. Edwards?"

"Yes, it is. However, Doctor Forrest and I were having dinner and–"

"Yes, of course you were." Adrian pulled on Sydney's hand. "But now that I am here I'm sure Sydney would prefer to join me at my table. Wouldn't you, darling?"

Sydney wouldn't let him pull her to her feet. "Actually, no I wouldn't. Blake and I were having a perfectly nice time and I'd like to continue to do so. If you want to have dinner then call me and we'll set a date. Now, if you'll excuse us."

Adrian's eyes flashed briefly but he smiled down at her. "Very well, if you insist, then I shall formally request your charming company for dinner tomorrow night at my house. Is that enough notice, my dear?"

"Yes." She smiled up at him. "I look forward to it."

"Then I shall see you promptly at seven." He leaned over her hand again. "I have something quite imaginative in mind, my pet - something to make the pirate adventure pale by comparison."

Sydney didn't comment and after a moment Adrian smiled and nodded to Blake then walked away.

"What was the pirate adventure?" Blake asked.

"I don't really want to get into that here, if you don't mind."

"Not at all," he said as he stood. "As a matter of fact, I don't think I want to be here at all, so let's go. We'll have Chinese delivered at your apartment. Right now I think we need to talk."

She nodded and stood. "Does that mean my apartment's safe or do you have it bugged?"

Blake felt the sting of her verbal jab and tried to ignore it. "No, your place is fine. Unless you don't want me there anymore. Would you prefer to join Mr. Zayne?"

Sydney shook her head and took his arm. "You know I don't. I want to be with you."

Blake felt his irritation and jealously fade but not disappear. As they reached the entrance of the dining room he glanced back and saw Adrian watching them with an amused smile on his face. Blake knew that his reasons were not entirely professional but at that moment he didn't care what the motivations were. All he knew was that he was really looking forward to putting Zayne away.

He walked Sydney to her car. "I'm parked across the street." He pointed to his car up the block.

"Okay, I'll be right behind you."

As Blake got in his car his thoughts were on the investigation and how he was going to make Sydney understand that she couldn't do things like have the Senator committed without clearing it first. He was so preoccupied with formulating the words that he paid little attention to the flow of traffic around him.

◌⃝

Adrian sipped his wine and thought about Sydney. In the beginning she had been little more than a slightly interesting diversion; another conquest in many ways.

While he had considered her beautiful and desirable at the onset, she had not been of any real consequence. He planned merely to use her to suit his needs then discard her as he had all the others. She was no more to him than the waitress who served his meal.

Now his opinion of her had undergone a change. Something about the way she looked at the FBI agent made Adrian experience a feeling he was totally unfamiliar with; jealousy.

He was quite amazed that he would feel that way. Sydney was a beautiful woman, but there were thousands of beautiful women in the world, and many who were much more compliant than she. In fact, he could not remember any woman ever resisting his charms the way she did. To even entertain the idea that she would choose someone like Blake Edwards over him was unthinkable and yet the way she looked at Blake told him that she felt something more for Edwards than she did for him. But only for the moment, he thought. He had made up his mind that he wanted Sydney Forrest. And what he wanted he got. Always.

CR

The sound of blowing car horns drew Blake's attention. He looked in his rear-view mirror a split second before a black Audi with tinted windows ran into the rear of his car. The jolt made him do more than sit up and pay attention; it sent adrenaline rushing through his body in a vibrating wave.

Blake swerved over in front of a taxi in the right-hand lane as the Audi roared up behind him again. The taxi driver blew his horn and gave him the finger but Blake didn't notice. His attention was on the Audi that was now racing up beside him.

The rear window behind him exploded in a shower of glass and he swerved back into the left lane, forcing another car to slam on brakes and squeal to a stop. He freed his handgun from the shoulder holster and jerked the car back over to the right lane into the side of the Audi.

The man taking aim from the rear driver's side window was thrown back by the impact but he recovered quickly and took another shot. Blake turned his head as the rear passenger's side window shattered then jerked the wheel hard to the right, slamming against the Audi.

The gunman fired two rounds. One hit the side of the car and the other passed through the opening in the back window to within inches of Blake's head. "Shit!" He swerved to keep from hitting a car in the left lane as the Audi rammed him. Another shot took out the rear window and that was when Blake reached his limit.

With a vicious jerk on the steering wheel he sent his heavier sedan ramming into the Audi. The driver of the Audi fought to keep from being forced off the road but was unsuccessful. For a few tense seconds the sound of grinding, screeching metal competed with the racing of the cars engines then the Audi swerved sharply to the left across traffic and merged into the traffic heading up Fort Myers towards the Key Bridge.

Blake cut a quick look in his side mirror. It would be a miracle if he didn't hit someone but he had to make the turn. With a pound on the horn he cut in front of a car and jammed the accelerator to the floor as he turned onto the exit. Behind him the sound of screeching tires and blaring horns let him know that no one was hurt.

He caught up with the Audi just as they were nearing the exit to the George Washington Memorial Parkway. He rammed the car from behind, steeling himself for the impact. The jolt was not the only worry he had. A moment after his car ran into the Audi, the rear windshield of the Audi exploded and bullets sprayed the front of Blake's car.

Blake threw his left arm up to protect his face as glass rained in on him. He felt the sting of the sharp slivers against his neck and hand but didn't let up on the gas petal. He was going to get the guys in the Audi if it was the last thing he did.

The Audi increased its speed and headed for the exit. It passed three cars and veered into the right-hand lane behind a sanitation truck that had just entered the freeway. The tires of the Audi screamed and blue smoke boiled as the driver tried to keep from running into the back of the truck. Unfortunately, his speed was a little too high or his reactions a little too slow. The Audi slammed into the rear of the truck and crumpled like an accordion.

Blake stomped his brake petal and sent his car into a slide. As his car collided with the rear of the Audi in a jarring impact he realized that he had been holding his breath.

He reached for the keys in the ignition to turn off his car at the same time a man jumped out of the back of the Audi and sprayed Blake's car with bullets from an Uzi. Blake threw himself down on the front seat of the car until the sounds of gunfire ceased then he jumped out of his car to see a man fleeing on foot down Fort Myers towards the bridge.

"FBI!" he shouted at the driver of the sanitation truck, who had, by that time dared to climb out and check the damage. "Get on your radio and have someone call the FBI. Officer Edwards in pursuit of a suspect on the Key Bridge. And call an ambulance!"

The man stared wide-eyed at Blake for a moment then turned back to the door of his truck Blake took off running after the suspect. He could see the man ahead of him, dodging in and out of traffic and causing cars to slam on brakes and swerve all over the road. If Blake didn't get to him fast he was going to cause a major wreck.

The man turned and looked at Blake which slowed him down for a moment. Blake put everything he had into a burst of speed and closed in. The man dodged through traffic to the north side of the bridge and pulled a gun from beneath his jacket.

Blake dove behind a car that had slid to a stop. "Get down!" he yelled at the driver, a pimply-faced teenager who gawked at him excitedly.

"Hey man!" the youth yelled at him, not bothering to do as he was told. "What the hell's going on? You some kind of hit man or something?"

"FBI," Blake shot back at him as he made his way to the rear of the car in a crouch. "Now get down!"

"Cool." The boy grinned. The grin was short-lived however. The suspect opened fire as Blake emerged from behind the car.

Blake knew he didn't have time to waste. If he didn't do something fast someone was going to get killed. Aiming his weapon as he ran, he shouted at the suspect. "FBI! Drop your weapon!"

"Fuck you, asshole!" the man shouted in reply and fired three rounds.

Blake hit to the ground and rolled to one side. As soon as he stopped he took aim. His first shot caught the man high on the right shoulder. Blake saw the man's arm drop and didn't wait to see if it would get back up. He jumped to his feet and ran towards the man.

"You're under arrest!" he shouted as he drew within a few yards of the man who was in the process of picking up the gun he had dropped. "Hands up where I can see them!"

"Not in this lifetime," the man snarled.

Blake saw what the man was going to do and charged him.. He made a grab for the man's leg as he climbed up on the protective rail but was a moment too late. His fingers closed around nothing as the man sailed off the bridge to the dark waters of the Potomac.

"Damn!" Blake holstered his gun and looked down to see the man splash into the water. He watched carefully for several seconds but did not see the man surface.

Someone ran up beside him and he instinctively reached for his gun. "Hey man, I'm a cop!" the short, African-American man held up both hands. "Off duty."

Blake removed his hand from his gun and pulled his credentials instead. "Special Agent Blake Edwards, FBI. You got a phone or a radio?"

"I've got a cell in my car. You want it?"

"Yeah, thanks." Blake leaned to look at the water again. There was no sign of the suspect.

Who the hell were those guys? He wondered as he waited for the policeman to return with the phone. That question made his heart leap. He had forgotten all about Sydney. The last he had seen of her was right after they had pulled away from the restaurant. He said a silent prayer that she was okay and took the phone the policeman handed him.

As he dialed FBI headquarters he thought about what had just happened. If anyone was after him then how would they know where he would be? Unless it was Zayne, he considered. Zayne had seen him with Sydney at the restaurant. Was he following Sydney? And if so, then why have muscle with him?

Once more Blake found himself with far too many questions and not an answer in sight.

༊

Sydney had given up trying to follow Blake. She had no idea what was happening and she was very worried but there was nothing she could do. The traffic on Arlington had slowed to a crawl because of something apparently on Fort Myers. As she passed the turn she could see that the traffic was at a stand-still. She hoped it had nothing to do with Blake but something inside told her it probably did.

Not knowing what else to do, she by-passed Fort Myers and continued to the Theodore Roosevelt Bridge, crossed the river and exited onto Virginia Avenue. She pulled up in front of her apartment and turned off the car. For a moment she just sat there, considering going back to look for Blake. Since she had no clue where to look she decided against that course of action and opted on another; to call GW and see if he knew anything.

She pulled out her cell phone as she took the elevator up to her floor. It went straight t voice mail. "It's Syd. I need to talk to you. Call me."

Sydney tossed her keys and purse on the table in the foyer and went into the study. She turned on her computer and sent GW a message for him to get in touch with her as soon as possible then exited and went into the kitchen.

There was nothing particularly appetizing in the refrigerator. Besides that her stomach was in knots. Now that she was home alone she was beginning to fear that something had happened to Blake.

Sydney grabbed a bottle of wine from the refrigerator, and a glass from the cabinet and went into the den. She turned on the television, sat down on the couch and poured a glass of wine.

She turned on the news and settled back on the sofa. Before she realized it her glass was empty. She refilled it and leaned back, wondering how long it would be before she heard something from or about Blake.

Fears that something had happened to him made her anxiety level rise. She tried to push the thoughts out of her mind and switched the channel to a movie. After fifteen minutes or so she put her empty glass down on the table and stretched out on the couch. Two glasses of wine on an empty stomach seemed to be having more of an effect than normal. She felt very sleepy; so sleepy in fact that it was almost impossible to keep her eyes open.

She sat up and tried to focus on the movie. Less than a minute passed before she lost the battle to stay awake. Her last thought before she fell asleep was that she would just rest for a few minutes then she would try and locate GW and see if he knew anything about Blake.

ଔ

It was almost dawn. The search had been ongoing all night, without success. Blake called a temporary halt and the boats came in for the night with plans to head out again at first light.

When he left the scene, he went directly to FBI headquarters. All night he'd thought about what had happened and he was convinced that Adrian Zayne was behind the attack. What worried him more than anything was that there was no word from Sydney. He'd tried to call her apartment several times but all he got was a busy signal and her cell phone went straight to voice mail. Even the texts he sent went unanswered.

Weasel was waiting for him as he entered the security door. "Any luck?" Weasel asked as soon as they were within speaking distance of one another.

"Not so far." Blake then gave Weasel a grateful smile as he accepted the cup of coffee Weasel offered. "Have you talked to Syd?" "Got a message from her last night on the answering machine and on my e-mail. She said she was at

home and needed to talk to me asap."

"Did you call her?"

"Not yet. Been busy on that car chace exhibition of yours."

"And?"

"And the body of the driver's been identified."

"Let me guess. " Blake pushed open the door of his office. "He works for Zayne."

"Baaah!" Weasel blurted. "Wrong. Seems like someone followed you from Jacksonville, my man. You pissed off a lot of drug dudes with that last bust and it looks like they decided to play get even."

Blake looked at him in surprise. "You sure about this?"

Weasel crossed his arms over his chest. "Does the Pope shit in the woods?"

"Let's see what you have."

"On your desk."

Blake picked up the folder and sat down at his desk. He spent the next fifteen minutes reading the stack of papers inside. When he finished he looked up at Weasel. "I would've bet the farm Zayne was behind it."

"Why's that?"

"He showed up at the restaurant when Syd and I were having dinner and made this big show of drooling all over her hand and calling her 'his darling' and shit like that. And he made some sly remark about outdoing some kind of pirate thing he did for Syd."

"Pirate?" Weasel raised his eyebrows. "As in rape, pillage and plunder? Sounds kinky."

Blake didn't think the comment was amusing. "Anything new on the Zayne investigation?"

"Nothing significant. If he's really behind this bombing thing then he's covered his tracks carefully. Like I told you before, I've made the connection with the NRA but that's hardly proof. It's not like it's a crime to be a member - hell, half the republicans in Washington are. I'm checking out some of the more - let's say, violent extremist groups to see if there's any connections but it's going to take some time."

"What about Donaldson and Peters?" Blake asked, referring to two of the other agents assigned to the case.

"They checked in a couple of hours ago. We got clearance to bug Zayne's house. They're going in as soon as they get a shot. It's not going to be easy. There's always someone at the house. Oh, Roberts and Turner are on surveillance right now. Turner took care of the wiretap and Roberts managed to plant a bug in one of Zayne's cars while he was downtown."

Blake rubbed his eyes and yawned. "Okay, I'm going to check on Syd and grab a couple of hours sleep. I'll meet you back here at ten."

Weasel nodded and followed Blake to the elevator. "This thing with Zayne," he said as they got in. "It's real personal with you, isn't it?"

Blake turned and gave him a hard look. "What are you trying to say? That I'm jealous of him?"

"Are you?" Weasel asked in return.

"Do you think I have a reason to be?"

"Let's not play this game," Weasel replied as the elevator doors opened. "But in answer to your question, no, I don't think you have a reason to be. Syd told you she didn't like the guy. And while we're playing question and answer I need to ask you one and I need a straight answer."

"Shoot," Blake said as he stepped outside and held the door for Weasel.

"This thing with you and Syd. It's not like the others, is it? You're not just playing her along until you get tired of her or something new comes along?"

"Is that what you think?"

"I don't know, man," Weasel stopped walking. "I've known you a while and in all that time since your divorce you've never been real serious about a woman. Hell, you even earned yourself a name because of all the women who pass through your life. I'm not knocking you for that - it's your life. But now you're messing with someone I care about and that changes everything."

"So you're looking out for Syd? Is that it? Big brother GW looking out for little sister?"

"Yeah, I guess so. Look, man—Syd's a real special person and she's been hurt, you know. That rotten son-of-a...that husband of hers really did a number on her and I just don't want to see her get hurt again. She might seem like she's made of stone—all professional and cool—but on the inside she's still a scared and vulnerable woman."

"Why don't we grab something to eat," Blake suggested. "Come on, we can take your car."

They started to the parking area. "So what's the story with Evan Mallory?" Blake asked. "Syd's never talked about him except to say that their marriage was a disaster and it made her determined not to care about anyone again."

"He was a real piece of work," Weasel replied. "He married her because she was Jack Forrest's daughter and he had political ambitions. He was having an affair with someone before they got married and continued it throughout the marriage."

Blake looked at him in surprise and Weasel nodded. "Syd was a mess when she found out. He really hurt her. Not because he was the love of her life or anything. To tell you the truth I don't think she was really in love with him. But he fit in her world and she felt like she wasn't ever going to be the kind of woman who fell madly in love so she settled."

"I can't imagine her having to settle. She could have her pick. She's beautiful and smart and—"

"And sees herself as less," Weasel interrupted. "Man you got to remember where she came from. Sheila Forrest was *the* hottest thing in Washington in her day. Every man who met her wanted her. She was from one of the most influential families in the country, was drop-dead beautiful, had money out the wazoo from her grandfather's estate and was some kind of up and coming star on the international social scene. Syd grew up in her shadow. She never felt like she could measure up to her mom so she didn't think she was anything special. Besides, Sheila thought Evan Mallory was the perfect man for Syd and she let Syd know about it constantly."

Blake thought about it for a few moments. "She's not like the others," he said softly.

Weasel looked at him and Blake faced him. "I love her, man. So much it scares me. After my divorce, I swore I'd never let myself care about someone that way. But then Syd came along and I realized that I'd never felt the way she makes me feel. It's like sometimes when she just reaches out and puts her hand on my arm it almost takes my breath away. Sometimes I just watch her, marveling that she would even waste her time with me. I thought I loved my wife. I did love her. But not the way I love Syd. It's like she's what I've been looking for all my life and the thought of losing her scares me more than anything ever has."

He laughed self-consciously. "Listen to me. I sound like a cheap romance novel."

"No." Weasel shook his head and stopped walking. "I appreciate you being honest with me Blake. She's family to me, you know? I just had to know where you stood."

"And now that you know how 'bout answering a question for me? Has she talked to you about me?"

"That's classified," Weasel's face split in a wide smile. "And my lips are sealed, dude. Listen, let's skip the grub. I want to get online before I pull the plug for the night. I'll catch you at the office."

"You sure?"

"Yeah, you go check on Syd. She's probably having a fit not knowing what happened to you."

"Okay." Blake started to unlock his car then stopped. "Weasel?"

"Yeah?" Weasel turned and looked back at him.

"Thanks."

"No problem. What are friends for?"

Blake smiled and got in his car. His smile faded as he remembered what he and Sydney had been talking about when they left the restaurant; her little scheme with Senator Tyler.

And Weasel never mentioned a word about Tyler. He suddenly realized. He was supposed to be trying to track Tyler down. *Strange. It's not like Weasel to forget something like that.*

The though nagged at him as he pulled out of the parking slot. Weasel didn't forget. Blake was willing to bet that Weasel had purposely not mentioned the Senator and had steered the conversation away from him to protect Sydney.

Come on, he chastised himself. *You don't think he had anything to do with it. No, surely not. But then again, he could have known about what she was up to and just covered for her.*

"Get a grip!" he murmured to himself. "You're starting to see plots at every turn."

Telling himself that he was just being paranoid, he headed for Sydney's apartment.

☙

Sydney tried to wake up when she felt Blake kiss the side of her neck but her eyes felt like they had lead weights on them.

"Come to bed," he whispered.

She wanted to answer him but she couldn't. It was all she could do just to make sense of his words. She managed an "umm" sound, but that was all. He must have understood that she was just too sleepy because the next thing she knew she was being lifted by strong arms.

Some time later she heard his voice again. "Did you see the Senator today?"

"Umm hmm," she hummed without opening her mouth.

"And what did you talk about?"

"Hmm." She went limp as he lay her on the bed and started undressing her. His hands felt warm on her skin. She felt him settle down beside her, tracing his hands down her body.

"Do you know where the Senator is?"

"Hmm."

"Sydney, I want you to tell me about Senator Tyler."

Sydney tried to force herself to complete consciousness so that she could respond to his caresses but something wouldn't let her. It was like she was locked in sleep and couldn't waken. She could hear Blake whispering, asking her questions about Senator Tyler as he touched her. She was torn between wanting to just enjoy the sensations and wanting to remind him that she couldn't divulge that information to him. In the end she did neither. With the sound of his whisper in her ear she sank into a dreamless sleep.

☙

177

Blake was a couple of blocks from Sydney's apartment when he decided to stop by his own place and get a change of clothes. When he got to the apartment he checked his voice mail on the land-land. Michael had called three times. On the third call he left a message that his ball team had won their division and he had been selected as the starting pitcher for the All Star team. He wanted Blake to call so he could give him a schedule of the games so that maybe he could come down and see one of them.

Blake made a mental note to call his son that afternoon then went into the bedroom. Clothes lay strewn on the bed and the hamper was full. If he didn't do some laundry soon he wouldn't have to worry about clean clothes because he wouldn't have any. He picked up all the dirty things and stuffed them in the hamper, then put a couple of things in a small bag, took a clean suit from the closet and left

He checked his watch as he got out of the car at Sydney's building. It was almost six. He might have already missed her. She liked to run early in the morning before getting ready for work.

He unlocked the door, set his suitcase down and draped his suit across the back of the couch as he walked down the hall toward the bedroom. Just as he reached the opened door he stopped short. Sydney was lying on her stomach on the bed with her face turned away from the man beside her.

Adrian Zayne sat up, letting the sheet fall away from his chest as he looked at Blake. "A bit early for visiting, isn't it, Mr. Edwards?"

"What's going on?" Blake barked without thinking.

Sydney blinked at the sound of voices and turned her face towards Adrian, reaching out for him. "Blake?"

"No, darling, it's Adrian."

She jerked her head up with a yelp of surprise then scrambled off the bed like she'd just found a snake in it, pulling the sheet with her to wrap around her naked body.

"What are you doing here?"

Adrian chuckled. "My, that does seem to be a popular question this morning. Mr. Edwards just asked me the same thing."

Sydney whirled around and saw Blake standing just inside the doorway. She looked from him to Adrian then back again. "I thought–I thought–"

Adrian seemed unconcerned with his nudity. "I was not aware that you were expected Mr. Edwards. Tell me, do you make it a habit to sneak into your friend's homes while they are sleeping?"

Blake felt a cold rage swell in his chest. To think that Sydney would take Zayne into her bed made him furious. To have to listen to Zayne's mocking words made him want to hit something.

"I wasn't aware you had company," he directed his comment to Sydney.

"Neither was I," she replied, clutching the sheet in front of her chest.

"And just what *are* you doing here so early, Mr. Edwards?" Adrian asked as he stood and slid on his pants.

"I don't think that's any of your business," Blake responded stiffly and looked once more at Sydney. "Sorry to intrude. I'll get out of your way."

"No!" she exclaimed and followed him down the hall. "Blake, wait!"

He stopped and turned to face her. "I swear by all that's holy, I didn't know he was here."

"Right." He crossed his arms in front of his chest as she tried to take his hand. "A man climbs into bed with you and you don't know it."

"I didn't!" she insisted.

"Tell someone who'll believe it," he said and turned away from her to head for the door.

"Would you please wait?" She reached out and grabbed his arm, tripping over the sheet as he continued to move.

Blake stopped again and at that moment Adrian walked down the hall, buttoning his shirt. "Darling, I hate to rush off, but I do have pressing matters that require my attention. Perhaps it would be best if we stayed at my house tonight where we will not be interrupted."

Sydney stared at him like he was a creature from outer space as he leaned over and kissed her on the cheek. "Say sevenish?"

She stared mutely at him as he smiled and looked at Blake. "I would say it has been a pleasure, Mr. Edwards, but we do seem to meet at the most inopportune moments. Please excuse me. "

He opened the door then paused and turned to look back at them. "Darling, it was a most memorable night. Try to get some rest, I know you must be exhausted." He smiled at Blake pointedly. "We didn't get much sleep."

Sydney watched him walk out the door then looked at Blake. "God as my witness I did not invite him here."

"And I guess you didn't have a memorable night with him either."

"Not that I remember, no."

"Cut the crap!" he snapped, angry at her dishonesty. "It's not like I didn't see it with my own eyes. What I want to know is why? Why did you do it?"

"Are you insane? I didn't spend the night with him! I came here when I couldn't keep up with you and called GW to try and find out if you were all right and I fell asleep on the couch waiting for you. Then when you came home you carried me in here and—and I don't really remember but I think you were asking me about seeing Tyler and—yes! You were asking me what Tyler told me and I wanted to tell you that I couldn't talk about it but I was so sleepy that I couldn't stay awake and then—"

"I wasn't here," Blake interrupted her. "I told you, I just got here. And Zayne was here. I saw him in your bed, remember?"

"And I'm telling you that I didn't know he was there! Look, I know it sounds like a lie but I swear that I did *not* go to bed with him, Blake. I wouldn't do that."

Blake studied her face. She didn't seem to be lying. In fact, she looked down-right frightened.

"I'm not lying," she said. "It happened just like I told you."

Sydney suddenly started like someone had jabbed her in the back. "God! Oh, god! It was him! He came in and—and he-he- " she whirled around and stared at him with the color draining out of her face. "Oh god, you don't think I—"

Blake watched in bafflement as she clamped her hand over her mouth and ran into the bathroom. Before he could reach the door, he heard her retching. He waited until he heard the water running in the sink then entered the bathroom. Sydney was standing in front of the mirror wearing a short robe and scrubbing at her teeth with her toothbrush like she was trying to brush the enamel off.

She rinsed out her mouth then lifted a bottle of mouthwash up and filled her mouth. When she had rinsed her face and was drying it, Blake walked up behind her. "Syd, what's really going on? Why was Zayne here?"

"I don't know." She looked up at him in the mirror with a haunted expression. "Blake, I swear to you I don't know."

"I think we better sit down and talk." He turned her around and steered her back to the bedroom. "Okay. " He pushed her down gently on the bed and sat down beside her. "Now, tell me what happened—everything."

"I was following you and suddenly there was this car and someone in it was shooting at you and both you and that car were swerving and running into one another. I tried to keep up but I lost you and I didn't know what else to do but come home and wait. I called GW and I left a message on his e-mail but I never heard from him. I was so scared that something awful had happened and I thought about going back out and trying to find you but then I was afraid you'd come here and—well, anyway, I decided the best thing to do was wait.

So, I had a couple of glasses of wine and watched television and—and I must have gone to sleep on the couch. I remember hearing you tell me I should come to bed but I was too sleepy to move or talk. Then you picked me up and—and I don' remember anything else except you whispering in my ear, asking me questions about Tyler. And then there's nothing until I woke up."

Blake thought about what she said. "And you don't remember letting Zayne in?"

"No."

"Then why was he here?"

"I don't know! I didn't even know he was here!"

Blake wanted to believe her and part of him did. But there was a small suspicious part of him that wouldn't give in and trust her. "Does he have a key?"

"No!" She jumped to her feet and started pacing. "I didn't invite him here and I didn't sleep with him—at least I don't—no, I know I didn't. I don't know why he was here or why I can't remember—damn!"

She stopped abruptly and looked at Blake. "The wine! That has to be it. He drugged me before using wine. He must have somehow gotten in and put something in the wine. That's why I couldn't wake up and why I can't remember. He—Blake, that's it. It was him whispering to me, asking me questions about Tyler. He was trying to find out what I know!"

Blake stood up to face her. "That's a little far-fetched."

"Are you saying I'm lying?"

"I'm just saying that it's a little unbelievable."

Sydney looked at him for a moment then ran out of the room. Blake followed her as she ran into the living room and picked up a wine bottle from the coffee table. "Here!" She held the bottle out to him. "If you think I'm lying then drink this."

Blake looked from her to the bottle. "I'm not drinking that."

"Why not? If you think I'm lying then there's nothing wrong with the wine."

He took the bottle from her and put it down on the table. "I didn't say I thought you were lying. I just find it hard to understand. If he did get in and drug the wine to try and get information out of you then why hang around till morning? And why the big show for me?"

Sydney suddenly laughed. "Why? Come on, Blake? Why else? The same reason he put on that display at the restaurant. Adrian likes playing games, making people believe what he wants them to believe. And look how good he is at it. You think I invited him into my bed and made up some story to cover for it. And that's exactly what he wants you to think."

Blake realized that she was probably right. Zayne played by a set of rules all his own and it was clear that he had his sights on Sydney. How better to get another man out of the picture than make it look like she had the hots for him. "I see your point."

"But you still don't believe me. Drink the wine."

Blake looked down at the bottle. "How about we have the wine tested instead—see what's in it?"

"And when it shows that there is some drug in it? Then will you believe me?"

"I already believe you." He stepped up to her and took her hands.

"Blake, I love you." She looked up into his eyes. "And I'd never betray you. Especially with Adrian."

He felt some measure of relief at her words, but something Adrian had said at the restaurant was still nagging at him. "Can I ask you something?"

She nodded. "Of course."

"What was he talking about when he said something about some pirate thing?"

Sydney flushed but didn't look away. "Adrian likes to role play–act out fantasies."

"And I surmise that you participated in one of his little fantasies?"

"Yes."

"And?"

"And what do you want to know? What we said, what we did, whether I had sex with him and if it was good or bad or indifferent?"

Blake felt a little embarrassed. He didn't know what to say, how to admit that the thought of Zayne touching her made him mad enough to kill, or that the thought that she would have liked it made him feel sick.

"It was just a game," she said softly. "And I wasn't raped, pillaged or plundered."

"But you did sleep with him."

"No."

"Do you want to?"

"No" She sighed and took a seat. "I don't know if you're–if we're ready for this, Blake. I love you and I want to be completely open and honest with you but quite frankly I don't know if we've reached a place where that's possible. Do you think we can survive the truth?"

"I think we have to find out," he answered and sat down beside her. "If we're going to have a future then we have to."

"All right." She nodded and her demeanor seemed to changed to one of detachment. "When I met Adrian I thought he was one of the sexiest men I had ever seen and I was attracted to him. But part of his appeal was that he was not the kind of man I could love. That's what I was running from, you know. Love. I was already in love with you but I was trying desperately not to admit it to myself. I saw Adrian several times but I never slept with him. Adrian could never excite me the way you do, don't you know that?"

"Honestly?" he asked, "No."

"Then I'll make it a priority in my life to prove it to you. And while we're being honest I have to tell you that if you ever scare me the way you did last night I might just kill you myself. What happened? Why were those men trying to kill you?"

Blake let himself be diverted from the topic of Adrian Zayne long enough to explain to Sydney what happened. She listened carefully, asking questions now and then. When he finished she had an odd expression on her face. She stood up and walked across the room with her arms wrapped around herself in a kind of protective embrace. For a few minutes she stood perfectly still, staring out of the window then she turned to face him.

"This is how it'll be, isn't it? Me being afraid that one day someone is going to come to the door and tell me you're dead - that someone just blew you up or shot you or stabbed you. This is just a preview of what's to come isn't it?"

"I suppose you could look at it that way," he said as he got up and walked over to her. "But then you could look at anyone's life that way. Who's to say that the CPA won't be hit by a car crossing the street or have an accident on the freeway on his way home, or drop over dead with a heart attack. Who's got a guarantee for tomorrow?"

"No one," she said softly and turned away. "I just don't think I could stand losing you."

"I'm not easy to lose." He tried to make light of it.

She turned and looked at him seriously. "I mean it Blake. As silly as it may sound to you, you're it for me. The one true love of my life. I didn't think it'd happen but it did, and it shocked the hell out of me to discover it had. But it did and now I'm scared of losing it."

"Then I'll work real hard to make sure you don't," he said in a more serious tone. "Syd, I need to ask you something. I know this is probably the wrong time but I have to know. I need to know what happened between you and Tyler."

"Oh, that's right." She looked away. "We didn't get to finish that conversation, did we?"

"No, we didn't."

"Well, then by all means, let's finish it," she said as she started out of the room. "Just as soon as I get out of the shower."

Blake watched her leave the room then sat down and put his head in his hands. *Here we are, right back where we started.* He thought as he rubbed his tired eyes. Him asking questions and her avoiding them. Much as he loved Sydney and wanted to trust her, sometimes she could be difficult to deal with.

Tuesday, April 25

"I want a full report and I want it by this evening." Adrian said into the phone. "I want to know every detail of Blake Edward's life." He cradled the receiver then look down from the window of the penthouse suite of the Watergate Hotel at the sights below. Since he left Sydney's apartment he'd been filled with an uncommonly intense feeling of animosity toward Blake Edwards. The way Sydney had jumped out of bed and run after Edwards and away from him made him angry enough to want to inflict severe and lasting pain on someone.

He smiled to himself. A way of dealing with both Sydney Forrest and Blake Edwards was about to be set into motion. A plan that would get him exactly what he wanted. He called for his driver and left the suite. The limousine was waiting when he walked outside. Adrian thought about his idea for a few minutes then placed a call. His conversation lasted the entire time it took to drive from Washington to his estate in Maryland.

When he arrived he went directly to his study, sat down at his desk, and picked up the phone to dial a long distance number. "Yes, good day. I want to place an order for fertilizer."

"Do you have an account with us?" the pleasant female voice on the other end of the line was so friendly a quick thought shot through his mind and he smiled to himself.

"No, I do not. Perhaps I could open one."

"Okay, then you'll need to talk to Judy," the woman said. "She'll take your application for an account. Hold on for a second while I transfer you."

Adrian rocked back in his chair and pushed the receiver away from his ear with a grimace as the blare of country music came through the phone. His smile changed to a smug smirk. *I can keep Edwards running in circles for years,* he thought with malicious glee.

After going through his personnel's history files, he had found just what he was looking for. An employee in need. That was when his initial idea had started to take shape. Byron Rogers had been selected by the puppet master to become the focal point in a very devious plot.

"This is Judy." Another female voice spoke in the earpiece. "How may I help you?"

"Judy, good day. My name is Adrian Zayne. I have just recently acquired the Roger's farm in Huntsville, Alabama and I understand that the account with you is, shall we say, quite delinquent."

There was a short pause. Adrian assumed that the girl was pulling up the account information on the computer. "Yes, sir, Mr. Zayne. The Rogers' account is currently on credit hold. Will you be paying off the account?"

"As a matter of fact, I will. And I will also be placing an order for five thousand pounds of ammonium nitrate, which is to be sent to the Rogers' farm as soon as it can be delivered."

Adrian imagined he'd just caused the girl's heart rate to increase. All orders over two thousand pounds were to be reported immediately to head of security. It was the standing order of the day for all supply companies.

"Uh…" she cleared her throat. "I'm sorry, but could you hold while I check the availability of our stock?"

Adrian rolled his eyes as the country music once more whined from the phone. He thought about his conversation with Byron Rogers when he had inquired about Byron's father's farm. Byron had seemed to find it odd that Adrian would ask, even a little suspicious. But his suspicions had quickly faded when Adrian offered to help..

"I have always admired the farmers of this country," Adrian claimed. "It's a shame we let the Chinese buy up all our good land the way we have. Don't you agree?"

Byron Rogers had agreed somewhat hesitantly. He didn't know that the Chinese were buying American farms.

"I would hate to see your father's farm end up in the hands of the Chinese," Adrian told him.

"My dad would never sell the farm," Byron assured him. "Especially not to the Chinese."

Adrian watched Byron with cold, calculating eyes. "Byron, you don'tt understand how the system works. Your father owes a lot of money to the bank. The bank he does business with is owned by the Chinese. Therefore, if the bank forecloses, they will sell your father's farm to the highest bidder, and I assure you the highest bidder will be of Asian descent."

"Mr. Zayne." Judy, came back on the line, interrupting his thoughts. "I'm sorry to keep you holding. We can make delivery in five days. If I could just get some information?"

Adrian answered all the questions and thanked Judy for all her help then called his secretary in. "Get AG up here and call Larry in legal. I want to meet with him as soon as he can get here. Then find me a Chinese interpreter."

Waving his hands at the secretary in a shooing motion as he rose, he strutted over to the bar where a set of pearl-handled Colt 45s hung in a leather studded holster. As he eyed the silver plating, he imagined himself sitting at a poker table, back in the days of the old west, as Bat Masterson.

William Barclay Masterson, the legend, was sophisticated and cunning. A ladies man with enough charm to woo the preacher's wife. Bat Masterson, the man, was Adrian's ancestor, on his mother's side. Adrian had always prided himself with the fact that he alone carried the Masterson blood. The Masterson line died out with Adrian's mother's generation.

A light knock on the door brought Adrian back to reality. " Come in, come in!" At another time Adrian would have hidden his excitement. But not this time.

AG's look of concern faded when he saw Adrian so happy. It was a big surprise. Few people ever saw Adrian in such a mood.

"Ah, AG!" Adrian smiled. "Come in. How are things going in accounting?"

"Huh?" AG stammered in surprise. "Uh, just fine, sir. We, uh, we were just printing last month's cash flow report."

"Fine, fine, splendid." Adrian moved to pat AG on the back. "Now, I need you to transfer some funds into a bank account in Huntsville, Alabama." He walked to his desk and picked up a piece of paper. "Here's the bank name and account number. We'll need an initial two hundred thousand to start with. I'll see that you get all the necessary info later."

"Yes, Mr. Zayne," AG looked down at the paper nervously. "How should I record this in my journal, sir?"

"We just purchased ourselves a farm." Adrian beamed and slapped AG on the back again to send him on his way. AG stumbled to the door just as Larry from legal pushed it open from the other side.

"Larry! Come in, come in. I've got a job for you." Adrian walked back to the bar and poured a stiff drink, propping one foot up on the bar stool rung. "Close the door and come join me."

Adrian downed his Scotch and poured one for Larry. "I want you to fly down to Huntsville and do a title search on this property." Adrian handed him a paper with the information on it.

"Title work is not my area, sir. This should be given to acquisitions."

"That's fine." Adrian dismissed it with a wave of his hand. "Take whoever you need. I just want you to oversee this personally. Make sure that everything is clean. No gray areas."

"Yes, sir."I'll see to everything personally."

Adrian picked up Larry's untouched glass and held it out to him. Just as Larry started to raise his hand to take the drink Adrian tossed it back in one gulp and let out a breath as the scotch scorched a satisfying path down his throat.

FBI Headquarters, Washington, D.C.

Blake was yawning when he walked into his office. He hadn't been to bed yet and he felt like his eyes were full of sand. By the time he and Sydney finished talking he had just enough time to get back to headquarters for the ten o'clock meeting.

He was still a little irritated with Sydney. While he believed that she had not invited Adrian into her bed he still found it hard not to be jealous. And her decision to commit Senator Tyler without consulting anyone was a thorn in his side. She explained her reasons for what she did and Blake understood them but it didn't change the fact that she'd acted unilaterally without considering the consequences.

Sydney's argument was that the plan had been to have Tyler committed all along so she didn't see what difference it made when it was actually done. The way she saw it, Senator Tyler was safe and out of the picture and that was all that mattered.

Blake agreed that they had planned to have the senator committed for his own protection but he reminded her that he had been put in charge of the investigation and could not afford to have her or anyone associated with the investigation acting alone in such a manner. Not only did it undermine his control but it could jeopardize the safety of others and the assignment in general.

In the end their argument had reached a stalemate. She believed she had done the right thing but did promise to talk with him before she took any other action in his investigation. He tried to make her understand that he wasn't coming down on her and reminded her that she was an important part of the investigation.

Now as he put the allegedly drug tainted bottle of wine down on his desk he wondered if it wouldn't be wise just to take her out of the picture all together. If what she said was true; if Zayne had somehow gotten into her apartment and drugged her then there was no telling what he would do next.

Also, as much as he didn't like to admit it, he'd just feel better if she was far away from Zayne and his advances. Blake didn't like the way Zayne looked at her; not like he was in love with her, but more like she was some sort of prize in some contest. Blake suspected that the contest Zayne was engaged in was with him and he didn't have any desire to be in competition with that man for anything.

Afraid you'd lose? A little voice asked in his mind. *He's filthy rich and has the kind of looks women go ga-ga over. Maybe you just don't think you can measure up. Maybe you really are scared that he'd beat you out - not only in the looks and money department but maybe bed as well.*

"But she loves me," he assured himself in a mumble.

"What?" Weasel asked from the door.

Blake looked up from his seat behind the desk. "Nothing, just thinking out loud."

"You look like hell," Weasel commented as he took the seat in front of the desk. "Thought you were going to get some sleep."

"Didn't get around to it. There was a surprise waiting for me at Syd's."

"Oh? What?"

"Zayne."

Weasel's eyebrows raised. Blake quickly explained what happened and what Sydney told him. "And you do believe her, right?" Weasel asked, eyeing the bottle of wine on the desk. "Or are you going to take that to the lab and have it checked?"

Blake considered it for a moment then nodded. "Yes. If it is drugged then I want to know with what."

Weasel's expression hardened and he stood. "I'll run it to the lab. I've got to pick up some printouts anyway."

Blake nodded and turned his attention to the report on his desk. He knew that Weasel was a little mad that he wanted to have the wine tested. He probably saw it as a lack of trust in Sydney. Blake told himself that it wasn't that at all. He just wanted to make sure that the drug in the wine wasn't dangerous.

Sure, that little voice in his mind spoke up. *You're just looking out for her. It doesn't have anything to do with trust.*

Blake wished that voice would shut up and leave him alone. The last thing he needed right now was more distractions.

❧

Sydney walked into the Galileo and gave her name to the maitre'd. "Yes, Doctor Forrest," he said politely. "Right this way."

She followed him to one of the private alcoves along the wall, curious who she would find waiting for her. When Blake had called her office he didn't give his name but said that her newest patient would like their initial meeting to take place somewhere other than her office. She didn't know what he was talking about but played along, thinking that it had to have something to do with the investigation on Adrian.

"Mr. Armand, your guest has arrived," the maitre'd nodded politely as he pulled Sydney's chair out for her.

"Thank you." The dark-skinned man inclined his head slightly. "Please bring us a bottle of your finest wine."

"Certainly, sir," the maitre'd replied and left.

"Mr. Armand?" Sydney raised her eyebrows.

Weasel smiled and adjusted the expensive silk tie he wore that complemented his even more expensive Italian silk suit. "Doctor Forrest, how kind of you to rearrange your schedule." His words were spoken in broken English as if he was not comfortable with the language.

Sydney's eyes darted from side to side, scanning the restaurant. "Why the act?" she asked softly, adjusting her napkin on her lap.

"Eyes and ears," he replied and pulled a thin gold case from his breast pocket to withdraw a slim cigarillo. Sydney watched as he fiddled with the case for a moment then put it down on the table between them. "Okay," he said as he lit the cigar, "we can talk now."

190

Sydney looked at the case on the table for a moment then at him. "What's that?"

"Something to give any listeners a headache," he said with a smile. "So, what do you think?

"Of the clothes or the accent?"

"Both."

"The clothes are fabulous. You look like a million. The accent? Well, just what kind of accent is that anyway?"

"The only one I can do," he said with a chuckle.

"So why are we here?"

"It's time you talked to your father."

"You didn't need to get me here to tell me that."

"We did if we want my cover to look authentic."

"Your cover?"

Weasel waited until the waiter poured their win and left. He took a sip of wine before speaking. "Are you having some?" he indicated her untouched glass.

"I think I'm swearing off wine, thank you," she declined, remembering her last couple of experiences with wine drinking.

"I get your drift." He nodded and pulled a leather memo book from his pocket and tore off the top page. "We had the wine tested and you were right. It was drugged. With this." He slid the paper across the table.

Sydney looked down at it then up at him. "You're sure?"

"Absolutely." He picked up the paper and held it above the flame of the candle on the table, letting it burn down almost to his fingertips before he dropped it in the ashtray. "You sure you're okay?"

"Fine," she said gruffly. "But just between you and me, I'd feel a lot better if Blake had just believed me to begin with."

"Give the man a break, Syd. I mean, put yourself in his place. Suppose you had walked into his place and found another woman in his bed? Do you think you would have been so quick to forgive?"

"I get your point, and you're right. But it still hurts."

"His plate's kind of full right now. And you didn't exactly help matters by having Tyler committed. Blake's supposed to be running the show, remember? How do you think that made him feel? Not to mention the fact that we had to do some skirting around the issue to make it look like he authorized it. And by the way, just where is Tyler anyway? We haven't been able to get any kind of lead on him."

Sydney smiled at him mischievously. "I guess that means I did a good job."

Weasel's face broke into a smile after a moment. "Okay, you did good. But I'd still like to know where you stashed him and how you covered your tracks so well. So, where is he?"

"Where no one would look." She opened her purse and took out a note pad to scribble down the address. "And unless you screw up and pass this around, no one will think to look."

Weasel took the paper and after reading in, put it in his pocket. "Okay, so on to business. Seems like you're having lunch with a dude who's got more money than morals. He's here to put a Senator in his pocket to make sure legislation goes the way he wants in what will prove to be the world's most efficient Advanced Encryption Standard cryptographic processing circuit.

"You're going to introduce me to dear old dad and we're going to make sure Zayne finds out about it and about my need for a Senator. And while we're at it, you're going to drop a few choice tidbits about your dad working to make sure the military budget gets slashed all to hell and back and that he has a lot of clout as to how the vote goes."

"I understand that part," she responded. "But why this act with the AES?"

"Let's just say we want to make sure Zayne finds an easy way to get to dear old dad. If he thinks he can blackmail him then so much the better."

"Okay, but don't forget that we still have to talk my father into going along with this."

"No problem," Weasel smiled. "Jack'll jump at the chance to put Zayne away when we tell him what's going on."

"But what about my mother? You know her mouth."

"What about her? She doesn't have to know."

"In case all those expensive clothes have clouded your mind, let me remind you that she already knows you. How do you think we're going to get her to go along with pretending that you've never met?"

"Leave Shirley to me." He said with a laugh. "Come on, Syd. You know she never could say no to me."

"That's true." Sydney reluctantly agreed. "But she can be very stubborn when she wants to."

"Then I'll play my ace in the whole."

"Which is?"

"Publicity." Weasel's smile widened. "We'll tell her about all the publicity that's going to ensue when this thing breaks. Why she'll be the media darling."

Sydney smiled despite herself. "That ought to do it all right."

Weasel polished off his wine then stood up. "So, shall we say tomorrow at noon at your father's house?"

She nodded and stood. "I'll go see him now and set it up. Are you coming by later? I'll fix dinner."

"No, I think maybe you and Blake should spend some time alone. You really need to get things ironed out, Syd. He's not the most secure man on the planet right now. He needs some reassurance."

Sydney thought about that and wondered how anyone could be more insecure or need assurance more than she did right now. Blake didn't trust her, Adrian made her feel like the fox in a hound hunt and the FBI had her office and car bugged. And he needed reassurance? She looked up at Weasel as they walked outside. "GW, I really do love Blake and I wouldn't ever invite Adrian to spend the night with me."

"I know. And I think deep down Blake does, too. But you have to remember that in this he has to think like an investigator first and a boyfriend second. A lot's riding on this gig, Syd. It could make or break his career."

Sydney considered his words. "Then I'll try very hard not to do anything to mess things up. In the meantime, could I ask a favor of you?"

"Name it."

"Just be careful. Blake told me you weren't a field agent and I just don't want your brilliant mind to get your skinny butt into something you can't get out of."

Weasel laughed good-naturedly. "I'll do my best to keep my narrow little ass in one piece. Catch you later."

Sydney watched him get into the back of the long black limousine that pulled up at the curb then she turned to walk down the block where her car was parked. Her mind turned to what she was going to say to her father. She was so caught up in thoughts, she didn't notice the two men who followed her.

❧

"What do you mean you think there's a conspiracy?" Jack Forrest demanded heatedly. "How would you know something like that?"

"Dad, if you'll just listen—" Sydney started but was cut off.

"Unless you heard it from someone involved. In which case . . . Sydney, are you part of this thing?"

"No, if you'll just give me a minute I'll explain."

Jack took a seat behind his desk and regarded her. "You have my full attention."

"Thank you." She took a seat in the chair in front of the massive desk. "Like I said to begin with, I can't tell you how I know this, only that I do. Apparently Ned Tyler took some money illegally from the man who was involved in that mortgage scandal decade ago. He thought he was safe but someone found out about it and used the information to blackmail him. He was asked to attend a meeting where there were several other men present; a congressman - I don't know who, a high-ranking general, and two other men. They told him about the World Trade Center Bombing and a plot to bomb the UN building that was thwarted by the FBI and all kinds of things. But what they were mostly interested in was the military budget and the impending budget cuts. They wanted him to try and sway the vote. He told them that the public would never go for more spending on the military and was told by the man who had arranged the meeting that he - the man, that is - had a plan to change the attitude of the people."

"That hardly sounds like a nefarious plot," Jack commented. "More like some unscrupulous, less than honest lobbyist."

"That's not all, Dad. Tyler's convinced that the man who arranged the meeting is behind what happened in Akron, and he thinks that was just the first of the bombings that are going to happen."

Jack looked at his daughter with a mixture of shock and disbelief on his face. "Are you telling me that Tyler's uncovered some terrorist plot?"

"In a manner of speaking, yes, that's what I think."

"Then you should have gone straight to the FBI." He stood up and walked around the desk to lean back on it. "Sydney, honey, this is very serious. If you have any information about who's responsible then you have to go to the FBI."

"I already have. Blake's in charge of the investigation and GW's working with him. That's really why I'm here, to try and enlist your help."

"Blake Edwards, the fellow you've been seeing off and on? I didn't know you two were still dating."

"It's moved passed dating. But that's beside the point. We need your help, Dad."

"In what way?"

"Blake and GW have come up with a plan." Sydney stood up and walked across the room so that she would not have to face her father when she told him. "They think that Adrian Zayne is the man behind all this and−"

"I should have known!" he exploded. "I've always suspected that he's . . . " Jack's face flushed and he bounded across the room. "Tell me that you're not seeing Zayne anymore."

"I sort of am." She looked away. "I'm what GW calls their 'inside man.' See, Adrian has some sort of thing for me for some weird reason and Blake and GW think that maybe I can get him to−"

"No!" Jack interrupted. "I absolutely will not stand for this. You have to disassociate yourself from this immediately. Do you have any idea what kind of danger you could be putting yourself in?"

"Yes, I know." She said quietly as she turned and faced him. "But I have to do this. And I need you to help me. Please, Dad. I know this is asking a lot but this is important, probably the most important thing I've ever asked you. Will you help me?"

Jack studied her for a few moments then sighed. "Just what exactly is it you want me to do?"

Sydney smiled at her father. "Just be yourself. GW is undercover as some hotshot with 'the' computer company who wants to make sure that legislation on the latest AES goes the way his company wants. They want me to pretend to introduce you to him and make it look like he's bribing you. At the same time, if Adrian really is behind this thing, then he's going to be looking for someone who has some clout who can sway the vote on the military budget. And–"

"I thought he had Tyler in his pocket?"

"Well, Tyler's kind of out of the picture."

"Kind of how?"

"He had a breakdown."

"I haven't heard anything about that. When did it happen?"

"Very recently. And as I understand it, he's tendering his resignation. So, like I was about to say, Adrian will be looking for a new power figure and if I play my cards right, he'll be looking at you."

Jack sat down on the leather couch along the back wall and looked at her in silence for a long time. "And the FBI wants me to pretend to go along with Zayne, is that it?"

"More or less."

"Do you have any idea how this will look if word of this gets out? The damage it could do to my reputation?"

"Not if we nail Adrian. Dad, just consider this. If we don't stop him then what happened in Akron could happen again. I just can't live with knowing that I could have done something to prevent it and didn't and quite frankly I can't imagine that you could either."

Jack's frown transformed into a grudging smile. "You know all the buttons to push, don't you?"

"I learned from the best," she teased, then became serious. "I know this is asking a lot, but I really believe that your reputation can stand the test. After all, you're a good, honest man. How can helping the FBI put away people who would kill innocents make you look bad?"

"I see your point. But let me ask you something. Are you doing this to see those people put away, or because you're involved with Blake and want to make him happy?"

"Neither. Or both maybe. But mostly just because it's the right thing to do. And you always told me that doing something because it was the right thing to do is enough."

"Indeed I did. Very well, I'll help you. But I'll need to discuss this with your mother and I'm not so sure she'll be thrilled with the idea."

"I think I've got that covered." Sydney grinned. "GW and I want to meet with you for lunch tomorrow and GW's going to work on Mom."

"Devious." Jack laughed. "Very devious, but very good. Shirley's always had a soft spot in her heart for that boy."

"Then we'll see you tomorrow. How about Maison Blanche?

"Noon." He stood and gave her a hug. "Will you promise your old dad one thing?"

"If I can."

"Be careful."

"Don't worry." She disengaged herself from his embrace and smiled up at him. "I have my own knight in shining armor watching over me."

Jack raised one eyebrow. "Well, that's all well and good but even knights sometimes get their armor pierced."

"I get the point. I'll be careful. But right now I have to go. See you tomorrow. And make sure that Mom doesn't act like she recognizes GW."

"I'll do what I can," he promised. "See you tomorrow."

Sydney left her father's office and got in the elevator. Two men got in with her and they all rode down to the ground floor. Sydney walked to her car and as she was getting her keys out of her purse she happened to see the two men's reflection in the window of her car as they got into a gray BMW parked nearby. She got in her car and started it, thinking it odd that they did not pull out of the parking lot.

That thought changed after she had gone a couple of blocks. She looked in her rear-view mirror and saw the same BMW behind her. A small jolt of fear ran through her as she realized she was being followed but she assured herself that it was nothing to worry about. Even if the men were working for Adrian, there was nothing odd about a daughter visiting her father. She forgot about the men completely and returned to her office.

Her secretary was not at her desk which was strange. Sydney thought that perhaps she had taken longer than normal for lunch and proceeded into her office. Just as she opened the door the chair at her desk turned around.

"Darling, I was beginning to think you were not going to return." Adrian smiled at her.

"Adrian, what are you doing here?"

"I'm your next appointment." He held up her appointment book.

"You need a psychiatrist?" she gave him a skeptical look.

"Desperately," he replied as he stood and started toward her.

Sydney dodged around him, put her purse on her desk and picked up a notepad. "Very well, then let's have a seat and get started."

Adrian gave her a wicked smile. "What? No couch? And I was so looking forward to it."

Sydney took a seat in one of the leather wing-chairs and gestured to the other. "I don't think you're ready for that. Shall we?"

He walked over and leaned down, placing his hands on the arms of her chair. "By all mean, let's."

Sydney looked up at him, feeling a sensation of butterflies in her stomach, wondering what kind of game he was playing this time.

Chapter Nine

Wednesday, April 26

Washington, D.C.

Blake was just getting out of the shower when he heard the persistent knocking on the front door. He hurried to get out and wrap a towel around his waist. "Okay!" he yelled as he started down the hall. "I'm coming!"

Sydney threw her arms around him as soon as he opened the door. "Thank god you're here!"

"What's wrong?" He untangled himself from her arms and closed the door.

"What's wrong?" she repeated the question incredulously.

"Yeah." He turned and walked away from her, trying to pretend that he did not know why she was upset.

He had gotten a message from her late the previous afternoon that she was having dinner with Zayne and would call as soon as she got in. When he had not heard from her by midnight he called her apartment. A man answered, sounding like he had been awakened by the phone answered and told him that Sydney did not want to be bothered.

"What's wrong with you?" She followed him into the bathroom.

"Just trying to get ready for work." He grabbed another towel and started drying his hair. "Do you mind?" He jerked his thumb in the direction of the door.

"Yes, I do!" She grabbed the towel from his hands and tossed it down on the sink. "Where were you last night?"

"Where was I? Shouldn't that be my line?"

A perplexed look came on her face for a moment before she dismissed the question. "I tried to call you a dozen times and you weren't here. You could have at least left you voice mail on."

Blake leaned back against the sink and crossed his arms in front of his chest. "Nice try, but no banana."

"What's that mean?"

"It means I called your apartment and your friend Mr. Zayne answered and told me that you didn't want to be disturbed. Funny, but I was sure you said something about not wanting to jump in bed with the guy. I must have been mistaken."

"That's insane! He wasn't at my apartment!"

"Oh, then it must have been one of your other boyfriends."

Sydney's jaw clenched and a flush stained her cheeks. "You...you bastard! How dare you. You know that's not true. I was right there where I said I'd be, trying to call you half the night!"

Blake heard the anger in her voice and read it in her body language and it seemed very genuine and very real. But he knew he had called her apartment. He had not gotten the wrong number. A man had answered and he was certain it was Zayne.

"Well, that's really amazing, considering that I was right here all night and the phone never rang."

Sydney stared at him wide-eyed for a moment then ran out of the bathroom and into the bedroom to jerk the receiver of the phone up to her ear. Blake walked into the room and looked at her. "There's nothing wrong with the phone."

"There has to be!" She dialed a number and waited for a few moments. "Hi, it's Syd. Will you call me right back at this number?" After reciting Blake's number she hung up.

Several seconds passed in silence. She looked over at Blake and arched her eyebrows then looked down at her wrist watch. Neither one of them spoke for what seemed a very long time. Finally, she broke the silence by picking up the phone and dialing again. "It's me again. Why didn't you call? ...Are you sure?... Okay, thanks. I'll see you at noon."

She hung up the phone and faced Blake. "That was GW. He tried to call your number and let it ring a dozen times but there was no answer."

"That's impossible!" Blake crossed the room, picked up the phone and punched the zero. "Hello, this is Special Agent Blake Edwards with the FBI. I think there's something wrong with my phone. Could you check and tell me what number I'm calling from?...Yes, I can give you my identification."

Sydney sat down and gave him a scornful look as he called out his badge number to the operator. "Yes, I need the number of the phone I'm calling from. Thank you."

After a couple of seconds, he looked sharply at Sydney. "Thank you very much," he said into the receiver then hung up.

"Well?" She looked up at him.

"Well, it looks like there is something wrong with the phone," he admitted. "Seems like my number and the number of a pay phone on the corner got switched somehow."

"You see!" she crowed triumphantly. "I told you! Now, would you like to apologize for those nasty little remarks you made earlier?"

Blake felt his hackles rise at the tone of her voice. His phone might not be working right but that had nothing to do with Zayne answering her phone in the middle of the night.

"I don't see what that has to do with you sleeping with Zayne."

"I did not sleep with him!" she shouted and jumped up. "Did it ever occur to you that if you're phone's been messed with then just maybe it's possible that mine has been too?"

Blake hated to admit it but until that moment he had not thought of that possibility. "Did you leave your voice mail on?"

"Yes, just like always."

He picked up the phone and dialed her number. After three rings a man answered. "Yes?"

"Is Sydney there?"

"Who is this?"

"Who's asking?

"Sydney does not want to be disturbed. Please do not call back."

Blake hung up the phone and turned to her. "I think I owe you an apology."

"Who was that?"

"I'm not sure. It could be Zayne."

"But..." she put her fingers to her temples. "But how could he manage that?"

"Enough money and you can do just about anything." Blake reached out and took her hands in his. "I'm sorry, Syd."

"You should be." She pulled her hands away. "Why is it that you're always so quick to jump to the wrong conclusion about me, Blake? If you love me then why don't you trust me?"

Blake sat down on the bed and looked down at the floor. He didn't know how to answer her. He did love her and he wanted to trust her. Part of him did. The other part; the part that had been lied to far too many times and been cheated on more than once had a hard time trusting anyone.

"I'm sorry," he said at last and looked up. "I want to trust you but...it's hard, Syd. I'm not used to trusting anyone but myself and to be honest, it's been my experience that people are basically–"

"Before you go any further," she interrupted as she sat down beside him. "Can I just say that I'm not just 'people?' I love you, Blake. More than anyone or anything in my life and I'd never deliberately betray you. I just want you to try and have a little faith. Otherwise, I don't see that we have any future together."

"I know." He nodded and put his arm around her to pull her close. "You're right and I'll try. Am I forgiven?"

Sydney put her hand on the side of his face as she looked up into his eyes. Her touch seemed to melt some rock-hard icy place in his heart where fear and mistrust dwelled, along with igniting a fire in other parts of his anatomy. He had never met a woman that could affect him so much by such a simple gesture.

"I love you," she whispered.

Blake pulled her to him. When their lips met his desire flared like gasoline being thrown on a fire. With a groan he pushed her back on the bed, feeling her lithe body mold against his. Her hands tugged at the towel around his waist and he pulled away from the kiss to look down at her. "You're all dressed and ready for work."

"So?"

"So, you might get all messed up."

"I certainly hope so," she said with a smile and pushed him away so that she could stand up and take off her jacket. Blake watched with mounting excitement as she slowly undressed. When she was naked she pushed him back on the bed and stretched out on top of him. "Now where were we?"

He forgot about being suspicious and angry as her lips met his. The doubts had not disappeared. There were still a lot of things he was unsure about. But wanting her was not one of them.

 са

As Sydney and GW were meeting Senator Forrest at the luxurious Maison Blanche for lunch, Blake was excitedly going over a report one of his agents had just handed him. "Are you sure about this?" He looked up at the younger, dark-haired man.

"Yes, sir," Special agent Matt Donaldson answered crisply. "Mr. We'zel checked it himself before he left and verified the information. In less than four days five thousand pounds of ammonium nitrate will be in transit to a farm to just outside Huntsville. There's also a shipment, another thirty-five hundred pounds being shipped from Muscle Shoals as well."

"That's a lot of fertilizer," Blake commented. "And there's no doubt that Zayne himself authorized the shipments?"

"None whatsoever, sir. In fact, he paid for everything on his personal Black American Express."

Blake whistled softly. "He must have one hell of a credit limit. Can we get a copy of the transactions?"

"We're working on that now, sir."

Blake sat back in his chair and looked at the younger man. "Okay, he's moving ammonium nitrate from one place to another. Alabama is farming country, isn't it?"

"Yes, sir, it is. But Mr. Zayne doesn't own any property in Alabama that we know of, and his business interests are not in farming, so why would he be buying ammonium nitrate?"

Blake nodded without comment. This was a good start but it wasn't enough. They needed more. "Good work, Matt. But I want you to dig a little deeper. Find out if there've been any large sales of fuel oil to Zayne or any of his businesses and if so, the amounts and destinations. I need transaction records from the sales of the nitrate from the people who sold it and copies of the credit card company's records."

"Yes sir." Donaldson nodded and left the room.

Blake looked down at the report on his desk and smiled for the first time. If this panned out and Zayne was buying material for another bomb then they could nail him inside a week. Then GW wouldn't have to continue with his undercover role and Sydney could get away from Zayne once and for all.

His phone buzzed and he picked it up. "Special Agent Edwards."

"Pete Roberts, sir. I think I may have something. There was a visitor to the Zayne estate this morning - a man in military clothing. We have video and I'm running an identity check as we speak. Turner's on duty."

Blake's mind went back to the meeting he'd had with the so-called general at the river. "I'll be right there," he said into the phone. He wanted to see for himself what this military man looked like. If it turned out to be the same man it would just be one more nail in Zayne's coffin.

Later That Evening

Sydney opened the door to find Adrian smiling down at her. "This is a surprise," she said as she stepped back to let him enter.

"I missed you," he replied and backed her up against the door as she closed it. "Have you missed me?"

"You can't imagine." She smiled, thinking to herself that if he knew how she really felt he would not be so eager to be close to her.

Adrian smiled and tilted her chin up to kiss her slowly. Sydney tried not to shrink from his touch but was not completely successful. The day before when he had come to her office it had taken all her willpower not to throw him out when he started making advances. He had not succeeded in having his way with her but she had let him kiss and fondle her briefly just to insure that he did not get too suspicious. Unfortunately, her capitulation had gotten her trapped into spending the evening with him.

She had to admit that the evening had not been completely intolerable. They'd gone to a show at the Kennedy Center and then to a late dinner at the Watergate. After dinner he had a small gathering in his penthouse suite. She had been quite surprised at the notable figures in attendance, but not nearly as surprised as she was when the President dropped in.

Adrian had been very attentive and the perfect gentleman the entire evening. Sydney had found herself thinking that he could be very pleasant to be with; interesting, witty and very charming. It was a shame that he was such a duplicitous person. If she did not know what she did about him she might actually be able to like him.

Sadly, she couldn't say the same for the President. He might have come into office hailing as one of the wealthiest men in America, and might have a very high opinion of himself and his own charm but she found him boorish, arrogant, petty and possessed of one of the worst cases of bad breath she'd ever had the displeasure to witness.

Nonetheless, she pretended to be very impressed and grateful to Adrian for allowing her the honor of meeting the President in person.

Adrian pulled back from the kiss. "I'm sorry to drop in on you unannounced, but there's something very important I needed to talk to you about."

"What?" She asked as she skirted around him to go into the living room.

"Actually, it's your father."

"My father?" Sshe turned in surprise to face him.

Adrian walked to her and took her hand. "Sydney, I hope this won't sound as if I'm meddling in your life. You see, an associate of mine mentioned that he saw you earlier today at Maison Blanche with your father and another gentleman, Ralton Armand."

"So?"

"I fear that you do not know who Mr. Armand is. Sydney, he is a very - how shall I put this - unscrupulous man. One who will stop at nothing to make sure he gets what he wants."

"How do you know that?"

Adrian looked away for a moment. "I had him checked out. And what I found was most disturbing."

Sydney felt a thrill of excitement run through her. If Adrian had been checking on GW and thought he really was Armand, then that meant the cover was secure. She wondered how GW had managed but right now that didn't matter. All that counted was that Adrian was fooled.

"What?" She tried to sound concerned.

"Please, let's sit." He pulled her over to the couch, still holding her hand as they sat. "Mr. Armand is desperate to have legislation on this AES cryptographic processing circuit go in his favor. You see, his company stands to either make or lose a great deal, depending on the outcome of the pending legislation. I fear that he is going to try and put pressure on your father to make sure things go his way."

Sydney laughed and pretended to relax. "Well, if that's what bothers you, you can stop worrying. Adrian, there isn't anyone who can make my father vote for anything or against anything he doesn't believe. Trust me when I tell you that my father will vote as his conscience directs and no one can change that."

"I've heard he is a very honorable man but even a saint can be tempted, my darling. And Armand has great resources at his disposal."

"He could have all the money in the world and it wouldn't matter," Sydney saw her chance and took it. "Just like this stupid wall and the military budget thing that has everyone in a knot. You wouldn't believe the campaigning that's going on behind the scene to try and sway his vote on that."

"Just what is the Senator's stand on that issue?"

"He's for the budget cuts. First of all, he sees that wall as a ridiculous waste of taxpayer's dollars. And Dad sees no reason to keep pouring money into the military when there's no need. Just think about it, Adrian and you can see he's right. Why keep spending needlessly on the military when the money could be put to so much better use elsewhere?"

"Yes, I see your point." He leaned back and regarded her. "But there are those who disagree. And from what I understand, their ranks are sizable."

"But not enough to defeat this in the Senate. And just between you and me, my father's so much in favor of these cuts that I'd be willing to bet it'll go his way.. You may not realize this, but he has a lot of influence - more than most people know. In fact, I don't think he's ever been on the losing side of a vote, if that's any indication of the influence he wields."

Adrian smiled and stroked her hand. "You're very proud of your father, aren't you?"

"Yes, I am. He's honest and kind and his heart's in the right place. Aside from being brilliant, of course."

"And is that that what you're looking for, Sydney? A man like your father?"

She didn't hesitate to speak the truth. "I don't have any complexes about my father, if that's what you mean. I'm not looking to replace him or find a Jack Forrest clone for myself, so I guess the answer is no."

"Then what are you looking for? Someone like your friend, Blake Edwards?"

She started at that question but tried to cover her surprise. "Blake is a very dear friend and–"

"I think he's much more than that." Adrian pulled her closed to him. "In fact, I'd be willing to wager that in reality, he's your lover. Isn't that so, my dear?"

"Yes." She decided that there was no point in lying. He probably had been having her followed all along so he knew that Blake had been spending the night at her apartment. "We've been seeing each other for a while."

Adrian dropped her hand and stood to cross the room and stare out of the window. Sydney remained where she was, unsure what to do or say. After a long silence he turned and looked at her. "I'd like to put aside all the pretense and just be honest if I may."

She nodded and he walked closer to the couch. "Despite my best intentions to the contrary, I find that I have become quite obsessed with you, Sydney. At first it was intoxicating and exciting - feeling so enamored of someone. Then it was disconcerting.

"I've never had my attentions cast aside the way you do - always running from me and behaving as if you are not interested. Quite frankly, it both enraged and frightened me. I did not know how to deal with it. I have never felt this way before. Oh, I have had a passing interest in women in the past, but the interest always disappeared quickly. You are different. In fact, I can say with complete honesty that I want you more today than I did the first time I saw you.

"And that, my darling, is very unnerving for me. I want you with me constantly and you - you seem to want to put as much distance as possible between us. What must I do to win you, Sydney? What does it take to attain your love?"

Sydney didn't know what to say. In fact, she was speechless. She had watched Adrian closely while he spoke and she could not tell that he was lying to her. He sounded as if he really was telling the truth and that was astounding to her. Since Senator Tyler had told her about Adrian she had been convinced that he was just using her; that his only interest in her was to make sure she did not tell anyone what Tyler had told her. Now, she wondered if she could be wrong about him. Was it possible that he was capable of genuine feeling?"

"Adrian, I don't know what to say. I didn't expect this and . . . and . . . "

"And you do not know how to tell me that you do not return my feelings." He dropped down on one knee in front of her.

"I don't fall in love easily. You're extremely handsome and sexy, charming and intelligent and any woman would be thrilled to hear you say such things to her. I'm flattered - no, I'm amazed - but I can't tell you that I love you because I just don't know you well enough for that. It takes me a longer—a lot longer. I need to make sure I'm not making another mistake. I've already made one and I don't relish the idea of repeating the experience."

"Is there a chance that you could come to love me?"

"Anything's possible." She said with a smile, hoping that she did not sound as phony as she felt.

"Then I shall not give up hope. I will find a way to win your heart, Sydney Forrest. One day you will come to me and want to be mine."

Sydney smiled. After a moment Adrian leaned forward and kissed her gently. "Would you consider going for a short cruise with me on my yacht this weekend?"

"A cruise? Where?"

"Just down the coast."

"I don't know," she hedged. "I have a lot of work to catch up on and—"

"And you would rather be with Mr. Edwards," his voice took on a rough edge.

"No," she insisted, perhaps a bit too soon. "It's not that. It's just that, I'm not sure I'm ready to spend the night with you."

Adrian smiled at her. "There is more than one bedroom on the yacht. You can have your pick of staterooms."

Sydney didn't see how she could refuse. She also didn't have any idea how she was going to make Blake understand. "All right," she agreed. "It does sound like fun. When will we leave?"

"Can you take Friday off?"

"I suppose I could reschedule my appointments for Friday."

"Then I will pick you up early Friday morning."

Sydney smiled as he stood up. "Okay, I'm looking forward to it."

Adrian took her hand in his. "As am I. Now, I will leave you to your evening. I will count the hours until Friday, my darling and I promise you, this will be a weekend to remember."

She nodded and walked him to the door. "I'm glad you came by, Adrian. Thank you for being so understanding."

"I want only to make you happy," he murmured as he leaned down to kiss her. "Until Friday, my love."

Sydney closed the door behind him and leaned back against it. She honestly didn't know if she could make it through an entire weekend with Adrian. With a sigh she pushed herself upright and went into the study where she'd left her phone. She might as well give Blake the news now and give him time to digest it before he came over.

Thursday, April 27

Washington

"I still think he's being unreasonable." Sydney insisted as she refilled GW's coffee cup then took a seat across from him in the dining room of her apartment. For the past forty-five minutes they'd been discussing Blake's and Sydney's argument the night before about her going on the cruise with Adrian.

"Maybe, maybe not," GW commented then held up his hands as Sydney started to argue again. "Syd, we've been over this so much that all we're doing now is going around in circles so let me just suggest that you look at this from his point of view. Here's some dude who might be the master-mind of one of the worst act of terrorism in this country's history who wants to take you on some cruise for the weekend. If the situations were reversed you can't honestly tell me that you wouldn't be just a little bit worried."

"I understand that and I agree. I can only tell you what I told Blake. I'm convinced that Adrian won't hurt me. Besides, I thought you and Blake wanted me to try and get information from him while I was steering him toward my father?"

"If this thing in Alabama pans out we may not need any of that."

Sydney shook her head. "Somehow I just can't believe that Adrian would be stupid enough to do something like that. He's a smart man, GW, and he knows that the FBI was investigating Tyler - plus the fact that I'm involved with Blake. Do you really think he'd take a chance on exposing himself by doing something so foolish? It just doesn't make sense and it doesn't fit the impression I have of the man."

"But the fact remains that two large shipments of ammonium nitrate are headed for Huntsville. And when you add that to the latest information, you come up with . . ."

"What information?" she interrupted him.

GW's eyes widened fractionally for a split second then he pressed his lips together and looked down at the coffee cup he twirled in his hands on the smooth surface of the table. "I, uh, I'm not at liberty to discuss this case without clearance."

"Not at liberty?" she sputtered in surprise then pinned him with a suspicious look. "What's going on? Why are you suddenly holding out on me? I thought—"

"Maybe you haven't." It was his turn to interrupt her. "Thought about it, I mean. Syd, in case you've forgotten, this *is* an FBI investigation and as such neither I nor Blake can discuss certain aspects with people outside the department. Not even you. It has nothing to do with you personally. It's just policy."

"Policy," she repeated the word as if it left a nasty taste in her mouth. In a way it did. When Blake got to her apartment the night before and they got into the argument about her planned trip with Adrian he had started spouting policy to her. She'd accused him of using 'policy' for his personal means and the argument had escalated.

As she silently observed GW she thought about her argument with Blake. He'd accused her of being interested in Adrian. He said that she must be more interested or involved than she was admitting or she wouldn't be so adamant about going on the cruise. She had denied having feelings for Adrian but did not admit that spending time with him had become personally consequential. She didn't want to admit that to anyone.

"Okay." She ended the silence that hung thick in the air. "Then can you tell me what you've uncovered about Adrian? I overheard Blake on the phone last night when you were talking saying something about double-checking the possible connections between Adrian and extremist groups. Did you find out—"

"You happened to overhear?" GW looked at her dubiously.

"Well…" She looked down in embarrassment. "Okay, fine, I was eavesdropping. That's not the point. Did you—"

"Whoa!" GW made a slashing motion with one hand in front of his throat. "Cut! Call me psychic or call me crazy but I'm picking up some peculiar vibes here. All these questions—it's not about the investigation at all, is it? This is personal. In fact, this is what you've been waiting on, isn't it, Syd?"

"I don't know what you're talking about!"

GW scoffed at her indignant tone. "You know exactly what I'm talking about. I was there, remember? I know your secrets and I know how your mind works. You've finally found it, haven't you?"

Sydney jumped up so fast that she overturned her chair. "That's ridiculous!" she insisted, turning away to right the chair so that he could not see her face.

"Is it?"

"Yes!" She could not look at him. "You know I gave up on—that I forgot all about that a long time ago."

"I know you tried to." He stood and started around the table to her. "But I don't believe for a minute that you ever really let go of it. And I think this Zayne guy is just what you've been waiting on. He represents just the kind of mystery that— "

"GW, just let it go!" She snapped and walked around him to go into the living room and stand in front of the picture window with her back to him.

He followed her but took a seat on the couch. "You've already started, haven't you?"

Sydney tensed at his words and immediately started to lie to him. But when she turned and looked at him she felt her intent to lie fade. She should have known that she wouldn't be able to hide this from GW.

"Yes," she admitted quietly.

"And?"

"And you're right." She couldn't keep the excitement out of her voice. "GW, it's like the words just flow without effort. I don't even have to think about it. It just happens and— "

"And what?" he gave her a verbal prod.

"And it feels so good!" She could not contain herself longer. "I feel like . . . like I've found myself again—like after all these years of hiding in the shadows I can finally step out into the sunlight."

GW nodded in silence and Sydney waited for him to comment. GW knew better than anyone what she was talking about. He was the only one who could understand. And he knew that this was something she had wanted since she was old enough to hold a book in her hands. Her biggest desire in life had always been to become a writer; to create stories that would allow people to lose themselves in another world, the way books had always done for her.

She had fully intended to see that dream become a reality when she entered college and she knew that it would have happened if it hadn't not been for Daniel Boorman. Daniel was a professor of philosophy. She became involved with him during her sophomore year in college.

He singled her out the first day of class, addressing his words to her as if they were alone in the vast auditorium instead of surrounded by over a hundred other students. She was flattered by his attention and intrigued with him. He was thirty-eight years old, worldly, intense and gorgeous in a brooding sort of way. Before fall semester ended they became lovers. By the middle of the next semester the trouble had already started.

During the time Sydney hadn't understood it. Daniel became increasingly possessive and would fly into a rage if he so much as saw her talking to another man. At first, she dismissed his irrationality, thinking it was kind of romantic and passionate. But his jealousy and possessiveness grew steadily to reach a point where she began to feel like a prisoner of his affections; constantly under surveillance and on guard not to do or say anything that would set him off.

It all came to a head the final week of exams of her junior year. As she stood there, looking out of the window of the living room in her apartment she let her thoughts travel back to that time.

She and GW sat on the living room floor of their apartment, cramming for an exam, surrounded by books, notes and discarded fast food bags and containers. Sydney got up to answer a knock at the door to find Daniel standing outside. He started to speak but GW yelled out, "Hey, Syd? Do you have the notes from McFarland's lecture on−"

GW never got to finish his question. Daniel's face turned red as a beet and he shoved Sydney backwards with an enraged scream. She stumbled backwards and before she could get her balance Daniel had rushed in and attacked GW.

Sydney screamed and ran at him, trying to pull him off GW, who was pinned on the floor while Daniel pounded on him. "Daniel, stop!" She tried to get hold of his arm and stop him. "Leave him alone!"

Daniel snarled and punched GW in the left temple. Sydney saw GW's eyes roll back and she screamed, thinking that he was dead. Daniel grabbed her and pushed her as hard as he could. She fell over the coffee table and he dove on top of her.

"I won't share you! You're mine, do you hear me? Mine!"

"We weren't doing anything!" She screamed as he raised his hand to hit her. "Daniel, no!"

But he did not listen to her. Sydney fought him with every ounce of strength she had as he started to hit her repeatedly. She managed to dislodge him and scrambled on all fours away from him. Unfortunately, she was not fast enough. He grabbed her around the waist and slung her. She collided with the dinette table and scrambled to right herself despite the feeling that her back was broken from impacting with the corner of the table.

Daniel was on her before she could stand, forcing her face down on the table like he was trying to drown her in the wood. Sydney kicked at him and tore at his hands with her nails but could not break free.

Sudden, overwhelming fear consumed her as she felt something cold and hard press against her temple. "I'll see you dead before I see you with another man," Daniel sobbed his words as he pressed the gun to her head.

"Daniel, I haven't been with anyone else," she insisted in a trembling voice. "Please, you have to believe me. I love you. I wouldn't –"

GW regained consciousness and groaned. Daniel jerked around to look at him, keeping the gun jammed against Sydney's head. "Hey, man, that ain't no answer!" She heard GW say weakly.

"Shut up!" Daniel screamed at him, grabbed Sydney and pulled her up in front of him. She looked at GW and saw her own fear mirrored in his dark eyes.

"Please, Daniel," she begged him. "Just put the gun down and we can talk. We can– "

"Shut up!"

Sydney felt like she was going to throw up she was so afraid. She knew she was going to die. But Daniel had other plans. He wrapped his hand in her hair and shoved her closer to GW. "So, you want my woman. Is that right, nigger?"

GW shook his head. "No, man. We're just friends. I don't—"

"Don't lie to me!" Daniel screamed and pushed Sydney again. "I've seen the way you look at her."

"Daniel please," Sydney cried.

He pushed her again and grabbed the phone to jerk it loose from the wall. "Tie him up!" he yelled at Sydney as he held the cord in front of her.

She took the cord but didn't move. He tapped the gun against the side of her head hard enough to make lights dance in front of her eyes and she yelped then took a hesitant step toward GW.

"Syd?" GW's voice brought her back to the present. "Where were you?"

She shook her head and took a seat beside him. "In hell."

"You mean Daniel."

She nodded and looked down at her hands in her lap. That night had been as close to being in hell as she could imagine. After Daniel made her tie GW up with the phone cord he had raped her repeatedly, threatening to kill her if she resisted him.

Sydney had never imagined that she could be so afraid or so humiliated. Knowing that GW was watching the things Daniel was doing made want to disappear. When Daniel finished he lay across her bruised body and cried. Then he abruptly jumped up and ran out of the apartment.

Sydney crawled over to GW and untied him then he took her to the hospital. They were both examined and the police were called. After all the photographs and examinations and interviews she was admitted to the hospital. GW was released but stayed there with her, holding her hand. The police came to her hospital room the next morning. When they went to pick up Daniel for rape they had found him dead. He'd shot himself.

That was the moment that Sydney gave up her dreams of becoming a writer. She couldn't understand what would drive a man to do the things that Daniel did but she couldn't find it in her heart to hate him. He had obviously been a tortured person. She decided she'd switch majors and the next fall she entered the pre-med program, determined to one day understand what made people like Daniel do the things they did.

"GW." She looked over at him. "I think I made a big mistake. I should never have gone to medical school. Don't get me wrong, psychiatry helps some people and it pays the bills, but there's just no– no passion or excitement. Sometimes I feel as cold and clinical as a hospital room and I'm just so tired of feeling that way."

He took her hand in both of his. "So, are you just going to chuck your practice and write or what?"

"I don't think I can afford to do that." She was grateful that he had not said anything more about the past. "But I have to continue this book. And to do that, I have to get inside Adrian's head. That's where the secrets are– and where this book is. I can't just let it go. Not now."

He shook his head and gave her a somber look. "I always figured that one day you'd return to writing. I guess you should. You're good at it. But this thing with Adrian - I'll be honest, it concerns me. If what we suspect is right he's a very dangerous man. He could make Daniel look like a boy scout in comparison, if you get my drift."

"I know. But I know he won't hurt me, GW."

"How can you know that?"

"I just do. Adrian's accustomed to getting what he wants and when he finds something he can't have it's like an obsession. He has to have it. I think maybe that's how it is with me. Because I haven't caved in and fallen all over him, it makes him want me. And don't forget, he knows that I'm seeing Blake - and with a personality like Adrian's, if he knows someone else wants something, it makes that something that much more desirable. So, if my estimation is correct, he'll be determined to win me over so that he can flaunt it in Blake's face. He wouldn't even consider harming me because that would deprive him of his victory."

"Maybe," GW conceded. "But what happens if he wins? If your assessment holds, then it's possible the object of his obsession won't be so desirable once he has it."

"By then I'll be out of reach," she said determinedly. "I don't have any intention on giving in to him. I just need to spend some time with him so I can get inside his head and figure out what makes him tick."

"All this for a book?"

"No. For my liberation from old ghosts and bad memories. I want to be free of it, GW - Daniel, Evan - all the mistakes. I want to be happy."

"And I want you to be." He squeezed her hand. "I think you and Blake can have a good thing if you can get over this hump with Zayne. But you're going to have to be honest with Blake, Syd. He deserves to know why you're being so stubborn about this."

"I don't know if I can talk about it to him," she admitted. "GW, I've never even told my parents. No one knows besides you and the police."

"Well, if you want to get rid of the ghosts you're going to have to stop carrying them around with you. And Blake's a smart, compassionate guy. Give him a chance."

"What if he can't handle it?"

"Then you didn't have much to begin with."

She nodded and put her arms around him. "Have I ever told you how much you mean to me?"

"You don't have to," he gave her a hug. "I know."

She pulled back with a smile. "So, does this mean you're going to support me?"

"Do I have a choice? I've gotta get going. Listen, do me a favor and take the laptop and your cell with you so we can stay in touch while your sailing uncharted waters with Zayne, okay?"

"All right. Oh! By the way, Dad wanted to know if you'd come by for drinks and dinner tonight? He wants to talk to you about this 'bribery' thing. He doesn't think a hundred thousand is enough to buy his vote."

GW laughed. "No, probably not. Not even if it is only make-believe. Okay, I'll give him a call. You be careful, okay?"

"I promise," she assured him as she walked him to the door. "Don't worry. Everything will be just fine."

GW left and Sydney returned to the dining room to clear away the coffee cups. She wished she was as confident as she tried to make GW believe. Not that she thought Adrian would do anything to hurt her. She really didn't believe he would do that. But she did think he would try to get her to sleep with him and she had to find a way around that without making him angry. Determined she'd find away, she pushed aside her doubts and fears and went into the bedroom to start packing for her trip.

ଔ

Blake put out his cigarette and got out of the car. It seemed like he'd smoked more the past couple of weeks than he had in the previous year. He knew that it was just his anxiety over this case. Worrying about Sydney didn't make matters any easier. Last night they'd gotten into a heated argument. In the end they compromised and agreed to table the discussion both of them were less tense. Blake fully intended to continue the discussion as soon as possible. He was still dead set against her going off on a cruise with Adrian Zayne.

That she would even entertain the idea was inconceivable to him. She knew as well as anyone what Zayne was capable of. *He drugged her, for God's sake!* He thought angrily as he entered headquarters and took the elevator up. *Why would she even consider isolating herself with him like that for three days? Surely she can't be so caught up in the excitement of being part of an FBI investigation that she can't see the danger?*

Blake knew from past experience that people could sometimes get over enthusiastic and caught up when they were involved with an investigation. People generally had the idea that being with the FBI was one thrilling adventure after another; days and nights filled with danger and intrigue. They didn't see all the work that went into making a case come together.

But then the danger's always been the lure for you, too, a voice inside his mind reminded him. He had always known that he was in large part a thrill junkie. Put him in a dangerous situation and he seemed to be more alive than at any other time.

I wonder if that's how it is with Syd? Is it possible that she's like me and I just didn't see it because of that cool facade of hers? His thoughts were interrupted by Matt Donaldson as he stepped off the elevator.

"Has Mr. We'zel filled you in on the latest info?"

Blake shook his head and continued walking as Donaldson talked. "We found out that a tanker of diesel fuel has been ordered to make delivery at the same location the fertilizer's going to. But the delivery date has been changed to Wednesday, the third of May."

"And I'm going to be there when the goods come in," Blake stated as he opened the door to his office. "Tuesday morning I leave before dawn. I've made arrangements for transportation and lodgings. The Birmingham office has agents assigned to assist and the local police will be brought in as well. I'll brief everyone fully before I leave."

"Yes, sir," Donaldson nodded. "Anything else, sir?"

"Proceed with your assignment," Blake answered absently and went into his office. He still had a lot of paper work to do before he met the other agents at ten.

He had been at it for almost an hour when Weasel walked into his office. "What's up?"

"Paperwork."

"So, I understand you and Syd had a row over her trip with Zayne?"

"She told you?" Blake looked up in surprise.

"She mentioned it in passing."

"I don't get it." Blake leaned back in his chair and looked across the desk at his friend. "Why's she so insistent on sticking her neck out? Am I just fooling myself thinking that we have something special or does she have a thing for Zayne?"

Weasel did not respond immediately and Blake got a sinking feeling in his stomach. "Is that it?"

"No." Weasel shook his head and took a seat in front of the desk, propping his forearms on his legs and lacing his fingers together with his index fingers extended. He studied his hands for a moment then looked up at Blake. "I really think this should come from Syd, not me."

"What?" "Look, man, I don't know how much Syd's told you about her past and I don't want to speak out of turn. I advised her to talk to you about this herself but to be honest I don't know if she will or not."

"Weasel, if you know something then please spit it out You're starting to worry me. Is something wrong with Syd?"

There was another long pause before Weasel answered. "Has she ever talked about college?"

"Not really."

"Did she ever say why she decided to become a shrink?"

"Just that she wanted to find out what made people tick."

"Yeah, well, it's a little more than that."

"So what does college and becoming a psychiatrist have to do with her obsession with Zayne?"

"Everything," Weasel replied and proceeded to tell Blake what had happened to Sydney. As he talked Blake got a sick feeling in his stomach. He couldn't believe that she'd been through something like that. But it did explain a lot about her; why she always kept that wall up between her and everyone else that was so hard to penetrate.

"And you were there?" he asked when Weasel finished. "He did that in front of you?"

Weasel nodded. "It was bad, man. Real bad. Syd was in the hospital for a week. She had two broken ribs and was beat up real bad. For a while the doctors thought she had internal damage and there was even some doubt as to whether she'd be able to have children. When he was beating her he - hell, I don't know how he did it, or with what, but he ruptured one of her ovaries and she had to have surgery."

"Jesus, Weasel, she never mentioned a thing about it."

"It's not something she likes to remember. But it was a turning point in her life. She was on the road to being the next Hemingway, man - and she would have made it. She was always winning awards for her writing and she had a lot of short stories published while she was in high school and college. But Daniel Boorman put an end to that and Syd retreated into a shell where she was safe and isolated. From then on she wouldn't let anyone get close to her except me and I guess that's because she felt safe with me, you know?"

"But she got married."

"Yeah, and that was her second mistake. Mallory was a prick, pure and simple. Syd married him because she let herself be pressured into it, not because she loved him. Don't get me wrong. She did care about him. But it was never the way it is between the two of you. She tried to start writing when things were bad with Evan - as a kind of escape. He found what she was working on and laughed at her - made fun of her. That was definitely not what she needed. But then, he really didn't give a shit about her. Now, it's different. She loves you, man. You're the one she's been waiting for. And now that she's finally come out of hiding and started writing again, I really think she can heal."

"Why couldn't she just trust me enough to tell me?"

"Maybe she will," Weasel replied. "And I'd appreciate it if you'd keep what I've told you between us. And while you're at it, maybe you could try and see Syd without all the emotions clouding your vision. See, this is the first time I've seen her be the real Syd in years. She was a bulldog, man, when she set her mind to something - afraid of nothing and willing to stick her hand in any hole, if you know what I mean. And she's determined to pick Zayne's mind so she can write this book."

"It's hard for me to imagine Syd being like that," Blake admitted. "She's always seemed so–so non-aggressive and kind of quiescent in a way."

"That's the mask she hides behind. The real Syd is a dynamo. I've missed the real Syd. I hope she makes it all the way back."

"I take that to be a mild hint for me to leave her alone on this one," Blake commented. "You think I should let her go on this trip and keep my mouth shut."

"I didn't say that. But I think maybe if you could just talk to her and try to trust the way she feels about you then maybe you could understand that just like you have to do what you do, so does she. Maybe even more. She was born to be a writer, man. She could be one of the best. I'd hate to think that you'd be one of the ones who'd squash that because it interfered with what you want."

Blake knew Weasel was right. He loved Sydney but he didn't own her and she had to do what was right for her. "Thanks," he said quietly. "I'm glad you've been there for her, GW. I'll try to do the same."

"GW?" Weasel arched his eyebrows. "What's this? No more Weasel?"

Blake smiled and shrugged. "Just seems kind of juvenile - considering."

Weasel stood up. "I gotta check out a couple of things. See you at the meeting."

Blake nodded and watched him leave then picked up the phone and dialed. "Syd? Hi, it's me. I was wondering if maybe you could knock off a little early today? Oh, I just thought it might be nice to take a drive into the country, stop for dinner at one of the inns in Virginia– maybe even stay the night. Wait. Let me finish. I promise to have you back in time to catch your boat tomorrow. Great! See you at the apartment. Ssay around two? Okay - and Syd? I love you."

He hung up the phone and blew out his breath, feeling like he had been holding it a long time. Talking about her trip was not as hard as he thought it would be, but then he wasn't watching her sail away with Zayne. He was quite sure he wouldn't find that task so easy.

☙

Adrian looked up as the man entered the room but didn't bother to stand. "You have something to report?"

"She's leaving with the FBI agent to go to Virginia for the night."

The urge to throw something rose inside him. His dislike of Blake Edwards was quickly turning into a deep-seated hatred. He couldn't believe Sydney would choose Blake over him, yet every time he turned his back she was with the man.

"I don't want that to happen." He knew his men would take care of the problem without having to fill him in on the details.

"Yes, sir." The man turned to walk away.

"Thomas?" Adrian called to him.

"Sir?"

"If the woman is harmed you should not return. Do I make myself clear?"

"Quite clear, sir."

"That is all."

He watched the man leave the room then turned his attention to the report on his desk. For a few moments he glowered at the page, then suddenly he smiled. Blake Edwards wasn't an insurmountable problem. Neither was Sydney's affection for him. That affection could quickly turn to disdain. She only needed the right incentive and Adrian knew just how to provide that. With a smile he picked up the phone.

☙

For a while Sydney and Blake rode without speaking. They left the Washington area, crossed the river and headed west on I-66. "Where are we going?" she asked as they turned off onto highway 50.

"I made reservations at the Ashby Inn." He looked over at her. "Have you ever stayed there?"

"No, but I've heard it's very nice."

"It is. The main house was built somewhere around the late 1820's and it's decorated in the Shenandoah style. Some of the rooms have cannonball and rope beds. There's an old schoolhouse that was converted and it has four suites that have big poster, canopy beds and fireplaces with their own private porches and these enormous six-foot tubs. The restaurant is very good. They serve candlelit dinners of mostly local fish and game."

"You sound like a travel brochure," she laughed and reached over to put her hand on his leg. "But it sounds heavenly."

"Not too tame?" he asked lightly.

"Tame?" She looked at him with a perplexed expression on her face. "Why would you ask that?"

Blake figured this was as good a time as any to broach the subject of her past. The only problem was he was not quite sure how to bring it up without divulging the fact that Weasel had filled him in. "Let's call it intuition," he replied. "Sometimes I get the idea that behind that cool and collected exterior beats the heart of an adventurer - someone who's more bold and daring than she lets on."

Sydney's expression changed to become guarded. "Are you sure you're not mixing me up with someone else? I'm just your average, garden-variety psychiatrist whose biggest risk is facing the morning rush-hour traffic."

"Has it always been like that?"

Sydney shrugged and looked out of the side window. "I guess."

"Well, what about when you were a kid or when you were in college? Were you a rebel or a trouble-maker? Did you ever get into−"

"You've been talking to GW, haven't you?" she interrupted him.

"I talk to GW all the time." He avoided answering her question directly.

"You've been talking about me. What is it you want to know, Blake?"

Blake reached for his cigarettes in his lapel pocket before he realized that he wasn't wearing a jacket. "Everything. That's not so odd is it? Most people want to know about the person they're in love with."

"True," she agreed. "But I get the distinct feeling that you want to know something very specific. So, instead of playing twenty questions and trying to steer me into a certain direction, why not just come out and ask me what it is you're curious about?"

"Syd, I..." He paused, thinking that he didn't want to cause a problem between her and Weasel, but not seeing a way around admitting he had talked to Weasel about her. Then an idea dawned on him. "Well, you know how us federal boys are. We run checks on everyone. And there are some interesting things in your past that we've never talked about."

"Such as?" she asked stiffly.

"Daniel Boorman." He decided to cut to the chase. He wasn't totally lying about checking her out. After Weasel had told him about Boorman and what happened, he had checked into it. There was not much in the files on the case except that she had been hospitalized with broken ribs, various cuts and contusions and serious internal damage caused by the rape.

"Daniel." She turned away from him and looked out the window once more. "What did GW tell you?"

"Only that you had a relationship with the guy and that he went whacko one night and attacked you then killed himself."

Sydney turned to him with an icy expression stamped on her face. "Then it would seem you already have all the facts."

"Syd, I'm not trying to make you mad. I just want to understand. I know you were hospitalized and I know you were raped. That had to have had an impact on you and I just wanted to know—"

"The gory details?" she snapped. "Is that what this little trip is all about? To question me about some mistake I made a million years ago?"

"No!" He reached out to try and take her hand. "Syd, please." He tried again when she pulled her hand away. "I wanted to be with you because I love you. But I need to know the real you if we're going to make it beyond this point and the only way I can do that is for you to let me through that wall you live behind."

Sydney looked down at his hand lying on the seat between them and slowly took it in hers. "Blake, I don't know if I can let anyone in. I want to, but I'm afraid of the pain. Remembering that time is like taking a trip into a nightmare. I don't know that I want you to see that. I don't know if you will still feel the same for me if you do."

Blake looked at her for a moment then made a left turn off highway 50 onto a small road marked as 629. Less than a mile down the road he turned again onto an unmarked dirt road and stopped the car. Sydney was looking out of the window as if she was afraid to look at him.

"Syd, look at me." He unfastened his seat belt and slid over closer to her. "I love you and nothing you can tell me will change that. But not being honest is the same thing to me as saying that you don't trust me and I don't think I can deal with that."

She nodded without speaking then turned to him. "Did GW tell you what happened that night?"

"Yes."

"It was the most horrible thing I've ever experienced. I couldn't believe that it was really happening to me. I really thought he loved me, you know? And I was too young and naive to realize that he was a sick man."

"GW said that's why you decided to go into psychiatry."

"Yes. When Daniel killed himself I knew I could never ask him why he'd done it and I had to know what made someone do something like that to someone they professed to love. I thought if I found the answer then I could prevent it from ever happening again."

"And so you gave up your dream of becoming a writer. Weasel told me that you're very good."

A hint of a smile fleetingly crossed her face. "He's a little prejudiced because of our friendship but yes, I gave up writing."

"Maybe you should get back into it." He watched her for a reaction to his words.

She looked up into his eyes and suddenly smiled. "He told you that too, huh? I'm really going to have to have a serious talk with GW. He's getting very gabby in his old age."

"He loves you," Blake responded in GW's defense. "And he wants you to be happy. Just like I do, Syd. He thought he was doing the right thing. Besides, if you want to blame someone, then blame me. I made him tell me."

She laughed and shook her head. "You made him? Sorry, but I don't think so. Don't forget, I know GW better than anyone and I know beyond the shadow of a doubt that it's next to impossible to make him do anything he doesn't want to."

"But I did. I forced−"

"It's okay," she interrupted gently. "I know he cares and I'm not really angry. Maybe it's time all of this was taken out of the closet, anyway. I've been hiding it for so long it's starting to weigh me down. I have started writing again and it's like coming home after being far away in some dark place where the sun never shines."

Blake figured he might as well try his luck at that point. "So does this book have anything to do with your determination to spend time with Adrian Zayne?"

"It has everything to do with it," she answered without hesitation. "Blake, I never imagined that something as horrible as this bombing would be the catalyst that would help me break free of all those old chains, but it has. And Adrian's a big part of it. He's not like everyone else. Not that anyone is ever really like anyone else - that's not what I mean. I mean Adrian's very different. The way his mind works fascinates me. I have to get inside his head! Otherwise the book will be stalled dead in the water and I've got to tell you that right now I just can't let that happen."

Blake considered what she said. In a way he understood where she was coming from. He was like that when he was involved in a case. Everything else came second because he became the case.

"I think I understand," he said at last. "But I'm still worried, Syd. You're probably in a better position to give an assessment of Zayne's personality and I wouldn't argue with you. But your own words make me nervous about you being with him. After what you went through with Boorman, do you really want to put yourself in the position to potentially be in danger from Zayne?"

"That's exactly why I have to!" she insisted. "But there's something you have to understand. Adrian is completely different from Daniel. He thinks he wants me but I'm convinced it's only because he doesn't have me.

"Think about it, Blake. Here's a man who's used to having anything he wants, when he wants it. When something or someone comes along that he can't have it drives him crazy until he gets it. I believe that's how it is with me. He doesn't really want me. He just thinks he does. So, as long as I don't give into him, I'm safe. He'll keep trying to win me over."

"Maybe," Blake replied. "But there's always the possibility that you could be wrong."

"And I'm prepared for that. I'm taking my laptop and cell with me. If I run into trouble I can call or at least get through via the computer to GW. Besides, there's always the possibility that he just might let his guard down and tell me something you can use against him. And believe me when I tell you that if he's responsible for all those people dying, I want to see him put away."

"We're going to," Blake promised. "But right now, you and I have a date at a romantic inn. So what do you say we get back on the road?"

Sydney smiled and looped her arms around his neck. "I say, yes. A canopy bed and fresh country air sounds divine."

Blake crushed her against him in a passionate embrace. They were both breathing harder when the kiss ended. "Much more of that and we won't make it to the canopy bed," he teased.

Sydney nuzzled his neck and he reluctantly pushed her away. "Damn, you sure make it hard on a man."

She laughed and moved back a little from him. "So, what are you waiting on? To the inn, driver!"

Blake reached for the keys in the ignition but before his fingers touched them a black van with tinted windows slid to a stop behind them, billowing dust and blocking the path. Two men dressed in camouflage fatigues jumped out of the front and started towards the car.

Blake reached for the glove compartment where his gun was hidden. It was locked. He didn't have time to unlock it before Sydney's door jerked open and one of the men grabbed her. She screamed and struggled with the man as he pulled her out of the car.

Blake's door opened and he looked at the man standing outside the car. "Who are you and what do you want?" he asked as he got out of the car and faced the man.

"I think we need to have a little talk, Mr. Edwards," the man replied then looked over at his partner who was trying to hold Sydney still. "Put her in the van."

"No!" Blake started to make a move to go around the car as Sydney started screaming and kicking at the man who held her. "Let her go. Whatever this is, she has no part of it."

"She shouldn't have, that's true," the man beside him agreed. "But you give us little choice, Mr. Edwards. You haven't upheld your end of the arrangement."

Blake's eyebrows drew together in a tight frown. "What the hell are you talking about? He whirled around and pointed at the man who had hold of Sydney's arm, twisting it up behind her. And don't make a move!"

"Blake!" she shouted as she tried to stomp the man's feet.

Blake reached his limit. He took a swing at the man beside him, feeling a satisfying crunch as his fist met the man's nose. Blood spurted but the man didn't go down. He staggered slightly then came back with a solid punch to Blake's midsection. Blake absorbed the blow, trying not to wheeze from the impact and went at the man again.

While they were fighting, the man holding Sydney was pushing her along towards the van. She kept kicking at him and landed one lucky kick that met his right knee. He stumbled and she managed to break free. He threw his free arm up as she snatched up a rock off the ground and threw it at him. It caught him in the middle of the forehead, hard enough to split the skin. As blood washed down his face he lunged at her and knocked her down. She hit the ground flat on her back.

By that time Blake had succeeded in overcoming his adversary. He left the man unconscious on the ground and raced towards Sydney. She was trying to catch her breath and scramble backwards at the same time as her attacker moved in on her. Blake jumped him from behind, driving him to the ground. This battle was brief. One blow to the back of the head and the man was out cold.

Sydney was on her knees when Blake looked up and saw the panel door of the van opening. He grabbed her arm, yanked her up and shoved her behind him. "Run!" he shouted, keeping his eye on the van.

"No, I won't leave you."

"Go!" he yelled. "Now!"

She hesitated for a moment then took off down the dirt road. Blake faced the two men who got out of the van. "Well, Mr. Edwards." The heavy-set man with cold-cropped gray hair smiled. "It seems that once again I've underestimated you."

"Who are you?" Blake watched the second man warily as he started moving away from the older man.

The older man laughed. "You can cut the crap. Your little friend's long gone. You reneged on our deal."

"Deal?" Blake looked at the man like he was crazy. "What the hell are you talking about?"

"Sir!" The younger man interrupted the conversation and pointed in front of Blake's car.

The older man and Blake both looked at the same time the younger man ran to the front of the car. Blake saw Sydney jump up from her hiding place and throw a large rock at the man. It hit him in the right cheek, drawing blood. She turned to flee as the man's hand went to his face but he ran after her and tackled her from behind. Sydney kicked and screamed like a wild animal but the man managed to get her to her feet and jerk her around, forcing her to the van where Blake stood.

"Get your hands off me!" Sydney barked, hitting at the man with both fists.

He released her by pushing her over to Blake. Blake caught her and pushed her behind him. "I think you people have me confused with someone else. I don't know you and I sure as hell don't have any deal with you. So, I suggest you get back in your vehicle and get the hell out of here."

The older man chuckled. "Very convincing, my friend. But I'm afraid it's gone too far for your little act now. I came to deliver a message. You have three days to live up to your end of the arrangement. After that the general will terminate your bargain. Do I make myself clear?"

"As mud," Blake replied. "I don't—"

"Save it for your lady friend," the older man interrupted. "Maybe you can fool her. For now, just remember what I said. Three days then we come looking for you. And next time, we won't be playing."

Blake didn't respond. He had no idea who the men were or what they were talking about. Mutely, he watched them gather up their comrades and load them into the van then pull away. Sydney watched in silence until the van pulled out onto the hard surface road and pulled away then she moved from behind him. "What was that all about?"

"I have no idea. I've never seen those guys before."

She looked at him doubtfully. "They seemed to know you. If this is part of something you can't talk to me about then just say so, I'll understand."

"It's not," he said earnestly. "God as my witness, I've never seen any of those men before and I have absolutely no idea what this was all about."

"Curious." She looked toward the road where the van had been. "How did they know where you were?"

Blake looked at the car then at her. "Either we're bugged or we were followed. Either way, I think it's time we got out of here."

"I tend to agree." She walked to the car and started to get in but stopped and looked at him over the roof. "But you do have to admit now that it's all over - it was exciting."

Blake could not have been more surprised if she had told him she used to be a man. He could admit to himself that now the danger had passed he was on a kind of adrenaline high but he would never in a million years have imagined that she would feel that way.

Just goes to show that you never really know anyone, he thought as he stared at her. "You think that was exciting?"

"Yes." She grinned and got in the car, sliding over close to him as he got in. "So did you," she continued, putting her hand on his chest. "I can feel it."

Blake reached for the keys but she stopped him. "Wait."

"For what?"

"This." She climbed on his lap, straddling his legs so that her back was pressed up against the steering wheel as she wrapped her arms around him and kissed him passionately.

"Syd," he tried to protest as her lips moved to his neck and her fingers fumbled with the buttons on his shirt. "It's broad daylight!"

"So?" She didn't pause in her actions.

"So, this isn't exactly the time or place."

"Yes it is," she argued huskily, continuing to kiss and undress him.

Blake couldn't deny that at that moment he was very worked up. And she wasn't making it easy to say no. She slid off him and knelt beside him to pull his shirt down over his arms. He pulled his hands free as she reached for the button on his pants. Before he could toss the shirt aside her hand closed on him and her lips met his.

There was no turning back after that. Clothes were thrown in disregard into the floorboard and out of the window. Sydney opened her door and got out of the car, pulling on Blake's hand for him to follow her. She led him to the front of the car, kissing and fondling him every step of the way.

He felt as if he would explode with pent up desire when she lay back on the hood of the car and pulled him to her, wrapping her legs around his waist as he slid into her hot center. His mind went blank to everything else as she writhed against him. At that moment the universe was composed only of her and their passion.

Friday, April 28

Washington, D.C.

Sydney turned to Blake as he pulled up in front of the Watergate Apartments. "I wish we could have stayed," she said softly as she put her hand against the side of his face. "It was so wonderful just to forget everything for a little while."

Blake took her hand and kissed it. "It was. Only, next time I think we should actually see the restaurant and the grounds."

"Oh, I don't know." She chuckled lightly. "I had a pretty fantastic view, myself. And I think I could live for days off champagne and strawberries."

He smiled and pulled her to him. "As soon as all this is over, we'll take a real vacation. We'll go somewhere exotic and warm where no one can find us and be beach bunnies."

"You promise?"

"You've got my word on it."

"I'll hold you to it," she promised and kissed him slowly. "Blake, will you promise me you'll be careful while I'm gone? If those men– "

He put his finger to her lips to silence her. "Syd, I swear I don't know who those men were but I assure you I'll be careful. And I'll breathe a whole lot easier when you get back so do me a favor. You be careful and if anything, however small makes you think you're in danger you call, okay?"

"I will." She looked down at her watch. "Well, I guess I better go. I'll call you as soon as I get back."

Blake nodded then kissed her once more and watched her get out of the car and walk away. He hated to see her go. Not only because he knew she was going to get on Zayne's yacht and sail away, but because last night had been the most memorable night of his life.

As if sensing or sharing his feelings, she stopped and looked back before she entered the building to blow him a kiss and wave. He returned the wave then put his car in gear and pulled out of the parking lot, thinking about her and paying no attention to the car that pulled out behind him.

If someone would have told him a week ago that she would suddenly turn into a wild, almost wanton lover, he would have laughed at them and told them that she was entirely too reserved for that. But he would have been dead wrong. From the time of the attack on the roadside until this morning when they left Virginia she seemed as if she could not get enough.

He was shocked at how excited the danger made her but he had to admit that her excitement sure stimulated his own. She had made him feel like he was twenty-two again, instead of forty-two. How long he could keep up with her in her present state was anyone's guess, but it would sure be fantastic while it lasted.

Sex wasn't the only thing that had been great, however. She really opened up and talked to him about things that happened in her past; about Daniel Boorman and her husband Evan Mallory. They had talked about her dreams to be a writer and he had even discovered that the reason she had such a good throwing arm was that she had played Little League baseball when she was a kid.

She'd been a pitcher, in fact and her team had gone to the Little League World Series when she was twelve and she had pitched three shut-outs before she was hit in the arm by a wild pitch and fractured the bone. That had been her last year playing baseball. By the time the next season rolled around she had blossomed into a young woman.

Blake felt like they had gotten closer the past twenty-four hours than they had in all the months they had known one another. And from the closeness came a new sense of trust that was a major relief to him. He felt sure that she had no romantic interest in Zayne and was equally sure that she did love him. That made it possible for him to keep his mouth shut about her taking the trip with Zayne.

His cell rang and he picked it up from the seat. "Hey GW. Yeah, I'm headed that way, want me to stop by and give you a lift? Sure, no problem. Be there in about fifteen minutes."

He put the phone down on the seat and lit his first cigarette since leaving Washington the day before. It tasted harsh and biting. He stubbed it out in the ashtray, still unaware of the car that followed close behind.

☙

Sydney had just finished dressing when the doorbell rang. She ran to answer it and found a man she had never met standing outside. "Can I help you?"

"Good morning, Doctor Forrest. My name is Gustave. I am in the employ of Mr. Zayne and am here to take you to his yacht."

"I thought Adrian was going to pick me up?" She felt a little uneasy about getting in a car with someone she didn't know.

"Unfortunately, Mr. Zayne was detained with some important business matters. He instructed me to assure you that he will meet you at the marina. If you like I will call and let you verify it with him."

"No, that won't be necessary." She felt a little foolish.

"Very well, may I carry your luggage?"

"That's it right there." She pointed to the two cases by the door.

He picked up the suitcases and she followed him out, making sure the door was locked. Downstairs he put the luggage in the back of the limousine then opened the rear door for her. Sydney got in and started in surprise. There was another man in the car.

"Good morning, doctor." Se smiled as he extended his hand toward her. She did not see the syringe in his hand until it was too late. A moment later she felt a sting in the side of her neck. She reached for the door handle but the man pulled her back and held onto her as she struggled and screamed. Her fight was short lived for within seconds she felt the effects of the drug. She tried to keep from losing consciousness but to no avail. Before they had traveled a block she was out cold.

232

THE TERRITORY OF LIES

Chapter Ten

Saturday, April 29
Washington, D.C.

Blake woke to the persistent sound of the doorbell. He ran his hands through his hair and yawned as he checked the time. It was just before seven in the morning.

He grabbed a pair of cotton pants with a drawstring waist and stepped into them as he made his way down the hall. When he opened the door he found Weasel smiling at him, holding a fast food bag that smelled temptingly of steak and egg biscuits and two large styrofoam cups of coffee.

"Wake up call, dude," Weasel said as he walked inside.

"Maybe for you," Blake remarked as he closed the door and covered another yawn with his hand. "I didn't get to bed until after four."

"Well, hell, if I'd known you were burning the midnight oil I'd have come by before you sacked out." Weasel started unloading the contents of the bag. "Got some news, chief."

Blake perked up at the words but held up one hand as Weasel started to continue. "How about giving me ten minutes then fill me in."

"Sure thing," Weasel started on one of the biscuits. "Take your time."

Ten minutes later Blake was showered and dressed and felt almost normal again. He walked into the kitchen, took a seat at the table, pulled the top off the cup of coffee Weasel pushed over in front of him along with a couple of biscuits.

"So, let's hear it," he said then took a bite of steak and egg.

"Our boy made contact," Weasel reported with a grin. "Got a call from Jack. Adrian wants to meet with him tonight."

Blake stopped in motion as he was lifting his coffee to his mouth. "Tonight? You sure about that?"

"Absolutely."

"But he's supposed to be on a cruise with Syd."

"So, maybe they decided to come back earlier than planned."

"Maybe," Blake considered the possibility with relish. He would like nothing better than to have Sydney off that yacht and away from Zayne. "So, what did Senator Forrest have to say exactly?"

"Zayne said he had something extremely important to discuss with the illustrious Senator - something regarding a certain Mr. Armand and some upcoming legislation."

"Sounds like the fish has taken the bait."

Weasel nodded enthusiastically. "Now all we have to do is reel him in."

Blake would like to think it would be that easy but something told him that Zayne would not be so simple to trap. So far he hadn't done what they predicted and Blake didn't want to be overconfident. "Get everyone in place, and make sure the meeting place is wired. I want audio and video on this one."

"Consider it done." Weasel said with a smile. "We've got him, man. Dead to rights."

"I hope you're right," Blake replied. "'Cause to be honest, I'm really getting tired of Adrian Zayne and this whole mess. I want to see him behind bars and I want to see it fast."

ભ

Sydney gasped as a combination of ice cold water and blinding white light brought her abruptly out of sleep. She covered her eyes with her hands, shivering in the cold and trying to determine if she was still alone or if there was someone else in the room.

She had no idea where she was or how long she had been there. All she knew was that she had awakened some time ago in this room, naked and cold. The room was completely devoid of furniture with white concrete walls and floor and a white ceiling that loomed at least twenty feet overhead.

Apparently, the temperature was controlled from some other location, as were the lights and the water controls in the ceiling. She'd experienced suffocating heat and frigid cold, along with blackness so deep that she couldn't distinguish her own hand in front of her face; and light so intense that it obliterated her sight.

Sydney didn't know why she had been brought to this place or why she was being treated in such a manner. All she really knew was that there seemed to be no way to escape and she was very afraid and confused.

The fear came from not knowing what was going to happen. The confusion stemmed from the fact that her internal clock was totally out of sync. She'd fallen asleep many times and had been wakened each time. How long she slept was impossible to determine. She tried very hard to concentrate, to determine approximately how long it had been since she left home but she had no beginning point to start with. She didn't know how long she had been unconscious from the drug so she could have been in the room for a few hours or days.

Or longer, she thought, realizing that the combination of drugs she had been given and sleep depravation could work to make her unable to think clearly.

"Are you cold?" A soft male voice came from above her.

"Who are you?" She tried to shade her eyes from the light so that she could look up and see who was speaking.

"Are you cold? Would you like to be warm?"

"Yes, I'm cold," she replied angrily. "And I'd like to leave."

"I'm afraid that is not possible. Would you like to be warm?"

"Why are you doing this?" she demanded, feeling around her for the owner of the voice. "Why won't you let me go?"

"Would you like to be warm?" the question was repeated.

"Yes!" she shouted. "Yes! Now will you please answer me?"

"Put this on."

Sydney felt something brush against her leg and she felt around with one hand. "What is this?"

"Put it on."

She wished she could locate the man speaking. If she could she would scratch his eyes out. His calm, monotone manner of speaking was grating on her nerves. However, since she could not see, there was little chance of that happening and she knew her best chance of getting though this ordeal was to try and go along with whoever the man was.

"Can you turn down the lights so I can see to dress?"

There was no answer to her question. "Did you hear me? Can you please turn down the lights?"

Still there was no answer. Forgetting about the clothes she stretched her hands out in front of her, feeling around on the floor as far as she could reach. "Are you there?"

"Put on the clothes."

"I will if you'll just turn down the damn lights!"

"I cannot permit disobedience or offensive behavior."

Sydney didn't know what was going to happen. She huddled up with her knees to her chest and her arms wrapped tightly around her legs. For a long time she waited in tense silence for something to happen. When it did, it was not what she expected. The temperature of the room became increasingly colder by the minute and a light spray of cold water fell from above.

"Please stop!" she called out to whoever might be listening. No one replied and the temperature continued to fall. Not knowing what else to do she fumbled with the clothing, trying to figure out what the articles were. When she did realize what she held she felt a sick dread take hold of her.

Oh, god! She shivered violently, as much from fear as from cold. What kind of deranged lunatic am I dealing with and how can I get out of here? She did not have any answers but she knew that she did not want to freeze to death in that room and the only way she could possibly avoid that was to do like the man said. With trembling hands she began to put on the rubber outfit.

ↂ

After Weasel left Blake couldn't stop thinking about the meeting that was supposed to take place between Zayne and Senator Forrest. He tried to put himself in Zayne's place and it made no sense. If he were on a cruise with a woman he was crazy about, he wouldn't cut it short just to have a meeting that could be delayed for a day or two without any consequence. The more he thought about it, the more he felt that something wasn't right.

He chain smoked and paced the floor as he considered it. The phone rang and drew his attention away from Zayne. "Hello?"

"Hi Dad!" His twelve-year-old son's voice came over the line. "What'cha doin'?"

"Hey, Mike. Not much, how about you?"

"Just hanging out." Michael's voice changed.

"Everything okay?"

"Yeah, I guess."

"Come on, Mike, what's going on?" Blake knew that something was wrong.

"It's...Dad, these men came to see Mom. They told her that you were involved in something illegal and asked her all kinds of questions."

"What men?" Blake felt his alarm bells go off. "Why didn't your mother call and tell me?"

"I don't know who they were. There were three of them and they all had on dark suits and white shirts - kinda like FBI guys, you know? Mom told me to go to my room but I stayed on the stairs so I could hear and they were asking her about some dude named Sydney and how involved you were with him and they said this Sydney guy was in deep shit with the feds and if you were part of it you could go down with him. Then they started asking if Mom knew anything about your bank accounts and the Swiss account and how much money you gave her and stuff like that."

Blake knew that whoever the men were, they were not FBI. If he was under investigation he would know about it; in fact he would not still be working for the bureau. The only logical answer was that Zayne was behind this. Why, he had no idea.

Unless he's trying to set me up for something. If the men in Florida were trying to put ideas into his ex-wife's head about Swiss bank accounts then Zayne must be trying to make it look like he was on the take.

"Mike, don't worry about it," he tried to reassure his son. "I'm not in any trouble and I can promise you that I don't have any Swiss accounts. Besides that, I'm not into anything illegal - and Sydney isn't a dude. She's a lady I've been seeing."

"You mean someone you dated?"

"It's a little more than that. I really care about her, son. She's a real special person."

"You mean you like...love her? Are you going to marry her, Dad?"

"That's possible," Blake answered. "One day - if she says yes. And I want you to meet her. I think you'll like her. She's beautiful and smart and fun to be around. She even likes to roller blade and I know you're into that. And hey, get this. She was a pitcher for a Little League team that went to the Little League World Series. She threw three straight shutouts."

"A girl?" Disbelief sounded in Michael's voice.

"Yeah," Blake laughed lightly. "She's pretty amazing. You think you'd like to come spend the weekend soon and meet her?"

"Sure, I guess so."

"Great! Tell your Mom I'll be in touch to make arrangements and in the meantime, don't worry about those men. I think someone's just trying to pull a fast one on your mom. I'll take care of it."

"Okay, Dad. Listen, Danny's here now and we're gonna go out and ride the ramp for a while. I'll see ya, okay?"

"Okay, you have a good weekend and I'll talk to you soon. I love you, Mike."

"Me too, Dad. Bye."

Blake hung up the phone and stared at it for a few moments. He wished he had more time to spend with Michael. He knew it was hard for a boy to grow up without a father and he would like to take more of an active role. But the divorce had pretty much prevented that. He had visitation rights but little else and his ex-wife didn't appreciate his opinions concerning Michael.

Out of the blue he was filled with anger; anger that someone would involve his son and his ex-wife in some plot against him. Zayne had to be behind it. *Or it could be one of the drug boys I pissed off, he considered.* Either way, he needed to find out who was behind it and put a stop to it. And the best way he knew to start was to talk to the one man he knew could find answers that were hidden from everyone else.

He picked up his phone to place a call. "GW, hey. Where are you?"

"On my way home."

"Can you come back over. Something's come up I need your help on."

"Time to go to town, Tonto," GW replied. "I'm headed your way."

"Thanks." Blake hung up the phone and lit a fresh cigarette as he walked to the spare bedroom where the computer was. He turned it on, sat down at the desk and called up the file he had on Zayne. A picture appeared in a small window of the screen and Blake looked at it. "What are you up to?" he asked the still picture of Adrian Zayne.

Every time he thought he had a handle on the man, something new was thrown into the mix. Blake's brow furrowed in concentration as he thought about the case and the new element that had been added. His eyes widened as something occurred to him.

"That's it, isn't it?" he asked the picture. "It's just to lead me another step away from the original investigation, isn't it? By diverting my attention - making me play the defense, you can lead me away from the truth - away from your involvement in the bombing. This is all just diversionary tactics."

His frown returned as another idea occurred to him. "So, what about Syd? Where does she fit in?"

He had no answer to that question.

◌

Sydney felt as if she were about to turn into a block of ice. She had put on the garments as instructed but little had changed. A fine spray of water still fell from the ceiling, making the concrete floor slick; and the temperature had dropped low enough that breathing was painful. She tried to keep moving, but walking on the slippery floor was difficult, especially since she couldn't see. She had to keep her eyes covered. The light was so bright that it felt like knives in her eyes when she uncovered them.

A sickly sweet smell made her stop. She turned around, listening with increasing dread as the water stopped and a hissing noise interrupted the silence. Then the choking sensation began.

"Stop!" She gasped, trying to cover her mouth and nose as she dropped to the floor and felt her way along to crawl into a corner. "Please."

The gas got thicker and her breath came in strangled gasps as her lungs filled. She felt herself becoming limp and knew that soon she would lose consciousness. Sure that she was dying, she tried to force her mind away from the fear. She pictured Blake's face in her mind, remembering the time they spent in Virginia. She tried to hold onto that memory as darkness claimed her.

What seemed like years or possibly only moments later she woke screaming in pain. It felt like someone had either stabbed her or stuck a live wire to the sole of her right foot. She tried to move away from the pain but found that she could not, she was immobilized.

After several seconds the pain subsided and she opened her eyes, blinking away the tears so that she could focus. She was lying face down on a hard surface that was about four feet off the floor. Her wrists were tied together to a thick metal post that extended up from the head of the platform above her head and her legs were somehow fastened securely as well.

She turned her head from one side to the other, seeing a figure dressed entirely in white standing beside her. There was a cart, similar to a hospital tray beside the figure. A white cloth covered something on the tray.

Sydney tried to see the face of the person beside her but it was covered with a white ski mask. Only the eyes were visible. She could tell it was a man due to the build and the shape of the face.

"Why are you doing this?" She tried not to let her voice break with fear.

"Are you warm now?" The voice was the monotone she remembered.

"Who are you?"

The man pulled the white cloth off the tray to expose the implements. He picked up a sharp scalpel and turned it back and forth in his hands. Sydney's eyes grew round in fear. "What do you want, Sydney Forrest?"

"I want to get out of here!"

"That is not the right answer." He turned and walked out of her range of vision.

Sydney heard what sounded like the muffled sound of a door opening and then a slight creaking noise. Two men rolled a platform like that which she was tied to into the room, placing it in front of her so that she could see the woman who was strapped down on it. Like Sydney, her arms were stretched out over her head and her legs were spread wide and fastened with thick leather straps at the knees and ankles.

The woman's eyes were wide with fear and small whimpering noises came from her mouth. The men left and the woman began to cry softly. "Who are you?" Sydney asked. "And where are we? Why are we here and who are those men?"

The woman looked at her with tears falling rapidly from her eyes. "My name's Maggie Robinson. I'm from Richmond. Those men - they drugged me and brought me here and they…"

"They what?" Sydney's voice sounded shrill and frightened even to her own ears. "Tell me!"

"They do things," the woman finally replied. "They put these red hot iron things on you and these electric things - they put them on you - in places that hurt so much you want to die."

"What do you mean?" Sydney asked in terror.

"It's like little clamps," the woman tried to explain between her tears. "They fasten them on your nipples and your . . . genitals and then they turn on the current. Sometimes they put these things inside you. And if you don't answer right, then they make it hurt so bad that you just scream until you pass out. But they don't kill you - they don't want to do that. They want to keep hurting you."

"Why?"

"I don't know!" the woman cried harder. "That one man keeps asking me what I want and I don't know the answer. And when I give the wrong answer he hurts me. I don't think I can take this! I just want to die so I won't have to hurt anymore."

Sydney didn't know what to say. She was too afraid to trust her voice anyway. She could not imagine suffering through what the woman had described.

"Hello Maggie," the monotone voice sounded behind Sydney.

Maggie screamed as the white-suited man walked to the head of her platform and started to push it. Sydney followed with her eyes until the man and the platform bearing Maggie disappeared somewhere behind her.

"Are you ready to begin, Maggie?" Sydney heard the man's voice, followed by a whimpering sound from Maggie.

"What do you want, Maggie?" the man asked.

"Please don't hurt me," Maggie begged. "I don't want to hurt anymore."

"That is not the correct response, Maggie."

Sydney yelped in fright as the man appeared beside her, holding a metal rod about one inch in diameter and about six inches long. The rod was mounted on a plastic base that looked like a handlebar grip on a bicycle with a switch along the side. From the bottom of the base an electric cord emerged.

"This is a most effective tool," the man showed it to her. "As you can see, it can be adjusted according to need, from a very mild charge to one quite intense and excruciating."

"What are you going to do?" Sydney whispered weakly.

"There are many uses for this particular instrument," the man replied in the same monotone as always. "It can be used eternally to deliver a very effective electric current - for example to the base of the spine or the bottom of the feet. Additionally it can be inserted into the vagina or rectum. Both orifices are excellent receptacles. Maggie is particularly susceptible to internal stimulation, as are many females. Please take note, Sydney Forrest."

The man moved away and a few seconds later she heard Maggie. "No, please don't. Please, please .... Nooooooo!" Her last word merged into an agonized scream that seemed to go on forever. Sydney wished she could cover her ears; blot out the sound. Her heart was beating so fast she thought it would explode from fear.

At last the screams began to diminish and after what seemed a very long time, they transformed into whimpers. Sydney was covered with sweat and trembling with fear but jerked violently as she felt a touch on her back.

"What do you want, Sydney Forrest?" the soft monotone voice asked.

She had no idea what the right answer was and was terrified of giving the wrong one. "I want you to tell me who you are and why you're doing this."

"That is not the correct response, Sydney Forrest."

"Then tell me what you want me to say!" she screamed as the man moved out of sight. "Just tell me . . . " she felt cool hands on her thigh and tensed even more. " . . . stop it!" she screamed as she felt something slippery and cold being smeared on her. " Please, don't touch me. I mean, it! Get away from−"

Her words changed into screams as the pain began.

CR

Weasel sat back and whistled softly. "Someone's really done a number on you this time, man. This one even has me stumped."

Blake felt like he had just eaten something that disagreed with him. His stomach was churning like it wanted to expel its contents. "Are you sure you can't trace it back to its point of origin? The money had to have come from somewhere"

"I can try." Weasel attacked the keyboard again, his eyes squinted as he stared at the screen.

Blake watched him work for a few minutes in silence then got up and paced around the room. This could be very bad if word of it got out. Somehow, someone had opened several accounts in his name in the Caymen Islands and in Switzerland. In each of the accounts was over three million dollars; for a grand total of six million, two hundred, seventy-five thousand. What was worse were the dates of the deposits.

The Swiss account was opened, according to what they had been able to find, a little over a year ago. The initial deposit was one and a half million dollars. Over the last year, four additional deposits of a little over a million had been made. The Caymen account had been opened two days after the date of the bombing of the federal building in Ohio. Three million dollars had been deposited in one lump sum.

Blake couldn't imagine the drug cartel being responsible. It wasn't their style to devise so elaborate a scheme, not to mention waste their own money, just to make a federal agent look bad. He believed that Adrian Zayne was behind it.

"Sweet Jesus!" Weasel exclaimed, capturing Blake's attention. "This is bad, man. This is real bad."

"What?" Blake took a seat beside him and looked at the screen.

"Whoever did this was clever," Weasel said with a hint of admiration in his voice then looked at Blake and winked. "See, here's the trail. You can see how the money was channeled though a series of banks throughout the world. That's the clever part. Whoever did this made it look like you were the one transferring the money to cover your tracks. They made it look like you were trying to cover the origin of the money."

"And?" Blake could not tell by looking at the screen what Weasel was getting at.

Weasel keyed in a command and hit the enter button. "So, here's the skinny. The funds originally came from an account in a bank in Iran."

"Iran?" Blake's eyebrows and voice rose at the same time. "You have a name for the account?"

Weasel nodded and pointed to a line on the screen. Blake read it and flopped back in his chair in shock. "You've got to be kidding!"

"Afraid not," Weasel leaned back and looked at him. "Man, if I didn't know this was a set up even I'd think you were hip deep in this shit. And considering the money came from the dude highest on America's shit list, if this gets out you'll be lucky if the bureau puts you under a prison somewhere. All it'd take is one whiff of this getting to the media and people would be breaking down the door to lynch your white ass."

Blake nodded mutely. Weasel was right. "But there's one thing that doesn't fit. No one's trying to pin anything on me so what's their angle? I'm a fed on the take? The take for what? And what's worth over six million dollars from the bad boy in Iran?"

Weasel tapped Blake on the forehead with his index finger. "Duh huh, dude. Remember how the press was screaming 'middle east' involvement right after the Ohio? What kind of parallels do you think they'd draw from a federal agent on the griff from Mr. Iran himself? Not only will they bury you, it'll add fuel to the fire from the administration and Potus' desire to shut down the borders and declare martial law."

Blake felt another wave of sickness wash over him. "Holy shit! Someone's trying to set me up for this bombing!"

Weasel nodded silently then turned to the computer. "Man, we've got to do something about this and we've got to do it like yesterday. The trouble is, this is going to take time and I don't know how much of that we have. It'd be my guess that whoever's behind this isn't going to wait long to let the hammer fall." He looked at his watch and cursed. "Damn! And we're supposed to be at Forrest's in half an hour!"

Blake stood up and gave the screen one last look. "Okay, let's get over there and see if we can nail Zayne. If he's behind this then we can stop it before it goes any further."

"We hope," Weasel added as he turned off the computer. "Otherwise, my friend - your goose is cooked."

Blake grimaced slightly then a look of cold determination took hold of his face. "I don't like goose. I'm going to bust this bastard, Weasel and I'm going to enjoy every moment of it. When we get through with him, he'll wish he'd never laid eyes on me."

Weasel didn't comment as he followed Blake out of the house but the expression on his face said that he was not so confident.

ભ

Sydney jerked awake as the lights came on. Her body ached and her head felt like someone was hammering inside it. She covered her face with her hands and rolled over onto her stomach on the cement floor.

"What do you want, Sydney Forrest?"

That question, issued from that unchanging, emotionless, monotone voice was more frightening than the sound of a wild beast charging at her with fangs bared. For what seemed like an eternity she had gone from excruciating pain to total unconsciousness, only to be awakened time and again to be asked that same question. She had given every answer she could think to give and none of them had been right. She could not even remember the number of times she had been asked. Her entire existence seemed to be nothing more than a hole of empty blackness, interrupted by pain and that one dreaded question.

She was so afraid of answering wrong that she hesitated. If only she had some clue as to what the man wanted then maybe she could come up with the right answer to the question. But he offered no clues.

A cold hand touched her back and she stiffened then curled up tight in a fetal position. "What do you want?" the question was repeated.

"An end to this," she whispered.

"That is not the correct response," the man replied then directed his words to someone else in the room. "Take her to the table."

Sydney screamed and fought as she felt hands take hold of her arms and lift her from the floor. Unfortunately, her strength was near depletion. Unable to do little more than struggle feebly she was blindfolded and carried from the room. She felt her feet dragging on a smooth surface for a little ways then she was lifted higher and strapped down to a cold surface. Her arms and legs were stretched out tight and strapped down and the blindfold was left on.

"What do you want, Sydney Forrest?" the voice came from beside her right ear.

"I don't know," her voice was barely audible.

"That is unfortunate."

She didn't have time to steel herself against the pain as it came. All at once nothing existed but pain. In sheer desperation she tried to focus on something to lessen the agony. Blake's face appeared in her mind and without realizing it she screamed his name.

The pain suddenly stopped and she heard a voice at the foot of the table. It sounded exactly like Blake. "You should have stayed out of it, Syd. You should have just forgotten what Tyler said and quit digging for answers. Then this wouldn't have had to happen. But you wouldn't let it go, would you? You just had to know everything. You had to know who the mystery man was, didn't you?"

"Blake?" she croaked, straining at her bonds. "Is that you? Please help me. Make them stop."

"What do you want?" the monotone voice of her captor sounded in her ear.

"I want to be rescued," she replied without thinking.

"And who will rescue you, Sydney Forrest?"

"Blake," she answered hopefully.

"I am sorry. That is incorrect."

She opened her mouth to speak but a scream erupted instead as once more the pain consumed her.

❦

Blake and Weasel were secreted in Jack Forrest's private study at the rear of the mansion in front of a bank of monitors when Adrian Zayne arrived. Thanks to the equipment that had been set up earlier they could see and hear everything. In the garage was another set-up connected to recording equipment so that the meeting could be documented.

"Mr. Zayne." Jack Forrest greeted Adrian as the butler showed him into the darkly paneled den. "Good evening."

"A pleasure to see you again, sir." Adrian smiled winningly and extended his hand to Jack. "How is your lovely wife?"

"Fine." Jack gave Adrian's hand a cursory shake then gestured towards the bar. "Would you care for a drink?"

"Not at this time, thank you," Adrian declined politely.

"Then perhaps we should just get to the point of this meeting, Mr. Zayne."

"Yes, I quite agreed," Adrian replied as he took a seat in a deep leather arm chair across from the couch where Jack sat.

Neither man spoke for a moment. Adrian looked around the room for a moment then looked directly at the corner of the room where a camera lens was hidden in the massive bookshelves. He smiled fleetingly then turned his gaze to Jack Forrest.

Blake's jaw tightened as he saw Adrian smile up at the camera. "Senator," Adrian began speaking. "I felt it important that we speak man to man on this matter. As it happens your daughter and I are very much in love."

Blake jumped in his seat at the same time he saw Jack tense. "What?" Jack stammered in surprise.

"Yes, I'm afraid it's all too true." Adrian's smile never wavered. "And, being somewhat traditional in such matters, I felt I should formally ask for her hand in marriage from her father."

"That's what you wanted to discuss? Your relationship with my daughter?"

"I can think of nothing more important, sir."

Jack stood up. "Could you excuse me for a moment?"

Adrian nodded and Jack left the room. A few seconds later Blake heard a tap at the door of the study. Weasel opened it and Jack walked in. "What the hell is this crap about that scum and Sydney?"

Weasel tried to calm him. "Jack, listen, he's probably just trying to rattle you or something. I don't know. But you need to just go along with him. We can't take a chance on spooking him so just play along and maybe you can steer the conversation away from Syd and back to Zayne's blackmail threats.

Jack frowned and looked over at Blake. "He's lying, isn't he? She isn't really in love with that shyster, is she? I thought you and she were–"

"No, she isn't in love with Zayne," Blake answered. "And yes, Syd and I do care very much for each other. Zayne's just up to his games. But since he's on the subject of Syd, how about asking why she didn't come with him to give you the big news about their supposed undying love?"

"Why?"

Blake did not want to worry Jack with his fears so he just shrugged. "See if it trips him up."

"Is there something you're not telling me?" Jack's question sounded more like a demand.

Weasel intervened, putting his arm around Jack's shoulders. "Don't worry. Everything's fine. But you better get back in there before he gets suspicious."

Jack left and Weasel turned to Blake. "You have any ideas what trip Zayne's on now?"

Blake just shook his head and turned his attention back to the screen that showed Adrian Zayne smiling up at the camera.

◌

It was nearly midnight when Blake and Weasel returned to his apartment. Blake unlocked the door, marched inside, hurled his keys across the room then drove his fist into the wall, smashing through the sheetrock.

"Son of a bitch!" he shouted, pulling his fist free and watching the plaster dust and debris fall to the carpet. "Just what the hell was all that?" He turned to Weasel.

"Beats me," Weasel said tiredly. "It doesn't add up. When I talked to Jack earlier he said Zayne almost came right out and said he was going to blackmail him. So, why does he show up tonight and say nothing? Also—" he paused for a moment. "Where's Syd?"

"I wish to hell I knew," Blake grumbled. Nothing had gone right the entire night. Zayne had showed up at Senator Forrest's as planned, but he had spent the entire evening talking about how much in love he and Sydney were and how it would mean so much to them to have Jack and Shirley's blessings.

Jack had followed their suggestion and tried his best to steer the conversation around to Weasel's role as Armand and the blackmail, but Adrian had ignored all attempts. Finally, Jack had given up and Adrian had returned to his original conversation of plans he and Sydney had of spending their lives together.

Late in the visit Jack had excused himself again to go to the restroom but slipped into his study where Blake and Weasel were listening in to the conversation going on in the den. "What do I do?" he asked.

Weasel started to make a suggestion but Blake cut him off. He was bothered not only by Zayne's reluctance to discuss what the meeting had been called for, but he was worried about Sydney. She was supposed to be with Zayne on his yacht. So, if he was there with Forrest, then where was she? He didn't want to alarm Jack, but he wanted to know where Syd was so he told Jack again to try and pin Zayne why Sydney hadn't come with him if he wanted to discuss their future.

Jack had done as Blake suggested and Zayne had suddenly taken on a very worried demeanor. He told Jack that he hadn't wanted to worry him but that he had tried to get in touch with Sydney for the past couple of days. He said that they had originally planned on taking his yacht out for the weekend but she never shown up. He also told Forrest that the last he had heard from her she had said she was taking a drive into Virginia with an old boyfriend, Blake Edwards, to tell him that she and Adrian were in love and she would not be seeing him anymore. He went on to say that he was very worried for her safety, as she'd told him that Blake Edwards was an insanely jealous and often abusive man.

Jack had stammered around in surprise for a moment and Adrian suggested that if Sydney hadn't returned by morning that he and Jack go to the police and have them pick Blake up for questioning. Jack agreed and after a few minutes Adrian had left.

That was when all hell broke loose.

"Where's my daughter?" Jack demanded as soon as Blake and Weasel walked into the room.

"As far as I knew she was with Zayne on his yacht," Blake answered.

"And what about this trip she took with you?" Jack demanded. "Where exactly did you take her, Mr. Edwards? And where is she now?"

Blake explained as best he could without going into intimate detail. Jack listened without interruption until Blake fell silent then he walked over to stand in front of him. "You listen to me, Mr. Edwards. If you've done anything to harm my daughter I'll see you get the chair, do you understand me?"

Weasel jumped in, in Blake's defense. "Jack, listen to me. He hasn't done anything to Syd. He's telling you everything we know. Syd said Zayne was going to pick her up Friday morning and they were going out on his yacht for the weekend. Blake dropped her at her apartment Friday morning and that's the last either of us have seen or heard from her. But before you get in a knot, let me just say that she had her cell and her laptop with her. With those she could have gotten in touch if she was in some kind of trouble."

"This has gone too far!" Jack exclaimed. "I never agreed to put my only child's life at risk for this insane plan. I want Sydney found and I want her found now. Both of you listen to me. I want to see my daughter safe and unharmed. You find her and bring her here. If I don't see you arrive here first thing in the morning I'm going to pay a visit to the Director of the bureau. Is that clear?"

"Yes, sir," they both said in unison.

"Then get to it!"

Blake and Weasel left the house. Outside in the garage the surveillance team was loading their equipment into the van. One of the men walked over to Blake. "Sir, about the recordings. I, uh, I . . . I have to turn them over to the CD director, sir. It's regulations. Charges were made against you sir and I −"

"I understand," Blake interrupted. "You do what you have to do."

"Thank you, sir," The younger man turned away then stopped and looked back at Blake. "For what it's worth, sir. All of us are behind you. We know you didn't do what Zayne said."

"Thanks." Blake tried to smile. "I appreciate that. Now, you guys get moving. Until you hear otherwise, the investigation proceeds as planned."

He and Weasel watched the men get in the van and leave then they got in Blake's car. Neither one of them spoke the entire way back to Blake's apartment.

Finally, Blake looked at Weasel. "You don't think he's done something to her, do you?"

Weasel shook his head. "I don't know, man. I hope not."

"We've got to find her, GW."

Weasel nodded. "And fast. Jack's as good as his word. "If we don't produce her, he'll go straight to the top."

Blake sighed and took a seat, staring vacantly across the room. It seemed as if suddenly his entire world was crumbling around him and he did not have a clue how to stop it.

Sunday, April 30

Blake was pacing the floor when Weasel arrived. "Well?" Blake looked at him.

"Nothing." Weasel's voice sounded tired and defeated. "Man, it doesn't make sense! His yacht's anchored, Syd's apartment's empty and no one has heard diddly from her."

"And she apparently isn't at Zayne's either," Blake commented.

Weasel's eyebrows rose. "What makes you say that?"

"I had a team check out his mansion and the penthouse at the Watergate. "They came up empty handed on both counts."

Weasel looked at his watch. "Well, we've about run out of time, dude. What do you want to do?"

"Do you think you could stall Forrest for a while, give us some more time?"

Weasel frowned for a moment then nodded. "I'll give it my best shot. You gonna hang around here or go home?"

"Might as well stay." Blake sat down on the corner of his office desk. "If Forrest won't agree to give us more time it'll save a trip when he comes down to blow me out of the water."

"Hey, man." Weasel walked across the room and put his hand on Blake's shoulder. "Don't give up yet. Maybe I can convince Jack. Meanwhile, have you checked all the flights and trains out the past couple of days?"

"That was at the top of the list," Blake grumbled. "Weasel, just between us, I'm getting scared that something's happened to her. What if she's—"

"She's not!" Weasel's voice sounded rough and harsh. "Syd's alive, I know it. If she was— well, I'd just know it. But she's not - and we will find her."

"I hope you're right. I really hope you're right. "

CR

Awaken by a sudden blast of noise Sydney jerked and looked around wild-eyed. She was strapped down to the table and the room was completely dark. Her head felt as if it would burst from the noise. It was like a confused din of sirens, alarms and horns all blaring at the same time.

She tried to wiggle her arms free from the straps that held them but they were fastened too tightly. After several minutes the pain in her head from the noise became too much to bear and she started to scream; the sound of her voice blending with the cacophony.

All at once the noise stopped. Simultaneously the lights came on. Sydney's scream lingered for a moment longer, stopping only when the man entered the room.

She watched him through bleary, tear filled eyes as he approached her. By now she had learned not to try and anticipate what would happen when he appeared. It could be any of a wide varieties of torture that would be used.

"What do you want, Sydney Forrest?"

That question. She had reached a point where she would have preferred for him just to put a gun to her head and pull the trigger, rather than ask that question. She shook her head, biting her bottom lip to keep from crying.

"I require an answer." He raised his hands to let her see the hypodermic needle in one and the cattle prod in the other.

Sydney's heart jumped painfully in her chest then began to race. Sweat poured from her body and she trembled as if having a seizure. Two more men entered the room. One wrapped a rubber cord around her arm, just above the elbow and the other pushed a cart containing a car battery and jumper cables.

The monotone man, as she had labeled him, inserted the needle in her arm at the crease of the elbow then released the rubber binder. She felt the rush of the drug like fire through her veins and gasped.

"I require an answer," Monotone Man repeated. "What do you want, Sydney Forrest?"

The man's shape swam in her eyes, shifting and distorting. "I–" she looked at the other men, seeing one transform to a creature with the head of a frog and the body of a goat and the other seem to dissolve into nothingness. "I want...I want to be saved."

"And who will save you, Sydney Forrest?"

She started to say Blake's name. She had cried his name many times. Each time it was a mistake. Each time she had heard his voice saying things that brought her no comfort, no hope. He condemned her, accusing her of betraying him by listening to Senator Tyler. He told her that she should have left things alone and then they could have been rich beyond their wildest dreams and could have gone away together. But she wouldn't so she had to be punished.

Sydney didn't know what to say. Who was there that could save her from this hell?

"Tell me the name of your savior, Sydney Forrest."

She opened her mouth and closed it a few times, trying to think through the effects of the drugs. A face appeared in her mind and she spoke without thinking. "Adrian," she mumbled. "Adrian Zayne."

Monotone Man smiled and let the cattle prod fall to the floor. Sydney felt the knot in her throat start to ease in relief then screamed as a current caused her body to arch and spasm convulsively.

Monotone Man nodded to the man with the jumper cables then leaned over close to Sydney's face as the pain subsided. "Are you quite sure, Sydney Forrest? Is Adrian Zayne your salvation?"

She was too afraid to answer; too afraid of the pain. But her words would have been just as effective as her silence. Another spasm wracked her while Monotone Man smiled into her face. "Are you sure?" he had to lean down and speak into her ear. "Is Adrian Zayne your deliverance?"

Sydney heard him through the sound of her own tortured screams. "You need only answer the question, Sydney Forrest and the pain will cease. Is Adrian Zayne the man you wish to save you?"

"Yes!" she screamed.

The cables were removed and she twitched spasmodically for several seconds then fell limp, staring in horror at Monotone Man's cold eyes and white teeth; the only features visible in the white ski mask that covered his face.

"I do not believe you are sincere, Sydney Forrest. Do you truly believe that Adrian Zayne is your deliverer? Is he the answer to the question?"

Another bout of pain consumed her, this one more intense than the last. "What do you want, Sydney Forrest?" the question was shouted in her ear.

"Adrian!" she screamed. "Adriiiiiaaan!"

Before she could find out if she had answered correctly pain sent her catapulting into blackness.

Monday, May 1

Washington, D.C.

Blake spotted Weasel sitting at a table in the back of the cafe as he entered. With Weasel were two of the men from the surveillance team. "What's up?" he asked as he reached the table and took a seat beside Weasel.

Ray Peters, one of the surveillance men answered his question. "We wanted to talk - away from the office, sir."

"I'm listening."

"It's the tapes, sir." Peters cut a look at the man seated next to him, John Turner. "From Senator Forrest's house."

"What about them?"

Peters cut his eyes at Weasel, which didn't go unnoticed by Blake. He turned his attention back towards Blake and cleared his throat. "It seems that the tapes were defective, sir. We have video but the audio is worthless - it's nothing but garble."

Blake looked at John Turner. "If I remember correctly, you can almost walk on water when it comes to this stuff. You sure they're worthless?"

"Yes sir." Turner nodded. "Completely,"

"Well, " Blake sat back in his seat and regarded the three men for a few moments. "How fortunate for me."

Weasel rolled his eyes while Turner turned bright pink and Peters stared at the table top. Blake leaned his elbows on the table and looked at the two men. "Listen, I appreciate what you're trying to do, but there's no need. I don't have anything to hide. I didn't do anything to Syd—to the Senator's daughter, so you don't have to do this. File your reports."

"We can't do that, sir." Peters looked up with a set to his jaw. "There's no way we're going to let Zayne do this to you. We all know he's a scumbag and we all want to see his ass nailed to the wall. And we can't do that if your butt's in a sling because of some trumped up allegations he made just to turn up the heat and get you off his ass."

Blake was surprised at how much it meant to him that his team had that kind of faith in him. It made him feel a little self-conscious because of the emotion it invoked. "I appreciate that," he said simply then smiled. "So, what are you doing sitting here? We have a job to do, so let's get at it."

"Yes, sir!" Peters grinned and stood.

Turner stood and extended his hand to Blake. "Thank you, Mr. Edwards."

"For what?" Blake looked up as he took Turner's hand and shook it.

"For being one of the good guys. That's why I joined the bureau, to work with people like you."

"Thanks." Blake smiled. "Now get out there and get me something on Zayne."

Blake moved to the opposite side of the table and looked across it at Weasel. "Was that your doings?"

"No way, man." Weasel shook his head. "They came to me and I just went along with it. Besides, you know me. Company man through and through. I'd have left you swinging in the breeze."

Blake chuckled, letting go of a little of the tension he had been carrying. "Yeah, I forget. It wasn't you that convinced Forrest not to run to the Director screaming about me kidnapping his baby."

Weasel laughed but the cheer was short-lived. "Man, I'm really getting worried," he said as his smile vanished. "There's no trace of her. I've put feelers out everywhere and I've called everyone she knows and nothing. It's like she just disappeared into thin air."

Blake felt a hard knot form in his throat. He was beginning to think that they weren't going to find Sydney. He had called in every favor he had coming from the bureau to the local police and so far there had been no leads.

"I wish I could disagree with you," he said finally, making no attempt to hide the despondency that colored his words. "But I can't and I don't know what to do at this point besides list her as a missing person."

"Jack will never go for that," Weasel responded. "He won't even let anyone mention the idea that she's—that she's not coming back." His eyes blinked rapidly a few times, but not before Blake saw the tears that gathered in them.

"We'll find her," Blake tried to sound confident.

"What if we don't?"

Blake shook his head and looked away. He could not even think about that.

⬩

The sounds of children laughing brought Sydney to consciousness. She started as her eyes opened and she looked around. Instead of white concrete surrounding her on all sides, the sight and smell of blooming flowers assaulted her senses.

She was sitting on a path that wound through plants with her back propped against a low planter. Two little girls, about five-years-old appeared on the path, pointing at her and giggling. "Mommy, mommy!" One of them turned around and called out. "Look, mommy! A lady's sleeping in the flowers."

Sydney pushed herself up, noticing that her suitcases and purse were sitting a few feet away. She looped the shoulder strap of her purse over her right shoulder and picked one of the suitcases up in each hand to hurry down the path in the opposite direction of the children who were jumping up and down, calling to their mothers about the lady who was sleeping in the flowers. She recognized where she was; the National Arboretum. How she had gotten there was a mystery. The last thing she remembered was pain.

As she hurried to the exit, she tried to think. *How did I get here? And why did they let me go?* She had no answers to her own questions and the more she thought about it the more afraid she became. *Suppose this is some kind of trick? What if they're toying with me and planning on grabbing me and taking me back to that room?*

The thought of going back was enough to make her break out into a run. She ran to the exit on Maryland Avenue and M Street NE and looked around fearfully. She didn't see anyone looking at her but she was still scared. She flagged down a taxi, threw her suitcases in and climbed into the back seat.

"Where to?" the driver asked over his shoulder.

His question sent another spike of panic through her. Suddenly she realized that she didn't know where to go. She couldn't go to Blake and didn't understand why. She felt like he was the enemy, someone she could not trust. If she couldn't go to him for help then where?

She heard herself giving the driver Adrian's address before she realized that she'd started speaking. She stopped in mid-sentence and the driver turned to give her an odd look. She stammered nervously, wondering why she had been giving Adrian's address but managed to squeak out her own address. The driver shrugged and pulled out into traffic. Sydney looked out the window, wondering why she was suddenly filled with an overwhelming need to be with Adrian. Somehow just the sound of his name made her feel safer.

She leaned her head back and she tried to push all thought out of her mind as she watched the scenery pass by. She was too tired and scared to think about anything at the moment. She would figure it all out later, when she reached safety.

Chapter Eleven

Monday, May 1, 2006

Washington, D.C.

Sydney set the lock on the doorknob of the front door of her apartment then engaged the deadbolt and the security chain. She leaned back against the door and looked around warily. Everything looked the same as when she left but somehow it felt different.

After a minute, she eased away from the door and slowly walked through the apartment, stopping here and there to pick up some personal item. It's like I'm not even the same person who lived *here*, she thought as she looked at the picture of her mother and father sitting on her desk in the study. *What did those people do to me?*

Intellectually she realized that more had happened during her imprisonment than she realized. Her memory was fragmented; the only clear memories were of the pain and that was not something she wanted to remember. The rest was hazy, like a dream you try to remember upon waking that slips away like morning fog in sunshine.

She walked into the bedroom and stopped, staring at the bed and feeling her heart suddenly race and a cold sweat break out on her body. Images of Blake flitted through her mind; of him walking towards her as she waited on him in bed, of the way his eyes darkened with desire as he looked at her. She felt the memories swell within her like a flower blooming. With the memories feelings began to assert themselves on her. She moved to the bed and picked up one of the pillows, putting it to her face. She could smell the scent of his aftershave.

As fast as a serpent's strike, fear suddenly consumed her. She threw the pillow away as if it was tainted. Thoughts of Blake now filled her with an overwhelming fear. *He is the enemy,* a low voice seemed to chant in her head. *He is the one Tyler was protecting. The one who wants you dead for what you know. He cannot let you live with the knowledge you possess.*

Sydney cried out, pressing her palms against her ears in an attempt to still the voice in her mind that refused to be silenced. She fell to her knees and sobbed quietly as the voice relentlessly went on and on.

଼

As he neared his office door, Blake could hear the persistent ring of the phone from within. He rushed to his desk and snatched up the receiver. "Special Agent Edwards."

"She's been spotted!" Weasel's excitement caused his voice to have a higher pitch than normal.

"Where?" Blake felt his own pulse accelerate.

"Getting out of a taxi in front of her apartment."

"I'm leaving now." Blake didn't wait for Weasel to reply, but hung up the phone and ran out of his office at full tilt, headed through the building like it was on fire.

He drove like someone possessed all the way to the Watergate Apartments, his attention entirely on getting to Sydney and making sure she was all right. When he arrived at her door he rang the bell several times then knocked impatiently on the door. "Syd? Are you in there? Can you hear me?"

He heard the clink of the deadbolt being unlocked and a moment later the door opened a crack. Sydney peered out with a terrified expression on her face. "W—wh—what do you want?" she stammered.

Blake could not have been more surprised if she had just turned green in front of his eyes. "What do I want? What's wrong? Syd, open the door."

She shook her head and started to push the door closed but Blake put his hand against it. "What's wrong?" he repeated. "Will you just let me in and tell me?"

"Go away!" She whispered like she was scared to death.

"Open the door!" Blake's anxiety was getting the best of him, making his voice rise in timbre and volume.

Sydney backed away from the door, shaking her head and Blake drew back and gave it a swift kick. The chain snapped and he rushed in. "Syd, what—"

"Stay away from me." Her words were a frightened plea.

Blake moved toward her and she backed away, pressing herself against the wall of the entrance and watching him like he was a monster. "Please." Her voice came out in a choked whisper. "Leave me alone. Please!"

"Syd!" Blake grabbed her by the arms and tried to pull her up against him. He was beginning to panic. Something was very wrong with her.

"Nooooooo!" She screamed like a tortured animal and fought to get away from him.

Blake struggled to hold her still without hurting her, trying to calm her down. She was like something wild, screaming and fighting like her life depended on it. "Please, Syd. Just - try and - listen. I'm . . . not going to . . . hurt . . . you." His words were oddly spaced and accented due to the struggle.

She didn't ease in her efforts and he started to think that she had simply lost her mind. "Stop it!" He shouted to be heard above her screams.

"What is the meaning of this?" A male voice came from behind him.

Blake turned and saw Adrian Zayne coming toward him. A split second later Sydney saw Zayne and tore free from Blake.

"Adrian!" She ran into his arms. "Oh, thank God, you're here."

Adrian wrapped his arms around Sydney and glared over her head at Blake. "Would you care to explain why you are here, assaulting my fiancé?"

"Your..." Blake could not bring himself to say the word. "Just what are you doing here, Zayne?"

"That is none of your concern, I am sure," Adrian replied haughtily.

"Adrian, please get me out of here." Sydney whispered urgently. "Please!"

"Yes, of course, my darling," he crooned and kissed the top of her head.

"You're not taking her anywhere!" Blake made a move to block the way.

"Is that so?" Adrian's tone turned to ice. "Well, perhaps you'd rather I called the authorities and let my fiancé tell them how you broke into her apartment and attacked her? Would that be to your liking, Mr. Edwards?"

Blake's eye narrowed into slits. He would have liked nothing better than to grab Zayne around the throat and squeeze the life out of him but he knew Zayne had him in a corner. With Sydney in the condition she was, there was no telling what she would tell the authorities and he couldn't afford the hassle. So, he did the only thing he could do. He stepped aside.

Adrian smiled coldly and led Sydney out of the apartment. Blake watched them leave then went to the phone. "We've got big trouble," he said as soon as Weasel answered the phone.

"You want to be more specific?"

"I'll tell you everything when I get back, but in the meantime, I want surveillance stepped up on Zayne. I want him followed twenty-four hours a day and we're not going to be discrete about it. Get the guy staking out Syd's apartment on the horn and have him follow Zayne. He's leaving Sydney's apartment now."

"Is Syd there?"

"Not anymore. Just hang on, I'll fill you in with all I know when I get there."

He hung up the phone and sat down on the arm of the couch. "What the hell's going on?" he asked aloud. There was no reply; only the silence of an empty room.

CR

Sydney woke to find herself in unfamiliar surroundings. She sat up straight, clutching the sheet to her chest as she looked around wildly. Adrian stood from where he sat in a chair by the window and walked to the bed. "Adrian!" she breathed in relief. "I...I didn't know where I was."

"Everything is fine," he assured her as he sat down facing her and took her hands in his. "You're safe, now. You don't have to be afraid."

She nodded mutely. Part of her felt it was wrong to be there. An almost indistinguishable little voice inside her mind was whispering to her but she couldn't understand what it was saying.

"Darling, do you think you're strong enough to tell me what happened?" he asked softly. "I was so terrified when you didn't show up Friday at the yacht. I had people looking for you everywhere. Where were you?"

Sydney opened her mouth to speak then closed it and shook her head. She wasn't ready to talk about what she had been through. First, she had to make sense of things that were happening now. Like why she

261

was suddenly so scared of Blake. Before she had been sure he was the man she loved. She could remember trusting him and loving him but now she couldn't seem to grasp those feelings.

It was all so confusing. She could remember everything and how she had felt before she had been taken to that room but nothing seemed real anymore. All the feelings were gone; replaced with new ones that she didn't understand.

Such as how she felt about Adrian. She knew she wasn't supposed to trust him; that she hadn't trusted him. He was supposed to be the enemy, an evil man who had caused pain and suffering. But she couldn't find the hatred that had once been inside her. Instead, being with him made her feel safe and loved and she was afraid to let go of that.

"What time is it?" She noticed that it was dark outside as she looked at the window.

Adrian glanced at his wristwatch. "A little after two in the morning."

"How long have I been asleep?"

"Almost seventeen hours."

Sydney leaned back against the pillows and looked at Adrian. "Have you been here all that time?"

"Where else would I be?"

She didn't speak and for a few minutes the only sound in the room was the chirping of insects that drifted in on the breeze from the opened window. "Adrian, I don't think I…" she hesitated, unsure how to put into words what she wanted to say. "…something happened – something– something horrible. I don't know if I'm whole anymore. I feel…"

"How do you feel?" he prompted her.

"Tampered with," she said flatly. "I can't trust myself. Not now."

"Then trust me." He moved closer and cupped her face in his hands. "I'll take care of you and I promise no harm will come to you. I love you, Sydney."

She nodded, trying to stem the tears that sprang to her eyes. Adrian kissed them away then moved his lips to hers for a soft kiss. He pulled back and looked into her eyes. "I want to love you."

Sydney wasn't sure she was ready for that but she did not know how to say no. He was her deliverer. How could she refuse him? She nodded and he stood o undress. Sydney watched him, barely noting his physical beauty. A question consumed her mind. *Why do I think of him as my deliverer?* That was an extremely odd way to feel. What prompted her mind to use that word? What had he delivered her from?

She had no time to ponder the question as he pulled back the sheet and lay down to take her in his arms. She pushed the questions back as their lips met and let the sensations of his hands on her body release her for a brief time from the uncertainty and confusion.

ℂℭ

Blake tossed the empty beer can in the general direction of the trash can. It bounced off the rim of the container and landed on the floor, rolling a couple of inches before it came to a stop. Blake paid no attention as he fished the last cigarette from the pack and lit it.

"This is stranger than strange," Weasel commented, shifting positions in his chair and setting his barely touched beer on the end table. "Tell me again what she—"

"I've told you a dozen times!" Blake snapped. "And no matter how many times I tell it, it's going to end up the same. She acted like I was some kind of ogre and Zayne was her goddamn white knight!"

Weasel frowned but said nothing for a few moments. "Something happened to her, man. Something severe. Unless she's playing some kind of game and she couldn't let you know. You did say Zayne showed up just minutes after you did, right?"

Blake nodded and Weasel sprang to his feet to pace back and forth. "So, what if Syd knew that he was there and she couldn't let on to you? Maybe this is part of her plan to sucker Zayne!"

"If that's the case then she should have been an actress. If you'd seen her . . . she was terrified. It was—spooky."

"But we can't rule out the possibility!"

"Then why wouldn't she take my calls?"

"Zayne's people probably didn't tell her you called."

Blake shook his head and got up to get another beer. He opened it and walked back into the den to set it down, untouched on the table. "I've got a real bad feeling about this," he said as he took his seat. "Right here." He rubbed the back of his neck. "It's like alarms going off. Something's very wrong and I don't know what the hell to do about it."

"You go to Alabama and get the goods on Zayne so we can put him away," Weasel said determinedly.

"And what about Syd? Do I just abandon her?"

"We've got around the clock surveillance on the house," Weasel reminded him. "She's okay. Besides, I think it's time her father found out she's back. Maybe I'll take a run over to Zayne's tomorrow with Jack and pay a visit on them. Then I can talk to Syd and find out what's going on. In the meantime, you've got about two hours until your flight leaves. Maybe you should clean up and we'll go grab some breakfast. A couple of cups of coffee might do you some good."

Blake rubbed his eyes tiredly. "You're probably right." He got up and went into the bathroom. As he turned on the light he saw his reflection in the mirror. Superimposed on the reflection was a mental image of the way Sydney had looked at him.

Something's very very wrong, he told himself. He had seen that look before. In textbooks - on the faces of people who have witnessed unspeakable horror. His chest tightened and he closed his eyes, trying to drive the image from his mind. It tore his heart out to know that seeing him had caused her to look that way. He had to find a way to make things right again. And the only way he knew to do that was to put Adrian Zayne away for the rest of time.

When he opened his eyes he looked at himself in the mirror. This was one case he was going to win. He had to.

Tuesday, May 2

Sydney jumped as the downstairs maid touched her lightly on the shoulder from behind. "Sorry, Miss," the woman apologized. "You have visitors. Shall I show them out here to the terrace or would you prefer to receive them inside?"

"Who?" Sydney asked anxiously. She was afraid it might be Blake and she didn't want to see him.

"Your father, Miss and a Mr. Armand."

"My father?" Sydney stood and looked into the opened French doors. "Is Adrian still in his study?"

"Yes, miss."

"All right. Why don't you show my father and Mr. Armand out here. And will you please ask Adrian if he can join us?"

The maid nodded and returned inside. Sydney took her seat and tried to stem the rising panic she felt inside. She didn't know why she should be anxious about seeing her father or GW, but the thought of it made her palms clammy and her heart beat accelerate. Only when she was with Adrian did she feel safe.

As soon as Jack Forrest stepped outside and saw Sydney he broke into a run. "Sydney!" he grabbed her up in a hug. "Oh, god, honey! I thought I'd lost you! Where were you? Why did you disappear like that?"

Sydney pulled back from the embrace. "Why don't we all sit down and I'll try to explain."

Jack released her and moved to the chair beside her. GW stepped forward and extended his hand. "Miss Forrest, please forgive me intruding on you this way, but your father requested that I accompany him."

Sydney realized that GW was still in his role as Mr. Armand. His words belied none of the concern she saw in the depths of his dark eyes. "It's quite all right, Mr. Armand." She replied, giving his hand a squeeze, thinking that at least she did not feel afraid being around GW. He still seemed the same as always. " I'm pleased to see you again. Won't you have a seat?"

GW sat down and Sydney dismissed the maid. "Clarise, would you mind bringing my guests some iced tea?" As soon as the maid left Jack looked at Sydney. "I want to know what happened to you? Zayne claims that you were supposed to meet him on his yacht and you never showed up and he seems to think that Blake did something to you. He said something about you and Blake going to Virginia and—"

"Dad, please!" Sydney couldn't take the barrage. "Just slow down, okay? First of all, I was supposed to go away with Adrian for the weekend. But I... "

She stopped, unable to go on. Even remembering what had happened was enough to freeze her with fear. She began to shake violently and Jack reached out for her. "Sydney, honey, what's wrong? Did someone hurt you? Please, I want to help you. Just tell me what—"

"Well, this is a pleasant surprise." Adrian interrupted as he stepped outside onto the terrace. "I didn't know you were expecting company, darling."

Sydney jumped up and met him as he walked to the table. She wrapped one arm around him and pressed against his side. He draped his arm around her and kissed the top of her head. "My father was worried," she said softly. "He wants to know what happened."

Adrian led her to the table and seated her. He stood behind her, placing his his hands on her shoulders. "I share your concern, Senator. You cannot imagine my relief when I was informed that Sydney had been found."

"You received word?" Jack asked. "From whom, if I may ask?"

"I hired a private detective agency to look for Sydney. They had her apartment under constant surveillance."

Jack looked at Sydney. "Can you tell me where you were, honey?"

"No." She shook her head, reaching up to touch Adrian's hand on her shoulder.

"But—" Jack stammered and looked up at Adrian. "Then perhaps you can tell me."

"I have no idea, sir. Sydney has been reluctant to speak of where she was."

"This is crazy!" Jack exploded and jumped to his feet. "You have us scared out of our minds, thinking that something dreadful's happening to you then you just show up out of the blue and refuse to even tell us where you were? Do you have any inkling of the hell you put us— "

"I don't know where I was!" Sydney shouted. She felt as if walls were closing in around her all at once, suffocating her. "Please." Her voice fell to almost a whisper. "Please don't ask me anymore. I can't tell...I can't talk…"

Jack dropped down to one knee beside her and took her hand in his. "I'm sorry, it's just that I was so worried. We didn't know if you were alive or dead or if something horrible had happened or —"

"Yes," she whispered.

"Yes?"

"Something horrible happened." Pent-up emotions suddenly exploded to the surface and she gasped at the gripping pain that seemed to consume her. "They... they hurt−" she tried to talk through the flood of tears and sobs that wracked her. "they−they did things...I−I... wanted...I wanted to...die."

A scream tore from her throat and she bolted to her feet, throwing herself in Adrian's arms and burying her face in his chest. He wrapped his arms around her and held her close, looking over her head at Jack who was standing up with a look of confusion and anger stamped on his face.

"I think it might be best if Sydney rested now," Adrian said quietly. "She has obviously been through some kind of terrible trauma. Perhaps you could postpone your visit until she is feeling stronger."

"No," Jack refused. "I think it would be best if you gave me some time alone with my daughter."

"I do not think that is wise."

"And I really don't care!" Jack snapped and reached out to touch Sydney on the back. "Syd, honey?"

She turned to look at him, wiping her eyes with her fingers. "Honey, I just want to talk, all right?"

Sydney looked over at GW for a moment. He was the one she really wanted to talk to. But she could not say that in front of Adrian or her father. For a moment she did not speak then she looked at Adrian. "I'm all right now. I'm sorry I fell apart like that, but I'm fine now. And I want to talk with my father. If you don't mind."

"Of course," he agreed. "I have some things to attend to. If you need me ring me in my study."

"Thank you." She tilted her face up for his kiss.

Sydney watched Adrian leave then turned and took a seat, pulling her chair up close to the table. "Why don't you sit beside Mr. Armand?" she suggested to her father. If he was sitting beside GW then she could talk to GW without it appearing as if she were directing the conversation at him.

Surprise registered in her mind as she realized she was still trying to protect GW's cover. That made confusion rise. Protecting GW's cover was also protecting Blake. *Why would I protect Blake? He's the enemy. I should be interested in exposing him instead of covering for him. God, what's wrong with me?*

"Sydney?" Jack reached across the table for her hand.

She drew her hands back out of his reach and looked at GW. "I went with Blake to Virginia for the night. On the way, a van load of men attacked us. Blake told me to run but I hid and I heard him talking to the men. They were saying something about him living up to his end of the bargain. After it was all over I asked him about it and he said he didn't know what the men were talking about. He brought me home Friday morning. He knew I was planning on going away with Adrian for the weekend and he wasn't happy about it but I was going anyway."

She paused to collect her thoughts. "I was in the apartment and the doorbell rang. I answered it and a man was there, saying he was Adrian's driver and was going to take me to the yacht, that Adrian would meet me there. When I got in the car there was another man. I didn't get a good look at him. He stabbed me in the neck with a hypo and the next thing I knew I..."

Sydney didn't know if she could tell the rest of it. She looked into GW's eyes and saw how concerned and anxious he was. "Please, Syd," he whispered. "Let me help."

She nodded and looked down at the table as she began to speak. "I woke in a room that was white. Everything was white concrete. There was no furniture—nothing. I –I don't remember everything.

"Light - bright, blinding light . . . heat . . . suffocating heat then cold, water raining down on me. Sometimes it was black. No light at all. I didn't know how long I had been there. They wouldn't let me sleep then they would gas me and knock me out and wake me up - over and over. I lost track of time. It seemed to . . . it seemed to stop. Time. Time stopped."

"Then..." She took a deep breath to steel herself. "Then the pain started. They—they strapped us down to these tables and used– used electric things...they..."

She wrapped her arms around herself as she began to shake. "I'm sorry... I can't. I just can't."

GW looked at Jack then back at Sydney. "How did you get away?"

"I don't know," she replied tiredly. "I was. He was...I don't know. One moment there was nothing but pain and the next I was waking up, dressed in the clothes I had left home in Friday, sitting on a path at the National Arboretum."

"Why didn't you call me?" Jack asked. "Or GW?"

"Or Blake?" GW added softly.

Sydney jerked her head up to pin him with a cold stare. "He is the enemy." She heard her own voice say the words in a cold, emotionless monotone, unable to stop herself.

GW's eyes grew round and he leaned back in his seat, staring at her in shock. She didn't blink or move a muscle. All that was in her mind at that moment was that Blake was the enemy. He was the one to be afraid of. He wanted her dead because she knew too much and only Adrian could save her.

"Sydney?" Jack touched her hand on the table. "Honey? What is it? Why is Blake the enemy?"

"He wants to kill me," she said in the same emotionless tone, like she was speaking by rote.

"Wants to kills you?" Weasel blurted. "That's crazy! He loves you! He'd never do anything to—"

"He is involved with the people who are responsible for the bombing." She interrupted in the same flat monotone.

Weasel's eyes narrowed as he regarded her. For several long seconds no one spoke. Then Weasel leaned forward slightly meeting Sydney's eyes and holding the gaze. "What makes you think that, Syd? I was under the impression that Tyler told you himself it was—well, you know, someone else."

"I… " She paused, trying to think clearly. She could remember Tyler being at her apartment and telling her to get away from Adrian. He so much as told her that Adrian was the man responsible. But somewhere along the way she had gotten other information; information that led her to think it was Blake that was behind everything. She couldn't remember where she had gotten the information or who had told her. "I must have—I guess I made a mistake."

"A mistake?" her father asked. "Are you telling me that we've been going along with this scheme to try and frame Adrian Zayne for something he didn't do?"

"Adrian has not done anything." Her voice reverted to a monotone.

Jack and Weasel looked at one another for a moment then Weasel turned to Sydney. "Syd, why don't you let us take you to the hospital? It might be a good idea to get someone to look you over after—ell, you know, after what you've been through. Maybe they can help you get things straight in your head. You're probably just confused because of . . . "

"I am not confused!" She jumped up from her seat. "I know what I know and that's all there is to it! Why can't you just accept that we all made a mistake and trusted the wrong person? He's been fooling all of us. He made you think he was your friend and he . . . he made me think he loved me but all along he was just using us. And now that I know the truth he wants to eliminate me like some bug that flew into his car."

"That's not true," Weasel said calmly. "Sydney, you've been through a traumatic experience and it's enough to confuse you. Let us take you to−"

"I think you should leave now," she interrupted angrily. "I'll have someone show you out. Excuse me, I need to find Adrian."

"Sydney!" Jack started after her as she dashed inside the house. Weasel took his arm and stopped him. "Let her go. We're not getting anywhere this way. We'll have to come up with something to get her away from him."

"Such as?"

Weasel shook his head. "Not here. Come on, let's go."

Once inside the privacy of the car, Weasel looked at Jack. "Did you notice anything strange about her?"

Jack looked at him with an incredulous expression on his face. "Anything strange? Everything was strange! She doesn't even seem like my daughter anymore. God, GW, what was done to her?"

"Aside from torture, I think she's been programmed," Weasel replied. "You could tell from the way she'd go into some sort of trace-like state when she was asked certain things. She'd talk like she was some kind of automaton, repeating what she'd been rehearsed to say. I think we need to get her into a hospital and we need to do it fast. Also, we have to find Tyler and get him to tell us exactly what he told Sydney."

"Couldn't we just have her committed for psychiatric observation? I am her father, I could sign the papers?"

"I don't know," Weasel said as he started the car. "That's something we've got to find out."

"Then let's go!" Jack looked back at the house as they started to pull away. "I don't want to leave her there a moment longer than necessary."

Inside the house, Sydney was standing in front of the window in the living room, watching the car move down the driveway when Adrian walked in. "Did you have a nice visit with your father?"

She shook her head without responding. He walked up behind her and put his hands on her shoulders. She didn't tense at his touch as she once had. That pleased him. He had decided that Sydney was going to be a permanent fixture in his home and having her compliant made things much more uncomplicated.

Adrian was surprised that he wanted her as much as he did. He had expected to find that she no longer held appeal once she stopped running from him, but that had not happened. Instead, he found that he wanted her more than ever. He was unaccustomed to feeling that way about anyone. Up until now, people had been as disposable as any material item. Sydney was different. He could see spending the rest of his life with her by his side. It was an idea that pleased him. They would have everything and she would adore him and give him a son to whom he could pass on his fortune, his legacy.

Sydney turned from the window and looked up at him. He smiled and cupped her face in his hands. "Darling, I know this may seem a rather peculiar time to discuss this, but I simply can't wait any longer. I spoke to your father this past weekend and told him of my intentions and now I would like to declare those intentions to you."

A puzzled look took hold of her features and he smiled and kissed her. "I want you to marry me, Sydney."

"Marry you?" She looked at him in surprise.

"I love you," he said as he looked into her eyes. "More than I thought I could ever love anyone. I want you to be my wife."

Sydney blinked and stepped back. "I don't know what to say."

"That's the easy part," Adrian advanced on her. "Just say yes."

She did not say yes as he took her in his arms. But neither did she say no.

Wednesday, May 3

Alabama

Blake sat in the Sheriff's office in Huntsville with his head in his hands; elbows on the desk, staring in exasperation at the papers that lay in front of him.

Ray Watkins, the Sheriff; a tall, stocky man walked in. "Hell of a mess, ain't it, young fella?"

Blake looked up from reading. "That's a mild way of putting it."

Watkins chuckled, took a seat, lit a fat cigar and puffed furiously for a few seconds until he had the tip of the cigar glowing and smoking like a locomotive. "Well, that's how it goes. Win a few, lose a few and sometimes break even. Don't get your shorts in a wad over it. Hell, boy, the whole damn county's in a tail-spin over that Ohio thing. Anybody could've made the mistake you did."

"You want to put that in writing for the director of my division?" Blake asked.

Watkins laughed and shook his head. "Nope, like I my daddy always liked to say, shit don't stink near as bad if you don't stir it."

"Meaning?" Blake asked.

"Meaning this is your pile, young man. I got enough trouble of my own without taking on any of yours."

"Well, thanks for your help, Sheriff," Blake gathered up his papers and stood. "Sorry it was all for nothing."

Watkins shook Blake's hand enthusiastically. "Not for nothing. It was pretty exciting around here for a minute."

Blake just stared at him. He wouldn't describe the fiasco they'd just gone through as exciting. In fact the only word he could find to adequately describe it was 'disaster.' He had no doubt that his superiors would be able to find a lot more colorful words.

"I'll be getting out of your way. Thanks again," he said and left the office. He walked outside and looked up at the clear sky. *Better enjoy it while you can,* he thought to himself as he started for the rental car. *The storm's going to hit soon enough.*

Blake stared the car and headed for the airport. There was no need to stay the night. The entire operation had been for nothing. The only thing that was going on at the Rogers' farm was an old man trying to hang on the only way he knew how.

Blake's team had apparently not dug deep enough or they would have discovered that the Rogers' farm had been sold to Adrian Zayne. It turned out that Rogers' son, Byron, worked for Zayne. As the elder Rogers told it, Zayne found out that they were in trouble and that the bank was about to foreclose and had offered to buy the farm and let

272

them work it, giving Rogers fifty-percent of the profits each year to apply toward buying back the farm at no interest.

Needless to say, it made Blake, the agents from the Birmingham offices of the FBI and the ATF look like complete fools when they had raided the farm only to find out that the most dangerous thing going on there was Mrs. Rogers' white gravy and biscuits.

Blake knew Adrian had manipulated him. He had set everything up and Blake had fallen for it. Now all that was left to do was go back to Washington with pie on his face and try to explain it.

Washington, D.C.

It was the middle of the afternoon when Weasel and Jack Forrest arrived at Adrian Zayne's Maryland estate. Weasel gave their names to the attendant on duty at the gate, then waited as the man walked back inside the glass and stone enclosed cubicle to pick up the phone and call the main house. A few moments later the gate began to swing open and the man stepped outside to inform them they could enter.

"Well, we made it past the first obstacle," Weasel commented as he drove up the long, curving drive toward the house.

Jack sat rigidly in the seat, clutching an envelope in his hand. Inside was a court order allowing him to have his daughter committed for psychiatric observation. Getting it had not been easy. He'd had to call in a lot of favors and even then it had been touch and go for a while. Since Sydney was no minor, nor financially dependent on Jack for her livelihood, it had required a bending of certain rules in order to get the judge to go along with him.

Weasel stopped the car in front of the house and got out as a valet approached the car. Jack stuffed the envelope in the inside breast pocket of his jacket then got out of the car and started up the steps with Weasel. They were greeted at the front door before either of them had a chance to ring the bell. Adrian Zayne opened the door, smiling and exuberant. "Senator Forrest, Mr. Armand! What a delightful surprise."

"I'd like to see my daughter," Jack said tensely, paying no attention to the man who walked out of the house behind Adrian.

"Of course," Adrian agreed. "She is waiting for you in the conservatory. Unfortunately, I will not be able to join you. I was just on my way out."

"Perhaps another time," Jack said impatiently. "May we go in?"

273

Adrian gestured toward the house with a smile. Jack walked inside without another word and Weasel followed him, giving Adrian and the man with him a curious look.

"I'm here to see my daughter." Jack said to the maid who was waiting inside.

"This way, please."

"Did that guy look familiar to you?" Weasel whispered to Jack as the maid led the way through the house. "I know I've seen him somewhere before but I can't place him."

Jack shook his head. "I don't care who he was. I just want to get my daughter out of here!"

Weasel didn't press the issue, but it nagged at him. He knew he had seen that man somewhere. The maid stopped at the door to the conservatory. "May I offer you gentlemen something to drink?"

"No." Jack brushed past her.

"Thanks anyway, " Weasel said with a smile as he followed the Senator into the enormous, glass walled room that was filled with lush green plants and artfully designed natural settings of pools and waterfalls.

Sydney was sitting on a low stone bench in front of a well-stocked koi pond, picking petals from a long-stemmed white rose and letting them fall into the water. She looked up as Jack walked up behind her.

"Hello, Dad." Her voice was soft and calm, a stark contrast to the day before when she had been alternately emotionless and terrified.

"Sydney, honey," Jack sat down beside her. "I want you to go with me somewhere."

"Where?" she asked, turning her attention back to plucking the few remaining petals from the rose.

Jack glanced back at Weasel who walked over and knelt down beside Sydney. "Syd, I know it's been really rough for you the past few days and we're not trying to make it worse, but your dad and I both think you should be checked out to make sure everything's okay."

"You mean go to a hospital," she stated rather than asking. "You think I've lost it and made up all that about being abducted, don't you?"

"No." Weasel shook his head. "We believe you. That's why it's so important for you to go with us. Syd, you're a doctor. You know that what you went through is enough to scar anyone, emotionally and mentally. Plus, you need to find out if there was any permanent physical damage done."

"I don't need a hospital," she said calmly. "I appreciate you worrying about me, GW, but I'm fine. I have everything I need and I don't—"

"Syd, try to think like a physician for a minute," Weasel interrupted. "If we could change places what would you recommend I do?"

She dropped the bare stem to the ground and looked at him. "You know what I'd do."

"Then as your friend I'm asking you to please use that advice for yourself," he pleaded. "Just let us take you to the hospital and once you've been checked out then we can take you home or—"

"I'd rather not," she refused.

"Then I have no choice," Jack spoke up and pulled the envelope from his pocket. "Sydney, I don't like doing this but you leave me no other choice. Either you come with us of your own accord or I'll call the police and have them come and take you. I have a signed order from the court that you be committed for a complete examination and psychological observation."

"You'd have me committed?" She turned to him in surprise. "My own father and you'd have me locked up just to get me away from Adrian?"

"It doesn't have anything to do with Adrian. Can't you understand that I'm worried about you? I just want to be sure that you're okay and if you won't be responsible enough to take the necessary steps then I will."

"Adrian won't allow you to take me," she said defiantly.

"He can't stop us." Jack tapped the envelope against his leg.

Sydney looked from her father to Weasel. "You'd really go along with this?"

"If it's the only way. So, what's it going to be?"

She looked away, staring at the fish in the clear pond for a long time then abruptly stood up. "Fine, let's get this over with."

Weasel started after her as she walked passed him but she stopped and looked back at him. "And when this is over, we're over too, understand? A friend would never betray me like this."

His mouth dropped open in surprise. In all the years he had known Sydney she had never acted like that. No matter what happened, he had always known that their friendship could survive anything. For her to suddenly turn on him told him clearer than anything that something was very wrong with her.

"If that's what you want," he agreed.

"It is." She turned away. "Now, let's get this over with. I want to be here when Adrian gets back. We have plans."

Thursday, May 4

Washington, D.C.

Jack Forrest stood as the doctor entered the waiting room. Weasel closed his laptop and rose as the doctor started speaking.

"Senator, I'm afraid that the news is not encouraging."

Weasel looked at Jack to see the color drain from his face. "Exactly what do you mean by not encouraging?" Jack asked shakily.

The doctor, a specialist brought in by the FBI to examine Sydney glanced briefly at Weasel. They were not strangers. Severl years ago a case Weasel helped break involved several people who had been taken hostage. Doctor Harrell had been brought in on that case. That was when they had met. During the years since then they had stayed in touch.

"Let's have it," Weasel said quietly. "All of it."

"Very well. As you know, Senator, the staff physicians and psychiatrists suspected from the initial examination that your daughter had been subjected to both physical and psychological torture. That's why Mr. We'zel requested that I be brought in. I've had some experience with this type of thing."

"Just what are you getting at?" Jack's voice was not as strong and hearty as normal.

Doctor Harrell made himself more comfortable in his seat. "Let me explain. Your daughter has been subjected to what is commonly referred to as brainwashing or 'thought reform.' Essentially, even though methods and techniques vary, the end result desired is to force someone to change his or her beliefs, for example, to accept as true what they had previously believed to be false."

"And you think that's what's been done to Sydney?" Jack looked like he was going to be sick. "Can you tell what they did to her?"

"From what we have been able to determine thus far, it would seem someone followed a fairly standard procedure," the doctor replied. "You see, most brainwashing will begin by isolating the victim in a cell or room where they are starved, deprived of sleep, drugged and even tortured. This type of mental and physical torment will eventually cause most people to give up their own beliefs and accept the ideas and beliefs their persecutors want them to."

"She was put in a prison?" Jack shook his head in confusion. "Are you telling me that she was locked up somewhere and–"

"Actually," the doctor interrupted, "we are not sure exactly what happened. She has been less than willing to discuss much of what happened to her. All we've learned from questioning is that she was hurt by something electric and that there was apparently another woman there."

"So how do we get to the truth?" Weasel asked.

"Most victims will return to their own beliefs after a period of time," Doctor Harrell said. "However, that period of time varies dependent upon the techniques used and length of time the victim was imprisoned. It is my belief that our best course of action at this point is to try a form of regression therapy; to get her to remember what happened. If we can determine what was done to her it will give us a better idea of how to treat her."

Jack nodded. "So, do it."

"She seems less than agreeable to the suggestion, sir. And without either her or her husband's permission, I am hesitant to continue."

"Her husband?" Weasel blurted. "What does Evan Mallory have to do with anything? They've been divorced for . . . "

"I was referring to her present husband," Harrell cut in. "Mr. Adrian Zayne."

Weasel's mouth worked for a moment, opening and closing, with no sound emerging. "Zayne?" he finally managed to croak. "What makes you think she's married to Adrian Zayne?"

"She told me she and Mr. Zayne were married yesterday at his house in Maryland by a Judge Beckford."

"Beckford!" Weasel jumped up and looked at Jack. "That's who that was at the house! I knew I'd seen that guy before. Damn! He married her just minutes before we got there!"

"Can't you do the hypnosis anyway?" Jack asked. "I mean if she's been brainwashed then can't you just say she's unstable or something and . . ."

"I would need a reason to proceed," Harrell looked at Weasel pointedly.

Weasel blew out his breath and jammed his hands in his pockets, staring up at the ceiling for a few seconds. Then he turned to Harrell. "Okay, you need a reason, you've got one. Sydney Forrest was working as a civilian for Blake Edwards, Special Agent with the bureau. One of her patients came to her with information that ties Adrian Zayne with the bombing of the federal building in Akron, Ohio. She was our informant, trying to get information on Zayne to use in the case against him. If she's been brainwashed there's a good possibility that Zayne's behind it. His marrying her just hours before we arrived with the court order to have her admitted for observation suggests that he's trying to cover his tracks. After all, as her husband he has the final say if she's incapable of making her own decisions. Add to the that the fact that as his wife she can refrain from testifying against him and you have one hell of a reason."

"I still need clearance," Harrell said. "From the agent in charge."

"That'd be Blake Edwards."

"Then get him here and we'll proceed." Harrell stood. "Until then all I can do is keep her here for observation. But only for another twenty-four hours."

Weasel nodded and picked up his computer, setting it inside the case and closing it. "I'll have him here no later than this afternoon."

Jack stood up as Weasel started out of the room. "GW?"

Weasel stopped and looked back. "What if she was telling the truth? What if it wasn't Adrian? What if it's really—"

"No way!" Weasel cut him off, not wanting him to voice in front of Harrell the accusations Sydney had made against Blake. "Trust me on this one, Jack. I'll get Blake here and then we'll get the truth."

Jack nodded tiredly. "I hope you're right."

"I am," Weasel said confidently then turned and left the room. He had no doubt about Blake's innocence. He just hoped that after the fiasco in Alabama and the new information he had dug up he and Blake both did not end up looking the wrong direction through prison bars.

◌

Blake walked into Doctor Harrell's office with Weasel. "Doctor Harrell, I'm Blake Edwards. I understand you needed to see me."

"Yes, Mr. Edwards," Harrell walked around his desk to shake Blake's hand. "Please, won't you have a seat?"

Blake and Weasel took seats as Harrell picked up a file from his desk and pulled a paper from it. "As I'm sure GW has explained, in order to proceed with the hypnosis session with Mrs. Zayne, I need official clearance. As the agent in charge this permission must come from you."

Blake was still reeling from the news that Sydney and Adrian Zayne were married. He felt like someone had kicked him in the stomach when Weasel told him and even now he had a dull ache in his midsection like his insides were twisted into a knot.

"Where do I sign?"

Doctor Harrell put the paper down on the desk and indicated where Blake's signature was required. Blake scrawled his name and stood. "I'd like to see Mrs. Zayne before you proceed, Doctor. There are a few questions I need to ask her."

"I'm not sure you'll get any answers."

"I still want to see her."

"Very well." Harrell put the signed paper back in the folder. "I'll take you to her."

"Mind if I tag along?" Weasel asked. "I haven't seen her since we brought her in."

Blake nodded and they followed Doctor Harrell to the elevator. They got off on the psychiatric floor and were led to a private room. Doctor Harrell stopped at the door. "She's been sedated so she may be a bit groggy for a while longer. Try not to upset her. I'll set up the session."

Blake pushed the door open and entered the room. Sydney was lying on her back on the bed; her arms strapped securely to the bed rails. He turned and looked at Weasel but found no comfort in his friend's dark eyes.

"Syd?" Blake said softly as he sat down in the chair beside the bed. "Can you hear me?"

"Adrian?" she asked without opening her eyes.

"No." Blake felt a pang of hate for Zayne stab at him but tried to keep it out of his voice. "It's Blake."

Sydney's eyes flew open wild and frightened. "What are you doing here?" she whispered in a strained voice, tugging to free her arms from the restraints.

Blake could not believe how afraid she was. "Syd, calm down. I'm not going to hurt you."

"I haven't said anything.I swear. I haven't told anyone. I won't tell them. I promise. No one has to know it was you. Just leave me alone. I won't tell, I promise. Please, don't let them hurt me anymore. Please—"

Her words were choked off by sudden crying. Blake stared at her in shocked silence. *What's happened to her?* He asked himself. *What's she carrying on about?*

"Sydney, you don't have to be afraid," he tried to speak soothingly. "No one's going to hurt you. I'm here to make sure you're all right. I just need to know what happened. Can you tell me—"

A hysterical laugh cut him off. "Here to make sure?" her voice was a shriek. "Here to make sure what? That I don't tell anyone what you let those men do to me? How they —"

"What is going on here?" Adrian's angry voice cut her words short. "What are you doing to my wife?" He demanded of Blake.

"I'm simply trying to talk to her." Blake stood to face Adrian.

"Well, it's obvious to me that she has no interest in talking with you, so I suggest you leave."

"Or what?" Blake asked with rising anger. "You'll call the cops? Try again, Zayne. I'm the one in charge here. This is an official investigation and unless you suddenly have higher rank than I with the bureau, you'll button it up and stay out of my way, or I'll have you removed. You got it?"

280

"Get away from my wife." Adrian stepped closer. "Or I'll move you myself."

"You can try." Blake barked. He'd like nothing better than to have Zayne take a swing at him. That would give him the perfect excuse to beat him to a pulp.

Adrian started towards Blake. Weasel jumped between them, holding up his hands in a placating manner. "Hey, this is very uncool, dudes. Why don't we– "

"Get out of my way!" Adrian shoved Weasel, causing him to topple over backwards on the bed, on top of Sydney's legs. Then he took a swing at Blake.

The blow never landed. Blake saw it coming and deflected it with his forearm, countering with a solid punch to the face. Adrian's head whipped back but he righted himself in moments and came at Blake. Weasel was pushing himself upright and Sydney was just lying in bed, staring at the two men fighting as if she were in a trance.

"I'll see you rot in jail, you sorry– " Blake's sentence ended in a grunt as Adrian kicked him in the mid-section.

"You're the one who'll be imprisoned!" Adrian countered. "After what you've done to my wife, you deserve to die!"

Blake delivered an uppercut to Adrian's chin, sending him reeling backwards. "You lying bastard!"

"Lie?" Adrian started towards him. "That's funny coming from you. How many lies have you told? How many women have you tortured like you tortured Sydney and Sheila? How many, Mr. Edwards? Lost count?"

Blake struck out in rapid succession, landing three blows. But Adrian did not stop coming. He issued a hard blow to Blake's stomach, followed by a low front-kick. Blake's breath whooshed out and he stumbled back, with Adrian advancing on him.

The noise drew the attention of a nurse who ran in the room to see the fight that was taking place. She ran out of the room at full tilt, shouting for someone to call security. Weasel pushed himself off the bed and tried to get between the two men. Unfortunately his timing was bad. He stepped right in front of a punch Blake was throwing at Adrian. Blake's fist met the side of Weasel's head and sent him crashing back into the bed and pushing it halfway across the room.

The table beside the bed overturned as Adrian slammed into Blake, ramming him into it. The plastic water pitcher spilled crushed ice and water all over the floor, making both men slip and slide as they battled. Weasel pushed off the bed and tried to grab Adrian but succeeded only in losing his footing on the slick floor and falling. Adrian tripped over him which gave Blake the advantage. He grabbed Adrian by the hair of his head and jerked up. As soon as Adrian's face turned up, Blake slammed him with two quick punches.

Adrian roared and jabbed his fist into Blake's stomach, breaking Blake's hold. Adrian stood and dove at Blake just as the door to the room opened and two security guards ran in. Blake had his back to the door and did not see them until one of them grabbed him in a choke hold around the neck and ordered an end to the fight.

Adrian straightened his tie and brushed back his hair. "Officer, I think perhaps you should place a call to this man's superior at the Federal Bureau of Investigation. He just attacked me while I was visiting my wife."

Blake jerked away from the security guard and pulled his identification from his pocket. "Special agent Blake Edwards. This is a federal matter. I'm going to have to ask you to leave."

"I think maybe we should all leave," Weasel suggested and nodded his head in Sydney's direction. She was looking around blankly as if she were in a stupor.

Blake looked at her in concern. She seemed totally removed from what had just happened. There was something very wrong with her. He realized that the best thing he could do at that moment was to follow Weasel's suggestion and get doctor Harrell to start the hypnosis as soon as possible,

He nodded at Weasel then turned to the guards. "Gentlemen, why don't we step outside?"

One guard opened the door and led the way. The other waited until Blake and Weasel had left the room then spoke to Adrian who had by then gone to sit on the edge of Sydney's bed. "Sir?"

"I think I should remain with my wife," Adrian said. "Please have someone call her doctor. She seems to be in some type of shock."

The guard nodded and left the room, informing his partner that he was going to find Mrs. Zayne's doctor. Inside the room, Adrian loosened the restraints on Sydney's wrists and pulled her up into his arms. She came unresisting.

"My poor darling," he whispered, stroking her hair. "That Edwards chap is obviously quite insane. Imagine him coming here after all he's already done to you."

Sydney closed her eyes as she sat with her head against Adrian's chest, listening to him. The fight he had just had with Blake had confused her. Both of them seemed so sincere in their accusations of the other. But one of them had to be lying. The trouble was, she didn't know which one it was. She was still afraid of Blake but watching him fight she had been seized with the feeling that he was somehow fighting for her. It didn't make any sense.

Suddenly she became attentive and alert. Something Adrian was saying made her mind shift gears. " . . . all that abuse and torture. It cuts into my soul knowing the fear you had to endure at the hands of those cold-hearted men in white, my darling. If I could find them I would kill them with my bare hands."

Sydney's eyes flew open. How could he have known the men were wearing white? She had not told Adrian that. Then it dawned on her that he had referred to the other woman she had seen while she was being held. She knew she had never mentioned the woman's name. And yet Adrian knew it. But how?

Some of the fog that had been clouding her mind dissipated and she felt a tightening in her chest. Adrian pulled back from her and she lowered her eyes. "I don't want to talk to any more doctors," she whispered. She was beginning to realize that the answers didn't lie in talking about what had happened. There was nothing that could be done about what had happened and she could not find answers in the hospital. She had to get out.

"Please," she looked up at him. "Do something so I don't have to talk to them, Adrian. I just want to go home."

"I will see to it," he said and leaned over to kiss her.

Sydney smiled slightly as he stood up. "Will you be back?"

"As soon as I have taken care of things."

She nodded and watched him leave the room. Only moments later the sound of raised voices in the hall could be heard. She got out of bed and went over to the door, listening to what was being said. She heard Blake tell Adrian that he had no choice. The session would talk place, by order of the FBI. Adrian threatened to go over Blake's head and Blake told him to go ahead.

Sydney jumped back in bed just a moment before the door opened and Blake walked in with Weasel. "Doctor Harrell will be here shortly. He's going to regress you so that you can remember what happened. I want you to cooperate with him."

"There's no need," she said without emotion. "I remember what happened."

"Then I want to know," he said as he crossed the room to her.

She shrank away from him as he reached for her hand. She couldn'tt help it. Part of her still did not trust him. But she nodded. "All right."

Blake looked at Weasel. "You want to record this on your phone?"

Weasel nodded. Blake picked up the overturned chair and put it beside the bed.. "Are you ready?" he asked Sydney as he took a seat.

She nodded and he nodded to GW who stood behind him. "Start recording."

Sydney looked at him and then Weasel, closed her eyes and started to talk. "I was at my apartment. I had just left you in the parking lot a few minutes earlier and gone inside. The doorbell rang and there was a man there who said he had come to take me to Adrian's yacht. I went down to the car with him and . . . "

Almost two hours later her voice was reduced to a hoarse whisper. "Then I got a taxi and went home. You know the rest."

Blake motioned for GW to end the recording and closed his eyes for a moment. The things she had told him made him both sick and enraged. He couldn't imagine the pain she had endured or the terror she had been put through. That made him mad enough to kill. The part that sickened him was her thinking that he was the one who had put the men up to what they did. It tore at his heart that she had been made to believe that he was responsible for her pain. But in her story was the key. The fact that she had been led to name Adrian Zayne as her savior told him that someone had worked very hard to turn her against him and send her running to Adrian.

"May I ask you a personal question?"

She looked at him for a moment. "What?"

"Why did you marry him?"

"I don't think you have the right to ask that. My personal life is none of your business anymore. Now, if you don't mind, I'd like to see my doctor. Unless there's something more you need from me."

"No," Blake stood. "That's all for now."

She looked away from him, refusing to turn back until he had left the room. Then she slumped back against the pillows. Talking about what had happened had both exhausted and freed her. It also had made her question things she had not bothered to question up until now.

But she still was not going to trust Blake. Just like she was no longer going to trust Adrian. In fact, until she could find some answers she was going to trust no one but herself.

❧

Blake stopped just outside the security door and drew in a long breath. After a moment he exhaled and swiped his card through the reader. The door latch released and he pushed open the door. Weasel followed him to his office. They had just walked inside when the door opened and Steve Greenland looked in. "Director of the Criminal Division wants to see the two of you in his office. Now. Donaldson, Peters, Roberts and Turner are already there."

Blake nodded. Fastening the top button on his shirt, he straightened his tie and followed Steve out. "I guess you heard?" he asked as they walked down the long corridor.

"Yeah."

"You catch any flack?"

Steve shrugged. "Aside from losing Tyler and not being able to locate him I'm not exactly in the loop. So, my fat behind is relatively safe." He stopped at the director's door. "I wish I could say the same for you."

Blake watched him walk off then knocked on the door. A muffled directive from inside directed him to enter.

"Sir?" Blake stopped just inside the door with Weasel behind him.

The director of the criminal division, Ross Braswell looked in his direction. "Have a seat."

Blake and Weasel took a seat. Blake looked at the other four agents who were staring straight ahead as if their eyes were glued in place. "Do you have any idea the amount of time and money you've wasted on this - investigation, agent Edwards?"

"Yes, sir," Blake answered. "According to my calculations, this investigation has cost the bureau . . . "

"I'm not interested in your calculations!" Braswell cut him off. "What I am interested in is seeing this entire matter put to a rest. To that end, I now ask you. Is there any reason - any at all that I should not stop this operation right now?"

"Yes, sir, there is," Blake answered with conviction.

"Then by all means, enlighten me," Braswell leaned back in his chair and stared coldly at Blake.

Taking a slow breath, Blake stood and started to talk. A long time ago one of his law professors had written that he had the uncanny ability to make people believe what he said was what they believed as well. Blake hoped that he still had just a little bit of that ability left. Because if he could not convince the director to have Adrian brought in, his case was ashes in the wind.

THE TERRITORY OF LIES

Chapter Twelve

Friday, May 5

Washington, D.C.

Doctor Harrell finished signing Sydney's discharge papers then looked at her as she ran a brush through her hair. "I still think it would be in your best interest to see a therapist, Mrs. Zayne. After what you've been through there are bound to be residual–"

"I know," Sydney stopped brushing her hair as she interrupted. "I'm a psychiatrist, remember? And I'll consider it, Doctor Harrell. But right now all I want to do is go home. So, unless there's something more we need to discuss, I'd like to call and have someone come for me."

"No, there's nothing else," he replied and extended his hand to her. "I wish you all the best, Mrs. Zayne."

"Thank you." She gave him a quick smile as she shook his hand.

He left the room and she turned to reach for the phone. Just as she was lifting the receiver the door opened. Weasel walked in, followed by Blake. Sydney cradled the receiver and looked at them coolly. "This is a surprise."

"We have orders to take you to headquarters for questioning in the investigation of your husband, Adrian Zayne." Blake's words were spoken in a brusque manner.

She looked from him to Weasel. "Has Adrian been arrested?"

"He's been asked to come in for questioning," Weasel replied and walked to her. "Syd, you have to come with us. You played a part in this from the start and–"

"I understand," she cut him off. "Am I under arrest?"

"No." Blake shook his head. "There's no law against stupidity."

Sydney's brows rose and a pink flush stained her skin. "Just what do you mean by that?"

"You tell me, Mrs. Zayne." His words were clipped and hostile.

She opened her mouth to retort but decided against it. There was no point in getting into an argument over her marriage to Adrian. And there was nothing she could say that would make Blake understand. She picked up her purse and looped the strap over her shoulder. "I'm ready."

Without another word Blake opened the door and held it for her. She followed Weasel out. At the Hoover building she was taken to what looked like a conference room. Inside were three men, seated at one end of a massive table. They stood as she entered with Blake and Weasel.

"Mrs. Zayne." A stocky man with light brown hair and sun-weathered skin stepped forward. "My name is Ross Braswell. I'm the director of the Criminal Division. This is deputy Frank Wright of the Justice Department and Inspector Mark Daniels of the FBI."

Sydney nodded to each man in turn. "Please, have a seat." Director Braswell indicated to a chair at the table.

She took a seat at the end of the table on the opposite side of the director. Weasel sat down beside her and Blake took the chair beside Weasel.

"Mrs. Zayne." The director looked up from a notepad on the desk in front of him. "Before the others arrive, I'd like to talk with you about the information you received from Senator Ned Tyler concerning—"

He was interrupted by someone opening the door. "Sir?" A dark-suited man looked in. "Mr. Zayne and his . . . representatives are here."

Sydney turned toward the door as Adrian walked in, followed by half a dozen people. Adrian walked over and leaned down to kiss Sydney on the cheek. "Darling, I had no idea they would drag you into this. I'm so sorry."

"That's okay," she murmured, wondering what in the world his entourage was up to. They were moving around the room, setting up large artists easels, televisions and video equipment and taking stacks of bound folders from briefcases.

Adrian looked at the head of the table where director Braswell sat. "Adrian Zayne," he said and inclined his head slightly.

"Ross Braswell. May I ask just what this is all about, Mr. Zayne?" Braswell gestured to the people who were busy setting up their equipment.

"I was under the impression that you had some interest in my involvement with Senator Ned Tyler," Adrian replied with a smile.

Braswell frowned. "I fail to see what this has to do with the Senator, Mr. Zayne."

Adrian took a seat at the opposite end of the table. "Director Braswell, we are both busy men, with little time to waste. I felt it would be expedient to bring my people with me so that we can clear up this unfortunate misunderstanding that your agent Edwards seems to have precipitated."

Braswell looked at Blake for a moment then back at Adrian. "You do understand the nature of the accusations being brought against you?"

"Of course," Adrian said. "Agent Edwards seems to have the misguided notion that I am somehow responsible for the hideous events that took place in Akron."

"You have been associated with Senator Ned Tyler, have you not?" Wright, from the Justice Department asked.

"Yes, I have," Adrian answered and held up his hand as Wright started to speak again. "If you will indulge me for a few minutes, I think I can clear this unfortunate misunderstanding up to everyone's satisfaction."

Wright looked at Braswell and Braswell nodded. "Very well, Mr. Zayne. Proceed."

Adrian stood up. "As all of you here are aware, over the past few years the military budget has been consistently cut, year after year. There are those in this country who believe this to be a profound and possibly dangerous mistake. "

He moved to one side of the room to stand between a television that had been set up and a large display easel. "Some time ago, at a charity function I had the opportunity to speak with Congressman Blackburn about this matter. He made a remark that he expected the military budget to be slashed again this year and thought it a mistake to weaken our military even more. A few weeks later, Congressman Blackburn came to my house with General Samuel Worth. We spoke again on the matter of the military budget and later that week I was invited to the White House to meet with the President. The statement was made that if the military had the support of the people, the house and senate might not be so eager to cut the budget. That gave me an idea."

He gestured to the television and the man beside it turned it on and started a video tape. Everyone watched as a series of advertisements played out, stressing the importance of a strong military, playing on the emotional impact by referring to past wars and the like. When the tape ended, Adrian pulled back the cover sheet on the large easel.

"As you can see, my advertising department has done quite a remarkable job in coming up with what I consider a brilliant advertising campaign." He flipped through the drawings, showing a variety of ads that would run in major publications, both newspaper and magazine. There were even audio ads for radio. Adrian waited until all of the advertising material had been shown then took his seat.

"It is no secret that lobbying takes place for one thing or another," he said as he looked around. "You might say that I have been acting in the role of a lobbyist in this particular matter. I contacted Senator Tyler concerning the military budget and he met with me, Congressman Blackburn and General Worth on several occasions to discuss the matter."

"And I suppose Congressman Blackburn and General Worth will back you up on this?" Deputy Wright asked.

Adrian smiled and gestured to the door. "Why don't you ask them yourself. They are just outside."

Wright looked at director Braswell in surprise. "Edwards!" Braswell barked. "See the gentlemen in."

Blake got up and opened the door. Just as Adrian had said Congressman Blackburn and General Worth were waiting outside. He asked them to come in. They entered and took seats after greeting Adrian and being introduced to everyone else. Deputy Wright asked them several questions, then director Braswell added a few of his own. Blake listened with an increasing sense of defeat. Within minutes the battle was over. He knew he had been outmaneuvered.

Braswell looked at Sydney. "Mrs. Zayne, I understand that you made audio recordings of sessions you had with Senator Tyler in which he claimed that Mr. Zayne and his associates were in fact, responsible for the bombing, and that he specifically told you that Mr. Zayne was responsible. Is that correct?"

"No, it is not." She looked directly at him.

"No you did not make any such recordings, or no Senator Tyler did not make those accusations?"

"I did make recordings."

"Will you voluntarily turn those over to me?"

"No, I can't do that."

"You can't or you won't?"

THE TERRITORY OF LIES

"I can't. I don't have them."

"Then where are they?"

"I destroyed them."

"And you have no written records or transcripts?"

"No sir."

"All right, let's move away from that for a moment. Did Senator Ned Tyler tell you, at any time that your husband was responsible for the bombing?"

"He told me he didn't think I should be involved with Adrian."

"Why is that?"

Sydney leaned forward and laced her hands together on the table in front of her. "Sir, Senator Tyler was, at the time, a very disturbed individual. Why he thought or said what he did during that time is hardly relevant. He was and is mentally ill. I'm sure you know that the Senator has tendered his resignation and is at the present institutionalized due to a complete nervous breakdown."

"Let's talk about this breakdown." The director referred to the report in front of him. "Is it not true that you falsified his records and that in fact, he did not suffer from any psychological problems?"

"No, it is not."

"And the institution where the Senator is confined?"

"That is privileged information."

"I could order you to provide me with the information."

"I suppose you could," she replied calmly. "However, the point is moot. The physicians caring for the Senator would give you the same diagnosis as I. He is suffering from a nervous breakdown and is not competent. Besides that, Senator Tyler never told me that Adrian was the one who bombed the federal building."

"What did the Senator say, specifically about Mr. Zayne?"

"That I shouldn't be involved with him."

"And you had no idea what his reasons were for saying that?"

"To be honest, I didn't put much stock in what the Senator thought I should do with my personal life. After all, sir, he's the one who was troubled. Not me. And if I may, I'd like to say that I resent all these accusations and innuendoes. My husband, as you can clearly see, has done nothing wrong. He merely supported a position he believes in. And as far as I know, there's no law against that."

"It was my understanding that it was initially your accusations against your husband that prompted agent Edwards to start this investigation, Mrs. Zayne."

Sydney looked straight at the director as he continued. "Is it not true that up until quite recently you had a relationship with agent Edwards?"

"Yes, that's true."

"And what was the nature of your relationship?"

"We dated."

"Dated. Nothing more?"

"Do you mean did I have sex with him?" she looked at him pointedly. "That's a little personal, but if it'll satisfy your curiosity then yes, I had sex with him."

"So you and agent Edwards were lovers?"

"I suppose so."

"Until when Mrs. Zayne?"

"Last Friday."

"The day you were abducted."

"That's correct."

"And when you miraculously returned from your ordeal, you suddenly ended the relationship. Is that correct?"

"Yes."

"Might I inquire as to why?"

"I realized that I loved Adrian and wanted to marry him.

"I see. Just like that, you decided you did not love one man and did love another."

"Yes."

"A bit sudden wasn't it, Mrs. Zayne?"

Sydney smiled at him. "Director Braswell, have you ever fallen hopelessly in love?" When he didn't reply she shook her head. "Then I suppose you wouldn't understand, would you?"

Braswell stared at her for a moment then looked at Blake. Sydney turned and saw Adrian watching her. As their eyes met he smiled at her. She dropped her eyes as the room resounded with silence.

After a moment, Braswell stood. "Mr. Zayne, I am sorry to have inconvenienced you. Please accept my sincere apologies. You are free to go."

Adrian stood as well. "There is one other thing I would like to discuss with you, if I may. In private."

Braswell frowned for a moment then nodded. "Please excuse us. Mr. Zayne?"

Adrian took a briefcase from one of his men as he followed the director from the room. Everyone else sat in tense silence for the next twenty minutes. The door opened and the director walked back in, carrying a folder in his hand. Adrian followed him with a smug smile on his face.

"Mrs. Zayne, if you would please remain. Agents Edwards and We'zel, you as well. The rest of you are free to leave. Thank you for your time and cooperation."

Everyone who had not been directed to stay left the room. Braswell opened the folder and took a black and white photo from it. "Do you know this man, agent Edwards?"

Blake took the photo that was slid across the table to him. It was a shot of him and the man who had identified himself as a general the day he was taken out in the boat on the Potomac. "I believe I covered this in my report, sir."

Braswell nodded. "And these men?"

Blake looked at the series of pictures. The men shown in them were the ones who had taken him to the river to meet with the man who called himself the general and several of the men who were on the boat. "As I said, this was all explained in my report, in the incident that took place in front of Doctor Forrest's office and later at the river."

"And you have no idea who these men are?"

"No sir."

Braswell picked up the phone on the table and dialed three digits. "Do you have the information? Please bring it in."

A few seconds later the door opened and a clerk walked in, handing the director a stack of papers. Braswell looked through them then looked up. "Thomas Harridan, age fifty-eight," he said as he held up a grainy black and white photo of the man that had identified himself as a general to Blake that day at the river. "Do you know who this man is, agent Edwards?"

"No sir."

Braswell read from one of the printouts. Blake felt a sinking sensation take hold of his stomach. The man was one of the leaders of a very active and often violent extremist group. "You have never seen this man before that day, agent Edwards?"

"No, sir."

Braswell picked up another photo. This one was of Sydney and a dark-haired man. The man was opening the door of a limousine for her. "This picture was taken on the day Mrs. Zayne was allegedly abducted. Do you recognize the man in the picture, agent Edwards?"

"No sir."

Braswell held another picture beside it. It was one of the shots of the bogus general and Blake on the boat. Behind Blake stood the dark-haired man from the picture with Sydney. Blake's eyes widened. It was the same man in both pictures.

Braswell put the pictures down and picked up a printout. "Agent Edwards, do you have a foreign bank account?"

"No sir."

"You have no banking interests in any institutions outside the continental United States?"

"No sir."

"Then how do you explain an account in your name with your social security number in the Grand Cayman's with a little over two million dollars in it?"

"Sir?" Blake could not believe what he was hearing.

"Do you deny knowledge of such an account, agent Edwards?"

"Yes, sir. I do."

Braswell looked at him then at Adrian. "Mr. Zayne, I want to personally speak with the detective agency that took these pictures. Beyond that, there is nothing further I need from you. You are free to leave and you may take your wife with you. Agent Edwards, you and agent We'zel will remain."

Adrian stood up and waited for Sydney to stand. She walked over to him and he held out his hand to her. She put her hand in his and he smiled down at her. Without looking back they left the room. Two agents escorted them down to the lobby. Adrian's driver was waiting outside with the car.

As soon as they were inside the car Adrian pulled her into his arms. "You have no idea how much it meant to me to hear you defend me the way you did, my darling."

She put her arms around him and held tightly to him. "What else could I do? You're my husband—my life."

Adrian smiled and crushed her against him. "Forever, my darling. You are mine until the end of time."

Sydney didn't reply but merely closed her eyes and reclined in his arms, listening to the inner voices in her own mind.

Weasel stared at some point across the room while Blake looked stone-faced at director Braswell. "You do realize the implications of this, don't you, agent Edwards?" Braswell asked as he stacked up the printouts and photos and returned them to the file folder.

"Yes, sir, I do. However, the information is false."

"There is no validity to the charges being made against you? Am I to understand that you are denying the allegations made against you?"

"Yes, sir. I most certainly do. That information is totally false. Obviously, Mr. Zayne has gone to some lengths to make it appear genuine but the fact remains that it is not."

"Then you will have no objections to an investigation being instituted in accordance with these allegations," Braswell said as he stood. "Until such time as this matter has been cleared up to my satisfaction, you are on leave of absence. I'll have to ask for your weapon and your identification."

Blake pulled his gun from the shoulder holster and put it on the table, along with his identification and security pass card. "I need not remind you that leaving the city, much less the country at this point in time would be viewed as a possible flight from justice, do I agent Edwards?"

"No sir."

Braswell nodded and started to walk away then stopped and looked once more at Blake. "Agent Edwards, you have an excellent record and I would personally hate to see it tarnished. I sincerely hope that the allegations made against you prove to be false."

"They will sir."

Braswell nodded and walked to the door. "Please escort Mr. Edwards to the exit. Agent We'zel, please report to your supervisor. I'm sure your talents can be put to good use."

Blake stood and looked at Weasel who finally stopped staring across the room and looked up at him. "I'll find the proof we need to clear you," Weasel said quietly. "You've got my word on that."

Blake forced himself to smile. "Thanks, buddy. I'll catch up with you later." He followed the agent stationed outside the door down the long corridor, trying not to notice the mixture of curious and suspicious looks he got from those he passed.

℣

It was a little after three in the afternoon when they arrived at Adrian's Maryland estate. The first thing Sydney did was plead fatigue and tell Adrian that she was going to go upstairs and lie down. He did not detain her but escorted her to the bedroom. She undressed, put on a short robe and took a bottle of pills from her purse.

"What's that?" Adrian asked as she shook one pill from the container.

"Just a mild sedative," she replied, putting the pill in her mouth and tucking it under her tongue as she poured a glass of water from the decanter on the dressing table and took a sip.

Adrian did not comment on the matter any further but kissed her and said that he would be downstairs in his study if she needed him. She smiled and told him she would be fine after a couple of hours sleep. As soon as he left the room she ran to the bathroom and spit the partially dissolved sedative into the toilet, watching it disappear as she flushed.

Now what? She asked herself as she walked back into the bedroom and sat down on the bed. After what she had heard in the meeting with the FBI she was more confused than ever. That confusion stemmed from the fact that her feelings were undergoing a metamorphosis. She no longer felt terrified of Blake. In fact, it seemed that the more time passed, the more she regained feelings that she thought had disappeared.

She attributed it to the fact that like most victims of brainwashing, after a period of time away from the control, the original feelings and beliefs began to resurface. She only wished that it had begun earlier, before she agreed to marry Adrian.

But maybe it's better this way, she considered. When she had spoken up in Adrian's defense at the meeting with the FBI he had been both surprised and delighted. She was sure that he now thought she was completely devoted to him and she wanted it to stay that way. At least until she discovered the truth. Now all she had to do was figure out how to find the truth.

Her stomach growled and she stood, remembering that she had barely eaten the last few days. She the bedroom she headed downstairs to see what she could find in the kitchen to snack on. To keep from being noticed she took the back stairs to the ground level. As she passed Adrian's study on her way she heard voices. One voice in particular made her stop and stare wide-eyed at the door.

"If there is ever a way in which I can be of service to you in the future, please contact me, Mr. Zayne." The emotionless voice of the man she had dubbed Monotone Man said.

Adrian chuckled. "I must say that for someone so unemotional, you certainly have a passion for your work. However, I do not think that I will be requiring your particular talents in the foreseeable future. I would suggest that you and your lovely companion take advantage of the opportunity to do a bit of traveling. The West Indies are delightful at this time of year. Perhaps a trip out of the country would be advisable."

A woman's giggle made Sydney inch closer to the partially opened door. As she peeked in the crack between the door and the frame she heard another familiar voice. "We put on a pretty good show, huh, honey? She thought for sure I was a goner with all that screaming and panting I was doing. You should have seen it, Mr. Zayne. I should have won an Oscar for that performance."

Adrian stood and gestured to the door. "Yes, I'm sure. Now if you will excuse me, I have other matters to attend to."

"It's been a pleasure, Mr. Zayne," Monotone Man said as he put his hand on the woman's back.

Adrian nodded and the couple started for the door. Sydney ducked back and scurried down the hall, dashing into the restroom as the couple left the room. She waited for several seconds, listening to the sound of their footsteps recede down the marble hallway then crept from her hiding place and cautiously approached the door to the study.

Adrian was opening a wall safe and taking something from it. As she watched she saw him take a DVD from a black case and put it in the machine. A moment later a picture came on the screen. Sydney had to put her hand over her mouth to keep from making a sound as she saw what he was watching. The footage was of her being tortured!

A cold sweat broke out over her entire body as she stood transfixed to the sight. *Oh, god!* She backed away from the door. *He knew all along what was happening to me! He paid to have it done!*

With startling clarity the truth hit her. She turned and ran up the stairs to the bedroom and looked around wildly. Somehow she had to figure out a way to get the evidence and get away from Adrian. But how?

Footsteps in the hall made her jump in alarm. She quickly got into bed and covered up, trying to slow her breathing. A moment later the door opened and Adrian entered.

She did not open her eyes until he sat down on the bed then she blinked and tried to pretend that she was having trouble waking. "Adrian? I'm sorry, have I been asleep long? I took two more of those pills and I'm just so . . . " She paused to yawn behind her hand then smiled sleepily. "I feel like I could sleep for a week."

"Darling, I wish you had waited before taking more medication," he said somewhat peevishly. "I have to go out of town and had planned on taking you with me."

"For how long?"

"Just overnight. My business will be concluded by tonight and I will return sometime mid-morning tomorrow."

"Well, why don't you go on," she suggested. "With all those sedatives floating around in me I'll probably sleep through the night. You can wake me up when you get in and we'll have a late breakfast in bed together."

He smiled at the suggestion. "That sounds delicious. But are you sure you will be all right without me? I do hate to leave you alone."

"With all the staff you have I'll hardly be alone," she said tiredly as if the effort of talking was wearing her out. "I'll be fine. Just hurry back to me, okay?"

He gave her another smile and leaned over to give her a lingering kiss. She smiled as he took her hand and lifted it to his lips. "I do love you, darling. More than you know."

"And you'd never be able to imagine the depths of my feelings for you," she replied, thinking that at least she was not lying about that. Right now she could not imagine hating someone as much as she hated him.

"I'll see you in the morning." He released her hand and stood. She smiled and blew him a kiss then snuggled back down under the covers. After the door closed she waited several minutes then got up and carefully opened the door and looked out into the hall. When she didn't see anyone she ran to the top of the stairs and listened.

She could hear voices downstairs. Adrian was directing his staff not to disturb her and informing them he could be reached on his private jet or on his cell phone. The front door closed and she ran to one of the bedrooms in the front of the house and looked out of the window to see his limousine pulling down the driveway.

Sydney ran back to the bedroom, threw off her robe, and dressed in a pair of old jeans and a faded T-shirt. She put on her running shoes, she pulled her hair back in a pony-tail and went downstairs, being careful not to run into anyone.

Adrian's office was empty. She closed and locked the door, then walked over to the side wall and pulled back the hinged abstract that covered the safe. As expected the safe was locked.

So where would he hide the combination? She asked herself as she looked around the room. Her eyes fell on the computer and she smiled. "Bingo!"

She sat down and turned on the computer. A window appeared on the screen requesting the password. Sydney frowned for a moment then a slow smile started to spread across her face as she saw the network icon at the bottom of the screen. *Clever, but not clever enough, Mr. Zayne,* she thought with some measure of satisfaction and hit the enter key twice.

After that she had to proceed slowly and carefully, looking for hidden files in the system. After several hours she still had not found anything referring to the safe. She opened one of the few hidden files remaining and drew back in surprise. A schematic appeared on the screen. "What's this?" She studied the screen. When she realized what she was seeing she straightened in surprise. It was a blueprint. She directed the drawing to the printer, got up and took the sheet of paper the laser printer ejected.

As she studied the drawing , she realized the study she was in was shown on the blueprint. And unless she was mistaken a door was supposed to be somewhere on the wall behind her that was lined with bookcases. She put the drawing aside and she went to the bookcase. There did not appear to be any hidden door mechanisms. She ran her hands along the bottoms of the shelves and felt behind the books but could find nothing. Then something caught her eye. One of the shelves seemed to stick out farther than the others, like it had slid forward just fractionally. She pushed on it and suddenly a section of the bookcase slid forward. She jumped back and watched as the entire section moved two feet into the room.

Sydney took a look behind the bookcase and saw a dark passageway. With a deep breath to summon her courage she stepped into the darkness, holding her hands out to her sides to feel the walls as she inched along. Just inches inside the passage her right hand touched something cool and metallic on the wall. Light flooded the darkness as she pressed the switch mounted on the metal plate.

The corridor extended about ten feet to end at the top of a steep stairway. She followed the hallway and took the stairs down. "God, it must be at least two floors!" she exclaimed to herself as she continued down. The stairs came to a halt in a small room. There was one door, mounted in the wall facing her. It was a heavy metal door with no knob or handle. A plate mounted on the wall beside the door with a control panel apparently controlled it. She pressed one of the buttons but nothing happened. She pressed the other button and jumped as the door swung inward.

One look had her grabbing the wall for support. Fear bubbled up inside her as memories of what had happened to her in this room took control of her mind. She stumbled back from the door, and fell back against the stairs, panting as she stared at the opened door.

"It was right here! I was right here!"

Her heart beat wildly as she pushed herself up. She forced herself to enter the room. The metal table sat in the center of the room. Beside it was a cart on which implements she was all too familiar with lay. She looked around the room and noticed for the first time the camera lens that was mounted high on the wall above the door. She had never noticed it before.

"That sick monster!" She allowed anger to take the place of fear. "He watched the whole thing."

Even her anger could not keep chills from running rampant up and down her spine. She could not stay in that room. She closed the door, climbed the hidden stairs and returned to the study. She had to find the combination to the safe.

Where would it be? She looked at the grandfather clock in the corner. It was after seven already. She began searching the room, starting with the desk. By the time she had gone through the study it was almost nine o'clock and still she did not have the combination. "Where is it?" She fumed and flopped down on the couch, staring morosely at the picture that covered the safe. She had no idea how long she had sat staring at the picture when something seemed to jump off the canvas at her.

Sydney laughed at the irony. Adrian had put the combination where no one would ever think to look for it. Right out in plain sight. She jumped up, ran across the room and pulled back the picture, twisting the dial to the left, back to the right and then all the way around left again.

She turned the handle and the safe door swung open. Inside was a stack of DVD's, a large amount of cash and a leather-bound journal. She took the DVDs and she sat down in front of the television. She put them in the video player one by one, fast-forwarding through each one. Six were of her torture.

Two were of Blake. One was of him meeting with some men at the river. The other was of the incident that took place when she and Blake were on their way to Virginia. She gathered up the DVD's and the journal, closed the safe and hurried through the house to the video room where the large screen television and bank of video equipment was located.

There was a spindle full of blank DVD's in a cabinet. Sydney wasted no time making copies of all the discs she's taken found in the safe. During the waiting time she looked through the journal. What she found shocked her. Not the contents so much as the fact that Adrian had been stupid enough to keep a handwritten account of his activities.

There were records of meetings described as well as records of payments made to many individuals. Sydney read Adrian's own words about the extent he had gone to in order to frame Blake. All of it was described in detail.

What was the most shocking was that he hadn't acted alone. By the time the last DVD was copied she had read the entire journal. There was enough evidence in it to convict Adrian. Combine that with the tapes and the hidden room and it was enough to put him behind bars for a very very long time.

Sydney put the original DVD back in the safe, used her phone and took photos of every page of the journal then replaced it in the safe with the DVD's and locked it.

She took all her evidence upstairs to the bedroom and put it in a big shoulder-bag. She then called the driver and asked him to have one of Adrian's sports cars brought around to the front for her. Hoping that she would not get any grief from the staff she went downstairs and walked outside.

The driver was just pulling up in front. "Would you like me to drive you, Mrs. Zayne?" He asked as he got out of the car.

"No, but thanks anyway," she replied as she moved around him and got in behind the wheel. "I'm going to do a little shopping." She looked up at the driver and smiled. "Just between you and me it's a little secret. You know that Adrian and I are newlyweds, right? Well, I really wanted to get him something special for a wedding present. You know, something to show how I feel? And I haven't had a chance to, so I thought this would be the perfect time. That way I can surprise him in the morning. By the way, do you have any ideas on what he'd like? It's kind of hard to buy for a man who has everything, if you know what I mean."

The driver smiled. "Yeah, I can imagine. And I'm afraid I can't be much help."

"Oh, well," she said as started the car. "Thanks anyway. See you later."

She breathed a sigh of relief as she pulled away. Step one of her half-baked plan was underway. She put her hand on the bag in the seat beside her containing the copies of the DVDs and increased her speed. Depending on what happened the next twenty-four hours she could either end up seeing Adrian behind bars or . . . she did not want to consider what might happen if her plan failed.

Saturday, May 6

Washington, D.C.

Adrian walked in the house to find Sydney sitting on the bottom step of the gracefully curved staircase, dressed in a flowing white dress of lacy gauze-like material. "Well. " He smiled and handed his attaché case to the man who accompanied him. "This is an unexpected surprise."

Sydney smiled as he walked over to her. "Welcome home," she said softly as he took her hand and pulled her to her feet.

Standing on the step put her at eye level with him. She wound her arms around his neck and pulled him close. "I have a surprise for you."

"Ummm," he murmured, running his hands down her back and kissing her neck as she arched her head back. "I can hardly wait."

Sydney laughed and pushed away to take his hand. "Come on."

Adrian let her pull him a few steps then paused and looked back. "That will be all for today, Matthew. Take the weekend off."

"Thank you, sir," the man replied. But Adrian did not notice as he was led through the house toward the arboretum.

Inside the massive indoor garden Sydney had instructed the staff to have a large tent erected beside the koi pond. Filmy white mosquito netting was draped from the frame, blowing slightly in the breeze that wafted in from the opened windows. The ground was covered with a soft thick white quilt on which a picnic basket sat along side a chilled pitcher of martinis. Stacks of fluffy pillows were scattered about.

"What is all this for?" he asked as she started helping him take off his jacket.

"Just to let you know how eager I was for you to return," she replied as she removed his tie and unbuttoned his shirt.

Adrian sighed with pleasure as her hands parted his shirt and her lips grazed his bare skin. He tried to take her in his arms but she darted away, laughing playfully. "First things first, darling. Sit and let me pour you a drink. I made everything myself."

He sat down and reclined back against a mound of pillows. Sydney poured him a drink and sat down, straddling his long legs. Holding the glass to his lips, she smiled as he took a long drink. Adrian's hands moved up her legs, pushing the flimsy material of her dress high on her thighs. She looked down at his hands but made no move to stop him as they crept higher.

"What about lunch?" she asked in a sultry tone, indicating the basket.

Adrian took the martini glass from her and polished off the drink then tossed the glass aside. With a look of smoldering need in his eyes he reached up and slipped the thin straps of her dress down over her shoulders. Sydney remained perfectly still as he lowered the dress. Once past the barrier of her breasts it slid unhindered to puddle around her hips, revealing the fact that she was wearing nothing beneath it.

For a moment Adrian did nothing but look at her, letting his eyes wander over her body. When his eyes met hers she moved her hands to his face and pulled him to her for a lingering kiss. "Tell me your desires," she whispered.

He took her by the shoulders and pushed her back to search her face. "Tell me," she repeated. "I want to know your fantasy, Adrian."

He started to speak then shook his head and lay back on the pillows, staring at her. She smiled and moved off him, letting the dress slid down her legs as she stood. Leaving it discarded at her feet she knelt and poured him another drink. She took a tiny sip then sat and offered him the glass.

He accepted, watching her as she lay down on her side and rested her head on his thigh, idly stroking his stomach in featherlight touches. "Did you miss me?" she asked, moving her hand near his manhood but never quite touching him.

"Did you miss me?" he asked in return.

"Isn't that obvious?"

"Yes, I suppose it is," he said and took a drink of his martini. "I must admit to some degree of surprise however. I did not expect you to be so fully recovered from your recent ordeal."

She sighed and rolled over on her back. "I thought about it all night and I realized that nothing would be served by clinging to it. I'm safe and protected and nothing can hurt me as long as I'm with you. Besides, I guess I exorcised all my demons in my mind so now I can move on."

"Oh? And how exactly did you go about exorcising your demons?" he asked and took another drink.

She raised her arms up above her head and stretched, watching his eyes rake over her. "I made up scenarios in my mind of what I would do to the people who hurt me." Suddenly she sat up and leaned forward on her hands. "What would you do?"

He raised his eyebrows and finished his drink. "Me? Well, I suppose if I found the people responsible I would give them what they deserve."

"And what would that be?" she asked and moved closer. "Adrian, if Blake really is responsible then I want him to pay for what he did to me. The trouble is, I'm not sure what just payment would be."

"I think it would be fitting for payment to be in kind," he said in slightly slurred words.

"You mean the person responsible should have to go through what he put me through?"

"Yes," he started to push himself up but fell back on the pillows. "Come here."

Sydney positioned herself on her hands and knees above him. He pulled her face down to his and she lowered herself on him as their lips met. The kiss began passionately but abruptly changed. Adrian's hands dropped loosely to his sides and his eyes rolled back.

Sydney smiled and sat up, reaching for her dress. She picked up the martini pitcher and poured the rest of it out on the ground. Step two was in progress.

∽

Blake was sitting at his kitchen table, staring gloomily at the stacks of notes and transcripts that had once been his case against Adrian Zayne. In hindsight he knew that he should have been more careful. He had underestimated Zayne and it had cost him dearly. Not only had he lost the woman he loved, but it looked like he would lose his career as well, and he would be lucky not to end up being prosecuted.

The doorbell rang and he pushed himself up to answer it. Weasel made a face as he got a look at Blake. "Man, you look like shit warmed over."

"Nice to see you, too," Blake commented bleakly and turned away to take his seat once more at the table.

"Thought you might need some sustenance," Weasel put a bag down on the table. "Steak and egg biscuits. Your favorite."

"Thanks, not hungry." Blake picked up a paper from one of the stacks and looked at it for a moment before wadding it up in his fist and throwing it across the room. "I let him lead me around by the nose, Weasel! Like a goddamn rookie!"

Weasel sat down and propped one elbow on the table, resting his chin on his palm. "Man, we were all suckered. You can't blame yourself."

"Then who can I blame?"

Weasel shook his head and for a few minutes neither one of them spoke. "I checked on those bank accounts," Weasel finally said. "The money trail's the same as before. I think if I can break into–"

He never got to finish his sentence because the doorbell rang. Blake got up and opened the door. A Fed-Ex delivery man stood outside. "Blake Edwards? Would you sign here, sir?"

Blake signed the paper attached to the clipboard and took the box the man handed him. "Thanks," he said as the man turned away. He kicked the door closed and looked up from reading what was printed on the box to Weasel. "It's from Syd."

Weasel stood up. "What is it?"

Blake shrugged and went into the kitchen. He put the box on the counter as he rumbled around in one of the drawers for a knife to cut the packing tape. As soon as he located one he sliced through the tape and opened the box. The first thing he saw was a handwritten note. He read it aloud.

Blake,

I'm sorry I ever doubted you. I have no excuse.

All I can say is that after what happened I thought

you were my enemy. I know that doesn't make

sense and I wish I had time to explain, but I don't.

I just wanted you to know that at the hospital,

when you and Adrian were fighting, I started to realize

the truth. I know everything now and I know you're

innocent. I hope one day you'll be able to forgive me.

I do love you, Blake. Please remember that.

The contents of this package should prove

that not only did Adrian set you up but that he's

responsible for what happened to me, as well.

These are only copies. The originals are in the safe
in his private study at his house in Maryland. The
combination of the safe is left 27, right 12 and
left to 31.

Use this to convince your superiors to
search the house. In particular, I think you'll find
a secret room in the basement quite interesting.
The only way in is through Adrian's study. Push in the
third middle shelf on the center bookcase and that will
open a secret door. As for Adrian, I've decided to
take care of him myself.

I love you.

Sydney

Blake dropped the note and reached in the box to remove a stack of
papers and a stack of DVDs. He carried everything into the den, put the
stack of paper down on the coffee table and put one of the DVD's into
the player.

"Jesus!" He breathed as the picture appeared on the television
screen.

Weasel looked up from reading the top paper on the stack and his
face got a sick look on it. "God almighty! Where did she get these?"

Blake shook his head and fast forwarded through the DVD. It
showed in vivid detail the torture Sydney was subjected to. When he
reached the end of the tape he put in another. In all there were six
DVD's of the torture. The last two were of him; one of him meeting with
the fake general and the other the run-in he and Sydney had with the
van full of men on their way to Virginia.

He stopped the DVD and turned to Weasel. Weasel tapped the
photocopies. "She's right, man. It's all here. Dates, times, places.
Records of conversations, payoffs. I don't know how she got it, but if we
can get our hands on the originals we can put that sucker away."

Blake jumped to his feet and grabbed the phone. "Hello, this is
Blake Edwards. I need you to put me through to director Braswell. . . ."

then give me his home phone number! . . . I don't care about that! I have to talk to him now. It's an emergency. Someone's life could be at stake. . . . okay, fine. I'll be here."

He hung up the phone and walked past Weasel and down the hall. A few moments later the phone ran. Weasel reached for it but Blake ran back into the room and snatched it up. "Edwards. . . . yes sir, I'm sorry to interrupt your weekend but this is urgent."

Weasel continued to read through the photocopies as Blake explained the situation to Braswell. When Blake finished explaining he listened for a few seconds then handed the phone to Weasel.

"Yes?" Weasel looked up at Blake questioningly as he answered. "Yes, sir. I have the copies in front of me. . . yes, I believe the source is reliable and I also agree with agent Edwards that Mrs. Zayne may be in danger. . . . yes, sir. We're leaving now."

He hung up the phone as he stood. "He's sending someone over to collect the DVD's and copies. We're to go to Zayne's. Backup is on the way."

Blake nodded grimly and headed for the door.

ᄋᆰ

Sydney stood silently waiting. Aside from a spotlight that shown down on the still figure on the table, the room was dark. There was a surreal, dreamlike quality to everything that she found odd yet comforting. A long time passed before a groan interrupted the silence.

Adrian blinked and looked around, squinting against the harsh light that shown down on him, blinding him to his surroundings. He tried to raise his hand to shield it eyes but the thick leather straps held him secure. He looked around nervously, his eyes wide with apprehension.

"Are you cold?" Sydney asked in a flat monotone voice.

"Sydney?" He squinted his eyes tightly, craning his neck to try and see beyond the light. "Is that you? What are you doing? Release me this instant."

"Not much fun, is it?" She stepped closer so that he could see her.

"What are you doing?" his voice rose. "Release me."

"I'm sorry." She smiled and put her hand on his bare chest. "I can't do that.

"Have you lost your mind?" he shouted. "This is insane! I demand that you–"

"You demand?" she laughed. "I hardly think you're in the position to demand anything."

"All right!" he shouted. "Then I ask you. Please stop this foolishness and release me."

"But I thought you liked surprises?" She taunted him as she bent down to pick up a large canister that the gardener used to water the flowers. "I thought you liked playing games?"

"What kind of insane game is this?"

She lifted the canister up and tipped it toward him so that a shower of water emerged from the spout, splashing down over his naked body. "There, isn't that nice and cool. Refreshing."

"Release me!" His voice increased in volume and pitch.

She finished dousing him with water then put the canister on the floor and moved to the cart that sat along side the table he was strapped to. "Remember this?" She picked up two metal rods about a half-inch in diameter and six inches long that were attached at one end to long cables that ran to a control panel mounted on the cart.

"Get away from me with that!" His voice sounded less demanding. "Sydney, stop! Don't come near me with that! I mean it."

"Or what?" She turned the switch on the control panel and touched the two rods together, watching a shower of sparks light the darkness beyond the circle of light. "Will you scream for help? Will you promise to do anything, say anything, believe anything I tell you just to keep the pain away? Or will you be brave and endure the pain - hold out until you pass out from the agony?"

Adrian shook his head as she moved closer. "Why are you doing this to me?"

"I could ask you the same question," she replied softly. "Why did you do it to me, Adrian?"

"I didn't! Sydney, you're confused. It was Blake Edwards. He's the one who–"

"Blake's done nothing!" She tapped the metal rods together over his wet chest. "I found the DVD's, Adrian. Just like I found this little room. And the journal. I know everything. I even heard you talking to the man you hired to torture me. Tell me, were you watching the whole time?

What did you think while you watched? Did you get off on it, darling? Seeing me naked, strapped down to this table, screaming for the pain to stop?"

"You've have it all wrong," he insisted. "Just put that down and release me and I can explain."

Sydney adjusted the current and lightly touched one of the rods to the sole of his right foot. Adrian groaned, gritting his teeth to keep from crying out as his body jerked. Sydney waited until his breathing slowed a little. "That was the lowest setting. That's how it started. The lowest setting, working up from the bottom of the feet. Painful isn't it?"

"I can explain!" he hissed.

"I'm sure. Just like you can explain how you set Blake up to look like he'd done something wrong."

"I don't know what you're talking about."

Sydney leaned over and looked into his eyes. "I really don't like this game very much, you know. All this talking and we're getting nowhere. It's starting to bore me. Tell me, darling. Do you have any idea what it's like to have something like this inside you?"

His eyes widened more and his skin paled as he stared at her. "It's actually very horrible," she whispered. "It makes you want to die. But you won't, you know. On the low setting the current's just enough to cause tremendous pain without inflicting trauma. Only, after a while it doesn't matter. You just can't take it anymore. Want me to demonstrate?"

"You're crazy!" he breathed. "You're absolutely insane! How did you—the martinis! You drugged me!"

"Nothing fatal, I assure you," she said with a smile. "Although I have to tell you that getting you down here was a real feat. You're a very big man. I'm afraid you're going to have a few additional bruises from the trip down the stairs. I had to roll you over onto a spread and drag you."

"Who's in on this with you?"

"Why no one, darling." She held out her hands and gestured around the room. "We're all alone. Just you and me. So, enough of this. I want you to do something for me. I want you to tell me all about how you set Blake up and why you did it."

"Blake Edwards!" He spit the name like it was dirty. "He's nothing! Why can't you just forget him and give us a chance to be happy? I can give you anything you can imagine."

"Not love," she said sadly.

"You're so wrong."

"No, I'm not." She extended one of the rods and touched him on the inside of his left thigh. This time a howl escaped his lips before he clenched his jaws tight.

"Tell me!" She lowered the rod toward his genitals.

"All right!" he screamed. "All right! Just don't . . . do . . . that."

She paused in motion and looked at him expectantly. "I did it for you," he said. "Because I love you. Can't you understand? I couldn't lose you and you were running away from me."

"So you what?" she prompted him.

"I set Edwards up," he admitted.

"How?"

Adrian quickly outlined his plan. Sydney was silent until he finished then she turned off the current and put the rods down on the table. She unfastened one of the arm straps and stepped back from the table.

"I'm leaving, Adrian. I've made copies of the DVDs and of your journal. At this moment they're on their way to the FBI. You're finished. The game is over. You lost."

With that, she turned, walked out of the room and climbed up the hidden stairs to his study. Then she proceeded up to the bedroom, picked up her suitcase and purse and turned to leave. Adrian was standing in the doorway.

"You can't leave me," he said as he stepped into the room. "I love you. I won't lose you."

"You already have," she replied calmly. "I don't love you and I don't want to be anywhere near you. Get out of my way and out of my life."

"No!" He grabbed her arm as she tried to walk past him. "I won't let you go."

"Get your hands off me!" She jerked away, swinging her suitcase as hard as she could against him. The case knocked him off balance and broke his hold on her arm.

"Sydney, please!" he pleaded with her. "We can go away - start over. It'll be like none of this ever happened. We can . . . "

"Shut up!" she yelled at him. "Don't you get it? I hate you. You cost me everything! My career's shot to hell, my professional reputation ruined and I lost the man I love. All because of you. I despise you and I don't ever want to have to lay eyes on you as long as I live."

Without giving him another chance to speak she ran out of the room and down the stairs. Just as she reached for the knob on the front door, she was jerked back. Adrian had one hand tangled in her hair and in the other he held a gun, a Baretta 9mm with a silencer attached. Sydney froze as she saw the gun.

Adrian grinned wickedly and backhanded her. The back of his fist caught her in the cheekbone; the barrel of the gun slamming into her temple. She fell, dazed by the blow. Looking up at him from the floor, she raised one hand.

He snarled and yanked her up from the floor by her hair. Jerking her head back at a sharp angle he jammed the gun under her chin and sneered at her. "Beg."

"Never," she refused.

He smirked and jerked hard on her hair. Sydney cried out as the gun rammed into the soft flesh under her chin. "You belong to me," Adrian rasped, pulling her up so that she was forced to stand on her toes. "I say when and if you leave. Do you understand? You're my property . . . just like this house and everything else. I own you."

Tears glistened in Sydney's eyes but she blinked them back. "Kill me," she whispered defiantly. "Go ahead. Pull the trigger. I'd rather die than live with you. Do it!"

He laughed in her face. "Kill you? No, my darling. I have other plans for you. To begin with I'm going to take you downstairs. That's going to be your new home. I'll make what was done to you before look like a romp in the park. Yes . . . " his eyes shown with maniacal glee. "You'll be begging me to take you back into my bed - willing to do anything I ask."

The thought of having to endure what waited in that room made Sydney crazy with fear. Without thinking of the consequences she started hitting at Adrian, screaming and kicking. He jerked her around by the hair, shouting at her to stop but she would not. Grabbing his hand holding the gun she bit down as hard as she could on the side of his hand, just below the knuckle of his last finger.

Blood filled her mouth as the skin punctured. Adrian roared and slung her around. The gun went off as she slammed into a marble table on one side of the foyer. She hit the floor and scrambled to push herself up. He was on her before she made it to her knees, driving her down under his weight.

Sydney screamed and thrashed around as he rose and jerked her over on her back. She raised her hands as his descended. The first blow made her head reel dizzily. She kicked at him, feeling her foot meet his leg. He cursed and hit her again. Still she would not stop fighting back. That enraged him even more. Over and over he shouted at her to stop as he pounded on her. She fought until her strength ran out. He continued to hit her until she was limp. Then he began to tear at her clothes.

She wanted to fight him but could not. Every inch of her body hurt and her arms felt like rubber. Still, she could not just lie there and take it. She tried to hit him, but he just grabbed her arms and pinned them over her head with one hand, laughing at her as he wedged his knees between her legs and forced them apart.

"Please, no," she cried. "Don't, Adrian, please don't."

"That's it," he chided. "Beg, darling."

She cried out as he viciously stabbed inside her. He pounded on her furiously as she writhed around, trying to get him off her. Unable to hold her still with one hand he released her wrists. As he did she went for his eyes, her fingers curved like claws.

Adrian howled as one nail tore a ragged gash from the corner of his right eye and down his cheek. Sydney pushed at him, managing to squirm back as he grabbed his face. She continued to push herself backwards and spotted the gun on the floor. She rolled over onto on her hands and knees and went for it. That was when Adrian reached her again. His foot caught her in the ribs and lifted her up off the floor.

She couldn't even scream. All the air was driven from her lungs. Another kick to her side and she was struggling just to breathe. He grabbed her hair and jerked on it, forcing her onto her knees. Sydney was dimly aware of him kneeling behind her. When she felt his erection against her and realized what he was about to do, it galvanized her into action.

She lunged forward, feeling her hair pull and tear. With a scream she drew her foot up behind her. Her heel made contact with Adrian's testicles and he screamed in pain and doubled over.

Drawing on strength she didn't know she possessed, she crawled across the foyer and grabbed a chair by the study door to pull herself to her feet. On wobbly legs she stumbled into the study. On the wall beside the bar was what she needed.

The pearl-handled Colt 45's beaconed her like a light in the darkness. With lurching steps she moved toward them. As she reached the holster she cut a look over her shoulder. There was no sign of Adrian. Her hand closed around one of the guns. It was heavier than she had thought. She pulled it free. Behind her Adrian's voice rang out.

"Put it down!"

She turned her head to see him standing in the doorway, cupping his injured testicles with one hand and pointing the Baretta at her with the other. She knew if she gave up the gun she didn't stand a chance. She ran behind the bar as Adrian ran toward her. He tried to reach across the bar and grab her but she snatched up a bottle and hit at him. It missed his hand and shattered on the top of the bar. Glass and liquor splattered all around them. Adrian made a noise as the liquor splashed in his face and eyes. He reached for his eyes, wiping at them.

Sydney saw her opportunity and took it. She ran unsteadily from the room, headed once more for the front door. Her only thoughts were of escape. The door was only feet away when her luck ran out. Adrian tackled her from behind. She lost the gun as she was driven to the floor.

For a moment neither of them moved. Then he pushed himself up and slapped her in the side of the head as he started to stand. "Look at me!" he ordered.

Sydney stayed as she was with her eyes glued on the pearl-handled gun that was just out of reach. "I said look at me!" Adrian shouted. "Damn you, look at me!"

Sydney knew that as soon as she turned over he would shoot her and decided that if she was going to die she might as well die fighting. With desperation she reached for the gun. Her fingers just touched it when the door suddenly burst open.

Blake rushed in. "Drop the gun!" He shouted as two other men ran in behind him.

With the pearl-handled gun now in her hand, Sydney rolled over. Adrian looked at her then at Blake. His face hardened and his finger tightened on the trigger. "Go to hell."

Two shots rang out at the same time. Sydney screamed as she saw Blake was thrown back against one of the other men. A red stain blossomed on the right shoulder of his shirt.

Adrian stood wavering for one moment then fell face forward. The back of his head looked like it had been ripped off. Sydney gagged and dropped the smoking gun. Weasel was now inside, holding onto Blake while one of the other men spoke into a cell phone.

"Syd," Blake's voice sounded weak as he called to her.

She looked at him and tried to get to her feet, fell and tried again. After several attempts she managed to stand. Blake was leaning on Weasel, moving toward her. "Blake." She reached for him. She never made it. She was unconscious before she hit the floor.

Saturday, June 24

Washington National Airport

Sydney sat with Blake and Weasel at a small table by the window in one of the airport bars. The waiter delivered their drinks and Weasel raised his glass. "Here's to being alive."

Blake clinked his glass to Weasel's with a smile. His smile faded as he looked at Sydney. She was staring pensively out of the window.

"Hey." Weasel tapped her on the arm. "This is supposed to be a celebration."

She turned and smiled. "Sorry. So, are you excited about your new assignment?"

He rolled his eyes but grinned. "Well, it does sound intriguing."

"Where is it you're going?" Weasel leaned forward and whispered. "Just between you and me . . . that's classified."

Sydney made a face at him. "So, how am I supposed to get in touch with you if you won't tell me where you're going to be?"

"There's always E-mail," he said with a chuckle.

She smiled and shook her head. Weasel took a sip of his drink and turned to Blake. "I still can't believe you took that position at the academy. I thought you were addicted to field work. Sure you won't get bored?"

Blake shook his head. "Nope, in fact, I think I'm ready for a change. I'm getting too old to keep up with these young bloods that are coming in. Let them handle it. I'll teach them how."

Weasel nodded his head in Sydney's direction, who was once more staring out of the window.

"Penny for your thoughts." Blake said softly.

She turned to look at him. "I was just thinking how strange it is. Here we are, new challenges and adventures, safe and sound - like nothing ever happened. The world goes on and people forget. Except that I can't forget. It happened and because it did, none of us will ever be the same."

The mood turned somber at her words. "Look, I know this is the last thing either one of you wanted to hear, so why don't I just shut up."

Weasel knew the thought of killing anything was against Sydney's nature. But having to actually kill another person . . . He pushed back the thoughts and spoke up, "Syd, I know it was worse for you than any of us and I can't blame you for . . . well you know, for being upset. But you've got to remember that you were the victim, Syd."

"Was I? I don't think so."

"How can you say that?" Blake interjected. "Zayne was insane. Dangerously insane. He damn near killed you and would have–"

"If you and Weasel hadn't come to my rescue," she cut in.

"I was going to say he would have killed me," Blake said. "If you hadn't . . . well, you know."

"You can say it." She put her hand over his on the table. "If I hadn't killed him. It's okay. I did it and I guess I'm going to have to learn to live with that."

"Syd, you can't let this drag you down," Blake spoke gently. "Like Weasel said, you were the victim."

"You don't understand." she looked at him then at Weasel. "I wasn't just the victim. I started this whole mess. Don't you see? I was just like all those people who started hurling accusations and pointing fingers after that bomb went off. Everyone was so eager to blame someone that they just started pointing fingers without any justification whatsoever. I did the same thing. I jumped to my own conclusion without knowing the facts."

"It's not the same," Weasel argued. "You were basing your suspicions on what Tyler told you. You thought he was telling you the truth. It was natural to come to the conclusion you did. We all did."

"No." She shook her head. "I let myself jump to the conclusion that Adrian was guilty because it was convenient."

"But you were right." Weasel pointed out. "And because of you everyone in this country is safer. We all could have been under a virtual dictatorship if you hadn't found Zayne's journal. That was the key to unraveling the whole ball of yarn."

"GW's right," Blake added. "If it were not for you this country would still be in the grips of turmoil, people squaring off at one another – some for and some against the new President but everyone angry and the country floundering. We were all being led into something that wasn't going to be easy to undo and would have been if it hadn't been for that journal and the evidence it led us too."

"Yeah, that's a real claim to fame I have going there," she commented. "I brought down the President. Do you have any idea how many people in this country hate me?"

"Do you have any idea how many people see you as a hero?" GW asked.

"I'm no hero."

"I disagree," Blake said and even when she made a face, continued. "Look, the truth is, the whole country was shell-shocked by what happened. Something like that - it cuts deep, Syd. Everyone in this country knew that the people in that building were killed by a madman. They just never dreamed that the madman was the man sitting in the Oval Office. No one would ever have thought to imagine that the President would cook up something like this with Zayne, all so he could declare martial law, close our borders, halt travel and basically isolate us from the rest of the world. We were all duped. A guy on the news put it well and said we'd all been living in the territory of lies for a while."

"That's what Tyler said." She felt sadness wash over her as she thought about the Senator. "I still have a hard time believing all this really happened," she admitted. "I mean our founding fathers were brilliant. They set up a system that should have been foolproof with all of the checks and balances built in. Three separate but equal branches so that no one branch of government could ever ride roughshod over the others and made such mistakes."

317

"Theoretically, it is foolproof," GW agreed. "But in this case, if Zane and the Oval had gotten your father under their thumb, they could have controlled the Executive and Legislative Branches and could have pretty much killed democracy in this country."

"It boggles the mind," she said. "And that aspect of things seems to have taken precedent over the lives lost in the bombing. At least in the media."

"I disagree," Blake said. "I know that's the sensational part of the story, and certainly what has had your photo plastered all of the news, but people haven't forgotten the bombing or the lives that were lost. I think that wound is still pretty raw. That hit everyone hard. It made us all realize that it could have been us or one of our family. It made us wake up and see that we can't take it for granted that we're safe. It's sad, but true. But it doesn't mean that we have to beat ourselves up or hide under our beds or suspect every person we pass on the street. And we don't have to be afraid of every person in a position of power. Steps are being taken to insure that this kind of thing doesn't happen again. But right now, all we can do is learn from whatever mistakes we've made and not make the same ones again."

Sydney stared at him for a moment then suddenly broke out in a smile. "Did anyone ever tell you that you'd make a half-way decent counselor, Mr. Edwards?"

"Half-way decent?" He raised his eyebrows then pouted. "And that was some of my best stuff,"

Weasel laughed and stood. "Well, my flight's boarding. You two take care, okay?"

Sydney stood and hugged him tightly for a long time. "I'm going to miss you," she said with tears in her eyes. "Will you promise to stay in touch?"

"You know it," he said and gave her a quick kiss then extended his hand to Blake. "It's been real, man."

Blake took his hand for a second then made a face. "What the hell?" he muttered and gave Weasel a big hug. "You stay out of trouble. But if you do get in over your head, you know where to call."

Weasel winked and picked up his laptop case. "Yeah, I know. So, I guess I'll see ya."

Sydney smiled, trying not to cry and waved as Weasel walked off. Blake offered her the handkerchief from his lapel pocket but she shook her head and wiped her eyes with a napkin from the table. "So, what do you have planned for the rest of the day?"

"I'm all yours," he said and took her hand as they left the bar. "How about you?"

"I have nothing planned until next week. I got a message from a publisher in New York who's interested in my manuscript."

"That's great!" Blake gave her hand a squeeze. "Maybe we should celebrate. Where would you like to go?"

"How about home?"

Blake grinned and leaned over to give her a kiss on the cheek. They passed the airport bookshop and a man stepped out in front of them with his head buried in a magazine. Blake stopped suddenly to keep from running into the man.

"Oh!" The man looked up. "Excuse me, I'm sorry. I was just–" he looked down at the magazine then at Sydney. "Hey! It's you! You're her. Adrian Zayne's wife – the lady who took down the President. I was just reading this article about you."

He showed them the magazine. Sure enough there was a photo of her, Adrian and the President, taken in Adrian's hotel suite.

"No, I'm sorry," Sydney said with a smile. "I'm not Mrs. Zayne."

"But," the guy looked down at the picture in the magazine. "Well, sorry," the man apologized. "Name's Lou Green. From Chicaco. Sorry I bothered you, miss–"

"Mrs." She corrected him and smiled up at Blake. "Mrs. Blake Edwards."

THE END

ABOUT THE AUTHOR

Ana is another pseudonym for Ciana Stone, what she likes to think of as the suspense/thriller/science-fiction aspect of her personality. As Ciana she write paranormal and western romance.

Married happily to the man of her dreams, Ana has two children, four grandchildren and calls Florida home for now. Who knows what the future will bring. That's the joy of the journey, just like reading a good book, you never know what's around the next corner until you turn the page.

Made in the USA
San Bernardino, CA
12 November 2019

59766257R00182